Sensing and Signal Processing in
Smart Healthcare

Sensing and Signal Processing in Smart Healthcare

Editors

Wenbing Zhao
Srinivas Sampalli

MDPI • Basel • Beijing • Wuhan • Barcelona • Belgrade • Manchester • Tokyo • Cluj • Tianjin

Editors
Wenbing Zhao
Cleveland State University
USA

Srinivas Sampalli
Dalhousie University
Canada

Editorial Office
MDPI
St. Alban-Anlage 66
4052 Basel, Switzerland

This is a reprint of articles from the Special Issue published online in the open access journal *Electronics* (ISSN 2079-9292) (available at: https://www.mdpi.com/journal/electronics/special_issues/sensing_smart_healthcare).

For citation purposes, cite each article independently as indicated on the article page online and as indicated below:

LastName, A.A.; LastName, B.B.; LastName, C.C. Article Title. *Journal Name* **Year**, *Volume Number*, Page Range.

ISBN 978-3-0365-0026-3 (Hbk)
ISBN 978-3-0365-0027-0 (PDF)

Contents

About the Editors

Wenbing Zhao (Professor) received his Ph.D. in Electrical and Computer Engineering at University of California, Santa Barbara, in 2002. Dr. Zhao joined Cleveland State University (CSU) faculty in 2004 and is a full Professor in the Department of Electrical Engineering and Computer Science at CSU. Dr. Zhao published over 200 peer-reviewed papers on smart and connected health, fault-tolerant and dependable systems, physics, and education. Dr. Zhao's research is supported in part by the US National Science Foundation, the US Department of Transportation, the Ohio Department of Higher Education, the Ohio Bureau of Workers' Compensation, and Cleveland State University. Dr. Zhao is currently serving on the organizing committee and the technical program committee of numerous international conferences. He has been invited to give keynote and tutorial talks at over ten international conferences. Dr. Zhao is an Associate Editor for *IEEE Access* and MDPI *Computers*, and an Academic Editor for *PeerJ Computer Science*.

Srinivas Sampalli (Professor) holds a Bachelor of Engineering degree from Bangalore University (1985) and a Ph.D. degree from the Indian Institute of Science (IISc.), Bangalore, India (1989), and is currently a Professor and 3M National Teaching Fellow at the Faculty of Computer Science, Dalhousie University. He has led numerous industry-driven research projects on Internet of Things, wireless security, vulnerability analysis, intrusion detection and prevention, and applications of emerging wireless technologies in healthcare. He currently supervises 5 Ph.D. and 10 Master's students in his EMerging WIreless Technologies (MYTech) lab and has supervised over 120 graduate students throughout his career. Dr. Sampalli's primary joy is in inspiring and motivating students with his enthusiastic teaching. Dr. Sampalli has received the Dalhousie Faculty of Science Teaching Excellence award, the Dalhousie Alumni Association Teaching award, the Association of Atlantic Universities' Distinguished Teacher Award, a teaching award instituted in his name by the students within his Faculty, and the 3M National Teaching Fellowship, Canada's most prestigious teaching acknowledgement. Since September 2016, he holds the honorary position of the Vice President (Canada) of the International Federation of National Teaching Fellows (IFNTF), a consortium of national teaching award winners from around the world.

Editorial

Sensing and Signal Processing in Smart Healthcare

Wenbing Zhao [1,*] and Srinivas Sampalli [2]

[1]   Department of Electrical Engineering and Computer Science, Cleveland State University,
    Cleveland, OH 44115, USA
[2]   Faculty of Computer Science, Dalhousie University, Halifax, NS B3H 1W5, Canada; srini@cs.dal.ca
*   Correspondence: w.zhao1@csuohio.edu or wenbing@ieee.org; Tel.: +1-216-523-7480

Received: 16 November 2020; Accepted: 16 November 2020; Published: 19 November 2020

1. Introduction

In the last decade, we have seen rapid development of electronic technologies that are transforming our daily lives. Such technologies often integrate with various sensors that facilitate the collection of human motion and physiological data, and are equipped with wireless communication modules such as Bluetooth, radio frequency identification (RFID), and near field communication (NFC). In smart healthcare applications [1], designing ergonomic and intuitive human–computer interfaces is crucial, because a system that is not easy to use will create a huge obstacle to adoption and may significantly reduce the efficacy of the solution. Signal and data processing is another important consideration in smart healthcare applications because it must ensure high accuracy with a high confidence level in order for the applications to be useful for clinicians to take diagnosis and treatment decisions. In this Special Issue, we received a total of 26 contributions and accepted 10 of them. These contributions are mostly from authors in Europe, including Italy, Spain, France, Portugal, Romania, Sweden, and Netherlands. There are also authors from China, Korea, Taiwan, Indonesia, and Ecuador. Soon after publication, all 10 papers have been cited. The average citation count per paper is 7. One of the papers [2] has already been cited 22 times. The accepted papers can be roughly divided into two categories: (1) signal processing, and (2) smart healthcare systems.

2. Signal Processing

Five of the 10 papers in this special issue are related to signal processing. Two of them used traditional methods, and the remaining three used machine learning algorithms.

In [3], Ricci and Meacci aimed to address the need to detect the weak fluid signal while not saturating at the pipe wall components in pulse-wave Doppler ultrasound. The weak fluid signal may contain critical information regarding the industrial fluids and suspensions flowing in blood pipes. They proposed a numerical demodulator architecture that auto-tunes its internal dynamics to adapt to the feature of the actual input signal. They validated the proposed demodulator both through simulation and through experiments. For the latter, they integrated the demodulator into a system for the detection of the velocity profile of fluids flowing in blood pipes. Their data-adaptive demodulator produces a noise reduction of at least of 20 dB with respect to competing approaches, and could recover a correct velocity profile even when the input data are sampled at reduced 8-bits from the typical 12–16 bits.

In [4], Pham and Suh proposed a method to improve the state-of-the-art of simulation data for human activities. The availability of high fidelity simulation data would help researchers experiment with different human activity classification and detection algorithms. The simulation data are based on position and attitude data collected via inertial sensors mounted on the foot. The position and attitude data are then used as the control points for simulation data generation using spline functions. They validated their data generation algorithm with two scenarios including 2D walking path and 3D walking path.

In [5], Torti et al. presented their study on the delineation of brain cancer, which is an important step that helps guide neurosurgeons in the tumor resection. More specifically, they addressed the performance issue on using K-means clustering algorithm to delineate brain cancer using a parallel architecture. With the improvement, the algorithm can provide real-time processing to guide the neurosurgeon during the tumor resection task. The proposed parallel K-means clustering can work with the OpenMP, CUDA and OpenCL paradigms, and it has been validated through an in-vivo hyperspectral human brain image database. They show that their algorithm can achieve a speed-up of about 150 times with respect to sequential processing.

In [6], Calamanti et al. reported an exploratory study on using machine learning methods to detect endothelial dysfunction, which is critical to early diagnosis of cardiovascular diseases, using photoplethysmography signals. For their study, they built a new dataset from the data collected from 59 subjects. They experimented with three classifiers, namely, support vector machine (SVM), random forest, and k-nearest neighbors. They show that SVM outperforms others with a 71% accuracy. By including anthropometric features, they were able to improve the recall rate from 59% to 67%.

In [7], Nurmaini et al. proposed to use deep learning to extract features in ECG electrocardiogram (ECG) data for machine-learning based classification on normal and abnormal heartbeats. Stacked denoising autoencoders and autoencoders are used for feature learning during the pre-training phase. Deep neural networks are used during the fine-tuning phase. They used the MIT-BIH Arrhythmia Database and the MIT-BIH Noise Stress Test Database on ECG to validate the proposed approach. They experimented with six models to select the best deep learning model and demonstrated excellent results in terms of the classification accuracy, sensitivity, specificity, precision, and F1-score.

3. Smart Healthcare Systems

Five papers in this special issue are related to systems towards smart healthcare. Two of the papers aimed at the detection of the presence of a human being at specific locations either using pre-placed sensors [2], or using Bluetooth signals (assuming that the person being monitored carries a Bluetooth device) [8]. The remaining three papers aimed at direct human activity detection using inertial sensors [9], time of flight sensors [9], near-infrared camera [10], and Microsoft Kinect sensor [11].

In [2], Bassoli et al. proposed a system for human activity monitoring using a set of sensors at specific locations, such as armchair sensor at kitchen area, magnetic contact sensor on the bedroom door, toilet sensor, passive infrared sensor in the bedroom. These sensors are directly connected to the Internet to report their data to a predefined cloud service. The contribution of the paper is to experiment with different ways of saving the battery power on these sensors without losing any monitoring accuracy.

In [8], Marin et al. presented their work on the implementation of intelligent luminaries with sensing and communication capabilities for use in smart home. The system consists of a server, smart bulbs, and dummy bulbs. The server is responsible to collect and store data collected from the bulbs, and generating reporting and alerting based on the data collected. The smart bulbs are connected to the server using WiFi. The dummy bulbs are connected to smart bulbs using Bluetooth. Both the dummy bulbs and smart bulbs are capable of sensing Bluetooth signals for indoor localization. They both have the logic to control the intensity of their LEDs. The smart bulb is powered by a Raspberry Pi 3 and is equipped with a variety of environmental sensors, such as temperature, humidity, CO_2, and ambient light intensity. It could also send data to connected medical devices. The system can generate two types of alerts. One type of alerts is when the room temperature has exceeded a predefined threshold. The second type of alerts is when the monitored person has been present in the bathroom for too long.

Electronics **2020**, *9*, 1954

In [11], Rybarczyk et al. described a tele-rehabilitation system for patients that have received hip replacement surgery. Two methods were experimented for rehabilitation activity recognition based on data collected by a Microsoft Kinect sensor [12]. One is dynamic time warping, and the other is hidden Markov model. The authors also conducted a cognitive walkthrough to assess the activity recognition accuracy as as well the system's usability.

In [9], Xu et al. proposed to use sensor fusion to improve the measurement accuracy with inertial-measurement-unit (IMU) and time-of-arrival (ToA) devices. The latter is used to mitigate drift and accumulative errors of the former. They used simulation to demonstrate the better performance over individual IMU or ToA approaches in human motion tracking, particularly when the human moving direction changes. In addition, the authors performed a comprehensive fundamental limits analysis of their fusion method. They believe that their work paved the way for the method's use in wearable motion tracking applications, such as smart health.

In [10], Wang et al. reported a non-intrusive video-based sleep monitoring system. They addressed some major technical challenges in detecting human sleep poses with infrared images. They first identify joint positions and build a human model that is robust to occlusion. They then derived sleep poses from the joint positions using probabilistic reasoning to further overcome the missing joint data due to occlusion. They validated their system using video polysomnography data recorded in a sleep laboratory and the result is quite promising.

Acknowledgments: We thank all authors and peer reviewers for their invaluable contributions to this special issue.

Conflicts of Interest: The authors declare no conflict of interest.

References

1. Zhao, W.; Luo, X.; Qiu, T. Smart Healthcare. *Appl. Sci.* **2017**, *7*, 1176. [CrossRef]
2. Bassoli, M.; Bianchi, V.; Munari, I.D. A plug and play IoT Wi-Fi smart home system for human monitoring. *Electronics* **2018**, *7*, 200. [CrossRef]
3. Ricci, S.; Meacci, V. Data-adaptive coherent demodulator for high dynamics pulse-wave ultrasound applications. *Electronics* **2018**, *7*, 434. [CrossRef]
4. Pham, T.T.; Suh, Y.S. Spline function simulation data generation for walking motion using foot-mounted inertial sensors. *Electronics* **2019**, *8*, 18. [CrossRef]
5. Torti, E.; Florimbi, G.; Castelli, F.; Ortega, S.; Fabelo, H.; Callicó, G.M.; Marrero-Martin, M.; Leporati, F. Parallel K-means clustering for brain cancer detection using hyperspectral images. *Electronics* **2018**, *7*, 283. [CrossRef]
6. Calamanti, C.; Moccia, S.; Migliorelli, L.; Paolanti, M.; Frontoni, E. Learning-based screening of endothelial dysfunction from photoplethysmographic signals. *Electronics* **2019**, *8*, 271. [CrossRef]
7. Nurmaini, S.; Darmawahyuni, A.; Sakti Mukti, A.N.; Rachmatullah, M.N.; Firdaus, F.; Tutuko, B. Deep Learning-Based Stacked Denoising and Autoencoder for ECG Heartbeat Classification. *Electronics* **2020**, *9*, 135. [CrossRef]
8. Marin, I.; Vasilateanu, A.; Molnar, A.J.; Bocicor, M.I.; Cuesta-Frau, D.; Molina-Picó, A.; Goga, N. I-light—Intelligent luminaire based platform for home monitoring and assisted living. *Electronics* **2018**, *7*, 220. [CrossRef]
9. Xu, C.; He, J.; Zhang, X.; Zhou, X.; Duan, S. Towards human motion tracking: Multi-sensory IMU/TOA fusion method and fundamental limits. *Electronics* **2019**, *8*, 142. [CrossRef]
10. Wang, Y.K.; Chen, H.Y.; Chen, J.R. Unobtrusive Sleep Monitoring Using Movement Activity by Video Analysis. *Electronics* **2019**, *8*, 812. [CrossRef]

11. Rybarczyk, Y.; Luis Pérez Medina, J.; Leconte, L.; Jimenes, K.; González, M.; Esparza, D. Implementation and assessment of an intelligent motor tele-rehabilitation platform. *Electronics* **2019**, *8*, 58. [CrossRef]
12. Lun, R.; Zhao, W. A survey of applications and human motion recognition with microsoft kinect. *Int. J. Pattern Recognit. Artif. Intell.* **2015**, *29*, 1555008. [CrossRef]

Article

Deep Learning-Based Stacked Denoising and Autoencoder for ECG Heartbeat Classification

Siti Nurmaini *, Annisa Darmawahyuni, Akhmad Noviar Sakti Mukti,
Muhammad Naufal Rachmatullah, Firdaus Firdaus and Bambang Tutuko

Intelligent System Research Group, Universitas Sriwijaya, Palembang 30139, Indonesia;
riset.annisadarmawahyuni@gmail.com (A.D.); ahmadnoviar.19@gmail.com (A.N.S.M.);
naufalrachmatullah@gmail.com (M.N.R.); virdauz@gmail.com (F.F.); beng_tutuko@yahoo.com (B.T.)
* Correspondence: siti_nurmaini@unsri.ac.id; Tel.: +62-852-6804-8092

Received: 16 December 2019; Accepted: 8 January 2020; Published: 10 January 2020

Abstract: The electrocardiogram (ECG) is a widely used, noninvasive test for analyzing arrhythmia. However, the ECG signal is prone to contamination by different kinds of noise. Such noise may cause deformation on the ECG heartbeat waveform, leading to cardiologists' mislabeling or misinterpreting heartbeats due to varying types of artifacts and interference. To address this problem, some previous studies propose a computerized technique based on machine learning (ML) to distinguish between normal and abnormal heartbeats. Unfortunately, ML works on a handcrafted, feature-based approach and lacks feature representation. To overcome such drawbacks, deep learning (DL) is proposed in the pre-training and fine-tuning phases to produce an automated feature representation for multi-class classification of arrhythmia conditions. In the pre-training phase, stacked denoising autoencoders (DAEs) and autoencoders (AEs) are used for feature learning; in the fine-tuning phase, deep neural networks (DNNs) are implemented as a classifier. To the best of our knowledge, this research is the first to implement stacked autoencoders by using DAEs and AEs for feature learning in DL. Physionet's well-known MIT-BIH Arrhythmia Database, as well as the MIT-BIH Noise Stress Test Database (NSTDB). Only four records are used from the NSTDB dataset: 118 24 dB, 118 −6 dB, 119 24 dB, and 119 −6 dB, with two levels of signal-to-noise ratio (SNRs) at 24 dB and −6 dB. In the validation process, six models are compared to select the best DL model. For all fine-tuned hyperparameters, the best model of ECG heartbeat classification achieves an accuracy, sensitivity, specificity, precision, and F1-score of 99.34%, 93.83%, 99.57%, 89.81%, and 91.44%, respectively. As the results demonstrate, the proposed DL model can extract high-level features not only from the training data but also from unseen data. Such a model has good application prospects in clinical practice.

Keywords: heartbeat classification; arrhythmia; denoising autoencoder; autoencoder; deep learning

---

1. Introduction

The electrocardiogram (ECG) is a valuable technique for making decisions regarding cardiac heart diseases (CHDs) [1]. However, the ECG signal acquisition involves high-gain instrumentation amplifiers that are easily contaminated by different sources of noise, with characteristic frequency spectrums depending on the source [2]. ECG contaminants can be classified into different categories, including [2–4]; (i) power line interference at 60 or 50 Hz, depending on the power supply frequency; (ii) electrode contact noise of about 1 Hz, caused by improper contact between the body and electrodes; (iii) motion artifacts that produce long distortions at 100–500 ms, caused by patient's movements, affecting the electrode–skin impedance; (iv) muscle contractions, producing noise up to 10% of regular peak-to-peak ECG amplitude and frequency up to 10 kHz around 50 ms; and (v) baseline wander caused by respiratory activity at 0–0.5 Hz. All of these kinds of noise can interfere with the original ECG signal, which may cause deformations on the ECG waveforms and produce an abnormal signal.

To keep as much of the ECG signal as possible, the noise must be removed from the original signal to provide an accurate diagnosis. Unfortunately, the denoising process is a challenging task due to the overlap of all the noise signals at both low and high frequencies [4]. To prevent noise interference, several approaches have been proposed to denoise ECG signals based on adaptive filtering [5–7], wavelet methods [8,9], and empirical mode decomposition [10,11]. However, all these proposed techniques require analytical calculation and high computation; also, because cut-off processing can lose clinically essential components of the ECG signal, these techniques run the risk of misdiagnosis [12]. Currently, one machine learning (ML) technique, named denoising autoencoders (DAEs), can be applied to reconstruct clean data from its noisy version. DAEs can extract robust features by adding noise to the input data [13]. Previous results indicate that DAEs outperform conventional denoising techniques [14–16]. Recently, DAEs have been used in various fields, such as image denoising [17], human activity recognition [18], and feature representation [19].

To produce the proper interpretation of CHDs, the ECG signal must be classified after the denoising process. However, DAEs are unable to automatically produce the extracted feature [15,16]. Feature extraction is an important phase in the classification process for obtaining robust performance. If feature representation is bad, it will cause the classifier to produce a low performance. Such a limitation in DAEs leaves room for further improvement upon the existing ECG denoising method through combination with other methods for feature extraction. Some techniques, including principal component analysis (PCA) or linear discriminant analysis (LDA) algorithms, have been proposed [20,21]. However, these cannot extract the feature directly from the network structure and they usually require a trial-and-error process, which is time-consuming [20,21]. Currently, by using autoencoders (AEs), extracting features of the raw input data can work automatically. This leads to an improvement in the prediction model performances, while, at the same time, reducing the complexity of the feature design task. Hence, a combination of two models of DAEs and AEs is a challenging task in ECG signal processing applications.

The classification phase based on ECG signal processing studies can be divided into two types of learning: supervised and unsupervised [22–27]. Such two types of learning provide good performance in ECG beats [26–28], or rhythm classification [27–29]. Among them, Yu et al. [26] proposed higher-order statistics of sub-band components for heartbeat classification with noisy ECG. Their proposed classifier is a feedforward backpropagation neural network (FBNN). The feature selection algorithm is based on the correlation coefficient with five levels of the discrete wavelet transform (DWT). However, for exceptional evaluation, DWT becomes computationally intensive. Besides its discretization, DWT is less efficient and less natural, and it takes time and energy to learn which wavelets will serve each specific purpose. Li et al. [27] focused on the five-level ECG signal quality classification algorithm, adding three types of real ECG noise at different signal-to-noise ratio (SNR) levels. A support vector machine (SVM) classifier with a Gaussian radial basis function kernel was employed to classify the ECG signal quality. However, ECG signal classification with traditional ML based on supervised shallow architecture is limited by feature extraction and classification because it uses a handcrafted, feature-based approach. Also, for larger amounts of ECG data and variance, the shallow architecture can be employed for this purpose. On the other hand, the deep learning (DL) technique extracts features directly from data [24,25]. In our previous work [30], the DL technique successfully worked to generate feature representations from raw data. This process is carried out by conducting an unsupervised training approach to process feature learning and followed by a classification process. DL has superiority in automated feature learning, while ML is only limited to feature engineering.

Artificial neural networks (ANNs) are a well-known technique in ML. ANNs increase the depth of structure by adding multiple hidden layers, named deep neural networks (DNNs). Some of these layers can be adjusted to better predict the final outcome. More layers enable DNNs to fit complex functions with fewer parameters and improve accuracy [27]. Compared with shallow neural networks, DNNs with multiple nonlinear hidden layers can discover more complex relationships between input layers and output layers. High-level layers can learn features from lower layers to obtain higher-order and more abstract expressions of inputs [28]. However, DNNs cannot learn features from noisy data.

The combination of DNNs and autoencoders (AEs) can learn efficient data coding in an unsupervised manner. However, the AEs do not perform well when the data samples are very noisy [28]. Therefore, DAEs were invented to enable AEs to learn features from noisy data by adding noise to the input data [28].

To the best of our knowledge, no research has implemented the DL technique using stacked DAEs and AEs to accomplish feature learning for the noisy signal of ECG heartbeat classification. This paper proposes a combination DAEs–AEs–DNNs processing method to calculate appropriate features from ECG raw data to address automated classification. This technique consists of beat segmentation, noise cancelation with DAEs, feature extraction with AEs, and heartbeat classification with DNNs. The validation and evaluation of classifiers are based on the performance metrics of accuracy, sensitivity, specificity, precision, and F1-score. The rest of this paper is organized as follows. In Section 2, we explain the materials and the proposed method. In Section 3, we conduct an experiment on a public dataset and compare the proposed method with existing research. Finally, we conclude the paper and discuss future work in Section 4.

2. Research Method

2.1. Autoencoder

Autoencoders (AEs) are a neural network trained to try to map the input to its output in an unsupervised manner. AEs have a hidden layer h that describes the coding used to represent the input [29]. AEs consist of two parts—the encoder ($h = f(a)$) and the decoder ($r = g(h)$) network. f and g are called the encoder and decoder mappings, respectively. The number of hidden units is smaller than the input or output layers, which achieve encoding of the data in a lower-dimensional space and extract the most discriminative features. Given the training samples D (dimensional vectors) $a = \{a_1, a_2, \ldots, a_m\}$, the encoder forms the x input vector into d (dimensional vectors), a hidden representation $h = \{h_1, h_2, \ldots, h_m\}$. This study implements the rectified linear unit (ReLU) as an activation function in the first hidden encoding layer. In addition, the activation function σ, $h = \sigma(W^{(1)}x + b^{(1)})$, in the output, where $W^{(1)}$ is a $d \times D$ (dimensional weight matrix), and $b^{(1)}$ is a d (dimensional bias vector). Then, vector h is transformed back into the reconstruction vector $r = \{r_1, r_2, \ldots, r_m\}$ by the decoder $z = \sigma(W^{(2)}h + b^{(2)})$, where r is a D (dimensional vector), $W^{(2)}$ is a $D \times d$ (dimensional weight matrix), and $b^{(2)}$ is a D (dimensional bias vector). The AEs' training aims to optimize the parameter set $\theta = \{W^{(1)}, b^{(2)}, W^{(2)}, b^{(2)}\}$ for reducing the error of reconstruction. The mean squared error (MSE) is used as a loss function in standard AEs [26,30]:

$$l_{MSE}(\theta) = \frac{1}{m}\sum_{i=1}^{m} L_{MSE}(x_i, z_i) = \frac{1}{m}\sum_{i=1}^{m} \left(\frac{1}{2}\|z_i - x_i\|^2\right) \tag{1}$$

AEs are usually trained using only a clean ECG signal dataset. For the further task of treating noisy ECG data, denoising AEs (DAEs) are introduced. In the case of a single-hidden-layer neural AE trained with noisy ECG data as input and a clean signal as an output, it includes one nonlinear encoding and decoding stage, as follows:

$$y = f(\widetilde{x}_i) = \sigma(W_2\widetilde{x}_i + b) \tag{2}$$

and

$$z = g(y) = \sigma(W_2 y + c) \tag{3}$$

where $\widetilde{x}$ is a corrupted version of x, b and c represent vectors of biases of input and output layers, respectively, and x is the desired output. Usually, a tied weight matrix (i.e., $W_1 = W_2^T = W$) is used as one type of regularization. This paper uses a noisy signal to train the DAEs before the automated feature extraction with AEs. DAEs are a stochastic extension of classic AEs. DAEs try to reconstruct a clean input from its corrupted version. The initial input x is corrupted to $\tilde{x}$ by a stochastic mapping $\tilde{x} - q(\tilde{x}|x)$. Subsequently, DAEs use the corrupted $\tilde{x}$ as the input data and then map to the corresponding hidden representation y and ultimately to its reconstruction z. After the reconstruction signal is obtained from DAEs, the signal-to-noise ratio (SNRs) value must be calculated so that the signal quality can be measured [30], as follows:

$$SNR = 10 * \log_{10}\left[\frac{\sum_n x_d^2(n)}{\sum_n (x_d(n) - x(n))^2}\right] \tag{4}$$

where x_d and x are the reconstructed and the original signal, respectively.

DAEs have shown good results in extracting noisy robust features in ECG signals and other applications [14].

2.2. Proposed Deep Learning Structure

The basis of DL is a bio-inspired algorithm from the earliest neural network. Fundamentally, DL formalizes how a biological neuron works, in which the brain can process information by billions of these interlinked neurons [30]. DL has provided new advanced approaches to the training of DNNs architectures with many hidden layers, outperforming its ML counterpart. The features extracted in DL by using data-driven methods can be more accurate. An autoencoder is a neural network designed specifically for this purpose. In our previous work [30], deep AEs were shown to be implemented in ECG signal processing before the classification task, extracting high-level features not only from the training data but also from unseen data. The Softmax function is used as an activation function, and it can be treated as the probability of each label for the output layer of the classifier. Here, let N be the number of units of the output layer, let x be the input, and let x_i be the output of unit i. Then, the output $p(i)$ of unit i is defined by the following equation,

$$p(i) = \frac{e^{xi}}{\sum\limits_{j=1}^{N} e^{xj}} \tag{5}$$

Cross entropy is used as the loss function of the classifier L_f, as follows:

$$L_f(\theta) = -\frac{1}{n}\sum_{i=1}^{n}\sum_{j=1}^{m} y_{ij}\log(p_{ij}) \tag{6}$$

where n is the sample size, m is the number of classes, p_{ij} is the output of the classifier of class j of the i_{th} sample, and y_{ij} is the annotated label of class j of the i_{th} sample.

In our study, the proposed DL structure consists of noise cancelation with DAEs, automated feature extraction with AEs, and DNNs as a classifier, as presented in Figure 1. DAEs structure is divided into three layers, namely the input, encoding, and output layer. There are two models of DAEs structured for validation—Model 1, which has an input, encoding, and output layer which each have 252 nodes, respectively, while in Model 2 the input and output layers have 252 nodes, respectively, and the encoding layer has 126 nodes. For all models, the activation function in the encoding layer is the rectified linear unit (ReLU) and in the output layer is sigmoid. The compilation of the DAEs model requires two arguments, namely the optimizer and loss function. The optimization method used in the DAE construction is adaptive moment estimation (Adam), with the mean squared error as the loss function. As the proposed DAEs structure, SNR −6 dB is used for the input as the noisiest ECG and SNR 24 dB for the desired signal as the best ECG quality in the dataset used in this study. After doing some experiments and completing the training phase, a good accuracy with a total of 400 epochs and a batch size of 64 is obtained. Then, the DAEs model can already be used to reconstruct the signal with SNR −6 dB, and the results of the reconstructed signal will approach an SNR of 24 dB.

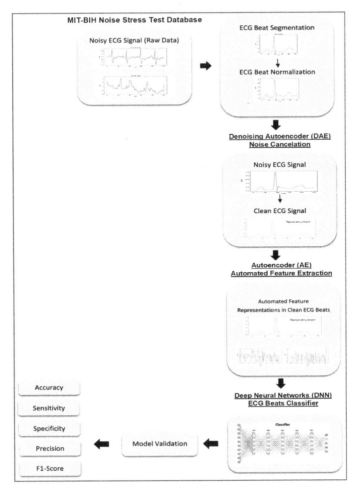

Figure 1. The proposed deep learning (DL) structures.

After all noisy signals have been removed by the DAEs, the next process is to extract the features of the signal. Automated feature extraction using the AEs [30] is the final step before the ECG heartbeat can be classified using DNNs. The ECG signal that has been reconstructed by the DAEs is carried out in a training process with 200 epochs and a batch size of 32 for the AE architecture. After completing the AEs' training phase, the reconstruction signal is used for prediction in the encoder, from the input layer to the encoding layer. After the signal is predicted in the encoder, a feature of the reconstructed signal is obtained. This reconstructed signal is used as the classifier input of the DNNs. Like the DAEs architecture, ReLU and Sigmoid were implemented in the encoding layer and output layer, respectively. The encoding layer of the AEs is used as an input for the DNNs classifier, which has five hidden layers and represents five classes of ECG heartbeat. In the input layer, there are 32, 63, and 126 nodes, which refer to the length of each feature signal. Then, in the output layer, there are 5 nodes, which represent the number of classified ECG heartbeat classes. Each of the hidden layers has 100 nodes. The DNNs architecture was conducted by ReLU in all hidden layers and by Softmax in the output layer. The loss function of categorical cross-entropy and Adam optimizer are also implemented in the proposed DNNs architecture. This DNNs architecture was trained to as many as 200 epochs with a batch size of 48.

2.3. Experimental Result

2.3.1. Data Preparation

The raw data were taken from ECG signals from the MIT-BIH Arrhythmia Database (MITDB), and the added noise signals were obtained from the MIT-BIH Noise Stress Test Database (NSTDB). The available source can be accessed at https://physionet.org/content/nstdb/1.0.0/. This database includes 12 half-hour ECG recordings and 3 half-hour recordings of noise typical in ambulatory ECG recordings. Only two recordings (the 118 and 119 records) from the MITDB are used for the NSTDB. From the MITDB's two clean recordings, the NSTDB records consisted of six levels of SNR, from the best to the worst ECG signal quality: 24 dB, 18 dB, 12 dB, 6 dB, 0 dB, and −6 dB. The NSTDB consists of 12 half-hour ECG recordings and 3 half-hour ECG noise recordings. Only two levels of SNRs were used in this study—the SNRs of 24 dB and −6 dB, the best and the worst ECG signal quality, respectively. The two levels consisted of four records; 118 24 dB, 118 −6 dB, 119 24 dB, and 119 −6dB were used in this study. SNRs of −6dB and 24 dB were processed by the DAEs. The ECG raw data are represented in Figure 2.

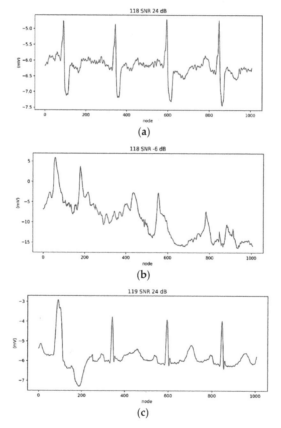

(a)

(b)

(c)

Figure 2. *Cont.*

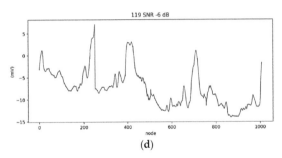

(d)

Figure 2. Electrocardiogram (ECG) raw data with noise. (**a**) Record 118 (24 dB), (**b**) Record 118 (−6 dB), (**c**) Record 119 (24 dB), (**d**) Record 119 (−6 dB).

2.3.2. ECG Segmentation and Normalization

In our previous work [30], ECG signal segmentation was used to find the R-peak position. After the R-peak position was detected, sampling was performed at approximately 0.7-s segments for a single beat. The section was divided into two intervals: t1 of 0.25 s before the R-peak position and t2 of 0.45 s after the R-peak position. The ECG records of 118 24 dB, 118 −6 dB, 119 24 dB, and 119 −6 dB were segmented into the beat (see Figure 3).

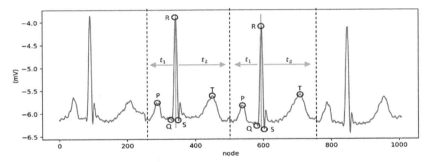

Figure 3. The ECG segmentation process.

The record of 118 contained four types of heartbeat: Atrial Premature (A), Right Bundle Branch Block (R), Non-conducted P-wave (P), and Premature Ventricular Contraction (V). The record of 119 contains two types of heartbeat: Normal (N) and Premature Ventricular Contraction (V). The total beats of each record were 2287 and 1987, respectively. The number and representation of each beat are represented in Table 1, and the sample of a heartbeat after segmentation in Figure 4.

Table 1. Heartbeat distribution after the ECG segmentation.

Beats	Record of 118	Record of 119	Total
N	None	1543	1543
V	16	444	460
R	2165	None	2165
A	96	None	96
P	10	None	10
Total	2287	1987	4274

11

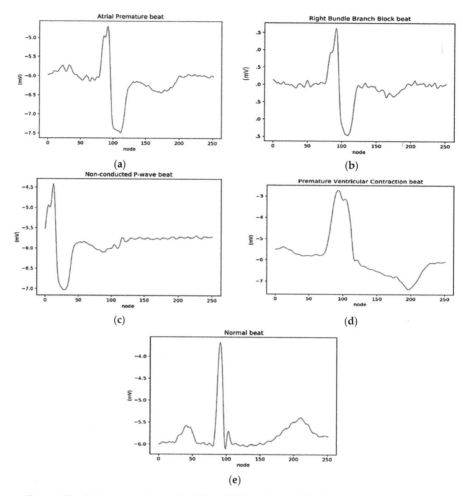

Figure 4. Heartbeat segmentation result. (**a**) Beat 959 label A (record 118), (**b**) Beat 72 label R (record 118), (**c**) Beat 2018 label P (record 118), (**d**) Beat 2323 label V (record 119), (**e**) Beat 2320 label N (record 119).

After the segmentation of each beat, the ECG signal was normalized into 0 and 1 using the normalized bound. Normalized bound changed the value of the lower limit (*lb*) and upper limit (*ub*) on the amplitude of a signal to the desired range without changing the pattern or shape of the signal itself. In this study, the data was acquired in the pre-process with the lower limit (0) and upper limit (1), respectively. The mathematical function of the normalization with normalized bound is as follows:

$$f(x) = x * coef - (x_{mid} * coef) + mid \tag{7}$$

where

$$coef = \left(\frac{ub - lb}{x_{max} - x_{min}}\right) \tag{8}$$

x_{mid} is the midpoint of the input signal:

$$x_{mid} = x_{max} - \frac{x_{max} - x_{min}}{2} \tag{9}$$

$x_{\max}$ is the peak point of the input signal, $x_{\min}$ is the lower point of the input signal, and *mid* is the midpoint of the specified limit:

$$mid = ub - \frac{ub - lb}{2} \tag{10}$$

The sample result of normalized ECG beats can be seen in Figure 5, in which the range of amplitude (mV) of signal is 0 and 1.

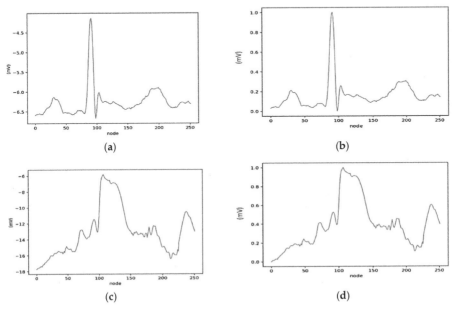

Figure 5. The sample of normalized beats in record 119. (**a**) ECG signal 24 dB before normalization, (**b**) ECG signal 24 dB after normalization, (**c**) ECG signal −6 dB before normalization, (**d**) ECG signal −6 dB after normalization.

2.3.3. Pre-Training and Fine-Tuning

The DL structure was formed by combining the pre-training DAEs' and AEs' encoding layers and the fine-tuning of the DNN algorithm with the fully connected layer. For the first model, ECG noise removal was based on the DAEs structure with 252 nodes in each of its encoding layers. Then, the second model used 126 nodes in the encoding layer. For the first model produced by the DAEs, the loss average was 0.0029, and the SNR reconstruction was 23.1527 dB. The DAEs' second model produced a loss of 0.0037 and a SNR reconstruction of 20.6129 dB. Both models had the desired SNRs of 25.8182 dB. Comparing the two models, the SNR reconstruction for the first model was 23.1527 dB and 20.6129 dB for the second. It can be concluded that the first model had a higher SNR than the second model. Higher SNRs were achieved, producing a better result for the reconstructed signal. Therefore, for the AEs' automated feature extraction, the DAEs' first model with 252 nodes was used, and the result of the ECG construction can be seen in Figure 6.

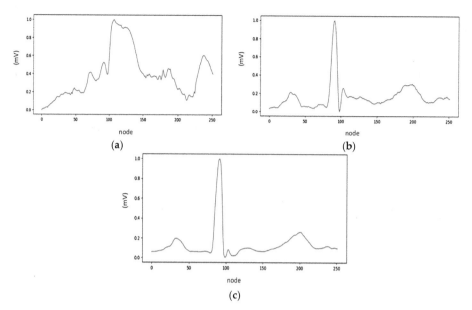

Figure 6. The sample of denoising autoencoders (DAEs)–autoencoders (AEs) process for ECG signal. (a) Noisy ECG Signal, (b) Target, (c) Reconstruction.

After the DAEs model was trained, a reconstruction result (clean ECG signal) was produced. A clean ECG signal was used as an input into the AEs model to extract features. The feature was learned through the encoder and decoder steps. After the AEs model was trained, the encoder part was used as the feature output, and all features (f1, f2, f3, ... fn) were used as an input into the DNNs model to classify the ECG heartbeat. All steps of feature learning are presented in Figure 7. In the third and fourth models there were five layers, in which there are 63 nodes in the encoding layer. For the fifth and sixth models, we propose seven layers, in which there are 32 nodes in the encoding layer. Based on our previous work [30], for all six models in this study, we propose ReLU and Softmax activation functions with Adam optimization (0.0001 as the learning rate). Adam optimization allows for the use of adaptive learning levels for each variable. The total epoch of each model is 200, with a batch size of 48.

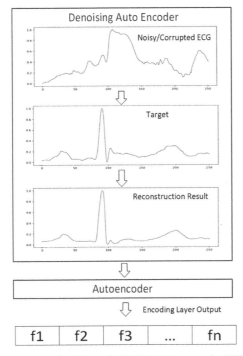

Figure 7. The sample of the stacked DAEs–AEs process for ECG signal.

To select a good classifier model, the DAEs, AEs, and DNNs change in some structures in the validation phase. Only DL with high performance is selected as the best DL model. This paper presents a total of six models for ECG heartbeat classification validation (see Table 2). The weights of the classifier are extracted from the pre-trained DAEs–AEs model, and the fully connected layer is added as an output layer with Softmax as an activation function and categorical cross-entropy as a loss function.

Table 2. Model validation of ECG heartbeat classification.

Model	DAEs	AEs	DNNs
1	(252-252-252) (ReLU-Sigmoid)	Autoencoder (252-252-252) (ReLU-Sigmoid)	(126-100-100-100-100-100-5) (ReLU-ReLU-ReLU-ReLU-ReLU-Softmax)
2	(252-252-252) (ReLU-Sigmoid)	Deep Autoencoder (252-126-63-126-252) (ReLU-ReLU-ReLU-ReLU-Sigmoid)	(63-100-100-100-100-100-5) (ReLU-ReLU-ReLU-ReLU-ReLU-Softmax)
3	(252-252-252) (ReLU-Sigmoid)	Deep Autoencoder (252-126-63-32-63-126-252) (ReLU-ReLU-ReLU-ReLU-ReLU-Sigmoid)	(32-100-100-100-100-100-5) (ReLU-ReLU-ReLU-ReLU-ReLU-Softmax)
4	(252-126-252) (ReLU-Sigmoid)	Autoencoder (252-126-252) (ReLU-Sigmoid)	(126-100-100-100-100-100-5) (ReLU-ReLU-ReLU-ReLU-ReLU-Softmax)
5	(252-126-252) (ReLU-Sigmoid)	Deep Autoencoder (252-126-63-126-252) (ReLU-ReLU-ReLU-ReLU-Sigmoid)	(63-100-100-100-100-100-5) (ReLU-ReLU-ReLU-ReLU-ReLU-Softmax)
6	(252-126-252) (ReLU-Sigmoid)	Deep Autoencoder (252-126-63-32-63-126-252) (ReLU-ReLU-ReLU-ReLU-ReLU-Sigmoid)	(32-100-100-100-100-100-5) (ReLU-ReLU-ReLU-ReLU-ReLU-Softmax)

The classification performances were measured by using the following five metrics in the literature: accuracy, sensitivity, specificity, precision and F1-score [22,30]. While accuracy can be used for evaluating the overall performance as benchmarking, the other metrics can measure the performance of a specific class of validation model. The five metrics that measured for model validation can be expressed as follows:

$$Accuracy = \frac{\sum\limits_{i=1}^{l} TP_i + \sum\limits_{i=1}^{l} TN_i}{\sum\limits_{i=1}^{l} TP_i + \sum\limits_{i=1}^{l} TN_i + \sum\limits_{i=1}^{l} FP_i + \sum\limits_{i=1}^{l} FN_i} \tag{11}$$

$$Sensitivity = \frac{\sum\limits_{i=1}^{l} TP_i}{\sum\limits_{i=1}^{l} TP_i + \sum\limits_{i=1}^{l} FN_i} \tag{12}$$

$$Specificity = \frac{\sum\limits_{i=1}^{l} TN_i}{\sum\limits_{i=1}^{l} TN_i + \sum\limits_{i=1}^{l} FP_i} \tag{13}$$

$$Precision = \frac{\sum\limits_{i=1}^{l} TP_i}{\sum\limits_{i=1}^{l} TP_i + \sum\limits_{i=1}^{l} FN_i} \tag{14}$$

$$F1 - Score = \frac{\sum\limits_{i=1}^{l} TP_i}{\sum\limits_{i=1}^{l} TP_i + \sum\limits_{i=1}^{l} FN_i} \tag{15}$$

where I is the number of beat classes; TP_i (true positives) is the number of class i^{th} that are correctly classified; TN_i (true negative) is the number of non-class i^{th} that are correctly classified; FP_i (false positive) is the number of non-class i^{th} that are incorrectly predicted as class i^{th} types, and FN_i (false negative) is the number of class i^{th} that are incorrectly predicted as non-class i^{th}.

3. Results and Analysis

In this study, the training process used 90% of the data, and the remaining data was used for the testing process. The testing set was used to make decisions on hyperparameter values and model selection in Table 2. The next procedure was the classification stage with DNNs after the feature had been extracted in the AEs. Firstly, in the input layer, different nodes were compared: 32, 63, and 126. Then, the fine-tuned nodes were used to obtain the best architecture in the input layer. As seen in Table 2, the first model of DNNs, with 126 nodes, was chosen because it outperformed the other nodes in the result. The architecture of the first DNNs model consisted of one input layer, five hidden layers (each with 100 nodes), and the output layers which represented five classes of ECG beat (i.e., A, R, P, V, and N). In the output layers, we applied the Softmax function. To evaluate our proposed DNNs model, five performance metrics were used: accuracy, sensitivity, specificity, precision, and F1-score. The comparison result based on these metrics of the six DL models in Table 2 is shown in Tables 3 and 4, for the training and testing sets, respectively. As displayed in Table 3, Model 1 yields the highest accuracy, specificity, precision, and F1-score in the training phase. For the testing results in Table 4, Model 1 also yields the highest results in all performance metrics. Therefore, Model 1 is our proposed DL architecture for ECG noise removal and AEs feature extraction to the DNNs classification task. Unfortunately, poor performances were shown in Models 5 and 6. This is because Models 5 and 6 use the DAEs' second model that produced a loss of 0.0037 and SNR reconstruction of 20.6129 dB. This reconstruction is not close to the target signal of 24 dB, meaning that the ECG is still noisy. This will affect the classifier's performance results at the end. The sensitivity, precision, and F1-score achieved only 56.97% to 59.19%. The sensitivity of Model 5 in training is inversely proportional to the testing set. In training, the sensitivity is 98.90%; however, in testing, it only achieves 56.97%. As seen in Tables 2 and 4, the number of AE encoding layers in Models 5 and 6 yields the worst result in the testing phase of the classifier.

Table 3. The performance evaluation of DL models in the training phase.

Training	Validation Model (%)					
Metrics	1	2	3	4	5	6
Accuracy	99.49	99.39	99.26	99.14	99.03	98.93
Sensitivity	95.94	96.83	93.00	94.59	98.90	98.84
Specificity	99.68	99.66	99.52	99.55	99.49	99.40
Precision	91.23	87.62	87.66	77.80	78.06	73.51
F1-Score	93.13	90.35	89.58	81.10	79.08	76.18

Table 4. The performance evaluation of DL models in the testing phase.

Testing	Model Validation (%)					
Metrics	1	2	3	4	5	6
Accuracy	99.34	99.06	99.06	98.97	98.22	98.41
Sensitivity	93.83	79.54	93.56	79.07	56.97	57.49
Specificity	99.57	99.33	99.35	99.43	98.75	98.94
Precision	89.81	87.63	89.42	79.90	59.19	59.37
F1-Score	91.44	81.80	91.11	79.48	58.04	58.40

As for classification, to analyze the prediction of the DL model in each class during the training and testing phase, the confusion matrix was applied. Tables 5 and 6 present the predicted ECG heartbeat class only for the first model as the proposed architecture. For the A-class (atrial premature beat), compared to the R class (right bundle branch block), there are 11 misclassified ECG heartbeats in the training phase and only two misclassified beats in the testing phase. From the result of the confusion matrix, the A-class is the worst result of all the classes. Beats were misclassified as R beats in both the training and testing phases. This may have occurred because of the larger amount of data for R beats compared to A beats. This may have occurred due to such a large amount of comparison data for the A and R beats. Later, the morphology between these two beats is similar.

Table 5. Confusion matrix in the training phase.

Class	A	R	P	V	N
A	49	37	0	0	0
R	11	1937	0	0	0
P	0	0	9	0	0
V	0	0	0	413	1
N	0	0	0	0	1389

Table 6. Confusion matrix in the testing phase.

Class	A	R	P	V	N
A	5	5	0	0	0
R	2	215	0	0	0
P	0	0	1	0	0
V	0	0	0	46	0
N	0	0	0	0	154

In this study, we compared the classification process of two types of feature-learning condition: with and without AEs. However, by excluding the AEs structure, the comparison is conducted only for the best models of DNNs structure. Such conditions help investigate what affects the DNNs' classifier performance without feature extraction. With the same DL architecture with DAEs, the result of the testing phase is presented in Table 7. Table 7 shows a significant gap between the DAEs–AEs–DNNs model and the DAEs–DNNs model. The DAEs–AEs–DNNs model outperformed the DAEs–DNNs model for all five ECG beat classes, with average scores of 99.34%, 93.83%, 99.575%, 89.81%, and 91.44% in accuracy, sensitivity, specificity, precision, and F1-score, respectively. Without AEs, the result of all the performance metrics decreases significantly, including a concerningly poor performance score of 78.67% in precision. DAEs are trained in a similar yet different way. When performing the self-supervised training, the input ECG signal is corrupted by adding noise. The DAEs, whose task is to recover the original input, are trained locally to denoise corrupted versions of their inputs. However, sometimes the input and expected output of ECG are not identical, which affects the DNNs classifier. Therefore, the DAEs are stacked with AEs as a solution to provide a good representation for a better-performing classifier. Intuitively, if a representation allows for a proper reconstruction of its input, it means that it has retained much of the information that was present in that input.

Table 7. The comparison results of DAEs–AEs–DNNs and DAEs–DNNs.

Architecture	Performance Metrics (%)				
	Accuracy	Sensitivity	Specificity	Precision	F1-Score
DAEs–DNNs (without AEs)	96.95	85.23	97.67	78.67	80.52
DAEs–AEs–DNNs (proposed model)	99.34	93.83	99.57	89.81	91.44

To verify the proposed DL model, the accuracy and the loss curve are shown in Figure 8a,b, respectively. In Figure 8a, the accuracy of the training set starts above 60% in the first epoch. Later, in the testing set, the accuracy of the model achieves a satisfactory accuracy of about 99.34%. Figure 8b shows decreasing error until 0.6%, along with increasing epochs in the training and testing set. Both curves produce suitable shapes, as the DAEs and AEs' reconstruction results show effective noise cancelation before processing with the DNNs. However, after 60 rounds of training, the DL cannot predict accurately when AEs are not included in the structure (see Figure 8c,d). This shows that while DAEs perform the denoising process to reconstruct the clean data, they fail to reconstruct the representation feature for the classifier. Without AEs, the input to DNNs is the DAE's encoding. Therefore, the output classifier reaches a 40% loss in the testing process and produces overfitting due to the ECG beats' signal being incorrectly predicted by the DNNs (see Figure 8c). As seen in Figure 8d, the training error is much lower than the testing error, thus producing a high variance.

The performance of the proposed DL structure was compared to three previous studies in the literature [26,27,31], due to limited previous research classifying heartbeats with noisy data using ML including SVM, FBNNs, and CNNs (see Table 8). The results found that, with an accuracy level of 99.34%, our proposed DL structure outperformed the SVM, FBNN, and CNN classifiers of ECG noise removal and feature representation algorithms (see Table 8). The proposed DL structure yields higher accuracy than FBNNs, SVM, and CNNs, which yield 97.50%, 80.26%, and 95.70% accuracy, respectively. We can clearly observe that the proposed DL model with stacked DAEs–AEs successfully reconstructs the heartbeat ECG signal from the noisy signal and is effective for arrythmia diagnosis. In our previous research [30], the DL model with DWT for noise cancelation was proposed with the MITDB dataset without noise stress. This study took the best DL model from [30] and added data from the NSTDB, producing a higher than 99% accuracy for two conditions of the ECG signal. This means the proposed DL model may be generalizable in arrhythmia diagnosis.

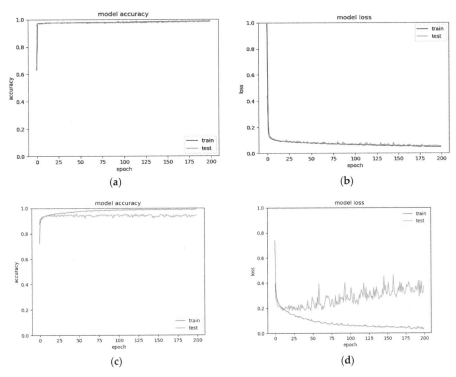

Figure 8. DL performance based on accuracy and loss curves. (**a**) Accuracy curve (DAEs–AEs–DNNs), (**b**) Loss curve (DAEs–AEs–DNNs), (**c**) Accuracy curve (DAEs–DNNs), (**d**) Loss curve (DAEs–DNNs).

Table 8. The benchmark of the proposed model with another DL structure.

Authors	Dataset	Noise Cancelation	Feature Extraction	Classifier	Case	Accuracy (%)
Yu et al. [26]	MITDB	DWT	Correlation coefficient	FBNNs	Beats classification	97.50
Li et al. [27]	MITDB	Filter	Variance	SVM	ECG signal quality	80.26
Ochiai et al. [31]	MITDB	DAEs	CNNs	CNNs 1D/2D	Beats classification	95.70
Nurmaini et al. [30]	MITDB	DWT	AEs	DNNs	Beats classification	99.73
Proposed	MITDB with NSTDB	DAEs	AEs	DNNs	Beats classification	99.34

4. Conclusions

ECG heartbeat classification is still an interesting issue in medical applications. The classification process is not a simple task because the ECG may get corrupted by noise during acquisition due to different types of artifacts and signal interference. The noise of the ECG can affect cardiologists' misinterpretation of arrhythmia cases. To overcome such problems, a deep learning (DL) approach is presented in this study. We exploit DAEs for noise cancellation, AEs for feature learning and DNNs for classification. In our DL structure, the DAEs and AEs structure is staked to produce good feature representation. To the best of our knowledge, this research is the first to stack autoencoders by using DAEs and AEs for feature learning. The encoding layer of the DAEs was implemented in the signal reconstructed with the AEs. Afterward, six DL models were compared to select the best classifier architecture. All DL models were validated by using the MIT-BIH Noise Stress Test Database. The result shows that the proposed DL model demonstrates superior automated feature learning as compared to a shallow ML model. ML requires human interference and expertise in determining robust features, making it time-consuming in the labelling and data processing steps. Moreover, the proposed DL structure is able to extract high-level features not only from the training data but also from unseen data. For all fine-tuned hyperparameters, the best model of ECG heartbeat classifier is the first model (Model 1) with one hidden layer in DAEs, one hidden layer in AEs and five hidden layers in DNNs. Such a DL model produces accuracy, sensitivity, specificity, precision, and F1-score of 99.34%, 93.83%, 99.57%, 89.81%, and 91.44%, respectively. Moreover, the proposed DL model with stacked DAEs and AEs, outperforms another DL structure without AEs. However, this study put greater focus on feature learning with denoising ECG signals. Therefore, the practicality and generalizability of multiple measurements of the ECG recording must be improved in the future to ensure the proposed method is suitable for clinical diagnosis with the widely used 12-lead ECG. With the collection of more abnormal ECG recordings, we hope to produce a good classifier for diagnosing more cardiac diseases with our proposed DL models.

Author Contributions: S.N. Conceptualization, resources, supervision, and writing—review & editing; A.D. Formal analysis, software, and writing—original draft; A.N.S.M. Software; M.N.R. Software and writing—review & editing; F.F. Writing—review & editing; B.T. writing—review & editing. All authors have read and agreed to the published version of the manuscript.

Funding: This work was supported by Basic Research Grants (096/SP2H/LT/DRPM/2019) from the Ministry of Research, Technology, and Higher Education and Unggulan Profesi Grants from Universitas Sriwijaya Indonesia.

Acknowledgments: The authors are very thankful to Wahyu Caesarendra, Universiti Brunei Darussalam, for his valuable comments, discussion, and suggestions for improving the paper.

Conflicts of Interest: The authors declare no conflict of interest.

References

1. Guaragnella, C.; Rizzi, M.; Giorgio, A. Marginal Component Analysis of ECG Signals for Beat-to-Beat Detection of Ventricular Late Potentials. *Electronics* **2019**, *8*, 1000. [CrossRef]
2. Castillo, E.; Morales, D.P.; Garcia, A.; Martinez-Marti, F.; Parrilla, L.; Palma, A.J. Noise suppression in ECG signals through efficient one-step wavelet processing techniques. *J. Appl. Math.* **2013**, *2013*. [CrossRef]
3. Antczak, K. Deep Recurrent Neural Networks for ECG Signal Denoising. *arXiv* **2018**, arXiv:1807.11551.
4. Wang, D.; Si, Y.; Yang, W.; Zhang, G.; Li, J. A Novel Electrocardiogram Biometric Identification Method Based on Temporal-Frequency Autoencoding. *Electronics* **2019**, *8*, 667. [CrossRef]
5. Meireles, A.J.M. ECG Denoising Based on Adaptive Signal Processing Technique. Master's Thesis, Instituto Politécnico do Porto, Instituto Superior de Engenharia do Porto, Porto, Portugal, 2011.
6. Joshi, V.; Verma, A.R.; Singh, Y. De-noising of ECG signal using Adaptive Filter based on MPSO. *Procedia Comput. Sci.* **2015**, *57*, 395–402. [CrossRef]
7. Sharma, I.; Mehra, R.; Singh, M. Adaptive filter design for ECG noise reduction using LMS algorithm. In Proceedings of the 2015 4th International Conference on Reliability, Infocom Technologies and Optimization (ICRITO) (Trends and Future Directions), Noida, India, 2–4 September 2015; pp. 1–6.
8. Aqil, M.; Jbari, A.; Bourouhou, A. ECG Signal Denoising by Discrete Wavelet Transform. *Int. J. Online Eng.* **2017**, *13*. [CrossRef]
9. Srivastava, M.; Anderson, C.L.; Freed, J.H. A new wavelet denoising method for selecting decomposition levels and noise thresholds. *IEEE Access* **2016**, *4*, 3862–3877. [CrossRef]

10. Kong, Q.; Song, Q.; Hai, Y.; Gong, R.; Liu, J.; Shao, X. Denoising signals for photoacoustic imaging in frequency domain based on empirical mode decomposition. *Optik (Stuttg)* **2018**, *160*, 402–414. [CrossRef]

11. Nguyen, P.; Kim, J.-M. Adaptive ECG denoising using genetic algorithm-based thresholding and ensemble empirical mode decomposition. *Inf. Sci. (N. Y.)* **2016**, *373*, 499–511. [CrossRef]

12. Yoon, D.; Lim, H.S.; Jung, K.; Kim, T.Y.; Lee, S. Deep Learning-Based Electrocardiogram Signal Noise Detection and Screening Model. *Healthc. Inform. Res.* **2019**, *25*, 201–211. [CrossRef]

13. Vincent, P.; Larochelle, H.; Bengio, Y.; Manzagol, P.-A. Extracting and composing robust features with denoising autoencoders. In Proceedings of the 25th International Conference on Machine Learning, Helsinki, Finland, 5–9 July 2008; pp. 1096–1103.

14. Chiang, H.-T.; Hsieh, Y.-Y.; Fu, S.-W.; Hung, K.-H.; Tsao, Y.; Chien, S.-Y. Noise Reduction in ECG Signals Using Fully Convolutional Denoising Autoencoders. *IEEE Access* **2019**, *7*, 60806–60813. [CrossRef]

15. Xiong, P.; Wang, H.; Liu, M.; Liu, X. Denoising autoencoder for eletrocardiogram signal enhancement. *J. Med. Imaging Heal. Inform.* **2015**, *5*, 1804–1810. [CrossRef]

16. Xiong, P.; Wang, H.; Liu, M.; Lin, F.; Hou, Z.; Liu, X. A stacked contractive denoising auto-encoder for ECG signal denoising. *Physiol. Meas.* **2016**, *37*, 2214. [CrossRef] [PubMed]

17. Xing, C.; Ma, L.; Yang, X. Stacked denoise autoencoder based feature extraction and classification for hyperspectral images. *J. Sens.* **2016**, *2016*. [CrossRef]

18. Yang, J.; Nguyen, M.N.; San, P.P.; Li, X.L.; Krishnaswamy, S. Deep convolutional neural networks on multichannel time series for human activity recognition. In Proceedings of the Twenty-Fourth International Joint Conference on Artificial Intelligence, Buenos Aires, Argentina, 25–31 July 2015.

19. Budiman, A.; Fanany, M.I.; Basaruddin, C. Stacked denoising autoencoder for feature representation learning in pose-based action recognition. In Proceedings of the 2014 IEEE 3rd Global Conference on Consumer Electronics (GCCE), Tokyo, Japan, 7–10 October 2014; pp. 684–688.

20. Nurmaini, S.; Partan, R.U.; Rachmatullah, M.N. Deep Neural Networks Classifiers on The Electrocardiogram Signal for Intelligent Interpretation System. *Sriwij. Int. Conf. Med. Sci.* **2018**. [CrossRef]

21. Martis, R.J.; Acharya, U.R.; Min, L.C. ECG beat classification using PCA, LDA, ICA and discrete wavelet transform. *Biomed. Signal Process. Control* **2013**, *8*, 437–448. [CrossRef]

22. Qin, Q.; Li, J.; Zhang, L.; Yue, Y.; Liu, C. Combining low-dimensional wavelet features and support vector machine for arrhythmia beat classification. *Sci. Rep.* **2017**, *7*, 6067. [CrossRef] [PubMed]

23. Hermans, B.J.M.; Stoks, J.; Bennis, F.C.; Vink, A.S.; Garde, A.; Wilde, A.A.M.; Pison, L.; Postema, P.G.; Delhaas, T. Support vector machine-based assessment of the T-wave morphology improves long QT syndrome diagnosis. *EP Eur.* **2018**, *20*, iii113–iii119. [CrossRef]

24. Faziludeen, S.; Sankaran, P. ECG beat classification using evidential K-nearest neighbours. *Procedia Comput. Sci.* **2016**, *89*, 499–505. [CrossRef]

25. Hejazi, M.; Al-Haddad, S.A.R.; Singh, Y.P.; Hashim, S.J.; Aziz, A.F.A. Multiclass support vector machines for classification of ECG data with missing values. *Appl. Artif. Intell.* **2015**, *29*, 660–674. [CrossRef]

26. Yu, S.-N.; Chen, Y.-H. Noise-tolerant electrocardiogram beat classification based on higher order statistics of subband components. *Artif. Intell. Med.* **2009**, *46*, 165–178. [CrossRef] [PubMed]

27. Li, Q.; Rajagopalan, C.; Clifford, G.D. A machine learning approach to multi-level ECG signal quality classification. *Comput. Methods Programs Biomed.* **2014**, *117*, 435–447. [CrossRef] [PubMed]

28. Übeyli, E.D. ECG beats classification using multiclass support vector machines with error correcting output codes. *Digit. Signal Process.* **2007**, *17*, 675–684. [CrossRef]

29. Sugimoto, K.; Kon, Y.; Lee, S.; Okada, Y. Detection and localization of myocardial infarction based on a convolutional autoencoder. *Knowl. Based Syst.* **2019**, *178*, 123–131. [CrossRef]

30. Nurmaini, S.; Partan, R.U.; Caesarendra, W.; Dewi, T.; Rahmatullah, M.N.; Darmawahyuni, A.; Bhayyu, V.; Firdaus, F. An Automated ECG Beat Classification System Using Deep Neural Networks with an Unsupervised Feature Extraction Technique. *Appl. Sci.* **2019**, *9*, 2921. [CrossRef]

31. Ochiai, K.; Takahashi, S.; Fukazawa, Y. Arrhythmia Detection from 2-lead ECG using Convolutional Denoising Autoencoders. In Proceedings of the KDD'18 Deep Learning Day, London, UK, 19–23 August 2018.

Article

Unobtrusive Sleep Monitoring Using Movement Activity by Video Analysis

Yuan-Kai Wang [1,2,*], Hung-Yu Chen [1] and Jian-Ru Chen [1]

[1]   Graduate Institute of Applied Science and Engineering, Fu Jen Catholic University, New Taipei 24205, Taiwan
[2]   Electrical Engineering, Fu Jen Catholic University, New Taipei 24205, Taiwan
*   Correspondence: ykwang@fju.edu.tw

Received: 29 June 2019; Accepted: 17 July 2019; Published: 20 July 2019

Abstract: Sleep healthcare at home is a new research topic that needs to develop new sensors, hardware and algorithms with the consideration of convenience, portability and accuracy. Monitoring sleep behaviors by visual sensors represents one new unobtrusive approach to facilitating sleep monitoring and benefits sleep quality. The challenge of video surveillance for sleep behavior analysis is that we have to tackle bad image illumination issue and large pose variations during sleeping. This paper proposes a robust method for sleep pose analysis with human joints model. The method first tackles the illumination variation issue of infrared videos to improve the image quality and help better feature extraction. Image matching by keypoint features is proposed to detect and track the positions of human joints and build a human model robust to occlusion. Sleep poses are then inferred from joint positions by probabilistic reasoning in order to tolerate occluded joints. Experiments are conducted on the video polysomnography data recorded in sleep laboratory. Sleep pose experiments are given to examine the accuracy of joint detection and tacking, and the accuracy of sleep poses. High accuracy of the experiments demonstrates the validity of the proposed method.

Keywords: sleep pose recognition; keypoints feature matching; Bayesian inference; near-infrared images; scale invariant feature transform

---

1. Introduction

Sleep disorders induce irregular sleeping patterns and sleep deprivation that have serious impacts on health. Obstructive sleep apnea (OSA) [1] is one of the most well recognized sleep disorders. OSA is characterized by repetitive obstruction of the upper airways during sleep, resulting in oxygen de-saturation and frequent brain arousal. It is a symptom that not only decreases sleep quality by sleep disturbance, but also has severe influence which may be life-threatening. Reduction in cognitive function, cardiovascular diseases, stroke, driver fatigue and excessive day time sleepiness are common among OSA patients.

Sleep monitoring systems [2] are an important objective diagnosis method to assess sleep quality and identify sleep disorders. They provide quantitative data about irregularity of brain and body behaviors in sleeping periods and duration. This information helps the analysis of sleep-wake state, diagnosis of the severity of disorders, and prompt treatment of sleep-related diseases.

Polysomnography (PSG) is a standard diagnostic tool in sleep medicine [3] that measures a wide range of biosignals, including blood oxygen, airflow, electroencephalography (EEG), electrocardiography (ECG), electromyography (EMG) and electro-oculography during sleep time. The subject monitored by PSG has to sleep by carefully wearing a lot of sensors with numerous electrodes attached to his whole body, which increases sleep disturbance and discomfort. A sleep technician has to read these overnight data and mark sleep status manually according to the standardized scoring rule. It is a complex, costly and labor-intensive instrument that is absolutely not adequate for sleep care at home.

Alternative approach with minimized contact-based sensors has been developed [3,4]. Unconstrained portable biosensors, accelerometer, RFID (Radio Frequency IDentification), pressure sensors and smartphone are individually-applied or combined to detect sleep behaviors such as limb movement, body movement and sleep position. Detected sleep behaviors are further analyzed to inference sleep-wake pattern and assess sleep disorder. Actigraphy is a good representative that is commonly used with a watch-like accelerometer device attached typically to the wrist. These alternatives apply contact-based sensors and are disadvantageous to the data acquisition and sleep quality.

The noncontact approach usually employs imaging sensors such as microwave, thermal imaging and near-infrared (NIR) camera to non-intrusively detect sleep behaviors. Among these imaging modalities, NIR camera is more desired for home sleep analysis because it is low-cost, easily accessible and highly portable. Sivan et al. (in 1996) and Schwichtenberg et al. (in 2018) [5,6] shows that NIR video alone is enough for effective screening of OSA. Manual analysis from NIR videos can result in high correlation to PSG based diagnosis. Automatic video analysis is then proposed for sleep-wake detection [7–10] and sleep behavior analysis [11–16]. The NIR video is analyzed to extract subject's motion information by the methods such as background subtraction, optical flow, image difference and edge filter. Classification methods are then employed to inference sleep states and body parts. However, robust methods for stable analysis remains a necessary concern.

Challenges of robust sleep video analysis come from the characteristics of NIR videos and sleep pose. Capturing sleep behavior using NIR camera in dark environment has the problems of non-uniform illuminance and bad image quality. NIR camera needs to actively project a near-infrared light source on objects. An unevenly illuminated image is usually obtained because the projected area is over-exposure but the other area is under-exposure. Moreover, NIR images have poor imaging quality because they has low resolution, low signal-to-noise ratio (SNR) and low contrast. In addition, noise is inevitably introduced to NIR images because of the low-light situation for sleep. Low contrast, high noise and uneven illumination degrade the distinctiveness of motion and edge features that are usually applied in existing studies. Therefore, extracting body movement from IR video suffers from the image degradation problem.

Sleep pose recognition from videos is highly challenging for the nonrigid characteristics of the human body. Deformable and partially occluded postures plus with irregular movements induce high variation and inconsistency of appearance and shape features of human body, and make it difficult to classify postures.

This paper proposes a nonintrusive method to recognize sleep body positions. The joint-based approach is adopted for our sleep pose recognition, including joint detection and pose recognition. The joint detection step finds body joints using keypoints extraction and matching, and builds human models from these joints. The tracking step updates the human model by an online learning approach to consider the constraint of sequential change of viewpoint of joints. The recognition step includes a Bayesian network and statistical inference algorithm to deal with the problems of self-occlusion and pose variations. A special scheme is developed for the detection of joints to conquer poor image quality and self-occlusion problems. A special design, called IR-sensitive pajamas, which attaches visual markers on human joints is proposed. Joint markers contain visual patterns distinguished with each other and each marker corresponds only to one specific joint. A human joint model is constructed from the detected joint markers within a sleep image and is recognized to the sleep pose being supine or lateral. An earlier version of this paper appeared in [11]. Compared to the prior paper, this study contains (1) a substantial number of additional survey, explanations and analysis, and (2) various additional experiments to investigate the impact an accuracy of infrared image enhancement for sleep analysis.

The rest of this paper is organized as follows. Section 2 reviews state-of-the-art sleep behavior analysis with contact- and noncontact-based approaches. Section 3 describes our method that includes three components: NIR image enhancement, joint detection and tracking, and sleep pose recognition. Section 4 presents the experimental evaluation compared with different methods. Finally, Section 5 concludes the characteristics and advantages of the proposed method.

2. Related Works

The medical foundation of sleep analysis from videos is the physiological interpretation of body movement during sleep, that is first reviewed and explained. Existing contact and noncontact methods for sleep pose recognition are also discussed. The final subsection introduces general posture and action recognition methods been developed in computer vision, and identify the importance of feature representation for detection and recognition problems.

2.1. The Relation between Sleep Behavior and Sleep Disorder

Several studies of sleep medicine [5,17] show that body movements are an important behavioral aspect during sleep. They can be associated to sleep states and connected to the sleep state transitions. In particular, major body movements have been described in non-rapid eye movement (NREM) sleep, whereas small movements predominantly occur during REM phases. Therefore, the frequency and duration of body movements are important characteristics for sleep analysis. Moreover, some study [18] has found correlations between sleep body positions and sleep apnea. There is also some clinical evidence that the analysis of body pose is relevant to the diagnosis of OSA. A sleep monitoring system that detects body positions during sleep would help the automatic diagnosis of OSA.

Body positions in sleep posture can be classified into supine, lateral and prone positions. Supine and lateral positions are dominant postures in adults, but children and infants may have prone positions [19]. Many patients with OSA exhibit worsening event indices while supine. Since supine OSA has been recognized to be the dominant phenotype of the OSA syndrome [20], objective and automatic position monitoring becomes very important because of the unreliability of patient's self-report of positions [21,22].

2.2. Contact Sensors for Sleep Analysis

The screening of sleep is typically obtrusive using contact sensors, like biosensors, accelerometers, wrist watches, and headbands [5]. Contact sensors have to be worn on user's body, have possible skin irritations and may disturb sleep. Saturation signal of oxygen in the arteries obtained through oximetry measurement or pulse oximetry is very effective for OSA diagnosis. Another attempt has been carried out by considering thoracic and abdominal signals, e.g., the respiration waveform. The use of EEG and ECG signals for the detection of sleep-wake and breathing apnea is a well-known standard. Actigraphy is a commonly used technique for sleep monitoring that uses a watch-like accelerometer based device attached typically to the wrist. The device monitors activities and later labels periods of low activity as sleep. It is a headband that users need to wear each night so that it can detect sleep patterns through the electrical signals naturally produced by the brain. The pressure sensitive mattress is an interestingly alternative of contact-based approach to identify occurrence of sleep movements [23]. It can monitor change in body pressure on the pad to detect movements. The main advantage of the pressure sensitive mattress is that users do not need to wear any device. But, it is a high-cost device and in some cases it may be uncomfortable to sleep on the pad and thus, they can affect sleep quality.

Sleep pose can be recognized by a contact-based approach [24]. Accelerometer [25], RFID [26], and pressure sensors [27] are used to acquire raw motion data of human, and inference sleep state from the motion data. While these methods are appropriate for sleep healthcare, their raw motion data is insufficient for accurate classification of sleep pose. More abundant data of human motions acquired by imaging sensors with both spatial and temporal information should greatly benefit sleep pose recognition.

2.3. Noncontact Sensors for Sleep Behavior Analysis

Noncontact approach usually employs imaging sensors to noninvasively detect sleep behaviors. The methods with microwave [28] and thermal imaging system [29] are advantageous to see through the bed covering to detect body movement. However, these imaging modalities are expensive, not portable, and is unable to perform long-time nocturnal video recording. More works adopted NIR camera [30,31] and computer vision techniques to extract body movement and chest respiration. The use of a NIR video camera to analyze movement patterns of a sleeping subject promises an attractive alternative.

Sleep posture has been analyzed in some studies. The system [12] detects posture change of the subject in bed by observing chest or blanket movement, and uses optical flow to evaluate the frequency of posture change. Wang and Hunter [14,15] addressed the problem of detecting and segmenting the covered human body using infrared vision. Their aim was to specifically tailor their algorithms for sleep monitoring scenarios where head, torso and upper legs may be occluded. No high-level posture is automatically classified. Yang et al. [13] proposed a neural network method to recognize the sleep postures. However, only edges detected by linear filters are applied as movement features of human body for the neural classifier, and recognition results were not satisfied. Liao and Kuo [16] proposed a video-based sleep monitoring system with background modeling approaches for extracting movement data. Since a NIR camera is often employed to monitor night-time activities in low illumination environment without disturbing the sleeper, the image noise can be quite prominent especially in regions containing smooth textures. They investigated and modeled the lighting changes by proposing a local ternary pattern based background subtraction method. However, none of these methods recognize positions of sleep body, especially supine and lateral positions that are strongly related to OSA. High-level postures can be robustly recognized by the modeling of articulated human joints.

Motion and texture features used for sleep pose recognition are sensitive to image degradation. Enhancing images before feature extraction [32] by recovering illumination, reducing noise and increasing contrast, can greatly improve the distinctness of features and increase detection and recognition accuracy [33]. Nonlinear filters, for example Retinex, have been successfully applied on many computer vision tasks [34] instead of vision based sleep analysis.

2.4. Pose Recognition by Computer Vision

Computer vision-based methods have been proposed for human pose recognition as a non-intrusive approach to capture human behavior with broad applications ranging from human computer interfaces, video data mining, automated surveillance, and sport training to fall detection. Appearance-based approach that directly adopts color, edge and silhouettes features for the classification of human poses has been widely applied [35]. However, nonrigid variations produced by limbs movement and body deformation make it difficult to the classification by appearance features. Joint-based approach [36] on the other way builds a structured human model by detected joints and/or body parts from low-level features, and then recognize poses by the structured human model. This approach tolerates not only high deformation but also self-occlusion issues in human poses.

Sleep poses are also highly deformable and partial occlusion often occurs. They should be tackled by joint-based approach [14]. Apart from partial occlusion, it is likely that limited motion information is available from partial and irregular movements, which seriously affects the usability of traditional feature extraction methods.

Local features such as scale invariant feature transform (SIFT) [37] and Speeded Up Robust Features (SURF) [38] are a new design scheme for salient feature representation of human postures. Its success on numerous computer vision problems has been well demonstrated [39]. Here we give only some examples of applying SIFT on action recognition. Scovanner et al. [40] proposed a 3D SIFT feature to better represent human actions. Wang et al. and Zhang et al. [41,42] applied SIFT flow to extract keypoint-based movement features between image frames and obtain better classification results than the features such as histogram of oriented gradients and histogram of optical flows. Local features have superior representability not only for visible-band images but also for NIR images. The paper [43] gave a comprehensive study of the robustness of four keypoint detectors for the three spectra: near infrared, far infrared and visible spectra. Robustness are demonstrated that performance of the four detectors is remaining for all the three spectra, although these interest point detectors were originally proposed for visual-band images. While these papers show the advantages of local features, it is still not easy to get articulated structure of human joints by local features.

In summary, sleep behavior is important and can be analyzed by non-contact approaches to achieve unobtrusive methods. NIR video analysis for sleep posture is challenging but innovative. A summary table of the reviews from related works is given in Table 1.

Table 1. Summary of reviews from related works.

Critical Points	Arguments
Sleep behavior is important to OSA diagnosis	• Body movements are an important behavior for sleep diagnosis • Body position is correlated to sleep apnea • Sleep behavior including body movements and body positions are relevant to OSA • Supine position is a critical posture
Non-contact and unobtrusive analysis are advantageous but have challenges	• Contact sensros have been well developed for sleep diagnosis • Non-contact imaging sensors are unobtrusive and better than contact sensors • NIR is a good non-contact sensor with many advantages • Challenges of NIR video analysis for sleep analysis are nonuniform illumination processing and nonrigid body deformation
Motivation of this paper	• Retinex is a nonlinear filter that could be applied to improve the NIR videos with nonuniform illumination • Joint-based methods are an important approach to traditional posture recognition in computer vision • Keypoints methods such as SIFT could be applied to joint-based posture recogntion

3. Sleep Pose Recognition

The proposed method analyzes near-infrared videos to recognize sleep poses by body joint model. The near-infrared images are first enhanced by an illumination compensation algorithm to improve the quality of feature extraction. SIFT-based local features are employed to perform joint detection of human body. Poses are recognized with a Bayesian inference algorithm to solve the occlusion issue.

A novel idea is developed for the joint detection and modeling in our method. One basic idea is that it becomes usual to delicately customize some bedding materials to facilitate more accurate monitoring, such as the mattress pad sensor. Therefore, we propose an unobtrusive passive way by revamping pajamas with NIR sensitive fabrics around the joint positions of human body. The fabrics that is sensitive to NIR light source can reflect more lights and show high intensity values in NIR images. With the NIR-sensitive fabrics we get more visual information of body joints and are able to detect and recognize sleep poses. Figure 1 gives an illustration of our design. There are ten joints that are common for posture and action recognition. We make ten NIR-sensitive patches with special fabrics sewing on pajamas.

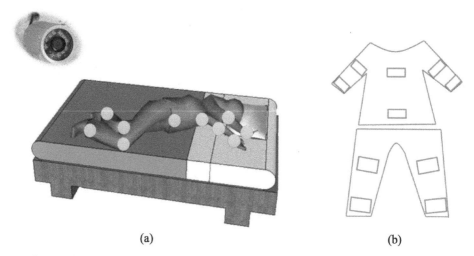

|(a)|(b)|

Figure 1. The proposed scheme for sleep pose recognition. (**a**) An infrared camera is used to acquire the sleep videos and analyze body joint positions. (**b**) Pajamas with ten near infrared (NIR)-sensitive patches are designed to facilitate the detection of body joints.

Another issue of the proposed method is to distinguish different joints. We apply the concept in augmented reality to design fiducial markers in order to not only reliably detect each joint, but also easily distinguish all joints. A fiducial marker supplements with image features originating in salient points of the image. However, we need to design a fiducial marker system that consists of a set of distinguishable markers to encode different joints. Desirable properties of the marker system are low false positive and false negative rates, as well as low inter-marker confusion rates. We adopt the markers designed in the paper [44] that derives the optimal design of fiducial markers specially for SIFT and SURF. Its markers are highly detectable even under dramatically varying imaging conditions.

3.1. Near-Infrared Image Enhancement

An illumination compensation algorithm [45] that includes single-scale Retinex and alpha-trimming histogram stretching is applied to enhance the NIR video. SSR is a nonlinear filter to improve lightness rendition of the images without uniform illumination. However, SSR does not improve contrast. The histogram stretching with alpha-trimming is then followed to improve contrast. Let I_t be an NIR image at time t and I'_t is the enhanced result, our image enhancement algorithm is a composition function of three successive steps as follows:

$$I' = m(f(R(I))), \text{ where } R(I) = \log(I) - \log(G(c) \otimes I). \tag{1}$$

$R(\cdot)$ is the SSR, $f(\cdot)$ is the alpha-trimming histogram stretching, and $m(\cdot)$ is a median filter for denoising. The SSR function $R(\cdot)$ uses a Gaussian convolution kernel $G(c)$ with size c to compute the scale of illuminant, and enhance the image by log-domain processing. The alpha-trimming histogram stretching applies a gray-level mapping that extends the range of gray levels into the whole dynamic range. Median filter is applied to eliminate the shot noise in the NIR images. The effect of the enhancement is majorly influenced by the size of Gaussian kernel size c. Figure 2 illustrates the influence with different kernel sizes. The original image has uneven illumination. The image in Figure 2b is still dark and the contrast of human body is low. It also has white artifact around image boundary. Figure 2f has better illumination compensation effect, better contrast on human body, and less artifact.

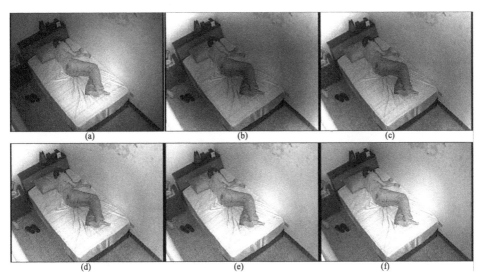

Figure 2. Enhanced NIR images with different Gaussian kernel sizes from 50 to 250. (**a**) Original image. (**b**) $c = 50$. (**c**) $c = 100$. (**d**) $c = 150$. (**e**) $c = 200$. (**f**) $c = 250$.

3.2. Detection and Tracking of Human Joints by Distinctive Invariant Feature

We propose a SIFT-based joint detection algorithm to detect joints in the first image, and a structured online learning to track those detected joints in the video. The SIFT analyzes an input image at multiple scales in order to repeatedly find characteristic blob-like structures independently of their actual size in an image. It first applies multiscale detection operators to analyze the so called scale space representation of an image. In a second step, detected features are assigned a rotation-invariant descriptor computed from the surrounding pixel neighborhood. The detail of applying SIFT to detect human joints is described in the following.

Given an enhanced image I'_t at time t and a set of joint markers M_i, $i = 1\sim10$, we apply SIFT to extract keypoint features of I'_t and M_i, and compute the correspondence set C_i to find all joints. The keypoints of I'_t is represented as a sparse set $X_t = \{x_t^j\}$ that is called image descriptor. The keypoints of M_i is a set $Y_i = \{y_i^k\}$ that is called a joint model descriptor. A correspondence set $C_i = \{(x_t^j, y_i^k) | s(x_t^j, y_i^k) > \tau\}$ is obtained for each joint marker M_i, where $s(\cdot, \cdot)$ is the matching score and τ is a matching threshold. The matching between X_t and Y_i is done by a best-bin-first search that returns the closest neighbor with the highest probability with pairwise geometric constraints. The set of matched joints $\widehat{J}$ is a set of joint coordinates J_i defined as follows:

$$\widehat{J} = \{J_i \mid J_i = median(C_i) \text{ and } |C_i| > \alpha\} \tag{2}$$

where σ is a threshold of minimum number of matched keypoints. A matched joint requires enough matched keypoints, i.e., $|C_i| > \sigma$. The coordinates of the ith are calculated as the median coordinates from $x_t^j \in C_i$ to screen outlier of keypoint-based joint detection, which can reduce the distance error of joint. While the keypoint-based matching is robust to illumination, rotation and scale variance, some joints may not be detected because of occlusion. That is, some joints are not detected if $|\widehat{J}| < 10$.

An example of keypoint detection is shown in Figure 3a. Most detected keypoints are clustered together around joint markers, that demonstrates the image descriptor X_t is a salient representation of the set of joint markers. Figure 3b shows an example of joint detection. The joint marker is shown at the left top of the image. These lines represent matched keypoints between the joint marker and the visual marker in the pajamas.

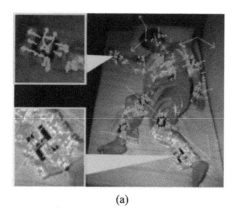
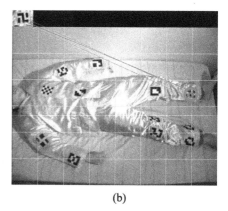

(a)   (b)

Figure 3. Keypoint detection and joint detection. (**a**) Image descriptor of an original lateral-pose image overlaid with keypoints of length and orientation information. Each arrow represents one detected keypoint. (**b**) A joint detection example for left ankle. It is detected by matching a specific joint marker representing the left ankle with a visual marker in the sleep image.

A structured output prediction with online learning method [46] is applied to perform adaptive keypoint tracking of the human joints. It is used for homography estimation of correspondence between frames and binary approximation of model. Structured output prediction is handled by applying RANSAC to find the transformation of the correspondence. To speed up the detection and description process, we adopt SURF instead of SIFT. This is achieved by not only relying on integral images for image convolutions but applying a Hessian matrix-based measurement for the detector and a distribution-based descriptor.

3.3. Sleep Pose Estimation by Bayesian Inference

The sleep pose model is mathematically formulated as a Bayesian network, and the estimation of pose class is achieved by probabilistically inferencing the posterior distribution of the network.

Bayesian network combining probability theory and graphical model for statistical inference is employed in this paper because of its great robustness capability with missing information. That is, pose class can be inferred even when there are undetected joints.

Our sleep pose model is a Bayesian network G with one root node representing the state of pose and ten child nodes J_i, $1 \leq i \leq 10$, corresponding to the states of joints. This network gives a probabilistic model to represent the causal relationship between sleep pose and joint positions: a given pose affects the positions of joints, and thus the pose can be inferred by Bayesian theory from a given set of joint positions. The property of conditional independence exists in this naïve model and is helpful for the inference of poses.

Let the undetected and detected joint sets be individually represented by U and $\hat{J}$. The conditional posterior distribution of p given $\hat{J}$ can be derived as follows:

$$P(p|J_1, \cdots, J_{10}) = \pi \sum_{J_i \in U} \prod_{J_i \in \hat{J}} P(p|J_i), \tag{3}$$

where π is the prior probability $P(p, J_1, ..., J_{10})$ that is in the form of full joint probability. The estimated sleep pose $\hat{p}$ is the maximum a posterior (MAP) estimate given by the following:

$$\hat{p} = arg\ max\ P(p|J_1, \cdots, J_{10}), \tag{4}$$

Both approximate and exact inference algorithms can be applied for the MAP calculation of our sleep pose model. While approximate inference algorithms are usually more efficient than exact inference algorithms, our sleep pose model could be solved more efficiently with exact inference approach. We employ clique-tree propagation algorithm [47] that first transforms the Bayesian model into undirected graph, then use query-driven message passing to update the statistical distribution of each node.

An example of sleep pose estimation is shown in Figure 4, which is a lateral pose with fully detected joints. The reconstructed human model is depicted with a cardboard representation.

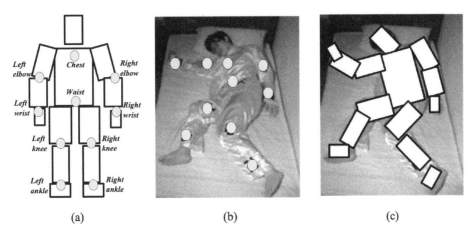

(a)   (b)   (c)

Figure 4. An example of reconstructed human model by fully detected joints. (**a**) A standard model with a standing pose. (**b**) A sleep image overlaid with the detected/tracked joints found by keypoint match and structured learning. (**c**) Reconstructed model of the lateral pose.

4. Experimental Results

We evaluated these components in our method: near-infrared image enhancement, joint detection and pose recognition. Accuracy and performance compared with existing methods are conducted and discussed. Two individual setups of experiments were established. The first setup was established to evaluate the efficacy of near-infrared image enhancement, whose accuracy was assessed by total sleep time (TST) measured from the sleep–wake detection results obtained after the enhancing of images. The second setup is built for joint detection and pose recognition. The detection of ten joints is assessed by pixel difference of joint positions, and the recognition of supine/lateral poses are assessed by classification precision.

The experimental setups were conducted in a sleep laboratory equipped with a PSG, near-infrared cameras and related instruments. The PSG was adopted to obtain ground truth. A full-channel PSG (E-Series, Compumedics Ltd., Melbourne, Australia) was employed to record overnight brain wave activity (electroencephalography from C3-M2, C4-M1), eye movements (left and right electrooculogram), electrocardiography, leg movements (left and right piezoelectric leg paddles), and airflow (oral/nasal thermister). The near-infrared video has the resolution of 640 * 480 pixels with the frame rate of 20 fps.

4.1. Effectiveness of Near-Infrared Image Enhancement

In this subsection, the assessment of image enhancement is carefully created from sleep experiments, because there is still no objective criteria to evaluate the quality of near-infrared images. Since our goal is to build a computer-vision based sleep evaluation system, it is reasonable to adopt a sleep quality criteria, TST, obtained in a sleep experiment to evaluate our image enhancement component. TST is the amount of actual sleep time including REM and NREM phases in a sleep episode; this time is equal to the total sleep episode less the awake time.

In this first sleep setup, eighteen subjects involved in the experiments are divided into two groups, including a normal group without a sleep disorder and an OSA group with sleep disorder. Table 2 gives statistics of the subjects in the two groups. From the data we confirmed that these subjects have only OSA symptom and have no PLM problems, because the means of body mass index and PLM are statistically identical, and the OSA group has higher RDI and lower sleep efficiency.

Table 2. Statistics of the two groups in the sleep-wake detection experiment. SD means standard deviation. RDI (respiratory disturbance index) is the number of abnormal breathing events per hour of sleep. PLM (periodic leg movements) is the number during nocturnal sleep and wakefulness. Sleep efficiency is the proportion of sleep in the episode, i.e., the ratio of total sleep time (TST) to the time in bed.

		Age	Body Mass Index	RDI	PLM	Sleep Efficiency
Normal group	Mean	42.63	24.39	4.23	1.28	91.44
	SD	14.37	4.18	2.44	1.61	4.7
OSA group	Mean	51.1	24.99	35.85	1.43	84.22
	SD	15.25	2.69	21.68	3.03	12.3

Both PSG data and IR videos were recorded overnight for each subject. Sleep stages were scored using the standard AASM criteria with thirty-second epochs. Obstructive apneas were identified if the airflow amplitude was absent or nearly absent for the duration at least eight seconds and two breaths cycles. A well-trained sleep technician was responsible for configuring the PSG for each subject. The ground truth of sleep state is manually labeled by the sleep experts working in hospital. The ground truth of the TST is obtained by the total sleep time calculated from the manual annotation.

Estimated TST is obtained from near-infrared videos by a process including the proposed image enhancement, followed by background subtraction and sleep-wake detection. We extract body movement information from the motion feature obtained from background subtraction. A statistical differencing operator is applied to measure the distance d_t between the enhanced infrared image I'_t and the previous background model B_{t-1} as follows:

$$d_t = |I'_t - B_{t-1}| \tag{5}$$

The background model B_{t-1} was recursively updated by the Gaussian mixture background subtraction method [48], and can successfully approximate the background of a given image which has a time-evolving model. The body movement BM_t at time t is obtained by accumulating the total motion pixels in d_t:

$$BM_t = \sum_x \sum_y M_t$$
$$where \ M_t(x,y) = \begin{cases} 1, \ if \ d_t(x,y) > threshold \\ 0, \ otherwise \end{cases} \tag{6}$$

Sleep activity feature was then calculated from BM_t by descriptive statistics such as mean, standard deviation and maximum, defined over an epoch of 30 s. Sleep activity is obtained by the sleep-wake detection algorithm that is modeled by the linear regression [49] of the sleep activity feature.

The proposed image enhancement algorithm is first qualitatively compared with four classical methods: histogram stretching, histogram equlization, gamma correction and single-scale Retinex, with regard to illumination uniformity and contrast. Figure 5b–d show the results of three global enhancement methods with raised image contrast, but the middle of these images is over-exposed. Figure 5e is the result of SSR filtering with uniform illumination but low image contrast. Figure 5f show the result of the proposed method that can solve both non-uniform illumination and low contrast issues.

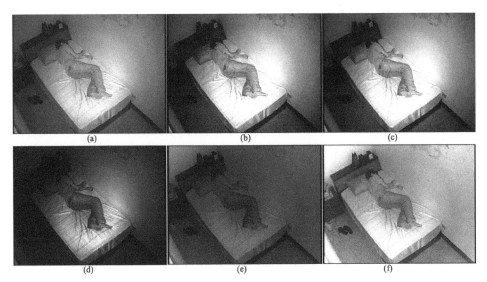

Figure 5. Enhancement of NIR images. (**a**) Original image. (**b**) Histogram stretching. (**c**) Histogram equalization. (**d**) Gamma correction. (**e**) Single-scale Retinex. (**f**) The proposed illumination compensation method.

Quantitative assessment of the proposed method was achieved by an index called TST error E_{TST}, that is defined as the normalized difference between estimated TST and ground truth of TST.

$$E_{TST} = \frac{|Estimated\ TST - Ground\ truth\ TST|}{Ground\ truth\ TST} \tag{7}$$

Its value is between [0,1]. Lower E_{TST} means better performance of our method.

The performance for a normal group with respect to three different sleep activity features, MA (moving average), MS (moving standard deviation), and MM (moving maximum), is shown in Figure 6. The three performances without image enhancement are not statistically differential. However, the performances with image enhancement are consistently lower than those without enhancement, and MA with image enhancement has the best performance.

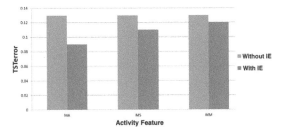

Figure 6. Effect of image enhancement (IE) for the performance improvement of the error of total sleep time.

The performance comparison of using image enhancement with respect to normal and OSA groups is shown in Table 3. MA is adopted as the only sleep activity feature in this comparison. Specificity (SPC) and negative predictive value (NPC) are also calculated for performance comparison. We can observe that while normal group has better performances with less standard deviation, OSA group still has good performances.

Table 3. Effect of image enhancement (IE) for the performance improvement of the error of total sleep time.

		E_{TST}	**SPC**	**NPV**
Normal group	Mean	0.09	0.95	0.91
	STD	0.16	0.04	0.10
OSA group	Mean	0.15	0.93	0.84
	STD	0.18	0.19	0.21

4.2. Evaluation of Pose Recognition

The second experiment has five subjects of various gender, height and weight wearing the custom pajamas and sleeping with free postures. Ten video clips were recorded with respect to the episodes of supine and lateral poses of various limb angles and occlusion. Half clips are randomly chosen for training of the classifier, and the remaining half for test. Ground truth of body positions and joint positions are manually labeled. The pose recognition in this experiment will not detect sleep and wake states. Therefore, background subtraction and sleep-wake detection algorithms are excluded, and the method in this experiment will include the three components in Section 3: image enhancement, joint detection and pose recognition. However, only the effectiveness of joint detection and pose recognition is validated here.

Figure 7 gives some example results of joint detection with respect to various poses. The positions of IR-markers are marked on the original image to evaluate the effectiveness of the proposed method. Some quantitative experiments are conducted to evaluate the localization accuracy of the proposed method. Figure 8a shows the effect of the threshold of matched keypoint numbers (σ) on detected joint numbers. High precision can be obtained with $\sigma = 1$. This result indicates that the design of joint markers is distinctive and so the joint localization does not need to match more numbers of keypoints. Figure 8b shows average detection rate of each joint position with mostly achieving high accuracy. The detection of right knee joint is a little not satisfactory because of perspective variations. Euclidean distance errors of each joint position is shown in Figure 8c. The average error of all joints is 6.57 pixels. The result indicates higher error in both ankle joints.

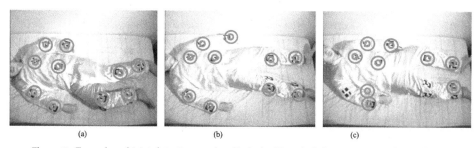

| (a) | (b) | (c) |

Figure 7. Examples of joint detection results. Each double-red circle represents a detected joint. (**a**) Lateral pose with ten successful detections. (**b**) Supine pose with ten successful detections. (**c**) Supine pose with eight successful detections. The right-knee and right-elbow joints are missed because of great distortion induced by perspective and cloth's wrinkles.

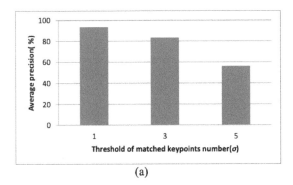

(a)

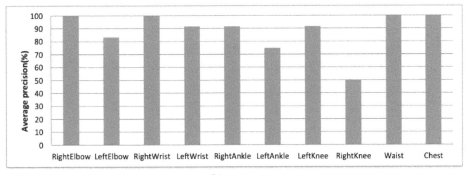

(b)

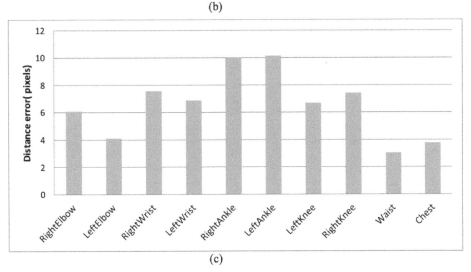

(c)

Figure 8. Accuracy evaluation. (a) The effect of the threshold of matched keypoint numbers. (b) Average precision of joint localization. (c) Average distance error of joint localization.

The performance of the proposed sleep pose model with clique-tree propagation inference was evaluated by comparing with five inference algorithms. Four are approximate algorithms: stochastic sampling, likelihood sampling, self-importance sampling, and backward sampling, and one exact algorithm: loop cutset conditioning. Figure 9 show execution and precision of the six algorithms. The result shows that clique-tree propagation algorithm takes the least time to achieve the best precision.

The positive predictive value, negative predictive value, specificity and sensitivity of the proposed method are 80%, 71%, 63% and 86%.

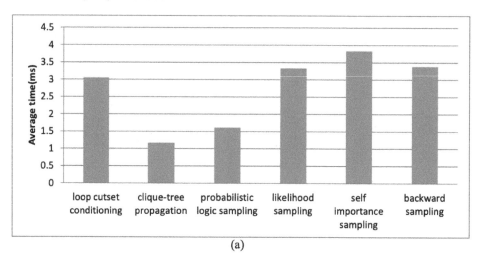

(a)

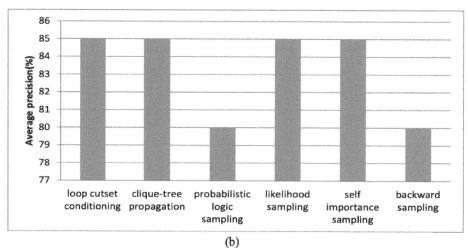

(b)

Figure 9. Comparison of six inference algorithms with respect to (**a**) execution time, and (**b**) accuracy.

The experimental results are compared with previous results: RTPose [14], MatchPose [15] and Ramanan [50]. The comparison is shown in Table 4. The previous results are obtained from their published publications. The results of our method were always superior than previous results except to right knee. Note that the accuracy of torso and head of our method are obtained from chest and waist, and the accuracy of ankles and knees in the table correspond to the lower legs and upper legs in previous publications.

Table 4. Comparisons with previous results. The numbers represent accuracy in percentage. N/A means the data are not available from their methods.

	Torso	Right Ankle	Left Ankle	Right Knee	Left Knee	Right Elbow	Left Elbow	Right Wrist	Left Wrist	Head
Ramanan	80	60	53	60	37	N/A	N/A	N/A	N/A	53
RTPose	93	N/A	N/A	70	80	N/A	N/A	N/A	N/A	80
MatchPose	97	45	69	75	80	N/A	N/A	N/A	N/A	94
Our	100	92	75	50	92	100	83	100	92	100

5. Conclusions

An automatic sleep pose recognition method from NIR videos is proposed in this paper. The method proposes keypoint-based joint detection and online tracking to persistently locate joint positions. Sleep poses are recognized from located joints by statistical inference with the proposed Bayesian network. Our method detects and tracks the human joints of great variations and occlusions with high precision. Experimental results validate the accuracy of the method for both supine and lateral poses. Further studies could incorporate more non-invasive sensors to develop a cheap and convenient sleep monitoring system for home care with long-term stability. With the reliable method proposed in this paper, an enhanced pajamas for home sleep monitoring can be further developed by costume designers.

Author Contributions: Conceptualization, Y.-K.W.; Funding acquisition, Y.-K.W.; Investigation, H.-Y.C.; Project administration, Y.-K.W.; Resources, Y.-K.W.; Software, J.-R.C.; Supervision, H.-Y.C.; Validation, H.-Y.C.; Visualization, H.-Y.C.; Writing—original draft, J.-R.C. and H.-Y.C.; Writing—review and editing, Y.-K.W.

Funding: This research was funded by the Ministry of Science and Technology, Taiwan, under contract number NSC 100-2218-E-030-004.

Acknowledgments: This research is jointly supported by the Sleep Center at Shin Kong Wu Ho-Su Memorial Hospital, Taiwan. The authors gratefully acknowledge the support of Chia-Mo Lin and Hou-Chang Chiu for their valuable comments in obstructive sleep apnea.

Conflicts of Interest: The authors declare no conflict of interest.

References

1. Berry, R.B.; Budhiraja, R.; Gottlieb, D.J.; Gozal, D.; Iber, C.; Kapur, V.K.; Marcus, C.L.; Mehra, R.; Parthasarathy, S.; Quan, S.F.; et al. Rules for scoring respiratory events in sleep: Update of the 2007 AASM manual for the scoring of sleep and associated events. *J. Clin. Sleep Med.* **2012**, *8*, 597–619. [CrossRef] [PubMed]

2. Procházka, A. Sleep scoring using polysomnography data features. *Signal Image Video Process.* **2018**, *12*, 1043–1051.

3. Roebuck, A.; Monasterio, V.; Gederi, E.; Osipov, M.; Behar, J.; Malhotra, A.; Penzel, T.; Clifford, G.D. A review of signals used in sleep analysis. *Physiol. Meas.* **2014**, *35*, 1–57. [CrossRef] [PubMed]

4. Park, K.S.; Choi, S.H. Smart Technologies Toward Sleep Monitoring at Home. *Biomed. Eng. Lett.* **2019**, *9*, 73–85. [CrossRef] [PubMed]

5. Sivan, Y.; Kornecki, A.; Schonfeld, T. Screening obstructive sleep apnoea syndrome by home videotape recording in children. *Eur. Respir. J.* **1996**, *9*, 2127–2131. [CrossRef] [PubMed]

6. Schwichtenberg, A.J.; Choe, J.; Kellerman, A.; Abel, E.; Delp, E.J. Pediatric videosomnography: Can signal/video processing distinguish sleep and wake states? *Front. Pediatr.* **2018**, *6*, 158. [CrossRef] [PubMed]

7. Scatena, M. An integrated video-analysis software system de-signed for movement detection and sleep analysis. Validation of a tool for the behavioural study of sleep. *Clin. Neurophysiol.* **2012**, *123*, 318–323. [CrossRef] [PubMed]

8. Kuo, Y.M.; Lee, J.S.; Chung, P.C. A visual context-awareness-based sleeping-respiration measurement system. *IEEE Trans. Inf. Technol. Biomed.* **2010**, *14*, 255–265. [PubMed]

9. Cuppens, K.; Lagae, L.; Ceulemans, B.; Huffel, S.V.; Vanrumste, B. Automatic video detection of body movement during sleep based on optical flow in pediatric patients with epilepsy. *Med. Biol. Eng. Comput.* **2010**, *48*, 923–931. [CrossRef]

10. Choe, J.; Schwichtenberg, A.J.; Delp, E.J. Classification of sleep videos using deep learning. In Proceedings of the IEEE Conference on Multimedia Information Processing and Retrieval, San Jose, CA, USA, 28–30 March 2019; pp. 115–120.

11. Wang, Y.K.; Chen, J.R.; Chen, H.Y. Sleep pose recognition by feature matching and Bayesian inference. In Proceedings of the International Conference on Pattern Recognition, Stockholm, Sweden, 24–28 August 2014; pp. 24–28.

12. Nakajima, K.; Matsumoto, Y.; Tamura, T. Development of real-time image sequence analysis for evaluating posture change and respiratory rate of a subject in bed. *Physiol. Meas.* **2001**, *22*, 21–28. [CrossRef]

13. Yang, F.C.; Kuo, C.H.; Tsai, M.Y.; Huang, S.C. Image-based sleep motion recognition using artificial neural networks. In Proceedings of the International Conference on Machine Learning and Cybernetics, Xi'an, China, 5 November 2003; pp. 2775–2780.

14. Wang, C.W.; Hunter, A. Robust pose recognition of the obscured human body. *Int. J. Comput. Vis.* **2010**, *90*, 313–330. [CrossRef]

15. Wang, C.W.; Hunter, A.; Gravill, N.; Matusiewicz, S. Real time pose recognition of covered human for diagnosis of sleep apnoea. *Comput. Med. Imaging Graph.* **2010**, *34*, 523–533. [CrossRef] [PubMed]

16. Liao, W.H.; Kuo, J.H. Sleep monitoring system in real bedroom environment using texture-based background modeling approaches. *J. Ambient Intell. Humaniz. Comput.* **2013**, *4*, 57–66. [CrossRef]

17. Okada, S.; Ohno, Y.; Kenmizaki, K.; Tsutsui, A.; Wang, Y. Development of non-restrained sleep-monitoring method by using difference image processing. In Proceedings of the European Conference of the International Federation for Medical and Biological Engineering, Antwerp, Belgium, 23–27 November 2009; pp. 1765–1768.

18. Oksenberg, A.; Silverberg, D.S. The effect of body posture on sleep-related breathing disorders: Facts and therapeutic implications. *Sleep Med. Rev.* **1998**, *2*, 139–162. [CrossRef]

19. Isaiah, A.; Pereira, K.D. The effect of body position on sleep apnea in children. In *Positional Therapy in Obstructive Sleep Apnea*; Springer Nature Switzerland: Basel, Switzerland, 2014; Volume 14, pp. 151–161.

20. Joosten, S.A.; O'Driscoll, D.M.; Berger, P.J.; Hamilton, G.S. Supine position related obstructive sleep apnea in adults: Pathogenesis and treatment. *Sleep Med. Rev.* **2014**, *18*, 7–17. [CrossRef] [PubMed]

21. Russo, K.; Bianchi, M.T. How reliable is self-reported body position during sleep? *Sleep Med.* **2016**, *12*, 127–128. [CrossRef] [PubMed]

22. Ravesloot, M.J.L.; Maanen, J.P.V.; Dun, L.; de Vries, N. The undervalued potential of positional therapy in position-dependent snoring and obstructive sleep apnea—A review of the literature. *Sleep Breath.* **2013**, *17*, 39–49. [CrossRef] [PubMed]

23. Liu, J.J.; Xu, W.; Huang, M.C.; Alshurafa, N.; Sarrafzadeh, M.; Raut, N.; Yadegar, B. Sleep posture analysis using a dense pressure sensitive bedsheet. *Pervasive Mob. Comput.* **2014**, *10*, 34–50. [CrossRef]

24. Hossain, H.M.S.; Ramamurthy, S.R.; Khan, M.A.A.H.; Roy, N. An active sleep monitoring framework using wearables. *ACM Trans. Interact. Intell. Syst.* **2018**, *8*, 22. [CrossRef]

25. Foerster, F.; Smeja, M.; Fahrenberg, J. Detection of posture and motion by accelerometry: A validation study in ambulatory monitoring. *Comput. Hum. Behav.* **1999**, *15*, 571–583. [CrossRef]

26. Hoque, E.; Dickerson, R.F.; Stankovic, J.A. Monitoring body positions and movements during sleep using WISPs. In *Wireless Health*; ACM: New York, NY, USA, 2010; pp. 44–53.

27. van Der Loos, H.; Kobayashi, H.; Liu, G. Unobtrusive vital signs monitoring from a multisensor bed sheet. In Proceedings of the RESNA Conference, Reno, NV, USA, 22–26 June 2001.

28. Xiao, Y.; Lin, J.; Boric-Lubecke, O.; Lubecke, V.M. A Ka-band low power doppler radar system for remote de-tection of cardiopulmonary motion. In Proceedings of the 2005 IEEE Engineering in Medicine and Biology 27th Annual Conference, Shanghai, China, 17–18 January 2005; pp. 7151–7154.

29. Bak, J.U.; Giakoumidis, N.; Kim, G.; Dong, H.; Mavridis, N. An intelligent sensing system for sleep motion and stage analysis. *Procedia Eng.* **2012**, *41*, 1128–1134. [CrossRef]

30. Sadeh, A. Sleep assessment methods. *Monogr. Soc. Res. Child Dev.* **2015**, *80*, 33–48. [CrossRef] [PubMed]

31. Deng, F.; Dong, J.; Wang, X.; Fang, Y.; Liu, Y.; Yu, Z.; Liu, J.; Chen, F. Design and implementation of a noncontact sleep monitoring system using infrared cameras and motion sensor. *IEEE Trans. Instrum. Meas.* **2018**, *67*, 1555–1563. [CrossRef]

Electronics **2019**, *8*, 812

32. Gao, Z.; Ma, Z.; Chen, X.; Liu, H. Enhancement and de-noising of near-infrared Image with multiscale Morphology. In Proceedings of the 2011 5th International Conference on Bioinformatics and Biomedical Engineering, Wuhan, China, 10–12 May 2011; pp. 1–4.

33. Holtzhausen, P.J.; Crnojevic, V.; Herbst, B.M. An illumina-tion invariant framework for real-time foreground detection. *J. Real-Time Image Process.* **2015**, *10*, 423–433. [CrossRef]

34. Park, Y.K.; Park, S.L.; Kim, J.K. Retinex method based on adaptive smoothing for illumination invariant face recognition. *Signal Process.* **2008**, *88*, 1929–1945. [CrossRef]

35. Maik, V.; Paik, D.T.; Lim, J.; Park, K.; Paik, J. Hierarchical pose classification based on human physiology for behaviour analysis. *IET Comput. Vis.* **2010**, *4*, 12–24. [CrossRef]

36. Wang, Y.K.; Cheng, K.Y. A two-stage Bayesian network method for 3D human pose sstimation from monocular image sequences. *EURASIP J. Adv. Signal Process.* **2010**, *2010*, 761460. [CrossRef]

37. Lowe, D.G. Distinctive image features from scale-invariant keypoints. *Int. J. Comput. Vis.* **2004**, *60*, 91–110. [CrossRef]

38. Bay, H.; Ess, A.; Tuytelaars, T.; Gool, L.V. Speeded-up robust features (SURF). *Comput. Vis. Image Underst.* **2008**, *110*, 346–359. [CrossRef]

39. Ouyang, W.; Tombari, F.; Mattoccia, S.; Stefano, L.D.; Cham, W.K. Performance evaluation of full search equivalent pattern matching algorithms. *IEEE Trans. Circuits Syst. II Analog Digit. Signal Process.* **2012**, *34*, 127–143.

40. Scovanner, P.; Ali, S.; Shah, M. A 3-dimensional SIFT descriptor and its application to action recognition. In Proceedings of the 15th ACM international conference on Multimedia, Augsburg, Germany, 25–29 September 2007; pp. 357–360.

41. Wang, H.; Yi, Y. Tracking salient keypoints for human action recognition. In Proceedings of the IEEE International Conference on Systems, Man, and Cybernetics, Kowloon, China, 9–12 October 2015; pp. 3048–3053.

42. Zhang, J.T.; Tsoi, A.C.; Lo, S.L. Scale Invariant feature transform flow trajectory approach with applications to human action recognition. In Proceedings of the International Joint Conference on Neural Networks, Beijing, China, 6–11 July 2014; pp. 1197–1204.

43. Molina, A.; Ramirez, T.; Diaz, G.M. Robustness of interest point detectors in near infrared, far infrared and visible spectral images. In Proceedings of the 2016 XXI Symposium on Signal Processing, Images and Artificial Vision (STSIVA), Bucaramanga, Colombia, 31 August–2 September 2016; pp. 1–6.

44. Schweiger, F.; Zeisl, B.; Georgel, P.F.; Schroth, G. Maximum detector response markers for SIFT and SURF. In Proceedings of the Workshop on Vision, Modeling and Visualization, Braunschweig, Germany, 16 November 2009; pp. 145–154.

45. Wang, Y.K.; Huang, W.B. A CUDA-enabled parallel algorithm for accelerating retinex. *J. Real-Time Image Process.* **2012**, *9*, 407–425. [CrossRef]

46. Hare, S.; Saffari, A.; Torr, P.H.S. Efficient online structured output learning for keypoint-based object tracking. In Proceedings of the IEEE Conference on Computer Vision and Pattern Recognition, Providence, RI, USA, 16–21 June 2012; pp. 1894–1901.

47. Huang, C.; Darwiche, A. Inference in belief networks: A procedural guide. *Int. J. Approx. Reason.* **1996**, *15*, 225–263. [CrossRef]

48. Wang, Y.K.; Su, C.H. Illuminant-invariant Bayesian detection of moving video objects. In Proceedings of the International Conference on Signal and Image Processing, Honolulu, HI, USA, 14–16 August 2006; pp. 57–62.

49. Cole, R.J.; Kripke, D.F.; Gruen, W.; Mullaney, D.J.; Gillin, J.C. Automatic sleep/wake identification from wrist activity. *Sleep* **1992**, *15*, 461–469. [CrossRef] [PubMed]

50. Ramanan, D.; Forsyth, D.A.; Zisserman, A. Tracking people by learning their appearance. *IEEE Trans. Pattern Anal. Mach. Intell.* **2007**, *29*, 65–81. [CrossRef] [PubMed]

 *electronics*

Article

Learning-Based Screening of Endothelial Dysfunction From Photoplethysmographic Signals

Chiara Calamanti *, Sara Moccia, Lucia Migliorelli, Marina Paolanti and Emanuele Frontoni

Department of Information Engineering, Universitá Politecnica delle Marche, 60121 Ancona, Italy; s.moccia@univpm.it (S.M.); l.migliorelli@pm.univpm.it (L.M.); m.paolanti@univpm.it (M.P.); e.frontoni@univpm.it (E.F.)

* Correspondence: c.calamanti@pm.univpm.it

Received: 29 January 2019; Accepted: 27 February 2019; Published: 1 March 2019

Abstract: Endothelial-Dysfunction (ED) screening is of primary importance to early diagnosis cardiovascular diseases. Recently, approaches to ED screening are focusing more and more on photoplethysmography (PPG)-signal analysis, which is performed in a threshold-sensitive way and may not be suitable for tackling the high variability of PPG signals. The goal of this work was to present an innovative machine-learning (ML) approach to ED screening that could tackle such variability. Two research hypotheses guided this work: (H1) ML can support ED screening by classifying PPG features; and (H2) classification performance can be improved when including also anthropometric features. To investigate H1 and H2, a new dataset was built from 59 subject. The dataset is balanced in terms of subjects with and without ED. Support vector machine (SVM), random forest (RF) and k-nearest neighbors (KNN) classifiers were investigated for feature classification. With the leave-one-out evaluation protocol, the best classification results for H1 were obtained with SVM (accuracy = 71%, recall = 59%). When testing H2, the recall was further improved to 67%. Such results are a promising step for developing a novel and intelligent PPG device to assist clinicians in performing large scale and low cost ED screening.

Keywords: endothelial dysfunction; photoplethysmography; machine learning; computer-assisted screening

1. Introduction

Cardiovascular Diseases (CVDs) refer to a class of cardiac disorders that, according to the European Heart Network, cause every year 3.9 million deaths in Europe, with estimated costs up to 210 billion euro per year [1]. As reported in the guidelines of the World Health Organization (https://www.who.int/cardiovascular_diseases/guidelines/Pocket_GL_information/en/) for the assessment and management of cardiovascular risks, several factors (e.g., physical inactivity, tobacco use, and obesity) have been shown to influence CVD onset.

Moreover, when these factors are present, there is also a high probability of Endothelial Dysfunction (ED), which is actually recognized to be of primary importance to early diagnosis of CVDs [2–4]. In physiological conditions, the endothelial tissue regulates many functions, among which the most important are to maintain vascular homeostasis and modulate the vascular tone by balancing the production of vasodilators, including nitric oxide, and vasoconstrictors. In presence of ED, the endothelium is liable to anatomical alteration (e.g., smooth muscle cell proliferation and migration, leukocyte adhesion and migration) and its regulation mechanisms are compromised [5,6].

The current gold standard technique for ED diagnosis is the Flow Mediated Dilatation (FMD), which uses high-resolution UltraSound (US) signals acquired on subject arm. FMD is measured after a 5-min arm compression followed by relaxation and measured as the percentage increase of the resulted maximum brachial-artery diameter with respect to the baseline diameter [7]. FMD computation is, however, operator dependent, expensive and requires an expert clinician, thus not suitable for screening purposes.

To overcome these limitations, studies in the clinical literature highlight the efficacy of PhotoPlethysmoGraphy (PPG) in assessing ED [8–12]. PPG is a noninvasive optical technique in which PPG sensors are applied on subject's fingers to measure changes in blood volume as a function of time [13,14]. From the PPG signal, similar to US-based analysis, the incremental ratio of the PPG signal amplitude (with respect to its baseline) is evaluated by clinicians in a sensitive, threshold-based way (not being compatible with the high variability of the PPG signals).

To successfully tackle data variability, different researchers in similar contexts exploited Machine-Learning (ML) techniques. For example, Weng et al. [15] adopted Random Forest (RF), Logistic Regression (LR), Gradient Boosting Machines (GBM) and Neural Networks (NN) with 30 features extracted from electronic health records (EHRs) (such as blood pressure, Body Mass Index (BMI), gender, etc.) to identify patients at risk of developing CVDs. They obtained overall classification recalls of 65.3% (RF), 67.1% (LR), 67.5% (GBM), and 67.5% (NN). Similarly, Boursalie et al. [16] used Support Vector Machines (SVMs) to classify features from wearable sensors and EHRs, achieving a classification accuracy of 90.5%. Work similar to that proposed in this paper is reported in [17], where several ML classifiers (such as SVM and RF) are investigated for the specific task of ED classification, although it focuses on features extracted from FMD data.

Considering the clinical relevance of early-diagnosing ED from PPG data (over the FMD ones), the goal of this research was to test if ML methodologies are suitable for ED classification starting from PPG-signal analysis, by providing a fast and low cost approach to the problem. Specifically, we investigated the following two hypotheses:

Hypothesis 1 (H1). *ML techniques can classify ED by PPG features.*

Hypothesis 2 (H2). *Including anthropometric features may improve classification results.*

Due to the lack of work in this field of research to test H1 and H2, a new publicly available dataset, the PPG Endothelial Dysfunction Dataset (ppgEDD), was collected (http://vrai.dii.univpm.it/content/ppgEDD-dataset).

The paper is organized as follows: Section 2 gives details on the EDD and the features used for endothelial dysfunction classification. Results and conclusions are presented in Sections 3 and 4, respectively.

2. Methods

This section presents the proposed approach to ED screening from PPG data (Section 2.1) and the experimental protocol used to investigate H1 and H2 (Section 2.2).

2.1. Endothelial-Dysfunction screening methodology

The proposed method consists of the following steps: (i) data collection (Section 2.1.1); (ii) feature extraction (Section 2.1.2); and (iii) classification (Section 2.1.3). The workflow of the approach is shown in Figure 1.

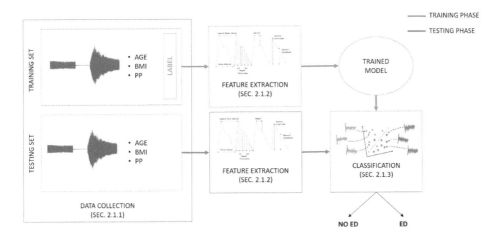

Figure 1. Workflow of the proposed learning-based approach to endothelial dysfunction (ED) screening from photoplethysmographic and anthropometric data.

2.1.1. PPG Endothelial-Dysfunction-Dataset Collection

The ppgEDD was built from 59 voluntary patients. Thirty-one subjects (F/M = 28/31, age = 39 ± 16 years) were healthy and the remaining ones had ED. The PPG-signal acquisition was carried out in the morning, in an environment with comfortable temperature and in absence of noise. Each subject was in the room at least half an hour before the exam to let his/her body to adapt to the temperature. All subjects respected the following instructions:

- Fasting for at least 8 h
- No drug consumption in the previous 6 h
- No smoking in the previous 6 h
- No intense physical activity in the hours immediately preceding the exam
- No nail polish

All participants were informed and provided a written agreement in accordance with the Declaration of Helsinki.

As shown in Figure 2, the medical equipment used to measure the PPG signal included:

- **VenoScreen**® (medis). VenoScreen was connected via a USB interface to a computer equipped with the CardioVascular Lab software package (MEDIS company, Ilmenau). The software verified, evaluated and displayed the measured PPG signals.
- **Prakticus II aneroid sphygmomanometer**® (Friedrich Bosch GmbH & Co. KG). The sphygmomanometer, applied above the elbow on the subject's left arm, was used to induce blood-flow blockage while measuring the blood pressure.

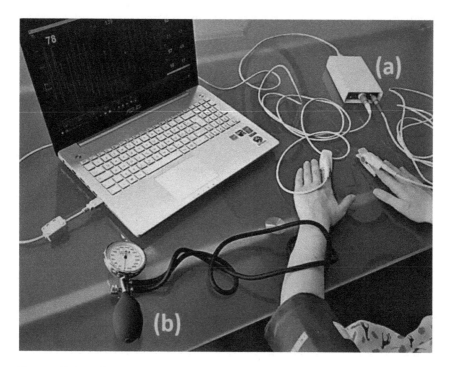

Figure 2. PPG-signal acquisition setup: (**a**) VenoScreen®(medis) with two photoplethysmography sensors; and (**b**) sphygmomanometer with cuff. Acquired signals were processed by the VenoScreen® (medis) software.

PPG processing

The PPG signal was obtained by measuring infrared light passing through finger skin. A LED light is diffused through the human tissue and then detected by a photo-detector located at the opposite side of the LED. The transmittance varies over time in accordance with variations in the blood volume. The device that records the PPG signal provides two different type of information: the signal that represents the light that is detected by a photo-detector (light transmitted) and the transmittance, which is the proportion of the incident (approaching) light that travels through the tissue to the photo-detector. The PPG signal is modulated by each cardiac cycle and may be influenced by several factors, such as breathing and movements. Moreover, the PPG signals may vary according to blood-oxygen saturation, skin temperatures, skin structure and external factors such as light in the environment. The aim of the pre-processing phase is reducing the PPG distortions, which may be observed in the wave profiles and may influence the features extraction, thus negatively impacting the subsequent phases of signal processing and the final diagnosis. For this reason, the following filters were applied on the PPG signal:

- **Noise**: Inevitably, the PPG signal contained high-frequency noise, which resulted from ambient light, thermal noise and other unclassified noise. The power line represented another noise source characterized by 50 Hz sinusoidal interference, probably accompanied by a number of harmonics [18]. To remove this noise, a simple filtering approach was applied, i.e., low-pass filter with 20 dB attenuation at 8 Hz [19].
- **Baseline wander**: Baseline wander filtering was required in order to minimize changes in beat morphology, which did not have cardiac origin [18]. The technique used for baseline wander

filtering consisted in down-sampling the PPG signal to 2 Hz, followed by forward/backwards filtering using a second-order low-pass Butterworth filter with a cut-off frequency of 0.5 Hz [20]. After that, the signal was unsampled and subtracted from the original PPG signal.

- **Outliers**: To remove outliers, the "isoutlier" function (The MathWorks, Inc., Natick, MA, USA), was applied to the PPG signal. A point was considered outlier when its value was more than three scaled median absolute deviations (MAD) away from the PPG signal median. The outliers were detected every 10 s and they were replaced by the mean value calculated in the same interval.

The sampling frequency of the PPG signal recorded by the VenoScreen device was 200 Hz.

ED gold standard classification was obtained by evaluating the PPG signal as in the actual clinical practice (Section 1).

2.1.2. Feature Extraction

PPG features

Inspired by the authors of [21,22], who proved the heart rate and augmentation index correlate with ED, and considering the work in [23], where a set of PPG features are shown to be potentially related to CVDs, in this work, we identified the following as features:

1. Systolic Amplitude (SA):

$$SA = M_{S_1} - M_{F_1} \tag{1}$$

   where M_{S_1} and M_{F_1} are the PPG signal amplitude in S_1 (systolic peak) and F_1 (dicrotic point before the systolic peak).

2. Inflection Point Area ratio (IPA):

$$IPA = \frac{A2}{A1} \tag{2}$$

   where area A1 and area A2 are obtained by dividing the pulse area into two areas at the dicrotic notch.

3. Pulse Interval (PI):

$$PI = t_{F2} - t_{F1} \tag{3}$$

4. Hearth Rate (HR):

$$HR = \frac{1}{t_{S_2} - t_{S_1}} \tag{4}$$

   where t_{S_2} is the time at which the second systolic peak occurred.

5. $Delta_T$, which is the time between the systolic and diastolic peaks:

$$Delta_T = t_{E_1} - t_{S_1} \tag{5}$$

   where t_{E_1} is the time of diastolic peak.

6. Stiffness Index (SI):

$$SI = \frac{H_P}{(t_{E_1} - t_{S_1})} \tag{6}$$

   where H_P is the subject's height.

7. Augmentation Index (AI):

$$AI = \frac{(M_{S_2} - M_{F_2}) - (M_{E_2} - M_{F_2})}{Delta_T} \tag{7}$$

   where M_{S_2} and M_{F_2} are the PPG signal amplitude in S_2 (systolic peak) and F_2 (dicrotic point before the systolic peak), and M_{E_2} is the PPG signal amplitude in E_2 (diastolic peak).

8. Recovery Time (*RT*). *RT* indicates how many seconds, from the maximum value of the PPG during the post-occlusion phase, are required to return to PPG pre-occlusion condition (Figure 3a).

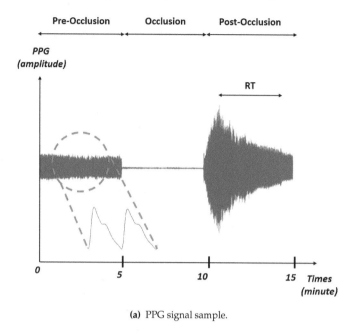

(**a**) PPG signal sample.

(**b**) Parameters for PPG-feature computation.

Figure 3. (**a**) The three phases of the photoplethysmography (PPG) signal acquisition: pre-occlusion (normal blood flow), occlusion (occluded flow), and post-occlusion (restored flow). Dotted lines highlights a zoomed signal portion. (**b**) From the zoomed signal portion, the parameters useful for computing PPG features are highlighted.

For the extraction of the features from the PPG signal, ten beats were selected randomly during the pre-occlusion phase. The fiducial points were identified for each beat (C1, C2, E1, E2, F1, F2, S1, and S2) to identify and quantify the parameters. Finally, the mean for each feature was calculated.

Anthropometric features

Considering our previous experience in this field [17], the following anthropometric features were investigated: age, BMI and pulse pressure (PP), (i.e., the difference between systolic and diastolic blood pressure at rests measured with the sphygmomanometer) [24].

2.1.3. Classification

To perform feature classification, SVMs were implemented [25]. Indeed, SVM decisions are only determined by the support vectors, which makes SVM robust to noise in training data. Here, SVM with the Gaussian kernel (Ψ) was used to prevent parameter proliferation while lowering computational complexity and limiting overfitting. For our binary classification problem, given a training set of N data $\{y_k, \mathbf{x_k}\}_{k=1}^{N}$, where $\mathbf{x_k}$ is the kth input feature vector and y_k is the kth output label, the SVM decision function takes the form of as follows:

$$f(\mathbf{x}) = sign\left[\sum_{k=1}^{N} a_k^* y_k \Psi(\mathbf{x}, \mathbf{x_k}) + b \right] \tag{8}$$

where

$$\Psi(\mathbf{x}, \mathbf{x_k}) = exp\{-\gamma||\mathbf{x} - \mathbf{x_k}||_2^2/\sigma^2\}, \qquad \gamma > 0 \tag{9}$$

b is a real constant and a_k^* is retrieved as follow:

$$a_k^* = max\left\{ -\frac{1}{2} \sum_{k,l=1}^{N} y_k y_l \Psi(\mathbf{x_k}, \mathbf{x_l}) a_k a_l + \sum_{k=1}^{N} a_k \right\} \tag{10}$$

with

$$\sum_{k=1}^{N} a_k y_k = 0, \qquad 0 \leq a_k \leq C, \qquad k = 1, ..., N \tag{11}$$

γ and C were retrieved with grid search, as explained more in detail in Section 2.2.

For the sake of completeness, the performance of other classifiers, i.e., k-nearest neighbors (KNN) [26] and RF [27], were investigated too.

Prior to classification, the feature matrices were normalized within each feature dimension.

2.2. Experimental protocol

To investigate the two hypotheses mentioned in Section 1, different set of features were considered (as introduced in Section 2.1.2):

- For H1, eight PPG features were used (Table 1).
- For H2, 11 features (three anthropometric features (Table 2) as well as eight PPG features) were used.

Table 1. PPG feature mean (±Standard Deviation (SD)) of the PPG endothelial dysfunction dataset (ppgEDD).

Features	Mean ± SD
SA	7.91 ± 5.68
IPA	0.61 ± 0.28
PI	172.92 ± 22.98
HR	69.19 ± 9.67
$Delta_T$	202.48 ± 40.29
SI	0.87 ± 0.18
AI	1.45 ± 0.38
RT	5.05 ± 0.66

Table 2. Anthropometric feature mean (±Standard Deviation (SD)) of the PPG endothelial dysfunction dataset (ppgEDD).

Features	Mean ± SD
Age (years)	39.0 ± 16.0
BMI (Kg/m^2)	25.7 ± 4.9
PP (mmHg)	44.15 ± 12.1

Considering the limited size of ppgEDD, Leave-One-Out (LOO) cross validation (CV) was implemented for testing purposes, as suggested in the ML literature (e.g., [28]). LOO-CV implies that, each time, 58 patients were used for training and the remaining one for testing.

During the training phase, classifier–hyperparameter tuning was implemented using a grid-search and LOO-CV approach. For SVMs, the grid-search space for γ and C was set to $[1, 0.1, 0.001, 0.0001]$ and $[1, 10, 100, 1000]$, respectively. The grid-search space for KNN number of neighbors was $[1, 3, 5, 7, 9]$ and that for the number of trees for RF was $[5, 10, 15, 20, 30, 40]$.

The performance of each classifier was evaluated in terms of accuracy (*Acc*), recall (*Rec*) and precision (*Prec*):

$$Acc = \frac{TP + TN}{TP + TN + FP + FN} \tag{12}$$

$$Rec = \frac{TP}{TP + FN} \tag{13}$$

$$Prec = \frac{TP}{TP + FP} \tag{14}$$

where TP and FN refer to subjects with ED that were and were not classified correctly, respectively, and TN and FP refer to subjects without ED that were and were not classified correctly, respectively.

All the experiments were implemented using scikit-learn Python libraries https://scikit-learn.org/stable/index.html.

3. Results

We tested our approach on the ppgEDD dataset to compare the endothelial function differences between patient with ED ($n = 28$) and patient without the disease ($n = 31$) based on the PPG signal. A full leave-one-out cross-validation was performed in our experiments procedure described in Section 2.2. In Tables 3 and 4, the performance of each classifier is shown for H1 and H2, respectively. For H1, the best performance in terms of accuracy (*Acc* = 71%) was obtained with SVM, with a recall of 59% and a precision of 73%. The confusion matrices for KNN, RF and SVM are shown in Figure 4a–c.

When investigating H2, as shown in Table 4, the SVM classification results were still the best, with a further improvement to 67% (*Rec*) and 69% (*Prec*). The normalized confusion matrices for KNN, RF and SVM are shown in Figure 4d.

The tested classifiers achieved encouraging results, with the best performance achieved by SVM (accuracy = 71%, recall = 67%). As reported in the literature [29]), similarity in performance metrics among the ML methods may be due to the fact that the analyzed dataset and the feature space were small.

Table 3. Investigation of H1: Classification performance obtained when classifying PPG features with K-Nearest Neighbor (KNN), Random Forest (RF) and Support Vector Machine (SVM) classifiers. Classification accuracy (*Acc*), recall (*Rec*) and precision (*Prec*) are reported.

Classifier	*Acc*	*Rec*	*Prec*
KNN	0.64	0.59	0.62
RF	0.66	0.63	0.63
SVM	**0.71**	**0.59**	**0.73**

Table 4. Investigation of H2: Classification performance obtained when classifying photoplethysmography and anthropometric features with KNN, Random Forest (RF) and SVM classifiers. Classification accuracy (*Acc*), recall (*Rec*) and precision (*Prec*) are reported.

Classifier	*Acc*	*Rec*	*Prec*
KNN	0.64	0.52	0.64
RF	0.49	0.44	0.44
SVM	**0.71**	**0.67**	**0.69**

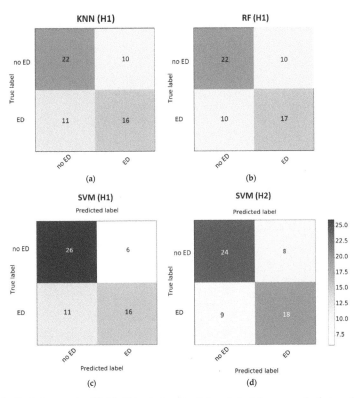

Figure 4. Confusion matrices (CMs) obtained when classifying photoplethysmography features (H1) with: (**a**) K-Nearest Neighbor (KNN); (**b**) Random Forest (RF); and (**c**) Support Vector Machine (SVM) classifier. (**d**) CM for SVM obtained when testing H2 (both photoplethysmography and anthropometric features).

4. Discussion and Conclusions

In this study, we presented and evaluated an innovative learning-based approach to ED screening from PPG data. Two different hypotheses were investigated for ED classification, i.e., using (H1) only PPG features and (H2) including also anthropometric features. Three ML classifiers (i.e., SVM, KNN and RF) were tested.

With H1 and H2, we showed that the proposed feature set can be promising for ED screening, even though further investigation is needed, e.g., to increase the ppgEDD dataset size numerosity. Results achieved when investigating H2 suggest that including anthropometric features is useful, as in accord with previous work in the literature (e.g., [17]).

The experimental results show that SVM outperformed KNN and RF. This is probably due to the SVM's ability to tackle: (1) the dimension of our feature space, which was high when compared with the number of ppgEDD subjects; and (2) the noise present in the PPG data.

The main novelty of this study relies on the fact that PPG features were used in combination with anthropometric ones to classify ED. The results verify that the ED SVM classification method significantly improved the generalization capability achievable with the SVM classifier. Another advantage of the SVM approach was found in its high sparseness, explained by the fact that the adopted optimization criterion was based on minimizing the number of support vectors.

As future work, we would like to investigate other anthropometric features, such as dyslipidemia and smoking habits, integrating PPG data with data coming from structured electronic-health-record datasets. Furthermore, we will investigate other features extracted from the PPG signal, such as those proposed in [30] to compute the diastolic and systolic pressure, and in [31,32] to analyze the ECG waveform. Our expectation is that research on this new ML approach based on PPG features will be empowered by the proposed work. Surely the prediction of ED based on this approach should be further explored using machine learning with other large clinical datasets and in other populations.

In conclusion, it is acknowledged that further research is required to ameliorate the algorithm as to offer all possible support for diagnosis, but the results presented here are surely a promising step towards a helpful intelligent PPG system to support the screening of ED.

Author Contributions: Introduction, C.C., E.F., S.M., L.M. and M.P.; Methods,C.C., S.M. and L.M.; Results, C.C., S.M. and L.M.; Discussion and Conclusion, C.C., E.F., S.M., L.M. and M.P. All authors contributed to the development and set up of the general idea.

Funding: This research received no external funding.

Acknowledgments: The work described in this paper was supported by STRUMEDICAL srl that provided us with the VenoScreen devices used in our studies.

Conflicts of Interest: The authors declare no conflicts of interest.

References

1. Wilkins, E.; Wilson, L.; Wickramasinghe, K.; Bhatnagar, P.; Leal, J.; Luengo-Fernandez, R.; Burns, R.; Rayner, M.; Townsend, N. *European Cardiovascular Disease Statistics 2017*; European Heart Network: Brussels, Belgium, 2017.

2. Hadi, H.A.; Carr, C.S.; Al Suwaidi, J. Endothelial dysfunction: Cardiovascular risk factors, therapy, and outcome. *Vasc. Health Risk Manag.* **2005**, *1*, 183–198. [PubMed]

3. Brunner, H.; Cockcroft, J.R.; Deanfield, J.; Donald, A.; Ferrannini, E.; Halcox, J.; Kiowski, W.; Lüscher, T.F.; Mancia, G.; Natali, A.; et al. Endothelial function and dysfunction. Part II: Association with cardiovascular risk factors and diseases. A statement by the Working Group on Endothelins and Endothelial Factors of the European Society of Hypertension. *J. Hypertens.* **2005**, *23*, 233–246. [CrossRef] [PubMed]

4. Anderson, T.J. Arterial stiffness or endothelial dysfunction as a surrogate marker of vascular risk. *Can. J. Cardiol.* **2006**, *22*, 72B–80B. [CrossRef]

5. Félétou, M. The endothelium, Part I: Multiple functions of the endothelial cells—Focus on endothelium-derived vasoactive mediators. Colloquium Series on Integrated Systems Physiology: From Molecule to Function. *Morgan Claypool Life Sci.* **2011**, *3*, 1–306.

6. van Hinsbergh, V.W. Endothelium role in regulation of coagulation and inflammation. In *Seminars in Immunopathology*; Springer: Berlin, Germany, 2012; Volume 34, pp. 93–106.

7. Corretti, M.C.; Anderson, T.J.; Benjamin, E.J.; Celermajer, D.; Charbonneau, F.; Creager, M.A.; Deanfield, J.; Drexler, H.; Gerhard-Herman, M.; Herrington, D.; et al. Guidelines for the ultrasound assessment of endothelial-dependent flow-mediated vasodilation of the brachial artery: A report of the International Brachial Artery Reactivity Task Force. *J. Am. Coll. Cardiol.* **2002**, *39*, 257–265. [CrossRef]

8. Zahedi, E.; Jaafar, R.; Ali, M.M.; Mohamed, A.; Maskon, O. Finger photoplethysmogram pulse amplitude changes induced by flow-mediated dilation. *Physiol. Meas.* **2008**, *29*, 625–637. [CrossRef] [PubMed]

9. Flammer, A.J.; Anderson, T.; Celermajer, D.S.; Creager, M.A.; Deanfield, J.; Ganz, P.; Hamburg, N.M.; Lüscher, T.F.; Shechter, M.; Taddei, S.; et al. The assessment of endothelial function: From research into clinical practice. *Circulation* **2012**, *126*, 753–767. [CrossRef] [PubMed]

10. Kuznetsova, T.; Van Vlierberghe, E.; Knez, J.; Szczesny, G.; Thijs, L.; Jozeau, D.; Balestra, C.; Dhooge, J.; Staessen, J.A. Association of digital vascular function with cardiovascular risk factors: A population study. *Br. Med J. Open* **2014**, *4*, e004399. [CrossRef] [PubMed]

11. Mashayekhi, G.; Zahedi, E.; Attar, H.M.; Sharifi, F. Flow mediated dilation with photoplethysmography as a substitute for ultrasonic imaging. *Physiol. Meas.* **2015**, *36*, 1551–1571. [CrossRef] [PubMed]

12. Moerland, M.; Kales, A.; Schrier, L.; Van Dongen, M.; Bradnock, D.; Burggraaf, J. Evaluation of the EndoPAT as a tool to assess endothelial function. *Int. J. Vasc. Med.* **2012**, *2012*, 1–8. [CrossRef] [PubMed]

13. Allen, J. Photoplethysmography and its application in clinical physiological measurement. *Physiol. Meas.* **2007**, *28*, 1–39. [CrossRef] [PubMed]

14. Moraes, J.; Rocha, M.; Vasconcelos, G.; Vasconcelos Filho, J.; de Albuquerque, V. Advances in photopletysmography signal analysis for biomedical applications. *Sensors* **2018**, *18*, 1894. [CrossRef] [PubMed]

15. Weng, S.F.; Reps, J.; Kai, J.; Garibaldi, J.M.; Qureshi, N. Can machine-learning improve cardiovascular risk prediction using routine clinical data? *PLoS ONE* **2017**, *12*, e0174944. [CrossRef] [PubMed]

16. Boursalie, O.; Samavi, R.; Doyle, T.E. M4CVD: Mobile machine learning model for monitoring cardiovascular disease. *Procedia Comput. Sci.* **2015**, *63*, 384–391. [CrossRef]

17. Calamanti, C.; Paolanti, M.; Romeo, L.; Bernardini, M.; Frontoni, E. Machine learning-based approaches to analyse and improve the diagnosis of endothelial dysfunction. In Proceedings of the IEEE/ASME International Conference on Mechatronic and Embedded Systems and Applications, New York, NY, USA, 2–4 July 2018; pp. 1–6.

18. Sörnmo, L.; Laguna, P. *Bioelectrical Signal Processing in Cardiac and Neurological Applications*; Academic Press: Cambridge, MA, USA, 2005; Volume 8,

19. Peng, F.; Zhang, Z.; Gou, X.; Liu, H.; Wang, W. Motion artifact removal from photoplethysmographic signals by combining temporally constrained independent component analysis and adaptive filter. *Biomed. Eng. Online* **2014**, *13*, 50. [CrossRef] [PubMed]

20. Solem, K.; Olde, B.; Sornmo, L. Prediction of intradialytic hypotension using photoplethysmography. *IEEE Trans. Biomed. Eng.* **2010**, *57*, 1611–1619. [CrossRef] [PubMed]

21. Maio, R.; Miceli, S.; Sciacqua, A.; Leone, G.G.; Bruni, R.; Naccarato, P.; Martino, F.; Sesti, G.; Perticone, F. Heart rate affects endothelial function in essential hypertension. *Intern. Emerg. Med.* **2013**, *8*, 211–219. [CrossRef] [PubMed]

22. McEniery, C.M.; Wallace, S.; Mackenzie, I.S.; McDonnell, B.; Yasmin.; Newby, D.E.; Cockcroft, J.R.; Wilkinson, I.B. Endothelial function is associated with pulse pressure, pulse wave velocity, and augmentation index in healthy humans. *Hypertension* **2006**, *48*, 602–608. [CrossRef] [PubMed]

23. Elgendi, M. On the analysis of fingertip photoplethysmogram signals. *Curr. Cardiol. Rev.* **2012**, *8*, 14–25. [CrossRef] [PubMed]

24. Beigel, R.; Dvir, D.; Arbel, Y.; Shechter, A.; Feinberg, M.S.; Shechter, M. Pulse pressure is a predictor of vascular endothelial function in middle-aged subjects with no apparent heart disease. *Vasc. Med.* **2010**, *15*, 299–305. [CrossRef] [PubMed]

25. Burges, C.J. A tutorial on support vector machines for pattern recognition. *Data Min. Knowl. Discov.* **1998**, *2*, 121–167. [CrossRef]

26. Keller, J.M.; Gray, M.R.; Givens, J.A. A fuzzy k-nearest neighbor algorithm. *IEEE Trans. Syst. Man Cybern.* **1985**, *SMC-15*, 580–585. [CrossRef]

27. Breiman, L. Random forests. *Mach. Learn.* **2001**, *45*, 5–32. [CrossRef]

28. Wong, T.T. Performance evaluation of classification algorithms by k-fold and leave-one-out cross validation. *Pattern Recognit.* **2015**, *48*, 2839–2846. [CrossRef]
29. Nasrabadi, N.M. Pattern recognition and machine learning. *J. Electron. Imaging* **2007**, *16*, 049901.
30. Rundo, F.; Ortis, A.; Battiato, S.; Conoci, S. Advanced bio-inspired system for noninvasive cuff-less blood pressure estimation from physiological signal analysis. *Computation* **2018**, *6*, 46. [CrossRef]
31. Rundo, F.; Conoci, S.; Ortis, A.; Battiato, S. An advanced bio-inspired PhotoPlethysmoGraphy (PPG) and ECG pattern recognition system for medical assessment. *Sensors* **2018**, *18*, 405. [CrossRef] [PubMed]
32. Dutt, D.N.; Shruthi, S. Digital processing of ECG and PPG signals for study of arterial parameters for cardiovascular risk assessment. In Proceedings of the 2015 International Conference on Communications and Signal Processing (ICCSP), Melmaruvathur, India, 2–4 April 2015; pp. 1506–1510.

Article

Towards Human Motion Tracking: Multi-Sensory IMU/TOA Fusion Method and Fundamental Limits

Cheng Xu [1,2], Jie He [1,2,*], Xiaotong Zhang [1,2,*], Xinghang Zhou [1,2] and Shihong Duan [1,2]

[1] School of Computer and Communication Engineering, University of Science and Technology Beijing, Beijing 100083, China; xucheng19880202@foxmail.com (C.X.); zhouxinghang@xs.ustb.edu.cn (X.Z.); duansh@ustb.edu.cn (S.D.)

[2] Beijing Key Laboratory of Knowledge Engineering for Materials Science, Beijing 100083, China

* Correspondence: hejie@ustb.edu.cn (J.H.); zxt@ies.ustb.edu.cn (X.Z.)

Received: 18 January 2019; Accepted: 27 January 2019; Published: 29 January 2019

Abstract: Human motion tracking could be viewed as a multi-target tracking problem towards numerous body joints. Inertial-measurement-unit-based human motion tracking technique stands out and has been widely used in body are network applications. However, it has been facing the tough problem of accumulative errors and drift. In this paper, we propose a multi-sensor hybrid method to solve this problem. Firstly, an inertial-measurement-unit and time-of-arrival fusion-based method is proposed to compensate the drift and accumulative errors caused by inertial sensors. Secondly, Cramér–Rao lower bound is derived in detail with consideration of both spatial and temporal related factors. Simulation results show that the proposed method in this paper has both spatial and temporal advantages, compared with traditional sole inertial or time-of-arrival-based tracking methods. Furthermore, proposed method is verified in 3D practical application scenarios. Compared with state-of-the-art algorithms, proposed fusion method shows better consistency and higher tracking accuracy, especially when moving direction changes. The proposed fusion method and comprehensive fundamental limits analysis conducted in this paper can provide a theoretical basis for further system design and algorithm analysis. Without the requirements of external anchors, the proposed method has good stability and high tracking accuracy, thus it is more suitable for wearable motion tracking applications.

Keywords: Cramér–Rao lower bound (CRLB); human motion; Inertial Measurement Unit(IMU); Time of Arrival (TOA); wearable sensors

---

1. Introduction

Human Motion Tracking (HMT) [1,2] has been a hot topic in the area of body area network (BAN) [3,4] during the last decade. It aims to obtain human body movement information via quantitative methods to capture and analyze human motion. The information obtained by HMT are mainly relative positions in 2D/3D space of various joints and limbs. With the booming of BAN [5–7], human-centric applications have been raising in both academic and industrial areas, such as interactive games, computer cinematography, animation, etc. [1]. Many entrepreneurial firms have been formed in these areas [8,9]. Besides, HMT also plays a big role in medical field [5], and military and security applications [6].

HMT systems could be classified into two categories: computer vision (CV)-based [10] and wearable sensor (WS)-based [6]. CV-based technology takes advantages of deployed web-depth cameras to monitor human activities, and has been applied in practical applications, such as film shooting [11], security monitoring [6] and so on. Many technology companies have also been working on the research and development of professional human motion tracking systems, such as Vicon [12] and Optotrak [13]. They perform with high accuracy when operated in controlled scenario, however they rely heavily on environment factors, such as shooting angle and lights [10]. These inevitable defects make it only suitable for smaller and controllable situations. WS-based HMT systems, by contrast, do not need to deploy devices in scenarios and are less sensitive to the environment. Thus, they are more suitable for large-scale and dynamic applications [14].

In the present stage, WS-based HMT systems are mainly composed of inertial measurement units (IMUs), such as accelerometers and gyroscopes. The basic principle is to measure the triaxial acceleration and angular velocity of the motion by these sensors, and obtain the trajectory of monitoring points through integral operations [15–18]. However, inertial sensors may inevitably throw off errors that accumulate over time [19–21]. The accumulative and drift error is the biggest challenge faced by WS-based HMT systems.

For better solving the drift error problem and improving HMT accuracy, the most common methods are as follows:

1. The hardware aspect uses inertial sensors with high precision, such as XSens [15] and Invensense [16] tracking units.
2. The algorithm aspect enhances the system by using multi-sensor data fusion means [1,19,22,23].

However, the above-mentioned methods cannot fundamentally solve the drift problem. High precision hardware used by wearable tracking systems is usually very expensive, and the cost of a single suit could be hundreds of thousands or even millions of dollars [15–18]. In the aspect of algorithms, filtering methods, such as Kalman and particle filter [24], can somehow slow down the accumulation process, but cannot eliminate it completely. Thus, the inevitable drift problem of inertial sensors has become a crucial constraint for wearable HMT systems, which limits its use in long term or large space applications.

In essence, human motion tracking can be viewed as a local multi-target real-time high-precision three-dimensional positioning problem [23]. Ultra-Wideband (UWB)-based time-of-arrival (TOA) ranging is the most commonly used high-precision localization technology, its measurement accuracy can reach the centimeter level, and it does not have the drawback of accumulative errors, compared with inertial-sensor-based HMT systems [23,25]. The size of TOA chip is small enough to be integrated into wearable devices. Thereinto, IMU/TOA fusion is an effective way to overcome the accumulative errors of drifting problem faced by solo IMU method [26].

Some achievements on IMU/TOA fusion have been reported in many studies (e.g., [20,21,23,25]) However, state-of-the-art studies, (e.g., [23,27]), mainly face the following two drawbacks:

1. Requirements of fixed external anchors: They need to be deployed in certain scenarios; for example, Zihajehzadeh et al. [23] introduced a magnetometer-free algorithm for human lower-body motion tracking by fusing inertial sensors with an UWB localization system. However, it is hard to realize wearable systems, and is not suitable for BAN applications.
2. State-of-the-art studies seldom concentrate on the fundamental limits of IMU/TOA fusion methods, and the error correction effects are not satisfying. For example, Nilsson et al. [27] proposed a cooperative localization method by fusion of dual foot-mounted inertial sensors and inter-agent UWB ranging, but the experiment results show that, compared with the performance lower bounds [22], there is still a lot of room for improvement.

Based on these considerations, we propose an external-anchor-free IMU/TOA fusion method, and analyze its fundamental limits to lay a theoretical foundation for realizing low cost and high precision motion tracking system that is suitable for medium and long term use in large space.

The rest of the paper is organized as follows: Section 2 briefly introduces the related works about human motion tracking techniques and Cramér–Rao lower bound (CRLB). Section 3 describes the problem definition, IMU/TOA fusion-based model and its error sources. Section 4 introduces our external-anchor-free IMU/TOA fusion method, and analyzes its fundamental limits. Sections 5 and 6, respectively, verify the spatial and temporal performance of proposed fusion-method. Section 7 presents a practical use case to verify the feasibility of proposed method when compared with state-of-the-art methods. Finally, Section 8 presents the conclusion.

2. Related Work

The development of HMT has been rising with the booming of Internet of Things (IoTs) and the rapid progress of human-centric applications [28–31] in the last decades. Particularly, HMT has become an essential task within the fields, such as clinical, military and security applications. In this section, we present a brief literature review on the following aspects: human motion tracking systems and applications, multi-sensory fusion methods and CRLB.

2.1. HMT Systems and Applications

HMT has shown a tremendous potential in the areas of industrial applications. Benefiting from the development of various systems, HMT has permeated into every aspect of social life, including clinical areas, emergency and rescue areas, security and entertainment, to name a few [5–9]. The most widely used HMT systems could be mainly classified into two categories: CV-based [10] and WS-based [6]. Next, we give a brief introduction and discussion about their merits and demerits.

Computer-vision-based systems, such as Vicon [12] or Optotrak [13], have a high accuracy when operating in controlled environments, e.g., several fixed cameras calibrated and correlated in a specific place and capturing configuration. Famous TV shows and movies, such as The Walking Dead, Game of Thrones and Guardians of the Galaxy, are all powered by human motion animators [15]. CV-based systems can provide a large amount of redundant data. Ambulatory systems, such as those using a Kinect [32] to capture human motion, are set in relatively uncontrolled environments and have a restricted field of view. These systems have a restricted margin of maneuverability and are more suitable for indoor use.

In contrast, a very promising frontier for reliable human motion tracking is WS-based [6] system, especially using IMUs. Iyengar et al. [33] defined a framework that managed common tasks for healthcare monitoring applications to aid development of BAN. Anwary et al. [34] utilized a pressure sensor array and IMU for gait analysis. Ghasemzadeh et al. [35] introduced a novel classification model that identified physical movements from body-worn inertial sensors while considering the collaborative nature and limited resources of the system. Inertial sensors are integrated with UWB localization system in [23] for simultaneous 3-D trajectory tracking and lower body motion capture (MoCap) under various dynamic activities such as walking and jumping.

WS-based HMT systems do not need to deploy devices in scenarios and are less sensitive to the environment. Thus, they are more suitable for large-scale and dynamic applications [2,6]. Currently, WS-based HMT systems [6] are mainly composed of inertial sensors, such as accelerometers and gyroscopes. However, inertial sensors may inevitably throw off errors that accumulate over time [8,15,25]. The accumulative and drift error is the biggest challenge faced by WS-based HMT systems.

2.2. Sensor Fusion and Filtering

Despite the advantages mentioned above, there still exist challenges when wearable sensors are applied to human motion tracking. As human motion tracking could be viewed as a multiple-target localization issue of human body joints, tracking accuracy is the most important consideration. However, sensor drift errors and distortion (especially in long time monitoring) are the main problems [8,15,25].

Kalman filter and calibration algorithms are the most widely adopted method to overcome drift errors. They are both used to overcome the instantaneous error problem and multiple sensor fusion problem. Yun et al. [36] realized a method to measure the orientation of human body segments using Kalman filter that takes into account the spectra of the signals, as well as a fluctuating gyroscope offset, and thereby improves the estimation accuracy. Zhao et al. [37] proposed a Kalman/UFIR filtering method for state estimation with uncertain parameters and noise statistics. Briese et al. [38] presented an adapting covariance Kalman filter based on the fusion of Ultra-Wideband (UWB) and inertial measurements. Since both sensor results are separately used in the Kalman filter, no registration between the implemented sensors is needed. Kim et al. [39] proposed a fusion algorithm based on a particle filter using vertical and road intensity information for robust vehicle localization in a large-scale urban area. However, filtering methods lack in terms of dynamic behavior and the algorithm performance varies with the change of state matrixes [38,39]. They can somewhat slow down the error accumulation process, but not eliminate it completely [40,41]. With the booming of artificial intelligence, deep neural networks [42] have been applied in the fusion of multi-sensors, while the requirement of a large scale of data still remains a big challenge in practical applications.

2.3. Cramér–Rao Lower Bound

The location of a target node is uncertain due to the influence of random factors, such as noise, fading, multi-path, and non-line-of-sight propagation, which ultimately affects the positioning accuracy [1,8]. Cramér–Rao lower bound (CRLB) defines the theoretical lower bound of the unbiased estimator variance and is used as a general criterion and benchmark for evaluating the performance of a positioning system [8].

Tichavsky et al. [43] provided the formulation of recursive posterior CRLB for nonlinear filters based on the Bayesian framework. For range-based wireless localization system, many research studies have provided CRLB results for different scenarios. Qi et al. [44] proposed a generalized CRLB (G-CRLB) of the wireless system for non-line-of-sight (NLOS) environment. Other similar works also give CRLB for different ranging techniques [45]. Although some other methods can be used for performance analysis [14], CRLB is still popular for wireless localization research due to its simplicity and general expression.

However, CRLB only focuses on the influence of the relationship between relative positions in spatial state on the accuracy of the positioning target, neglecting the time information, thus cannot meet the requirements of the time evaluation in the positioning system. The posterior Cramér–Rao lower bound (PCRLB) considers the time domain information [46] and can be used as another criterion for the performance evaluation of the positioning system. PCRLB has recently been used as the basis for determining optimal observer trajectories in bearings-only tracking (e.g., [47]). Recent interest in the PCRLB is primarily a result of an excellent paper [43] in which a computationally efficient (and general) formulation of the bound is derived. This has led to a number of further developments, including derivations of the bound and associated information reduction factors in cluttered environments [14] and the establishment of PCRLBs in multi-target tracking with either preprocessed [1,5] or raw sensor data [8,15].

To better comprehend HMT problems and provide a theoretical basis for the system verification and algorithm design, in this paper, we conduct a comprehensive analysis on performance evaluation of HMT system based on IMU/TOA fusion. By the derivation of CRLB and PCRLB, we present a feasible assessment means to evaluate IMU/TOA fusion system in both temporal and spatial aspects.

3. Problem Definition

The body can be viewed as an interconnected whole, and each movement is done in collaboration with a number of body parts. The part of body that is connected to each other is called the joint. We call this chain of rigid limbs and joints the "chain of motion". Therefore, HMT can be considered as a collaborative tracking process of the motion chain composed of multiple human joints.

3.1. Model Description

Generally speaking, a 3D human motion is considered as a set of multiple joints and limbs movement, which can be described using mathematical expressions of coordinates and direction. As shown in Figure 1, the whole body is divided into five connected parts, namely left upper limb, right upper limb, trunk, left lower limb and right lower limb. We use dots to represent joints and lines for limbs. The whole human body acts as a unity of these limbs and joints.

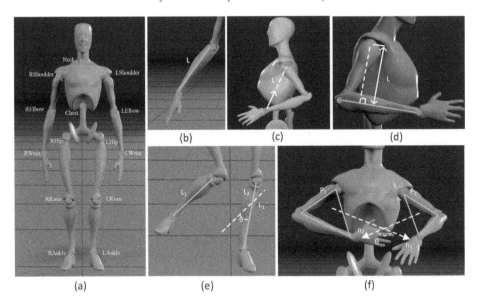

Figure 1. Human skeleton model, and the key distance and angle parameters related with human motion tracking. (**a**) the entire human body and (**b–f**) the distances and angles between joint and limbs.

As shown in Figure 1, the human body consists of 15 joints and 14 limbs. To better describe the complicated human body movements, Denavit–Hartenbe (D-H) equation [22,25] is generally used in the description of HMT features and parameters. Its measurement parameters mainly include the distances between joints (Figure 1b,c) joint and limbs (Figure 1d) and the relative angles between limbs (Figure 1e,f). To simplify the above tracking problem, we abstract the HMT serialization process as shown in Figure 1, representing the target's coordinate and measurement parameters in time sequence $T = \{t_0, t_1, \cdots, t_n\}$.

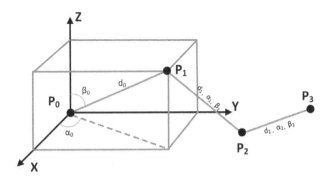

Figure 2. The definition of Gauss–Markov random process towards human motion tracking and its key parameters.

On the basis of random motion model [25], we assume a Gauss–Markov process to describe the movement of the joints of the body, as shown in Figure 2. Thanks to Inertial Measurement Unit (IMU), acceleration and angular data can be obtained and, furthermore, the rotation angle of the target position within the history frames can be calculated by means of Attitude and Heading Reference System (AHRS) [20]. In addition, distance-related information can be obtained using the TOA technique [19], after a few simple calculations. Compared with IMU-based dead reckoning method [25], TOA-based tracking method does not have to face the problem of drifting.

3.2. Error Sources

As mentioned above, the measurement parameters of the system are derived from IMU and TOA. The measurement error sources can be divided into two aspects: distance measurement error and angle measurement error. Thereinto, target node's distance parameter $\hat{d}_t$ at time t is defined as:

$$\hat{d}_t = d_t + n_d \tag{1}$$

where d_t is the actual distance value and n_d is Gauss distributed measurement noise whose variance is σ_d^2, namely $n_d \sim \mathcal{N}(0, \sigma_d^2)$. Vector $\hat{d}_t = [\hat{d}_1, \hat{d}_2, \cdots, \hat{d}_{n+m-1}]^T$ is introduced to collect distance information, namely the distance between target node and reference nodes, respectively, standing for one body joint.

Horizontal heading estimates from inertial-sensor-based approach α reads:

$$\hat{\alpha}_t = \alpha_t + u_t, u_t \sim N(0, \epsilon_t^2) \tag{2}$$

where α_t is the true value of actual horizontal heading. u_t is uncorrelated zero-mean Gaussian random variable with variance ϵ_t^2, which is independent from z direction and is also uncorrelated with $\hat{d}$. The horizontal heading is an instantaneous measurement parameters, which may introduce cumulative error by the characteristics of IMU. Namely, $\hat{\alpha}_t$ is a time-dependent parameter. Vector $\alpha_t = [\alpha_1, \alpha_2, \cdots, \alpha_{N_\alpha}]^T$ is introduced to collect α_t, i.e., the angular cumulative information in the past N_α frames.

Vertical elevation estimates from inertial-sensor-based approach β reads:

$$\hat{\beta}_t = \beta_t + v_t, v_t \sim N(0, \zeta_t^2) \tag{3}$$

where β_k is the actual vertical elevation. v_t is uncorrelated zero-mean Gaussian random variable with variances ζ_t^2, which is independent from z direction and is also uncorrelated with both $\hat{\alpha}$ and $\hat{d}$. $\hat{\beta}_t$ is also a time-independent parameter. Vector $\beta_t = [\beta_1, \beta_2, \cdots, \beta_{N_\beta}]^T$ is introduced to collect β_k, i.e., the angular cumulative information in the past N_β frames. As above mentioned angles α and β are all measured from IMU, thus, for ease of expression, we take σ_{IMU} as the variance of both these two parameters.

3.3. Model Presentation

In continuous human motion tracking process, some body parts remain relatively steady in comparison to the end joints or limbs of the human body, such as the trunk. Thus, these positions may be set as reference nodes, defined as $\mathcal{P}_a = \{1, ..., m\}$, in which the kth reference node's coordinate is defined as a_k. m indicates the number of reference nodes. In addition, the position state of the target is denoted by $p_t = [p_t^X \ p_t^Y \ p_t^Z]^T$, where p_t^X, p_t^Y and p_t^Z are the coordinates in the 3-D positioning system, and T is the transpose operator. The target nodes set is represented as $\mathcal{P}_x = \{1, 2, ..., n\}$, and the ith target node's coordinate is defined as p_i. n indicates the number of target nodes.

According to the Bayesian theorem [22,25], at time t, the state estimation x_{t-1} could be represented as:

$$p_t = f_t(p_{t-1}) + q_t \tag{4}$$

where Equation (4) is the prediction equation, and $\mathbf{f}_t(\cdot)$ is the transition equation, and the noise of x_t follows standard normal distribution with variance Q_t, namely $\mathbf{q}_t \sim \mathcal{N}(0, Q_t)$.

To describe the measurement parameters of human motion in a more general way, we define the measurement parameters of the system as:

$$\mathbf{z}_t = \mathbf{h}_t\left(\mathbf{d}(p_t, k), \boldsymbol{\varphi}\right) + \mathbf{r}_t \tag{5}$$

where the measurement vector $\mathbf{z}_t$, whose noise follows normal distribution, i.e., $\mathbf{r}_t \sim \mathcal{N}(0, R_t)$, contains two parts, namely TOA measurement parameter (distance) and IMU measurement parameter (acceleration, angular velocity, etc.). $\mathbf{h}_t(\cdot)$ is nonlinear observation equation, which is related with actual measurement values of target $\mathbf{p}_t$, including $\mathbf{d}(\mathbf{p}_t, \mathbf{k})$ (the distance vector at time t), and $\boldsymbol{\varphi}$ (the angle vector at time t). $\mathbf{k} = [k_1, \cdots, k_j, \cdots, k_{m+n-1}]$ is distance measurement indicator, such as line-of-sight (LOS)/non-line-of-sight (NLOS), the reference node accuracy indicator, etc. $m + n - 1$ is the total number of both reference and target nodes. $\boldsymbol{\varphi} = [\varphi_1, \cdots, k_i, \cdots, \varphi_s]$ is the vector of angle measurement values, whose amount is s. $\mathbf{k}$ and $\boldsymbol{\varphi}$ are auxiliary parameters that are not essential but may help increase the localization accuracy and could be calculated in real time. The effects of these parameters can be verified in subsequent simulation experiments.

4. IMU/TOA Fusion Based HMT Method

Our analysis considers the possible unknown random factors that may influence the human motion tracking. Considering the characteristics of sequential human motion tracking, we define the measuring variable at time slot t as $\boldsymbol{\theta}_t$ (for simplicity, it is abbreviated as $\boldsymbol{\theta}$), namely

$$\theta \triangleq \begin{bmatrix} p_t^T & p_{t-1}^T & k^T & \varphi^T \end{bmatrix}^T \tag{6}$$

where p_t is the target position vector at the moment, and p_{t-1} is historical target location information at the former time slot.

Cramér–Rao lower bound (CRLB) [22] is defined as the inverse of Fisher Information Matrix (FIM) and represents the theoretical lower bound of the observed variance of unbiased estimators [22,25]. Suppose that $p(\boldsymbol{\theta}, z_t)$ represents the joint probability density function of observation vectors z_t and $\boldsymbol{\theta}$, then FIM could be derived as the variance of its log likelihood function gradient, namely

$$\mathbf{J}(\boldsymbol{\theta}) \triangleq \mathbb{E}[\Delta_{\theta}^{\theta} \ln p(\boldsymbol{\theta}, z_t)] \tag{7}$$

where $\mathbb{E}\{\cdot\}$ represent the expectation of parameters. $\nabla_{\theta} = [\frac{\partial}{\partial \theta_1}, \cdots, \frac{\partial}{\partial \theta_n}]$, $\Delta_{\alpha}^{\beta} = \nabla_{\beta} \nabla_{\alpha}^T$. Thus,

$$\mathbf{Cov}_{\theta}(\tilde{\theta}) \succeq \{\mathbf{J}(\boldsymbol{\theta})\}^{-1} \tag{8}$$

where $A \geq B$ for the sake of simplicity, represents that matrix $A - B$ is non-negatively defined.

According to the Bayesian theorem, $p(\boldsymbol{\theta}, z_t) = p(z_t|\boldsymbol{\theta})p(\boldsymbol{\theta})$, then $\mathbf{J}(\boldsymbol{\theta})$ could be divided into two parts, namely

$$\mathbf{J}(\boldsymbol{\theta}) = \mathbf{J_D}(\boldsymbol{\theta}) + \mathbf{J_P}(\boldsymbol{\theta}) \tag{9}$$

where $\mathbf{J_D}$ is the information matrix obtained by measuring parameters. $\mathbf{J_P}$ is the information matrix obtained by prior information. We describe the representation of these two variables separately in the following section.

4.1. Measurement Parameter Information Matrix

Due to the measurement equation, we get $\mathbf{h} = \mathbf{h}_t\left(\mathbf{d}(p_t, k), \boldsymbol{\varphi}\right)$, and then, based on the chain rules [48], $\mathbf{J_D}$ could be represented as:

$$\mathbf{J_D} = \mathbf{H} \cdot \mathbf{J_h} \cdot \mathbf{H}^T \tag{10}$$

where $\mathbf{H} = [\nabla_\theta h]$, J_h is the FIM of h, namely

$$\mathbf{J_h} = \mathbb{E}\left\{\nabla_\mathbf{h}\ln p(\mathbf{z}_t|\boldsymbol{\theta})\left[\nabla_\mathbf{h}\ln p(\mathbf{z}_t|\boldsymbol{\theta})\right]^T\right\} \tag{11}$$

where transition matrix $\mathbf{H}$ could be further decomposed into four components

$$\mathbf{H} = \begin{bmatrix}\mathbf{H}_t & \mathbf{H}_{t-1} & \mathbf{K} & \boldsymbol{\Phi}\end{bmatrix}^T \tag{12}$$

where $\mathbf{H}_t = [\nabla_{p_t}h]$, $\mathbf{H}_{t-1} = [\nabla_{p_{t-1}}h]$, $\mathbf{K} = [\nabla_k h]$, $\boldsymbol{\Phi} = [\nabla_\varphi h]$. Because the distance is a instantaneous measurement parameter, it has no error accumulation problems. Thus, $\mathbf{d}$ has no relationship with prior information $\boldsymbol{p}_{t-1}$, namely $\mathbf{H}_{t-1} = 0$. Then,

$$\mathbf{H} = \begin{bmatrix}\mathbf{H}_t & \mathbf{0} & \mathbf{K} & \boldsymbol{\Phi}\end{bmatrix}^T \tag{13}$$

For $\mathbf{J}_h$, we can use diagonal matrices of order n to represent it,

$$\mathbf{J_h} = \boldsymbol{\Lambda} = \mathbf{diag}(\lambda_1, \ldots, \lambda_j, \ldots, \lambda_n) \tag{14}$$

where λ_j stands for the jth measurement value. Then, $\mathbf{J_D}$ is represented as a $(4 + m + n + s) \times (4 + m + n + s)$ matrix,

$$\begin{aligned}\mathbf{J_D} &= \mathbf{H} \cdot \boldsymbol{\Lambda} \cdot \mathbf{H}^T \\ &= \begin{bmatrix}\mathbf{D}_{11} & \mathbf{0} & \mathbf{D}_{13} & \mathbf{D}_{14} \\ \mathbf{0} & \mathbf{0} & \mathbf{0} & \mathbf{0} \\ \mathbf{D}_{13}^T & \mathbf{0} & \mathbf{D}_{33} & \mathbf{D}_{34} \\ \mathbf{D}_{14}^T & \mathbf{0} & \mathbf{D}_{34}^T & \mathbf{D}_{44}\end{bmatrix}\end{aligned} \tag{15}$$

where

$$\begin{aligned}\mathbf{D}_{11} &= \mathbf{H}_t\boldsymbol{\Lambda}\mathbf{H}_t^T & \mathbf{D}_{13} &= \mathbf{H}_t\boldsymbol{\Lambda}\mathbf{K}^T \\ \mathbf{D}_{14} &= \mathbf{H}_t\boldsymbol{\Lambda}\boldsymbol{\Phi}^T & \mathbf{D}_{33} &= \mathbf{K}\boldsymbol{\Lambda}\mathbf{K}^T \\ \mathbf{D}_{34} &= \mathbf{K}\boldsymbol{\Lambda}\boldsymbol{\Phi}^T & \mathbf{D}_{44} &= \boldsymbol{\Phi}\boldsymbol{\Lambda}\boldsymbol{\Phi}^T\end{aligned} \tag{16}$$

4.2. State Parameter Information Matrix

It could be known by the whole probability formula, for the variable θ, the probability $p(\theta) = p(\boldsymbol{p}_t|\boldsymbol{p}_{t-1})p(k)p(\varphi)$. Then, log-likelihood function could be represented as:

$$\ln p(\theta) = [\ln p(\boldsymbol{p}_t|\boldsymbol{p}_{t-1})] + \ln p(k) + \ln p(\varphi) \tag{17}$$

where $p(k)$ and $p(\varphi)$ are corresponding independent information of $\boldsymbol{p}_t$ and $\boldsymbol{p}_{t-1}$. We decompose the vector θ into two components, namely state vector $[\boldsymbol{p}_t \quad \boldsymbol{p}_{t-1}]^T$ and observation vector $[k \quad \varphi]^T$. Thus, J_P could be represented as:

$$\begin{aligned}\mathbf{J_P} &= \mathbb{E}[\Delta_\theta^\theta \ln p(\theta)] \\ &= \begin{bmatrix}\mathbf{J}_{\mathbf{P}_{11}} & \mathbf{J}_{\mathbf{P}_{12}} \\ \mathbf{J}_{\mathbf{P}_{12}}^T & \mathbf{J}_{\mathbf{P}_{22}}\end{bmatrix}\end{aligned} \tag{18}$$

where $J_{P_{11}}$ could be obtained with the recursion of vectors $\boldsymbol{p}_t$ and $\boldsymbol{p}_{t-1}$, which, according to Tichavsky et al. [43], could be described as:

$$\mathbf{J_{P_{11}}} = \begin{bmatrix}\mathbf{M}_{11} & \mathbf{M}_{12} \\ \mathbf{M}_{12}^T & \mathbf{M}_{22} + \mathbf{J}(\boldsymbol{p}_{t-1})\end{bmatrix} \tag{19}$$

where

$$\begin{aligned}
\mathbf{M}_{11} &= \mathbf{Q}_t^{-1} \\
\mathbf{M}_{12} &= \nabla_{p_{t-1}} f_t(p_{t-1}) \mathbf{Q}_t^{-1} \\
\mathbf{M}_{22} &= \nabla_{p_{t-1}} f_t(p_{t-1}) \mathbf{Q}_t^{-1} \left[\nabla_{p_{t-1}} f_t(p_{t-1}) \right]^T
\end{aligned} \tag{20}$$

$\mathbf{J}(p_{t-1})$ is the FIM of p_{t-1}. As $p(k)$ and $p(\varphi)$ are independent from p_t and p_{t-1}, $J_{P_{12}}$ is 0, namely

$$\mathbf{J}_{P_{12}} = \begin{bmatrix} 0 & 0 \\ 0 & 0 \end{bmatrix} \tag{21}$$

Similarly, the prior probability $p(p_t|p_{t-1})$ are independent from k and φ. Thus, $J_{P_{12}} = J_{P_{21}}^T = 0$. Finally,

$$\mathbf{J}_{P_{22}} = \begin{bmatrix} \mathbf{J_K} & 0 \\ 0 & \mathbf{J_\Phi} \end{bmatrix} \tag{22}$$

where $\mathbf{J_K}$ and $\mathbf{J_\Phi}$ are, respectively, the FIM of vectors k and φ:

$$\begin{aligned}
\mathbf{J_K} &= \mathbb{E}[\Delta_k^k \ln p(k)] \\
\mathbf{J_\Phi} &= \mathbb{E}[\Delta_\varphi^\phi \ln p(\varphi)]
\end{aligned} \tag{23}$$

4.3. Integral Information Matrix

Due to the analysis above, substituting Equations (15) and (18) into Equation (9), the FIM of variable θ could be represented as:

$$\mathbf{J}(\theta) = \begin{bmatrix}
\mathbf{M}_{11} + \mathbf{D}_{11} & \mathbf{M}_{12} & \mathbf{D}_{13} & \mathbf{D}_{14} \\
\mathbf{M}_{12}^T & \mathbf{M}_{22} + \mathbf{J}(x_{t-1}) & 0 & 0 \\
\mathbf{D}_{13}^T & 0 & \mathbf{D}_{33} + \mathbf{J_K} & \mathbf{D}_{34} \\
\mathbf{D}_{14}^T & 0 & \mathbf{D}_{34}^T & \mathbf{D}_{44} + \mathbf{J_\Phi}
\end{bmatrix}. \tag{24}$$

However, only the lower bound of p_t is of interest, namely a small submatrix of $\mathbf{J}(\theta)$, $\mathbf{J}^{-1}(p_t) = [\mathbf{J}^{-1}(\theta)]_{2 \times 2}$.

Furthermore, due to the Schur complement theorem [49], $\mathbf{J}(p_t)$ could be divided into two components, namely state matrix J_S and measurement matrix J_C, then

$$\mathbf{J}(p_t) = \mathbf{J_S} - \mathbf{J_C} \tag{25}$$

where

$$\begin{aligned}
\mathbf{J_S} &= \mathbf{M}_{11} + \mathbf{D}_{11} - \mathbf{M}_{12} \left(\mathbf{M}_{22} + \mathbf{J}(p_{t-1}) \right)^{-1} \mathbf{M}_{12}^T \\
\mathbf{J_A} &= \begin{bmatrix} \mathbf{D}_{13} & \mathbf{D}_{14} \end{bmatrix} \begin{bmatrix} \mathbf{D}_{33} + \mathbf{J_K} & \mathbf{D}_{34} \\ \mathbf{D}_{34}^T & \mathbf{D}_{44} + \mathbf{J_C} \end{bmatrix}^{-1} \begin{bmatrix} \mathbf{D}_{13} & \mathbf{D}_{14} \end{bmatrix}^T
\end{aligned} \tag{26}$$

As mentioned above, we demonstrate a comprehensive analysis of how distance and angle measurements are related with human motion tracking accuracy in IMU/TOA fusion systems. The detailed calculation process is shown in Algorithm 1. In the next two sections, we further evaluate the overall performance of the fusion system from two aspects, namely spatial and temporal performance, in theory.

Algorithm 1 Proposed IMU/TOA fusion-based human motion tracking method.

0: **Initialization:**

1: Define measuring variable at time slot t as $\boldsymbol{\theta}_t \triangleq \begin{bmatrix} \boldsymbol{p}_t^T & \boldsymbol{p}_{t-1}^T & \boldsymbol{k}^T & \boldsymbol{\varphi}^T \end{bmatrix}^T$. Set the time slot index
$t = 0$. Choose an initial value for $\boldsymbol{p}_{t-1}$ of variable $\boldsymbol{\theta}_t$, generally as 0.

Part 1: measurement parameter information

2: Calculate parameter matrix $\mathbf{H}_t$, $\mathbf{K}$, Φ.

3: Update the matrix parameters $\mathbf{H} = \begin{bmatrix} \mathbf{H}_t & \mathbf{H}_{t-1} & \mathbf{K} & \Phi \end{bmatrix}^T$.

4: Calculate parameter matrix $\mathbf{D}_{11}$, $\mathbf{D}_{13}$, $\mathbf{D}_{14}$, $\mathbf{D}_{33}$, $\mathbf{D}_{34}$ and $\mathbf{D}_{44}$.

5: Update the matrix parameter $\mathbf{J_h}$.

6: Update the information matrix obtained by measuring parameters, i.e., $\mathbf{J_D}(\boldsymbol{\theta}) = \mathbf{H} \cdot \mathbf{J_h} \cdot \mathbf{H}^T$

Part 2: state parameter information

7: Calculate parameter matrix $\mathbf{M}_{11}$, $\mathbf{M}_{12}$, $\mathbf{M}_{22}$, $\mathbf{J_K}$ and $\mathbf{J}_\Phi$.

8: Update the matrix parameters $\mathbf{J_{P_{11}}}$, $\mathbf{J_{P_{12}}}$ and $\mathbf{J_{P_{12}}}$.

9: Update the information matrix obtained by prior information, i.e., $\mathbf{J_P} = \begin{bmatrix} \mathbf{J_{P_{11}}} & \mathbf{J_{P_{12}}} \\ \mathbf{J_{P_{12}}^T} & \mathbf{J_{P_{22}}} \end{bmatrix}$.

Part 3: integral information

10: Update the FIM matrix by $\mathbf{J}(\boldsymbol{\theta}) = \mathbf{J_D}(\boldsymbol{\theta}) + \mathbf{J_P}(\boldsymbol{\theta})$

11: Update Schur complement parameters of $\mathbf{J}(\boldsymbol{\theta})$, namely state matrix J_S and measurement matrix J_C

12: Update the estimation result $\boldsymbol{p}_t = \mathbf{J}(\boldsymbol{p}_t) = J_S - J_C$

Part 4: recursive computation

13: $t + 1 \rightarrow t$, go to step 2.

---

5. Spatial Performance Analysis

When it comes to spatial performance, we suppose that the tracking system has time independence, namely $J(\boldsymbol{p}_t)$ and $J(\boldsymbol{p}_{t-1})$ are independent from each other. Thus, $\mathbf{M}_{12}$, $\mathbf{M}_{22}$, $J_{p_{t-1}}$, J_K, $\mathbf{D}_{13}$, $\mathbf{D}_{33}$ and $\mathbf{D}_{34}$ are all 0, namely

$$J(\boldsymbol{p}_t) = \mathbf{M}_{11} + \mathbf{D}_{11} - \mathbf{D}_{14}[\mathbf{D}_{44} + \mathbf{J}_\Phi]^{-1}\mathbf{D}_{14}^T \qquad (27)$$

Movement characteristics of each body part should be taken into consideration. Because of the spatial features of human motion sensing, it could be classified into two categories: 2-D and 3-D conditions. 2D motions refer to the body movements that can be captured by a plane, such as raising one's arms into Y pose or T pose. 3D motions refer to stereoscopic movements such as walking, running or swing hands. The different relative positions may contribute to various capture accuracy. Therefore, both the CRLB of human body in 2D and 3D scenarios are taken into consideration. CRLB of each location is derived as following demonstration and performance of proposed fusion method is verified. See Appendix A for the detailed derivation process of CRLB for spatial performance analysis.

5.1. Scenario Setup

As mentioned above, the trunk remains relatively steady in comparison to the end joints or limbs of the human body. In consideration of end-effector problem, we set the joints of neck, chest, left and right hip as reference nodes for error bounds estimation. A constrained scenario of 2 m $\times$ 2 m is set up for further experiments. The entire human body is supposed to located in the center of this region. In contrast, two sequences of reference nodes combination are considered, namely $Case1 = \{Neck, Chest, LHip, RHip\}$ and $Case2 = \{Neck, LShoulder, RShoulder, Chest, LHip, RHip\}$. The body is allowed to move freely in this space.

5.2. Performance Analysis

To demonstrate the typical calculation results, CRLB, when the variance of distance measurement σ_d is 0.2 and σ_{IMU} is 0.1, is selected upon common commercial motion sensing systems, such as Xsens. From the experiment results, as shown in Figure 3, the following conclusions could be obtained:

1. In the aspect of two-dimensional condition, shown in Figure 3a,b, lower CRLB is shown when the position is closer to the trunk. It is also lower in the lower limb than the upper, which is possibly due to the selection of reference nodes. To verify this, a comparison experiment was conducted when the reference nodes were chosen differently. Results shown in Figure 3a,b indicate that the relative position of the reference nodes cause different CRLB of human motion and the more uniform the nodes distribute, the relative lower CRLB it achieves. The same result can also be seen in Figure 3c,d when only distance measurement is applied in the human motion sensing process.

2. Since human motion is a three-dimensional process, stereoscopic presentation is shown in Figure 3e,f. The human is assumed to be placed in the XOZ plane when the y is set as zero. The 3D version of CRLB is likely to be a 2D one that stretches along the Z-axis. Similar results could be seen in 3D condition that, the closer to the trunk, the lower the CRLB that could be achieved.

3. For comparison, the CRLB under two measurement method were calculated, respectively, independent distance measurement and the fusion of IMU and distance measurement. Comparison results are shown in Figure 3a,c (also in pair of Figure 3b,d).

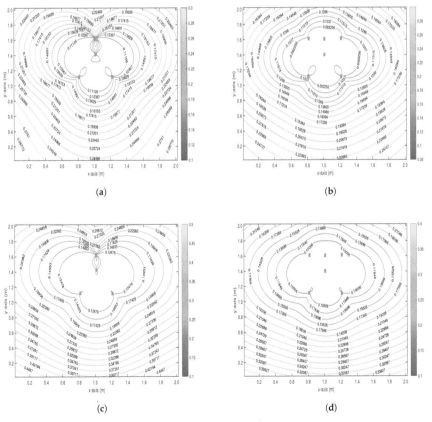

(a) (b)

(c) (d)

Figure 3. *Cont.*

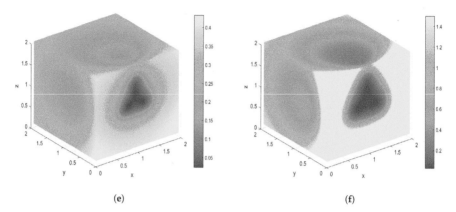

(e)   (f)

Figure 3. CRLB comparison in two-dimensional and three-dimensional condition: **(a,b,e)** CRLB in condition that both distance and IMU information are considered using proposed model; and **(c,d,f)** CRLB considered with distance information solely. σ_d is set as 0.2 and σ_{IMU} is 0.1.

To clearly show the different capture capability of distance measurement and IMU, Figure 4 is presented. As shown, under different σ_d^2, CRLB increases along with the increase of σ_{IMU}^2. When σ_{IMU}^2 is fixed, CRLB also increases along with the increase of σ_d^2. However, the change is more apparent when σ_d^2 is fixed. It means that the accuracy of IMU measurement matters more in the fusion process, but the distance measurement helps restrain the bounds of CRLB. It is worth mentioning that, for a given σ_{IMU}^2, CRLB shows little variation with the increase of σ_d^2 if it is larger than 0.2. It indicates that the distance measurement may be not the main limiting factor of CRLB, but σ_{IMU}^2 is.

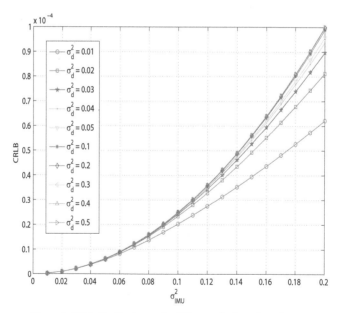

Figure 4. CRLB distribution under different σ_d^2 when σ_{IMU}^2 changes.

6. Temporal Performance Analysis

We suppose that the tracking system has cumulative recursion characteristics, namely $J(p_t)$ and $J(p_{t-1})$ are not independent from each other. Based on [22], Equation (26) could be simplified into a recursive form, namely Posterior Cramér–Rao Lower Bound (PCRLB) [22,25].

$$\mathbf{J}(x_t) = \mathbf{M}_{11} + \mathbf{D}_{11} - \mathbf{M}_{12}\left[\mathbf{M}_{22} + \mathbf{J}(x_{t-1})\right]^{-1}\mathbf{M}_{12}^{T} \tag{28}$$

See Appendix B for the detailed derivation process of PCRLB for temporal performance analysis.

6.1. Scenario Setup

Even though there are elegant expressions to recursively calculate the FIM, Equation (27) usually does not have analytical close-form solution. To deal with that, we employ the Monte Carlo approach [50] to convert those continuous integrals into discrete summations, and finally work out the PCRLB. The root-mean-square of PCRLB is given by $\frac{1}{L}\sum_{i=1}^{L}P_k^i$, where P_k^i is the PCRLB on the Root-Mean-Square Error (RMSE) of joint at step k in the ith Monte Carlo trial. L is the total Monte Carlo trial number ($L = 1000$ was used in this study). Note that, for each Monte Carlo trial, we randomly selected the initial location for PCRLB calculation to get a fair average of the entire human body moving process.

6.2. Performance Analysis

We mainly analyzed the influence of different factors on PCRLB from the following two perspectives: fusion method factor and topology factor.

(1) Fusion method factor: Considering different Q_t and R_t in IMU/TOA fusion methods, as well as using sole TOA or IMU method, may lead to different results of human motion tracking accuracy.

Figure 5 shows in IMU/TOA fusion methods, the lower bounds under different Q_t and R_t as well as in the use of sole TOA or IMU method. As shown in the figure:

1. When only inertial sensors are adopted in the tracking system, as indicated by the black solid line in Figure 5, the accumulative errors may tend to be diverging. Theoretically, this confirms that IMU based HMT system faces the problem of accumulative errors. However, IMU/TOA fusion method can avoid this divergence. The performance curves of proposed approaches achieve stability after certain steps, i.e., their errors converge.

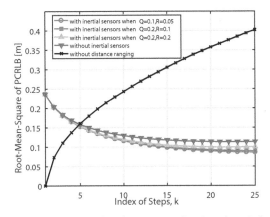

Figure 5. Temporal performance as a function of step index.

2. Compared with sole TOA tracking method, IMU/TOA fusion-based method can significantly increase the accuracy of human body motion tracking. The lower bound of proposed fusion method could drop below 8 cm.
3. With increase of Q_t and R_t, PCRLB also increases, which means that the accuracy is inversely proportional to these two parameters.

(2) Topology factor: As already indicated in Section IV-B, topologies have much influence on the performance of certain tracking systems. We work out the PCRLB of different topologies shown in Figure 6, where Q_t is 0.1 and R_t is 0.05. As shown in Figure 7, we could draw the following conclusions:

1. Under different topologies, the theoretical accuracy lower bounds of the tracking system are different.
2. The different topological conditions tend to be stable after the same iteration number (around 15), which means the convergence rate is roughly the same under various topologies.
3. Topology 3 suffers the largest RMSE, which may be due to the dense reference nodes. The minimum RMSE is less than 8 cm, as shown in Topology 4, which makes it a better choice for practice applications.
4. The proposed fusion HMT systems with TOA integrated share identical trend results with that of solely TOA ranging.

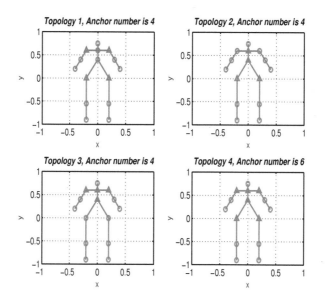

Figure 6. Topologies configuration. ○ represents free joints, and △ represents selected anchors.

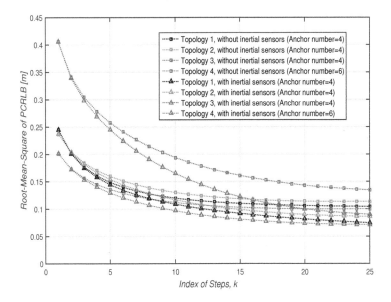

Figure 7. Root mean square of PCRLB as a function of index of steps. Different receiver topologies are considered.

7. Practical Use Case

In above sections, the theoretical effectiveness of our proposed human motion tracking method is verified in terms of both spatial and temporal performances. The introduced IMU/TOA fusion method utilizes both distance and IMU information to lower the expected error bounds in theory. In this section, we take advantage of this method in 3D practical application scenarios to verify its performance.

7.1. Platform Overview and Experiment Setup

A minimized wearable sensing platform was specially designed for the tracking of human motion in 3D scenario. It aimed to collect spatial and temporal information during the human motion process. Sensing nodes were designed and intended to be put on joints to capture the movement conditions. Target data included accelerated velocity, angular velocity and the distances between joints and body parts. Among these, distance information was especially different when compared with other platforms, such as Xsens and Invensense. We sampled data using above-mentioned platform at 10 Hz. All processing work were performed online in Matlab with PC (Intel Core i7-6700M CPU, 16GB RAM). The communication between wearable nodes and the PC was via Bluetooth.

Our integrated wearable sensor system was composed of two parts: one control unit and several data acquisition units. The control unit worked as a gateway to control the whole operation process via Bluetooth communication. Data acquisition unit was mainly responsible for data sensing. Each data acquisition unit had a six-axis sensor (MPU6050, which integrated a triaxial accelerometer and a triaxial gyroscope), a barometer sensor (MS5611) and a UWB-TOA ranging module (DWM1000) [19]. The MEMS sensors were connected to a micro-controller (STM32F103) for the sake of sampling efficiency at a rate of 10 Hz. Data were transferred to the control unit in real-time and also written into its SD card as backups for other offline analysis and applications. Three sensing nodes were mounted onto the ankle, knee and hip joint. Distance measurements were conducted between these nodes. The whole system architecture is demonstrated in Figure 8.

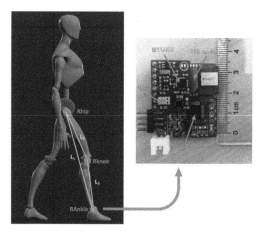

Figure 8. Experimental Platform Settings. Three sensing nodes were mounted onto the ankle, knee and hip joint. Each node mainly consisted of micro-controller unit (STM32), IMU unit (MPU6050 and MS5611) and TOA unit (UWB module).

We proposed an IMU/TOA fusion method for human motion tracking applications, introducing distance information into inertial systems. However, one of the most obvious difference between the proposed method and that in [23] is: the algorithm in [23] needs to take advantage of external UWB stations as reference nodes, namely anchors. However, in our method, we simply utilized internal tags (mounted onto body joints) to range and conduct the fusion process, which can significantly reduce the complexity of tracking systems.

Based on above considerations, human lower limb movement analysis in 3D scenario was chosen as a typical verification experiment, for better demonstrate the performance of proposed method when it is applied to human motion tracking.

7.2. Practical Use Case in 3D Scenario

A spiral-stairs (between two floors) scenario Was selected as a 3D use case and four UWB anchors were located at each floor (totally eight anchors were used), as shown in Figure 9. The location of anchors in each floor are referred to those in [23] and only used in comparative experiments. Three comparative algorithms were also tested:

(1)	Only IMU was used for human lower limb tracking. Zero velocity update (ZUPT) algorithm [51] was applied. For simplicity, we denoted it as "IMU" method.
(2)	IMU and TOA fusion method in [23] was applied. UWB based TOA tag nodes were mounted to the right lower limb and communicated with external anchor nodes, implementing TOA localization algorithm. For simplicity, and to separate it from our proposed method, we denoted it as "IMU/ex-TOA" method.
(3)	Optimal Enhanced Kalman Filter (OEKF)-based method in [52] was applied. The cumulative errors in attitude and velocity were corrected using the attitude fusion filtering algorithm and ZUPT, respectively. For simplicity, and to separate it from our proposed method, we denoted it as "IMU-OEKF" method.

Experiment results are shown in Figures 9 and 10.

For better comparison, ground truth and tracking trajectories applying all mentioned methods (the proposed method and three comparative ones) are drawn in Figure 9. It is clearly seen that, when applying the proposed method, the experiment results were far closer to the ground truth, while the results when applying methods of IMU [51], IMU/ex-TOA [23] and IMU-OEKF [52] were drifting away as time accumulates. The result remained similar at the very beginning; however, the gap became larger over time.

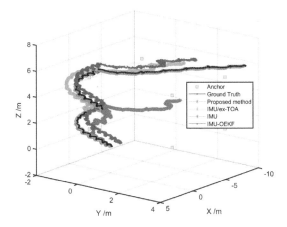

Figure 9. Walking trajectory when climbing a spiral-stairs with our proposed method and two comparative methods.

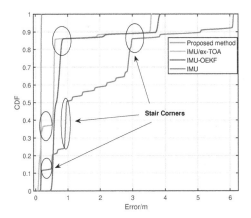

Figure 10. The accumulative distribution function (CDF) curve in 3D scenario when algorithms were applied.

Detailed accumulated errors are shown in Figure 10. IMU, IMU/ex-TOA and IMU-OEKF faced the problem of drift error, especially when the experimenter turned around at stair corners. Time accumulated errors were more likely to be caused when moving direction changes. With IMU/ex-TOA and IMU-OEKF methods applied into the algorithm, localization errors to some extent could be fixed, but still existed and were critical at turns. On the contrary, our proposed human motion tracking method showed a good stability and no clear drift errors were observed in our experiment. This is because, with the use of proposed method, body connections are considered and temporal transitions are estimated. Especially at turns, body constraints could to some extent fix time accumulated errors. The results suggest that our proposed method performed well while applied in human lower limb analysis. This also confirmed the conclusion obtained in theoretical simulation (Sections 4 and 5).

Methods with only inertial sensors faced the problem of drift errors, but our proposed model could fix time accumulative errors.

From above analysis, our proposed method had significantly higher accuracy, as well as little drift problem. Besides, compared with IMU/ex-TOA method [23] and IMU-OEKF method [52], our method did not need external anchors and had higher tracking accuracy, thus is more suitable for wearable motion tracking applications.

8. Conclusions

A IMU/TOA fusion-based human motion tracking method is proposed in this paper. IMU based HMT technique faces the tough problem of accumulative errors and drift. Time of Arrival (TOA) is considered to compensate the drift and accumulation caused by IMU. On this basis, Cramér–Rao lower bound (CRLB) is derived in detail with consideration of both temporal and spatial related factors. Simulation results show that the IMU/TOA fusion-based HMT method proposed in this paper has significantly higher accuracy, as well as little drift problem, compared with the traditional independent IMU or TOA tracking methods. The comprehensive fundamental limits analysis conducted in this paper can provide a theoretical basis for further system design and algorithm analysis. In the practical use case, proposed IMU/TOA fusion method also shows obvious performance advantages when compared with state-of-the-art methods. Besides, it does not need external anchors, thus it is more suitable for wearable motion tracking applications.

Author Contributions: C.X. and J.H. conceived and designed the experiments; C.X. and X.Z. (Xinghang Zhou) analyzed the data and contributed to the writing the manuscript. X.Z. (Xiaotong Zhang) and S.D. reviewed the analyzed data and contributed to the writing. C.X. and J.H. are co-first authors and contributed equally to this work.

Funding: This work was supported by The National Key R & D Program of China, No. 2016YFC0901303; National Natural Science Foundation of China (NSFC) project No. 61671056, No. 61302065, No. 61304257, and No. 61402033; Beijing Natural Science Foundation project No. 4152036; and Tianjin Special Program for Science and Technology No. 16ZXCXSF00150.

Conflicts of Interest: The authors declare no conflict of interest.

Appendix A. Derivation of the CRLB

CRLB is represented as a theoretical lower limit for any unbiased estimation and is widely used to assess localization performance. Thus, we comprehensively derive the CRLB for 3D localization of IMU/TOA fusion method in WSNs to evaluate its spatial performance. The following are some definitions. If p_k is an unbiased estimate of p_k, then

$$E(\hat{p}_k - p_k)^2 \geq CRLB = tr\left\{J(p_k)^{-1}\right\} \tag{A1}$$

where $J(p_k)$ is the Fisher information matrix [43,46]. Before solving the Fischer information matrix, we need to first define the joint probability density function as

$$
\begin{aligned}
&p(\hat{d}_k, \hat{\alpha}_k, \hat{\beta}_k, \hat{p}_k) \\
&= \left\{\prod_{n=1}^{N} p(\hat{d}_{n,k}|p_k)\right\} p(\hat{\alpha}_k|p_{k-1}, p_k) p(\hat{\beta}_k|p_{k-1}, p_k)
\end{aligned} \tag{A2}
$$

where $p(\hat{\alpha}_k|p_{k-1}, p_k)$, $p(\hat{\beta}_k|p_{k-1}, p_k)$ and $p(\hat{d}_{n,k}|p_k)$ can be obtained according to Equations (1)–(3).

According to the joint probability density function, we can define the Fischer information matrix as

$$J(p_k)_{i,j} = -E\left[\frac{\partial^2 \ln p(\hat{d}_k, \hat{\alpha}_k, \hat{\beta}_k, \hat{p}_k)}{\partial p_{k,i} \partial p_{k,j}}\right], i,j = 1,2,3 \tag{A3}$$

Bringing Equation (A2) into Equation (A3) can calculate each element of the Fischer Information Matrix, and further obtain CRLB.

Appendix B. Derivation of the PCRLB

Sequential tracking problem is a temporal as well as spatial problem. This continuous information could be used to evaluate the performance of given algorithms. Thus, we extend the above CRLB to PCRLB by considering posterior information.

Before the derivation, we redefine the joint probability density function as

$$
\begin{aligned}
& p(\hat{d}, \hat{\alpha}, \hat{\beta}, \hat{p}) \\
& = p(\hat{d}_0|\hat{p}_0) \prod_{k=1}^{K} p(\hat{\alpha}_k|p_{k-1}, p_k) p(\hat{\beta}_k|p_{k-1}, p_k) p(\hat{d}_k|p_k)
\end{aligned}
\tag{A4}
$$

To calculate the Fischer information matrix at state k, we define

$$
p_k = p(\hat{d}_{0:k}, \hat{\alpha}_{0:k}, \hat{\beta}_{0:k}, \hat{p}_{0:k},)
\tag{A5}
$$

where $\hat{d}_{0:k}$, $\hat{\alpha}_{0:k}$, $\hat{\beta}_{0:k}$, and $\hat{p}_{0:k}$ represent ranging, vertical angle, horizontal angle and target coordinate vector from the start state to state k, respectively.

Therefore,

$$
\begin{aligned}
& J(p_{0:k}) \\
& = \begin{bmatrix} E\left\{-\Delta_{p_{0:k-1}}^{p_{0:k-1}} \ln p_k\right\} & E\left\{-\Delta_{p_{0:k-1}}^{p_{0:k}} \ln p_k\right\} \\ E\left\{-\Delta_{p_{0:k}}^{p_{0:k-1}} \ln p_k\right\} & E\left\{-\Delta_{p_{0:k}}^{p_{0:k}} \ln p_k\right\} \end{bmatrix} \\
& = \begin{bmatrix} A_k & B_k \\ B_k^T & C_k \end{bmatrix}
\end{aligned}
\tag{A6}
$$

According to Tichavsky et al. [43], the sub-matrix J_k can be obtained by pseudo-inverse of the matrix $J(p_{0:k})$, i.e.,

$$
J_k = C_k - B_k^T A_k^{-1} B_k
\tag{A7}
$$

According to Equations (A5) and (A6), the joint probability density for the $k+1$ state is

$$
p_{k+1} = p_k p(\hat{\alpha}_{k+1}|p_k, p_{k+1}) p(\hat{\beta}_{k+1}|p_k, p_{k+1}) p(\hat{d}_{k+1}|p_k, p_{k+1})
\tag{A8}
$$

According to the joint probability density of state $k+1$, we can find that

$$
J(p_{0:k+1}) = \begin{bmatrix} A_k & B_k & 0 \\ B_k^T & C_k + H_k^{11} & H_k^{12} \\ 0 & H_k^{12} & \gamma_{k+1} + H_k^{12} \end{bmatrix}
\tag{A9}
$$

where H_k^{11}, H_k^{12}, and H_k^{22} reflect the posterior information from state k to state $k+1$, and γ_{k+1} reflects the location information based on TOA ranging [19].

From $J(p_{0:k+1})$ and J_k, we can get the Fischer information matrix for state $k+1$, i.e.,

$$
\begin{aligned}
& J_{k+1} \\
& = \gamma_{k+1} + H_k^{22} - \begin{bmatrix} 0 & H_k^{12} \end{bmatrix} \begin{bmatrix} A_k & B_k \\ B_k^T & C_k + H_k^{11} \end{bmatrix} \begin{bmatrix} 0 \\ H_k^{12} \end{bmatrix} \\
& = \gamma_{k+1} + H_k^{22} - H_k^{12}(J_k + H_k^{11})^{-1} H_k^{12}
\end{aligned}
\tag{A10}
$$

Due to the step error and the directional error obey Gaussian distribution, $H_k^{11} = H_k^{12} = H_k^{22} = H_k$ can be calculated.

The solution of H_k can be found in [53]. In summary, the posterior Fisher information matrix is

$$J_{k+1} = \gamma_{k+1} + H_k - H_k(J_k + H_k)^{-1}H_k \tag{A11}$$

According to the SMW (Sherman–Morrison–Woodbury) formula [54], it can be further simplified as

$$J_{k+1} = \gamma_{k+1} + (H_k^{-1} + J_k^{-1})^{-1} \tag{A12}$$

where γ_{k+1} reflects the information based on TOA, H_k reflects information based on IMU.

Then, sequential simulation can be conducted by Monte Carlo methods [50].

References

1. Gravina, R.; Alinia, P.; Ghasemzadeh, H.; Fortino, G. Multi-sensor fusion in body sensor networks: State-of-the-art and research challenges. *Inf. Fusion* **2017**, *35*, 68–80. [CrossRef]
2. Fortino, G.; Giannantonio, R.; Gravina, R.; Kuryloski, P.; Jafari, R. Enabling Effective Programming and Flexible Management of Efficient Body Sensor Network Applications. *IEEE Trans. Hum. Mach. Syst.* **2013**, *43*, 115–133. [CrossRef]
3. Sodhro, A.H.; Luo, Z.; Sangaiah, A.K.; Baik, S.W. Mobile edge computing based QoS optimization in medical healthcare applications. *Int. J. Inf. Manag.* **2018**. [CrossRef]
4. Sodhro, A.H.; Pirbhulal, S.; Qaraqe, M.; Lohano, S.; Sodhro, G.H.; Junejo, N.U.; Luo, Z. Power control algorithms for media transmission in remote healthcare systems. *IEEE Access* **2018**, *6*, 42384–42393. [CrossRef]
5. Cao, J.; Li, W.; Ma, C.; Tao, Z. Optimizing multi-sensor deployment via ensemble pruning for wearable activity recognition. *Inf. Fusion* **2018**, *41*, 68–79. [CrossRef]
6. Galzarano, S.; Giannantonio, R.; Liotta, A.; Fortino, G. A task-oriented framework for networked wearable computing. *IEEE Trans. Autom. Sci. Eng.* **2016**, *13*, 621–638. [CrossRef]
7. Abebe, G.; Cavallaro, A. Inertial-Vision: Cross-Domain Knowledge Transfer for Wearable Sensors. In Proceedings of the 2017 International Conference on Computer Vision, Venice, Italy, 22–29 Octorber 2017; pp. 1392–1400.
8. Fortino, G.; Galzarano, S.; Gravina, R.; Li, W. A framework for collaborative computing and multi-sensor data fusion in body sensor networks. *Inf. Fusion* **2015**, *22*, 50–70. [CrossRef]
9. Yang, X.; Tian, Y. Super Normal Vector for Human Activity Recognition with Depth Cameras. *IEEE Trans. Pattern Anal. Mach. Intell.* **2017**, *39*, 1028–1039. [CrossRef]
10. Bux, A.; Angelov, P.; Habib, Z. Vision Based Human Activity Recognition: A Review. *Adv. Comput. Intell. Syst.* **2017**, *513*, 341–371.
11. Zhao, H.; Ding, Y.; Yu, B.; Jiang, C.; Zhang, W. Design and implementation of Peking Opera action scoring system based on human skeleton information. *MATEC Web Conf.* **2018**, *232*, 01026. [CrossRef]
12. Vicon. Available online: https://www.vicon.com/ (accesed on 15 January 2019).
13. Optotrak. Available online: https://www.ndigital.com/ (accesed on 15 January 2019).
14. Hong, J.H.; Ramos, J.; Dey, A.K. Toward Personalized Activity Recognition Systems With a Semipopulation Approach. *IEEE Trans. Hum. Mach. Syst.* **2016**, *46*, 101–112. [CrossRef]
15. Xsens. Available online: https://www.xsens.com/ (accesed on 15 January 2019).
16. Invensense. Available online: https://www.invensense.com/ (accesed on 15 January 2019).
17. VMSens. Available online: https://www.vmsens.com (accesed on 15 January 2019).
18. Noitom. Available online: http://www.noitom.com.cn/ (accesed on 15 January 2019).
19. Decawave. Available online: https://www.decawave.com/ (accesed on 15 January 2019).
20. Cornacchia, M.; Ozcan, K.; Zheng, Y.; Velipasalar, S. A Survey on Activity Detection and Classification Using Wearable Sensors. *IEEE Sens. J.* **2017**, *17*, 386–403. [CrossRef]
21. Bao, S.D.; Meng, X.L.; Xiao, W.; Zhang, Z.Q. Fusion of Inertial/Magnetic Sensor Measurements and Map Information for Pedestrian Tracking. *Sensors* **2017**, *17*, 340. [CrossRef]
22. Xu, C.; He, J.; Zhang, X.; Yao, C.; Tseng, P.H. Geometrical Kinematic Modeling on Human Motion using Method of Multi-Sensor Fusion. *Inf. Fusion* **2017**, *41*, 243–254. [CrossRef]

23. Zihajehzadeh, S.; Park, E.J. A Novel Biomechanical Model-Aided IMU/UWB Fusion for Magnetometer-Free Lower Body Motion Capture. *IEEE Trans. Syst. Man Cybern. Syst.* **2017**, *47*, 927–938. [CrossRef]

24. Qiu, S.; Wang, Z.; Zhao, H.; Hu, H. Using Distributed Wearable Sensors to Measure and Evaluate Human Lower Limb Motions. *IEEE Trans. Instrum. Meas.* **2016**, *65*, 939–950. [CrossRef]

25. Fullerton, E.; Heller, B.; Munoz-Organero, M. Recognising human activity in free-living using multiple body-worn accelerometers. *IEEE Sens. J.* **2017**, *17*, 5290–5297. [CrossRef]

26. Chen, C.; Jafari, R.; Kehtarnavaz, N. A survey of depth and inertial sensor fusion for human action recognition. *Multimed. Tools Appl.* **2017**, *76*, 4405–4425. [CrossRef]

27. Nilsson, J.O.; Zachariah, D.; Skog, I.; Händel, P. Cooperative localization by dual foot-mounted inertial sensors and inter-agent ranging. *Eur. J. Adv. Signal Process.* **2013**, *2013*, 164. [CrossRef]

28. Sodhro, A.H.; Shaikh, F.K.; Pirbhulal, S.; Lodro, M.M.; Shah, M.A. Medical-QoS based telemedicine service selection using analytic hierarchy process. In *Handbook of Large-Scale Distributed Computing in Smart Healthcare*; Springer: Cham, Switzerland, 2017; pp. 589–609.

29. Lodro, M.M.; Majeed, N.; Khuwaja, A.A.; Sodhro, A.H.; Greedy, S. Statistical channel modelling of 5G mmWave MIMO wireless communication. In Proceedings of the 2018 International Conference on Computing, Mathematics and Engineering Technologies (iCoMET), Sukkur, Pakistan, 3–4 March 2018; pp. 1–5.

30. Magsi, H.; Sodhro, A.H.; Chachar, F.A.; Abro, S.A.K.; Sodhro, G.H.; Pirbhulal, S. Evolution of 5G in Internet of medical things. In Proceedings of the 2018 International Conference on Computing, Mathematics and Engineering Technologies (iCoMET), Sukkur, Pakistan, 3–4 March 2018.

31. Sodhro, A.H.; Pirbhulal, S.; Sodhro, G.H.; Gurtov, A.; Muzammal, M.; Luo, Z. A joint transmission power control and duty-cycle approach for smart healthcare system. *IEEE Sens. J.* **2018**. [CrossRef]

32. Kinect. Available online: https://developer.microsoft.com/en-us/windows/kinect (accesed on 15 January 2019).

33. Iyengar, S.; Bonda, F.T.; Gravina, R.; Guerrieri, A.; Fortino, G.; Sangiovanni-Vincentelli, A. A framework for creating healthcare monitoring applications using wireless body sensor networks. In Proceedings of the ICST 3rd International Conference on Body Area Networks, Tempe, AZ, USA, 13–17 March 2008.

34. Anwary, A.R.; Yu, H.; Vassallo, M. Optimal Foot Location for Placing Wearable IMU Sensors and Automatic Feature Extraction for Gait Analysis. *IEEE Sens. J.* **2018**, *18*, 2555–2567. [CrossRef]

35. Ghasemzadeh, H.; Jafari, R. Physical Movement Monitoring Using Body Sensor Networks: A Phonological Approach to Construct Spatial Decision Trees. *IEEE Trans. Ind. Inf.* **2011**, *7*, 66–77. [CrossRef]

36. Yun, X.; Bachmann, E.R. Design, Implementation, and Experimental Results of a Quaternion-Based Kalman Filter for Human Body Motion Tracking. *IEEE Int. Conf. Robot. Autom.* **2006**, *22*, 1216–1227. [CrossRef]

37. Zhao, S.; Shmaliy, Y.S.; Shi, P.; Ahn, C.K. Fusion Kalman/UFIR filter for state estimation with uncertain parameters and noise statistics. *IEEE Trans. Ind. Electr.* **2017**, *64*, 3075–3083. [CrossRef]

38. Briese, D.; Kunze, H.; Rose, G. UWB localization using adaptive covariance Kalman Filter based on sensor fusion. In Proceedings of the 2017 IEEE 17th International Conference on Ubiquitous Wireless Broadband (ICUWB), Salamanca, Spain, 12–15 September 2017.

39. Kim, H.; Liu, B.; Goh, C.Y.; Lee, S.; Myung, H. Robust vehicle localization using entropy-weighted particle filter-based data fusion of vertical and road intensity information for a large scale urban area. *IEEE Robot. Autom. Lett.* **2017**, *2*, 1518–1524. [CrossRef]

40. Bai, F.; Vidal-Calleja, T.; Huang, S. Robust Incremental SLAM Under Constrained Optimization Formulation. *IEEE Robot. Autom. Lett.* **2018**, *3*, 1207–1214. [CrossRef]

41. Sebastián, P.S.J.; Virtanen, T.; Garcia-Molla, V.M.; Vidal, A.M. Analysis of an efficient parallel implementation of active-set Newton algorithm. *J. Supercomput.* **2018**. [CrossRef]

42. Liu, Z.; Zhang, L.; Liu, Q.; Yin, Y.; Cheng, L.; Zimmermann, R. Fusion of magnetic and visual sensors for indoor localization: Infrastructure-free and more effective. *IEEE Trans. Multimed.* **2017**, *19*, 874–888. [CrossRef]

43. Tichavsky, P.; Muravchik, C.H.; Nehorai, A. Posterior Cramér-Rao bounds for discrete-time nonlinear filtering. IEEE *Trans. Signal Process.* **1998**, *46*, 1386–1396. [CrossRef]

44. Qi, Y.; Kobayashi, H.; Suda, H. Analysis of wireless geolocation in a non-line-of-sight environment. *IEEE Trans. Wirel. Commun.* **2006**, *5*, 672–681.

45. Yang, Z.; Liu, Y. Quality of Trilateration: Confidence Based Iterative Localization. *IEEE Trans. Parallel Distrib. Syst.* **2010**, *21*, 631–640. [CrossRef]

46. Geng, Y.; Pahlavan, K. Design, implementation, and fundamental limits of image and RF based wireless capsule endoscopy hybrid localization. *IEEE Trans. Mob. Comput.* **2016**, *15*, 1951–1964. [CrossRef]

47. Zhang, H.; Dufour, F.; Anselmi, J.; Laneuville, D.; Nègre, A. Piecewise optimal trajectories of observer for bearings-only tracking by quantization. In Proceedings of the 2017 20th International Conference on Information Fusion (Fusion), Xi'an, China, 10–13 July 2017; pp. 1–7.

48. Fisher/Information. Available online: https://en.wikipedia.org/wiki/Fisher_information (accessed on 15 January 2019).

49. Horn, R.A.; Johnson, C.R. *Matrix Analysis*; Cambridge University Press: Cambridge, UK, 2012.

50. Gasparini, M. Markov Chain Monte Carlo in Practice. *Technometrics* **1999**, *39*, 338. [CrossRef]

51. Nilsson, J.O.; Gupta, A.K.; Handel, P. Foot-mounted inertial navigation made easy. In Proceedings of the 2014 International Conference on Indoor Positioning and Indoor Navigation (IPIN), Busan, Korea, 27–30 Octorber 2014.

52. Fan, Q.; Zhang, H.; Sun, Y.; Zhu, Y.; Zhuang, X.; Jia, J.; Zhang, P. An Optimal Enhanced Kalman Filter for a ZUPT-Aided Pedestrian Positioning Coupling Model. *Sensors* **2018**, *18*, 1404. [CrossRef] [PubMed]

53. Xu, C.; He, J.; Zhang, X.; Tseng, P.H.; Duan, S. Toward Near-Ground Localization: Modeling and Applications for TOA Ranging Error. *IEEE Trans. Antennas Propag.* **2017**, *65*, 5658–5662. [CrossRef]

54. Deng, C.Y. A generalization of the ShermanMorrisonWoodbury formula. *Appl. Math. Lett.* **2011**, *24*, 1561–1564. [CrossRef]

Article

Implementation and Assessment of an Intelligent Motor Tele-Rehabilitation Platform

Yves Rybarczyk [1,2,3,*], Jorge Luis Pérez Medina [1], Louis Leconte [4], Karina Jimenes [1], Mario González [1] and Danilo Esparza [1]

1 Intelligent & Interactive Systems Lab (SI² Lab), Universidad de Las Américas, Quito 170125, Ecuador; jorge.perez.medina@udla.edu.ec (J.L.P.M.); karina.jimenes@udla.edu.ec (K.J.); mario.gonzalez.rodriguez@udla.edu.ec (M.G.); wilmer.esparza@udla.edu.ec (D.E.)
2 Department of Electrical Engineering, CTS/UNINOVA, Nova University of Lisbon, 2829-516 Monte de Caparica, Portugal
3 School of Informatics, University of Skövde, 54128 Skövde, Sweden
4 Ecole Normale Supérieure, 94235 Paris-Saclay, France; louis.leconte@ens-paris-saclay.fr
* Correspondence: y.rybarczyk@fct.unl.pt; Tel.: +351-2-1294-8545

Received: 18 October 2018; Accepted: 24 December 2018; Published: 4 January 2019

Abstract: Over the past few years, software applications for medical assistance, including tele-rehabilitation, have known an increasing presence in the health arena. Despite the several therapeutic and economic advantages of this new paradigm, it is important to follow certain guidelines, in order to build a safe, useful, scalable, and ergonomic tool. This work proposes to address all these points, through the case study of a physical tele-rehabilitation platform for patients after hip replacement surgery. The scalability and versatility of the system is handled by the implementation of a modular architecture. The safeness and effectiveness of the tool is ensured by an artificial intelligence module that assesses the quality of the movements performed by the user. The usability of the application is evaluated by a cognitive walkthrough method. Results show that the system (i) is able to properly assess the correctness of the human's motion through two possible methods (Dynamic Time Warping and Hidden Markov Model), and (ii) provides a good user experience. The discussion addresses (i) the advantages and disadvantages of the main approaches for a gesture recognition of therapeutic movements, and (ii) critical aspects to provide the patient with the best usability of a tele-rehabilitation platform.

Keywords: eHealth; software engineering; gesture recognition; Dynamic Time Warping; Hidden Markov Model; usability

---

1. Introduction

Over the past few years, alternative healthcare deliveries have been developed. For instance, the advances in the telecommunications have permitted the emergence of telehealth systems. One specialized field of telehealth is tele-rehabilitation, which allows for the implementation of a therapeutic program via an interactive multimedia web-based platform [1,2]. A remarkable increase in the number of patients treated by tele-rehabilitation has been noticed since the beginning of the 21st century, especially in physiotherapy [3]. Despite the several medical and economic advantages of this new paradigm, the development of a tele-rehabilitation platform has to follow specific rules to be safe and efficient. Two fundamental rules are (i) to build a platform based on an affordable system to capture the human movements and (ii) to make sure the patient is performing the therapeutic exercises correctly [4].

The present work proposes a web-based platform for motor tele-rehabilitation applied to patients after hip arthroplasty surgery. This orthopedic procedure is an excellent case study, because it involves people who need a postoperative functional rehabilitation program to recover strength and joint mobility. The development of a tele-rehabilitation system is justified by the condition of these individuals that makes difficult their transportation to and from the physiotherapist's office. The proposed approach considers two fundamental conditions for the development of a suitable tele-rehabilitation platform. First, the system is based on a modular architecture composed of a low-cost motion capture device, in order to ensure the viability and scalability of the tool. Second, the platform detects automatically the correctness of the executed movement to provide the patient with real-time feedback [5]. Since exercises are carried out in front of a machine instead of a therapist, the subjects may produce incorrect movements that could be harmful, especially after a surgery. In addition, the lack of human presence diminishes the motivation, which may slow down the recovery process. Here, two possible approaches are tested to assess the movements and display an appropriate feedback: (i) Dynamic Time Warping (DTW) [6], and (ii) Hidden Markov Models (HMMs) [5].

The remainder of the manuscript is organized into six parts. Section 2 is a presentation of related work. Section 3 is a general description of the web-based platform. Section 4 focuses on a first study to assess the movements and it is based on DTW. Section 5 presents a second study on movement assessments, which uses HMMs. The reliability of both approaches to discriminate between correctly and incorrectly performed movements is tested through laboratory experiments that compare the evaluation of the computer to the evaluation of the therapists. Section 6 consists of an analysis of the usability of the system, through an experiment that involves end users. Finally, the last section (i) discusses the results of the automatic assessments and the usability tests, and (ii) draws conclusions on the most suitable solutions to develop an efficient tele-rehabilitation system.

2. Related Work

Different approaches are proposed to provide the patient with a tele-rehabilitation system. The motion capture can be based on inertial wearable sensors or visual sensors. [7] propose a cloud-assisted wearable system (Rehab-aaService) that enables a general motor rehabilitation, even if the application is optimized for the upper limbs. The platform is scalable and can be integrated into a body sensor network (BodyCloud) [8] for the monitoring of different physiological parameters. However, the system does not have an artificial intelligent module that allows for a rigorous assessment of the rehabilitation exercises. In addition, the wearable devices require the inertial sensors to be precisely placed on the body and/or to involve a calibration stage. Thus, another approach consists of using a vision-based motion capture. This system also presents certain limitations, such as the occultation problem, but it has the advantage to provide an easy setup. The occultation refers to a configuration in which a body joint disappears temporarily behind a part of the individual's body. This situation can be overcome (at least partially) by asking the individuals to change the orientation of their body according to the plane in which the movement is performed. Most of the systems use the Kinect, because it is an affordable piece of equipment and its accuracy is good enough for functional assessment activities [9]. An experiment that consists of assessing the accuracy of the Kinect by comparison to an accelerometer shows a percentage of correlation between the two sensors equal to 96% [4]. An avatar evolving in a serious game is usually used to motivate the users to regularly practice their therapeutic exercises [10]. This gamification approach is also applied for physical exercises, such as Tai Chi [11]. The application can indicate how well the player imitates the instructor, even if the system is not designed to classify gestures. Another type of Tai Chi prototype platform is built to rehabilitate patients with movement disorders [12]. The patient's movements are compared with pre-recorded movements of a coach and further evaluated by using a fuzzy logic algorithm [13]. Additionally, a component-based application framework is proposed by [14] for the development of 3D games by combining already existing 3D visual components. The preliminary results indicate that the prototypes can be used as serious game for physical therapy. However, this framework is not open source and the matching between the avatar and the user is not robust, especially when occultations occur.

In general, it is very rare to find a system that provides both an attractive virtual environment and an algorithm to assess the quality of the rehabilitation movements executed by the patients. Instead of evaluating a spontaneous movement, other studies propose to guide the gesture through visual [15] or haptic [16] feedback, in order to avoid wrong motions. The disadvantage of these approaches is to induce a too stereotyped movement, which reduces the functional benefit of the rehabilitation. Thus, the technological implementation of an appropriate program of motor rehabilitation must involve an expert system that could substitute the therapist and provide the patient with feedback. Recent studies applied algorithms based on rules [17] or Dynamic Time Warping [18] for the recognition of therapeutic movements, and fuzzy logic [19] for the diagnosis of physical impairments. Nevertheless, the current systems are essentially able to discriminate between a correct and an incorrect gesture, but they do not give a targeted feedback on the type of error or they do not consider compensatory movements when an exercise is wrongly executed. To get such a feedback, it seems necessary to build a model of the therapeutic exercises as suggested by [20], who propose a theoretical modeling in UML for the reeducation of the upper limbs. Our work proposes a more advanced approach, since we developed and implemented a statistical model to assess the rehabilitation movements, which can be applied on any part of the body (upper and lower limbs) and can precisely identify the cause of a bad performance to provide the users of the platform with comprehensive feedback regarding the corrections to be made to the gesture.

3. Functionalities and Architecture of the Platform

As represented in Figure 1, the platform is composed of two main blocks dedicated to (i) the Core and (ii) the Real Time Evaluation.

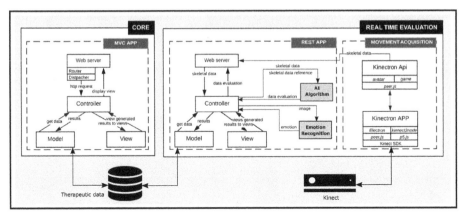

Figure 1. Architecture of the tele-rehabilitation platform.

3.1. Core

The core block allows for empowering patients, who can perform autonomously a set of rehabilitation activities from a program elaborated by health professionals (e.g., physiotherapists) [21]. Several functionalities are implemented in the platform, in order to support patients in their self-recovery process. They have access to a set of multi-modal learning resources on the appropriate use of the platform and the correct procedure to complete the therapeutic program. The patient can initially visualize a list of learning resources, select one of them and display an additional list of associated multimedia files. Then, it is possible to choose the preferred learning resources among different modalities, review the information and return to the general learning menu.

In addition, this block is connected to the database that contains a set of rehabilitation exercises. The computational implementation is based on Django 2.0.5. This web framework uses the Model-View-Controller (MVC) design pattern and works under the two central principles: (i) maintaining loose coupling between the layers of the framework, and (ii) Don't Repeat Yourself (DRY) [22]. According to this pattern, the application functionality is divided into three kinds of components. The model represents the knowledge and has the logic to update the controller. The view represents the visualization of the data. The controller determines the data flow into a model object and updates the view whenever data change. It keeps view and model separated and acts on both.

3.2. Real Time Evaluation

3.2.1. Functionalities

The rehabilitation sessions are planned by the physiotherapist. They are composed of a set of exercises. An exercise is based on the composition pattern [23], which means that it is a composition of simple or compound exercises. Before performing the exercises, patients have to answer a questionnaire regarding their health status. The responses are processed by the application to authorize or disavow them to start a rehabilitation session. If they are authorized to initiate a session, the system activates the execution interface of the exercises. An exercise consists of a set of repetitions predefined in the recovery plan. There is a short break between each repetition to provide the patient with a feedback regarding the quality of the movement. The trials are assessed in terms of range of motion (ROM) and compensatory movements. Before starting an exercise, the patients can consult a set of instructions to execute the movements correctly. During the completion of the exercise, an avatar that maps in real time the patient's movement is displayed in a game-based virtual environment (Figure 2). The movement quality and facial expressions are also assessed in real time by artificial intelligence algorithms. Once a trial is completed, the performance is graphically presented to the user. Finally, the patients have the possibility to suspend a rehabilitation session at any time. In this case, they must provide the physiotherapist with a reason to abort the session.

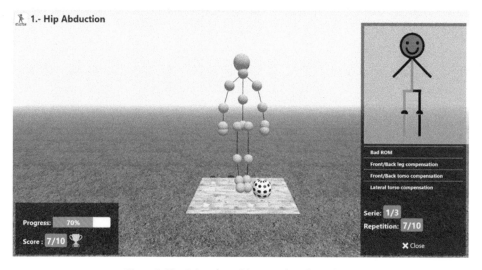

Figure 2. User's interface of the game-based exercises.

3.2.2. Implementation

The real time evaluation block is composed of two modules, the first one for processing skeleton data with a RESTful API, and the second one for acquiring movement data as a client application. They communicate to each other for processing the movement data and for giving the results using JSON data format. The RESTful API was developed using Django Rest Framework 3.8.2. It is a powerful and flexible toolkit of Django to build RESTful Web Services [24]. The client application is built with the Kinectron 1.4.2 and Processing 1.4.8. Kinectron is an open source tool to capture the movement data. It has two components: a server that broadcasts Kinect data, and an API that receives Kinect data [25]. A Kinect v2 camera is used to capture the movements of the patient and extracts the coordinates of the main body joints. A cross-browser JavaScript Library is incorporated (Three.js) to display in a web browser the game-based exercises, which are composed of 3D animated objects and the user's avatar. Additional technologies, such as Boostrap 4.1.13 and JQuery 3.1.14 are used to build the interface. Boostrap is a CSS framework that provides a characteristic of responsive web design. It allows developing interfaces compatible with different kinds of browsers and terminal platforms [26]. JQuery is a Javascript library which has CSS selector, flexible animation system and event system, rich plugins, and solutions for browser compatibility issues.

The API REST package works with the exercises packages and contains the intelligent modules to assess both the quality of the movements and the emotions of the patients when performing an exercise. It has a couple of services to process the skeleton and the images frames through different artificial intelligence algorithms. The first service processes the skeleton to evaluate if the patient is exercising correctly and the result is transferred as a JSON structure with a set of angles. Each angle has a type, a DTW metric that compares the performed movement to the reference movement. A graphical-based feedback is displayed on the user's interface to inform the patients on the quality of their performance (Figure 2). A red color represents bad movement amplitude for a determined limb or body part. This visual feedback is reinforced by a textual description of potential errors in the motion. Other information, such as a progress bar and a score are also displayed. The second service processes the image frame every second to determine if the patient feels pain. A machine-learning algorithm based on Support Vector Machine (SVM) is implemented to operate a Boolean classification of facial expressions in pain (1) vs. no pain (0). A sequence of 1 and 0 is obtained at the end of each repetition. This information is used by the therapist to identify if the intensity of the exercises is appropriate or not for a determined patient.

4. Movement Assessment: DTW Approach

4.1. Dynamic Time Warping

Dynamic Time Warping (DTW) is an algorithm for measuring similarity between two temporal sequences, which may vary in speed. It is perfectly adapted for the assessment of therapeutic movements for which the velocity of the execution is not relevant. This characteristic explains why we have chosen this technique, because it enables us to assess the quality of the movement by a single comparison to a reference. Any distance (Euclidean, Manhattan, ...) which aligns the i-th point on one-time series with the i-th point of another produces a poor similarity score. On the contrary, a non-linear alignment produces a more intuitive similarity measure, allowing similar shapes to match even if they are out of phase in the time axis. The implementation of such an algorithm is obtained through a matrix sized with the length of each signal (Figure 3). On each point of the matrix, the distance between the points associated with each of the two signals is calculated. The best alignment of two signals is given by the path through the grid that minimizes the total distance between these two signals. Our algorithm implements a quadratic distance (D), as defined in Equation (1).

$$D_{(i,j)} = (x_{(j)} - y_{(i)})^2 \tag{1}$$

Thus, a distance matrix is obtained. Then, a cumulated distance matrix (C) is created, based on the distance matrix (D). The latter is built thanks to a definition of distance very close to the 8-connectivity in a square tiling (mathematic topology) for each point of the matrix, as presented in Equation (2).

$$C_{(i,j)} = \min\left\{ C_{(i-1,\,j-1)},\ C_{(i-1,j)},\ C_{(i,j-1)} \right\} + D_{(i,j)} \tag{2}$$

Finally, we have to look for the path that minimizes the cumulated distance. To do so, we start from the last point and look for the point with the lower cumulated distance between all its three inferior neighbors (within the meaning of Moore neighborhood). We reiterate the process until we reach a side or the originate point C(0, 0). Then, we just have to calculate the length of this path. The result is small when signals are close, and becomes larger when signals differ. An optimization can be provided to this algorithm, using a warping window. It is based on the fact that a good alignment path is unlikely to wander too far from the diagonal and, thus, limits the window length. Since the Kinect frequency is about 33 Hz and the movements are short, we do not need to implement this optimization, because only few points (between 100 and 200) have to be analyzed.

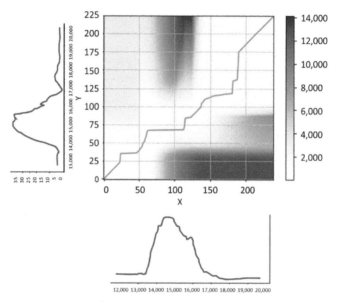

Figure 3. Cumulated distance matrix and its optimal path (in red), between a reference movement and a movement to be tested (blue signals).

4.2. Trigonometric Parametrization

As we expect our algorithm to be invariant to 3D translational motion and to different bodies, we have to focus not on coordinates of each joint, but on angles. This section describes the mathematical calculation of the (i) working angles (ROM) and (ii) compensation angles for the four main therapeutic movements: hip abduction, slow flexion hip and knee, hip extension, and forward-sideway-backward sequence. During a rehabilitation session it is important to identify both the movement amplitude the patient should reach (ROM) and the compensatory movements that should be avoid for an appropriate re-education of the injured limbs.

For hip abduction, we identified one working angle (Figure 4, picture on the left) and three compensation angles (Figure 4, three pictures on the right). To obtain the angle of the hip abduction (θ_{aw}), we have to project $\overrightarrow{16\_18}$ on the frontal plane, and proceed with the calculation of Equations (3)–(5).

$$n_1 = \left[\sum_{k=x,y,z} (k_{18} - k_{16})(k_{16} - k_0) \right]^2 \tag{3}$$

$$d_1 = (x_{16} - x_0)^2 + (y_{16} - y_0)^2 + (z_{16} - z_0)^2 \tag{4}$$

$$\cos\theta_{aw} = \frac{|y_{16} - y_{18}|}{\sqrt{\frac{n_1}{d_1} + (y_{16} - y_{18})^2}} \tag{5}$$

where n_1 and d_1 are intermediate variables used to calculate the angle θ_{aw}, and k is successively equal to x, y, and z in the calculation of the sum. '0' stands for spine base, '16' stands for left hip, and '18' stands for left ankle. The leg compensation angle (θ_{lc}) is obtained by the calculations of Equations (6)–(8).

$$n_2 = \left[\sum_{k=x,z} (k_{18} - k_{16})(k_{15} - k_{14}) \right]^2 \tag{6}$$

$$d_2 = (x_{15} - x_{14})^2 + (z_{15} - z_{14})^2 \tag{7}$$

$$\cos\theta_{lc} = \frac{|y_{16} - y_{18}|}{\sqrt{\frac{n_2}{d_2} + (y_{16} - y_{18})^2}} \tag{8}$$

where n_2 and d_2 are intermediate variables used to calculate the angle θ_{lc}. '14' stands for right ankle, and '15' stands for left foot. Equations (9)–(11) are used to calculate the frontal torso compensation angle (θ_{ftc}).

$$n_3 = \left[\sum_{k=x,z} (k_0 - k_{20})(k_{15} - k_{14}) \right]^2 \tag{9}$$

$$d_3 = (x_{15} - x_{14})^2 + (z_{15} - z_{14})^2 \tag{10}$$

$$\cos\theta_{ftc} = \frac{|y_0 - y_{20}|}{\sqrt{\frac{n_3}{d_3} + (y_0 - y_{20})^2}} \tag{11}$$

where n_3 and d_3 are intermediate variables used to calculate the angle θ_{ftc}. '20' stands for spine shoulder. Equations (12)–(14) are used to calculate the lateral torso compensation angle (θ_{ltc}).

$$n_4 = \left[\sum_{k=x,y,z} (k_{20} - k_0)(k_{16} - k_0) \right]^2 \tag{12}$$

$$d_4 = (x_{16} - x_0)^2 + (y_{16} - y_0)^2 + (z_{16} - z_0)^2 \tag{13}$$

$$\cos\theta_{ltc} = \frac{|y_0 - y_{20}|}{\sqrt{\frac{n_4}{d_4} + (y_0 - y_{20})^2}} \tag{14}$$

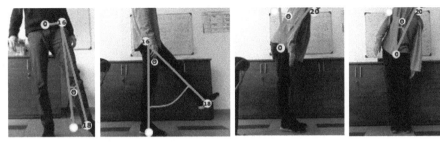

Figure 4. Expected and possible movements involved in hip abduction (from left to right): working angle, leg compensation, front torso compensation, and lateral torso compensation.

For slow flexion of hip and knee, we identified two working angles (Figure 5, picture on the left) and two typical compensation angles (Figure 5, two pictures on the right). Equations (15)–(17) are used to calculate the hip-working angle (θ_{hw}).

$$n_5 = \left[\sum_{k=x,y,z} (k_{17} - k_{16})(k_{15} - k_{14}) \right]^2 \tag{15}$$

$$d_5 = (x_{15} - x_{14})^2 + (y_{15} - y_{14})^2 + (z_{15} - z_{14})^2 \tag{16}$$

$$\cos \theta_{hw} = \frac{|y_{17} - y_{16}|}{\sqrt{\frac{n_5}{d_5} + (y_{17} - y_{16})^2}} \tag{17}$$

where n_5 and d_5 are intermediate variables used to calculate the angle θ_{hw}. '14' stands for right ankle, '15' stands for left foot, '16' stands for right hip, and '17' stands for left knee. Equations (18)–(20) are used to calculate the knee-working angle (θ_{kw}).

$$n_6 = \left[\sum_{k=x,y,z} (k_{18} - k_{17})(k_{15} - k_{14}) \right]^2 \tag{18}$$

$$d_6 = (x_{15} - x_{14})^2 + (y_{15} - y_{14})^2 + (z_{15} - z_{14})^2 \tag{19}$$

$$\cos \theta_{kw} = \frac{|y_{18} - y_{17}|}{\sqrt{\frac{n_6}{d_6} + (y_{18} - y_{17})^2}} \tag{20}$$

where n_6 and d_6 are intermediate variables used to calculate the angle θ_{kw}. '14' stands for right ankle, '15' stands for left foot, '17' stands for left knee, and '18' stands for left ankle. Equations (21)–(23) are used to calculate the thigh compensation angle (θ_{thc}).

$$n_7 = \left[\sum_{k=x,y,z} (k_{17} - k_{16})(k_{12} - k_{16}) \right]^2 \tag{21}$$

$$d_7 = (x_{12} - x_{16})^2 + (y_{12} - y_{16})^2 + (z_{12} - z_{16})^2 \tag{22}$$

$$\cos \theta_{thc} = \frac{|y_{17} - y_{16}|}{\sqrt{\frac{n_7}{d_7} + (y_{17} - y_{16})^2}} \tag{23}$$

where n_7 and d_7 are intermediate variables used to calculate the angle θ_{thc}. '12' stands for left hip, '16' stands for right hip, and '17' stands for left knee. Equations (24)–(26) are used to calculate the tibia compensation angle (θ_{tic}).

$$n_8 = \left[\sum_{k=x,y,z} (k_{18} - k_{17})(k_{12} - k_{16}) \right]^2 \tag{24}$$

$$d_8 = (x_{12} - x_{16})^2 + (y_{12} - y_{16})^2 + (z_{12} - z_{16})^2 \tag{25}$$

$$\cos \theta_{tic} = \frac{|y_{18} - y_{17}|}{\sqrt{\frac{n_8}{d_8} + (y_{18} - y_{17})^2}} \tag{26}$$

where n_8 and d_8 are intermediate variables used to calculate the angle θ_{tic}. '12' stands for left hip, '16' stands for right hip, '17' stands for left knee, and '18' stands for left ankle. The same frontal and lateral compensation movements of the trunk as described in hip abduction are also calculated for this exercise (Equations (9)–(14)).

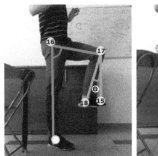

Figure 5. Expected and possible movements involved in slow flexion of hip and knee (from left to right): working angle for hip (in green) and knee (in blue), thigh compensation, and tibia compensation.

For hip extension, the working angle is the same as the compensation angle of hip abduction, and the compensation angle is equal to the working angle of hip abduction (Figure 6). The same frontal and lateral compensation movements of the trunk as described in hip abduction are also calculated for this exercise (Equations (9)–(14)).

Figure 6. Working angle for hip extension.

There are two working angles for the forward-sideway-backward sequence, which are the working and leg compensation angles of the hip abduction (Figure 7). Again, the frontal and lateral compensation movements of the trunk described in hip abduction are considered for this exercise (Equations (9)–(14)).

Figure 7. Working angle for forward–sideway–backward sequence.

4.3. Filtering and Implementation

Since the raw input data provided by the Kinect are too noisy, a low pass filter is applied to the signal (Figure 8). The Butterworth Filter available in the python library 'scipy.signal' is used to smooth the signal. It is necessary to create two different filters according to the noisiness of the data (a moderate and a strong one). The best ratio signal/noise for the moderate filter is obtained empirically with the parameters as follows:

- filter order = 2
- sample rate (Hz) = 40
- cutoff frequency (Hz) = 5

The settings of the strong filter are:

- filter order = 4
- sample rate (Hz) = 150
- cutoff frequency (Hz) = 5

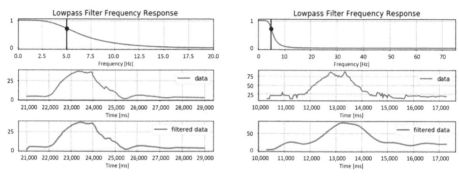

Figure 8. Examples of the filtering effect for the moderate (**left panel**) and the strong (**right panel**) filter.

The assessment module is implemented to compare the DTW cost of each described angle (ROM and compensations) to an empirically defined threshold (the optimum value is defined in the next section). If the distance calculated by the DTW is higher than the threshold, the angle of the movement is classified as wrong. Since different DTW run in parallel (one for each specific working and compensation movements), it is possible to provide the patients with a detailed feedback of their errors for helping them to correct their performance in the next trial. Whatever the correctness of the movement, a graphical message is always displayed to the users at the end of the trials (see Figure 2). Once a session is finished, a JSON file is created with every angle data cost, pictographic feedback (good, bad, or neutral smileys), and six possible messages that are displayed on the patient's interface (evaluation of the ROM and potential compensation movements). Then, these data are stored in the platform database.

4.4. Validation

4.4.1. Experimental Protocol

The experiment consisted of comparing the assessment performed by four physiotherapists to the assessment made by the algorithm. Seven healthy subjects participated in the study. They were informed about the purpose of the study and signed a consent form to take part to the experiment. They were asked to take place at approximately two meters distance from a single Kinect camera. The motion capture device was placed at the height of the subject's xiphoid apophysis. Each of the four movements described in Section 4.2 was repeated eleven times (one of them was used as reference). The participant had to introduce a different error in the execution of the movement at each repetition (e.g., wrong range of motion or different kinds of compensation). To do so, they followed a script unknown to the therapists and different from one participant to another. The only similarity between the scripts is the fact that they were composed of six accurate executions, two movements with an incorrect ROM, and three movements with compensation errors. For each trial, the physiotherapists were asked to evaluate all the angles (ROM and compensations) on a 4-point Likert scale (0–3). The data were processed with the python library *Pandas*. Due to the inter-individual differences between the assessments made by the physiotherapists, the scale of the marks was reduced to two levels. All the assessments of 0 and 1 were grouped in a single category that corresponded to a bad execution of the exercise. And the assessments of 2 and 3 were all classified as a good movement. The final therapist's evaluation was obtained by averaging the score of the four professionals. In case of draw, the trial was discarded. Then, these Boolean variables (bad vs. good) were compared with the assessment performed by the algorithm. The outcome was expected to be different depending on the decision threshold.

4.4.2. Results

Overall, the outcome of the algorithm matches at 88% with the assessment made by the physiotherapists. The accuracy of this matching depends on the threshold of tolerated difference between the reference movement and the analyzed movement (Figure 9). A certain variability in the performance of the classification is observed from one exercise to another. For instance, the best results are obtained for the assessment of the ROM for hip abduction and forward-sideway-backward sequence (percentage of accuracy >90%).

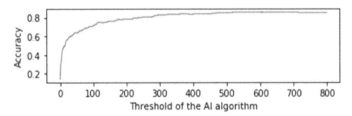

Figure 9. Overall variation of accuracy depending on the threshold.

A confusion matrix permits to identify the percentage of movements assessed as correct by the therapists and predicted as correct by the algorithm (True Positives—TP), the incorrect movements predicted as incorrect (True Negatives—TN), the correct movements predicted as incorrect (False Negatives—FN), and the incorrect movements predicted as correct (False Positives—FP). The accuracy of the algorithm to predict the TP and TN is almost the same, even if it is slight higher for the former than the latter (Table 1). This small difference can be explained by the fact that there is more diversity in the execution of the bad (errors of ROM and compensations) than the good movements.

Table 1. Confusion matrix providing a detailed comparison between the movement assessments of the physiotherapists and the algorithm.

		therapists assessment	
		good mvt	bad mvt
algorithm prediction — good mvt		TP = 91%	FP = 9%
algorithm prediction — bad mvt		FN = 15%	TN = 85%

The misclassified movements (FP and FN) can be explained by two main reasons. First, there is only a partial consensus between the assessments carried out by the four therapists. Nevertheless, the discrepancy between the health professionals is less than 8% and, consequently, the human judgment is considered as an acceptable reference to evaluate the algorithm. Second, some angles suffer from occultation and cannot be evaluated correctly by the computer. This situation happens occasionally when a body joint (e.g., the hip) disappears temporarily behind a part of the participant's body (e.g., the hand).

Table 2 provides a quantification of the missing data in terms of the percentage of sampling errors and occultations. Sampling errors are defined as technical issues caused by faults in the capture sampling rate of the Kinect. The occultations refer to situations in which the participants cross their arms, cross their arms in front of the torso or cross the legs while performing the exercises. They are computed considering the pose arrangement [27] that identifies intersections between the torso, the arms, and/or the legs. The results show that the sampling errors are almost insignificant (<0.01%) and the occultations represent less than 6% of the missing data. Some movements are more affected by occultation than others, which suggests defining an optimal orientation of the body with respect to the vision-based motion capture sensor, for each exercise.

Table 2. Missing data defined in terms of the percentage of sampling errors and joint occultations, for each exercise (slow flexion hip and knee—SFHK; hip abduction—HA; hip extension—HE; forward-sideway-backward—FSB).

Exercises	Sampling Error (%)	Occultation (%)	Total (%)
SFHK	0.01	14.35	**14.36**
HA	0.00	0.26	**0.26**
HE	0.01	1.17	**1.18**
FSB	0.00	7.61	**7.61**
Mean (%)	**0.005**	**5.85**	**5.855**

5. Movement Assessment: HMM Approach

5.1. Hidden Markov Model

Hidden Markov Model is a probabilistic approach that aims to model a given action into hidden states. It is composed of initial, transitional and emission probabilities. Initial probabilities are the distribution of probabilities of 'being in a state' before a sequence is observed. Transitional probabilities are represented by a matrix, in which the probabilities indicate the possible changes from one state to another. Finally, the emission probabilities model the variance of each state's associated values (mostly Gaussian Probability Density Functions—PDFs) obtained from continuous variable observations. These model parameters can be learned with the use of the Expectation-Maximization (EM) algorithm. Signals can be classified by looking at the probability that a signal is generated from a trained HMM. This is done by the use of the forward algorithm.

Learning the model parameters (states and transitions) by optimizing the likelihood is essential to make meaningful use of the HMM in classification. The distribution function defined by a Gaussian, Mixed Gaussian or multinomial density function, as well as the covariance type, needs to be characterized prior to this process. An observation is merely a noisy and variable representation of a related state. A state is a clustering of observations that relates to a distribution with a specific mean in the parameter space. A likely state is retrieved by finding the cluster that the observation is member of. Also, the transition probabilities between states creates a sequence of the most likely temporal succession of states. Estimating the model parameters is done by utilizing the Baum-Welch Expectation-Maximization algorithm, which is based on a forward-backward algorithm used in classifying Hidden Markov Chains [28,29]. The probabilities are calculated at any point of a sequence by inspecting previous observations, to find out how well the model describes the data, and following observations, to conclude how well the model predicts the rest of the sequence. This is an iterative process, in which the objective is to find an optimal solution (state sequence) for the HMM. This optimal sequence of states is inferred using the Viterbi algorithm. In addition, the forward algorithm can be used to calculate the probability that a sequence is generated by a specific trained HMM, making it applicable for classification.

This classification is based on training an individual HMM per subclass of an exercise. For instance, one HMM could be trained on 'running' while another one would be trained on 'walking' (both subclasses of the human locomotion class). When calculating the forward probabilities of a sequence of observations and comparing the probabilities of all the HMMs, the sequence is classified as the category that provides the highest probability, as described in Equation (27).

$$\text{Class} = \arg_{i=1}^{n} \max\left[\Pr(O|\lambda_i) * \Pr(\lambda_i)\right] \tag{27}$$

where λ_i represents a determined model and O is a sequence of observations. The amount of states in a HMM is a free parameter. The Bayesian Information Criteria (BIC) is a technique that aids to define a determined number of parameters by taking into account the possibility of overfitting the data when the number of states increases. BIC penalizes HMMs that have a high number of states, as described in Equation (28).

$$\text{BIC} = \ln(n)s - 2\ln(MLE) \tag{28}$$

where n is the data size and s the amount of states. Therefore, the optimal amount of states is retrieved by selecting the model with the lowest BIC score. HMMs trained with multiple states are evaluated by cross-validation on their Maximum Likelihood Estimation (MLE) and the previously mentioned penalizing term.

5.2. Gesture Representation

A skeletonized 3D image from a Kinect camera provides Cartesian x, y and z coordinates of twenty body joints. The gesture representation is chosen to be a skeletonized image as this has been shown to improve the model accuracy [30]. This representation depends on the position of the subject in relation to the camera and the roll, yaw and pitch angles of the device. The causal relationships between different joints are not captured by this representation. This means that physical constrains, such as a movement of the ankle that could be influenced by bending the knee, are not accounted for. To overcome these limitations, the joints are used to create a new representation that contains angles of multiple joints in respect to the frontal and sagittal planes, as well as multiple angles between relevant limbs. Figure 10 shows a graphical representation of the features in relation to the skeleton image. Table 3 describes the feature vector of the joint movements according to the anatomical terminology.

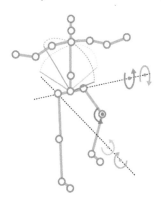

Figure 10. Graphical representation of the features used in the study. The movements in the egocentric frontal plane and sagittal plane are represented in green and red, respectively. The purple arrow represents the angle of the knee (independent from any plane).

Table 3. Feature vector describing the joint movements. For the purpose of the assessment these features are also transformed into speed and acceleration.

Right Hip	Left Hip	Spine Center	Knee
Right hip Frontal plane rotation (abduction)	Left hip Frontal plane rotation (abduction)	Spine center Frontal plane rotation (lateral left)	Right knee (flexion)
Right hip Frontal plane rotation (adduction)	Left hip Frontal plane rotation (adduction)	Spine center Frontal plane rotation (lateral right)	Left knee (flexion)
Right hip Sagittal plane rotation (flexion)	Left hip Sagittal plane rotation (flexion)	Spine center Sagittal plane rotation (flexion)	
Right hip Sagittal plane rotation (extension)	Left hip Sagittal plane rotation (extension)	Spine center Sagittal plane rotation (extension)	

In this study, the motion is defined from the following joints: ankles, knees, hips, and spine. The angles of the knees are obtained by calculating the angle between ankle, knee and hip. The orientation of the knees induced by hip activity are expressed in four angular representations, following the two opposite directions for both sagittal and frontal planes. The same method is applied to describe the orientation of the torso, by finding the displacement of the center between the two shoulders in relation to the hips. This leads to a description of the movement into fourteen features. It is the principal representation followed by a first order and second order derivatives of these features that provide speed and acceleration of the movement. Overall, a total amount of 42 features is used. Figure 11 represents a diagram of the HMM's implemented in this study, in which $State_{(t)}$ and $Observation_{(t)}$ are state id and associated feature values at t time, respectively.

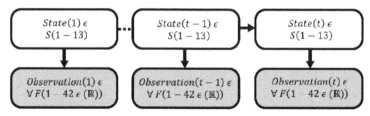

Figure 11. Graphical representation of the HMM for the exercise assessment. ϵ stands for: takes value out of; and $\forall$ stands for: out of all. F and S are the collection of features (42) and states (13), respectively. The definition of the optimal number of states is explained in Section 5.3.4. Each state is dependent on its previous state and observations are samples of the associated current state.

5.3. Experiment

5.3.1. Protocol

Four healthy subjects participated in the experiment. They were informed about the purpose of the study and signed a consent form to take part in the experiment. They were asked to stand at approximately two meters distance front of a Kinect camera. The motion capture device was placed at the height of the subject's xiphoid apophysis. Each participant executed 70 movements leading to a total of 280 records. The rehabilitation exercise was a sequence, in which the subjects had to do one step forward, one step sideways and one step backward, with variations. These variations are staged executions of errors or compensatory movements that can occur during the rehabilitation in practice. The exercise was performed in batches of ten and the experiment was divided into two independent parts. In the first part, the subjects had to execute the movements as follows: (I) correct execution, (II) steps too short, (III) execution without moving the center of mass, (IV) steps too large, (V) steps with bended knee, (VI) steps with bended knee and flexed torso. The objective of this first experimental part was to assess the accuracy of the models to classify the movements. In the second part, the subjects had to perform ten trials of a partially wrong executions of the exercise (VII), in which the faults II to VI are only occurring in the beginning, middle or end of the sequence. This second experiment is used to evaluate the real-time applicability of the HMM technique.

An application was created to capture the skeletonized image of the subjects performing an exercise. Python 2.7 was used to create a graphical user interface with the option to name, start and stop a recording. In addition, Python was used for the later processing steps, which were feature transformations and classifications. The application communicated with the Kinect SDK and wrote the data into a CSV file, with a frequency of 60 Hz, during the recording mode. The developed programs and raw data are available at http://docentes.fct.unl.pt/y-rybarczyk/files/programs.rar and http://docentes.fct.unl.pt/y-rybarczyk/files/data.rar, respectively. The HMMLearn package for python 2.7 was used for the training and application of the HMMs (https://github.com/hmmlearn/hmmlearn).

5.3.2. Evaluation Method

Using the BIC score to select the appropriate amount of states was done for each type of trained HMMs (I–VI). It provided insight on the semantic variation within the exercises. For instance, less states assigned to a faulty movement relative to the good execution implies that 'there was something missing in the execution', whereas the detection of extra states implied that 'there was something added to the movement'.

For each type of execution (I–VI) an HMM was trained, leading to a total of six distinct HMMs. In order to build a general model that could assess the movements of any subject, models that classified the executions of a subject were exclusively trained on the recordings of the other remaining subjects. This led to a total of 24 trained models (6 per subject). The initial model parameters were set with a Gaussian density function and a full covariance matrix type (the initializations of the model parameters were done randomly, HmmLearn standard initialization was used, and EM iterated a 1000 times unless log-likelihood gain was less than 0.01). The HMM topological structure was fully connected, because priory knowledge about the expected state sequence could not be estimated with sufficient certainty. In addition, as the outcome of six classifiers determined the most likely model that was associated with the sequence, unpredicted variance in a signal (or noise) should not drastically influence the likelihood of the signal. The outcome of the six classifiers was calculated by means of the forward probabilities. Then, these probabilities were ranked from 1 to 6, where 1 and 6 were assigned to the highest and the lowest probability, respectively. A confusion matrix was used to map these values in terms of average prediction rank of each type of execution. In addition, an indication of the similarity of a type of execution in relation to the combination of all the other executions was provided. Finally, a range of sliding temporal windows was used to evaluate the real-time suitability of the approach. It was applied to assess the correct detection of the present types of faults in executions VII. These windows classified a subsequence in a fixed number of samples, which partially overlapped over time.

5.3.3. Validation Method

To get a reliable result that validated the models, it was important that the test data were different from the training data. Both training and test sets had to be produced by independent sampling from an infinite population, which avoided a misleading result that would not reflect what it was expected when the classifier is deployed. This section describes the used method that enabled us to apply this mandatory rule in machine learning. A 10 times repeated random sub-sampling, Monte Carlo Cross-Validation (MCCV) was used to evaluate the performance of each model (6 per subject and 24 in total). Results with Gaussian mixtures on real and simulated data suggested that MCCV provided genuine insight into cluster structure [31]. This method selects the most appropriate model for classification. To assure the ability of the model to generalize well, the validation was executed by applying, for each subject, the other three subject's recordings. This means that each trained HMM was used as classifier of the data of an unrelated subject. Each fold contained a trial of the three subjects. The split (80% train, 20% validation) was newly created during every validation (10 times) with a random assignment of the trials in the training and test sets. This led to a model trained with 24 exercises (8 of each subject). To perform the random assignment, the python built-in random function that implements the Mersenne Twister regenerator method was used. During each validation, 6 HMMs (models I–VI) were trained such as the best performing (based on the validation score) set of HMMs was selected as models set for classification. Forward probabilities were calculated for each HMM. When the correct HMM output the highest probability, the classification value became 1 and contrary 0. Per fold, each HMM classified the remaining 6 exercises where the performance per fold was the fraction correctly classified exercises (sum of classification results) of the total classifications (36) of the 6 HMMs combined. The model's parameters differed slightly between the sets as the random data selection altered the learned state Probability Density Functions (PDFs) per fold. The best performing model set out of the 10 validations was then selected to perform the classification for the test subject.

5.3.4. Results

1. State assignment and classification

The MLE for each HMM up to twenty states was used to define the BIC scores (see Equation (28)) against the amount of states (Figure 12). The profile of the BIC score against the amount of states was similar between the HMMs. The consensual lowest BIC score was obtained for an amount of states equal to thirteen (value that corresponds to the minimum of the average curve—the blue bold broken line in Figure 12). Thus, thirteen states were used to model the six movements. This makes intuitively sense as the exercise was constructed out of three distinctive parts (a multiple of three is expected), plus an initial/ending part (inactive state). Hence, each part in the exercise was described by four states.

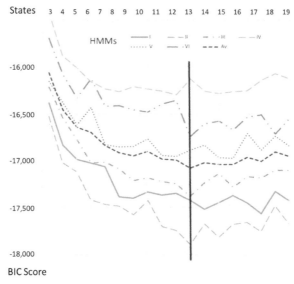

Figure 12. BIC scores for each type of execution (I–VI) and an averaged BIC score over these executions (blue bold broken line). The black vertical line indicates the optimal amount of states.

The classification performance shows a high level of accuracy (Table 4) in classifying a whole sequence into the classes (I–VI). A value of 1 means the model always gave the highest probability, with respect to the other models and for any sequence of the related movement, whereas a value of 6 indicates the lowest probability. The values in this table are averaged prediction ranks for each model of each movement (I–VI). The average prediction rank of HMM I is the highest (2.78), which means that the execution type I (correct movement) is most closely related to all the other types. The overall performance of the classification for each class (I–VI) is shown in Table 5. It is to note that the execution type III (i) is more likely to be classified as type I, and (ii) has the lowest prediction accuracy compared with the other classes. Movement III is the one that presents the subtlest difference from movement I. The only distinction between these two executions is the fact that the participants do not move their center of mass in the former case. In other words, the trunk does not go with the rest of the movement. This fine difference could explain the limitation of the algorithm to discriminate between the two types of movement. A solution to overcome this issue could be to implement a better staging of the execution III and/or getting a higher descriptive power in the gesture representation (e.g., including additional features related to the upper-part of the body).

Table 4. Confusion matrix of executions (I–VI). Each column represents the types of movement and each row the output prediction ranks of the HMMs (I–VI). The closer is the value to 1 (green cells) the better is the prediction.

Movements

Predictions	I	II	III	IV	V	VI	Average rank
I	1	2.27	1.4	3.97	4	4	2.78
II	2.7	1	2.8	6	6	5	3.92
III	2.3	2.74	1.57	5	5	6	3.77
IV	4.74	4	4.9	1.04	2	3	3.28
V	4.27	5	4.34	1.97	1	2	3.1
VI	6	6	6	3.04	3	1	4.18

Table 5. Performance of the classification of movements I–VI.

I	II	III	IV	V	VI
100%	100%	57%	97%	100%	100%

2. Real-time testing

The aim for the platform is not only to provide an overall classification of the movement (correct vs. types of fault), but also to identify a potential real-time transition from one classification to another during a single exercise. This can aid the patient to be aware on the phases of the movement in which certain errors tend to occur. The result of this instantaneous classification could be displayed as a real-time feedback when the patient is executing any exercise.

The samples of execution type VII are used to evaluate the ability for the trained models I–VI to classify partially incorrect movement (i.e., only certain phases of the movement are wrong). This execution is a rehabilitation movement in which the individual performs one step to the front, one step to the side and one step to the back, in a continuous sequence. The classification takes place over a selection of frames within the movement. The forward algorithm, as described previously, is used to perform this classification. Three different sizes of windows are used for the classification: 100, 60 and 20 frames. These different samplings are made to study the effect of the window size on the consistency and accuracy of the assessment. After classifying the frames of a determined window size, the window shifts half the number of frames in the total sequence and the classification is repeated until the end of the sequence is reached. This so-called overlapping window is used to obtain a smoother classification path over time. There are multiple classification values during the full exercise. At each newly created classification moment in the exercise the values of the six classifiers are normalized in a fashion that the highest value becomes 1 and the other values are expressed as a fraction of this value. Detection is considered accurate if the majority of the movement's phase where the error occurred assigns the value of 1 to the expected error type. In the case of the execution type VII, there are three phases: step forward, step sideways, and step backward.

Figure 13 shows that whatever the window size is the performance maintains quite accurate, even though the result is a little bit noisier when the sizes get smaller. For instance, there is a very high detection rate (21/24) when errors of types IV to VI are present in the sequence of the movements, for any sampling size. Detecting execution types II and III are less successful (9/16). It can be explained by the fact that these two types share high similarities with execution I (see Table 4).

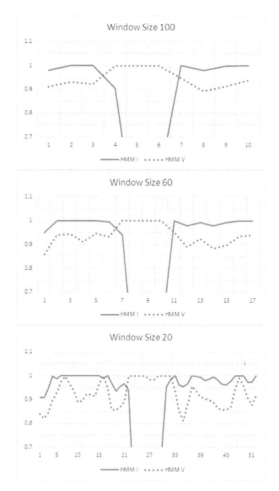

Figure 13. Execution of type VII where the middle part (i.e., step to the side) is performed as type V. Three different window sizes are represented: 100, 60 and 20 samples. The red dotted line represents the prediction of HMM V and the blue line indicates the prediction of HMM I (correct movement).

There is a certain trade-off for choosing the window size. A smaller window can provide a frequent feedback, but a slightly noisier prediction. Figure 13 presents the example of a correct sequence, except the middle part is performed as execution V (step with bended knee). In this figure the amount of feedback moments is represented on the *x*-axis and a normalized classification value on the *y*-axis. The sampling rate is 50 Hz (20 ms per sample). Window sizes of 100, 60 and 20 represent approximately every second, twice a second and five times a second feedback, respectively. This example shows that the accuracy of the prediction (identification of correct vs. incorrect executions) is not significantly altered by the window sizes, which confirms the pertinence of an HMM approach for real-time applications.

6. Usability of the System

6.1. Participants and Procedure

In order to evaluate if the platform can be easily used by the end users, a usability test was carried out. A total of 41 right handed participants (distributed in 32 males and 9 females) volunteered for the experiment. No specific skill was necessary to take part to the study. 92.3% of the subjects was between 18 and 30 years old. All participants reported that they had never used a tele-rehabilitation system before.

Participants were informed about the purpose of the study and signed a consent form to participate. Then, subjects were asked to take an accommodation phase, in which they followed a tutorial on the use of the platform. Once the scenario of tele-rehabilitation was clarified and after the participants were confident with the application, they were asked to complete five tasks described in the next section. The total duration for the completion of the tasks was around 15 min. Once the whole tasks were completed, the subjects were requested to fill in the IBM Computer System Usability Questionnaire (CSUQ) described in Table 6 [32]. CSUQ is a questionnaire based on a Likert scale, in which a statement is made and the respondent then indicates the degree of agreement or disagreement with the statement on a 7-point scale, from 'strongly disagree' (1) to 'strongly agree' (7).

6.2. Tasks

The rehabilitation program is implemented in the platform according to 3 chronological stages. The intensity of the therapeutic exercises increases progressively from stage 1 (the week following the surgery) to stage 3 (about 3 weeks after the surgery). During the usability test, participants had to perform five tasks related to activities implemented in these different stages.

6.2.1. Task 1: Consult Therapeutic Instructions of Stage 1

In this task, subjects were asked to access and understand the documentation provided by the core component regarding 'how to use the platform'. They could select among different learning modalities (text, audio, and video).

6.2.2. Task 2: Perform Rehabilitation Exercises of Stage 1

This task involved several subtasks. First, participants had to answer a questionnaire to self-assess their health status and unlock the exercise interface (meaning that they are in physical condition to pursue). Second, they had to select an exercise of stage 1 (low intensity exercises) and consult recommendations to perform it properly. Finally, the exercise had to be executed in front of the Kinect.

6.2.3. Task 3: Consult Therapeutic Instructions of Stage 2

Again, participants had to access and consult general recommendation documents developed for the therapeutic education of the patients in stage 2 (medium intensity exercises). At the end, and before continuing to the rehabilitation program, they had to accept the conditions by clicking a check-box.

6.2.4. Task 4: Perform Rehabilitation Exercises of Stage 2

As in task 2, subjects were requested to perform an exercise available in stage 2. An addition requirement for this task was to abort the series of repetition by using the functionality 'cancel' and, then, to fill in the questionnaire to justify the cause of the suspension.

6.2.5. Task 5: Consult and Send a Message to the Therapist

In this task, participants had to access the mailbox integrated in the platform, in order to consult new messages and send a text-based or audio-based email to their physiotherapists.

6.3. Results

Overall, the participants mostly agreed with the statements. In most cases, the averages of the responses were greater than 5 with a standard deviation (SD) less than 1.19. The global result to the questions (#09, #10 and #11) that belong to the information quality or INFOQUAL (Mean = 5.49, Median = 6.00, SD = 1.15) suggests the platform provides a good online aid and documentation. Nevertheless, question #09 is assessed less positively (Mean = 4.77, Median = 5.00, SD = 1.51), which means that users tend to consider the error messages as not helpful to solve problems. Finally, the result to question #15 (Mean = 5.92, Median = 6.00, SD = 0.84) clearly indicates that the participants agree on the organization of the information of the user interface.

Table 6. Structure and results of the IBM Computer System Usability Questionnaire.

Category	#	Question	Mean	SD
SYSUSE	01	Overall, I am satisfied with how easy it is to use this system.	5.82	0.88
	02	It was simple to use this system.	5.92	0.74
	03	I could effectively complete my work using this system.	6.03	1.01
	04	I was able to complete my work quickly using this system.	5.74	0.97
	05	I was able to efficiently complete my work using this system.	5.79	1.10
	06	I felt comfortable using this system.	5.82	0.99
	07	It was easy to learn to use this system.	5.90	0.94
	08	I believe I could become productive quickly using this system.	5.72	0.92
INFOQUAL	09	The system gave error messages that clearly tell me how to fix problems.	4.77	1.51
	10	Whenever I made a mistake using the system, I could recover easily and quickly.	5.31	1.51
	11	The information (such as online help, on-screen messages, and other documentation) provided with this system was clear.	5.38	1.04
	12	It was easy to find the information I needed.	5.72	1.15
	13	The information provided for the system was easy to understand.	5.69	0.95
	14	The information was effective in helping me complete the tasks and scenarios.	5.64	1.01
	15	The organization of information on the system screens was clear.	5.92	0.84
INTERQUAL	16	The interface of this system was pleasant.	5.54	1.19
	17	I liked using the interface of this system.	5.38	1.07
	18	This system has all the functions and capabilities I expect it to have.	5.59	1.09
OVERALL	19	Overall, I am satisfied with this system.	5.74	0.88

The average values for the IBM CSUQ measures are presented in Table 6. Concerning the category SYSUSE (Mean = 5.84, Median = 6.00, SD = 0.94), the results show that the participants tend to consider the system as useful. The results to the INFOQUAL category (Mean = 5.49, Median = 6.00, SD = 1.15) also suggest a good quality of the information presented on the user interface. The participants have indicated that the information provided by the system was easily understood and helpful to complete the tasks and scenarios. Nevertheless, future work will concentrate on improving the feedback provided by the system, especially when errors occur. Interface quality or INTERQUAL (Mean = 5.50, Median = 6.00, SD = 1.11) shows that the user interfaces of the platform are adapted to the end user. However, it seems that the tool requires some additional improvements, such as: (i) a simplification of the visual interface for the execution of the rehabilitation exercises, and (ii) the incorporation of a speech-based remote interaction with the application. Overall satisfaction or OVERALL (Mean = 5.74, Median = 6.00, SD = 0.88) suggests that the system is positively evaluated by the users. It can be concluded that the system usability of the current version of the platform is assessed positively by the participants, who seem to like the general organization and functionalities of the application, even if some upgrades are required.

7. Discussion

This study describes the development of a tele-rehabilitation platform to support motor recovery. Exercises designed for patients after hip arthroplasty are presented as a case study. Nevertheless, this platform is built on a modular architecture that facilitates its adaptation for any other physical rehabilitation programs (e.g., hemiparetic patients). In addition, an artificial intelligence module is integrated in the platform, in order to assess the quality of the therapeutic movements performed by the patients. Two possible methods are tested: Dynamic Time Warping and Hidden Markov Models.

First, a DTW approach was used to evaluate the motion by comparison to a reference. The experimental results show a high correlation between the assessment performed by the computer and by the health professionals. The slight discrepancy between the two evaluations has both technical and human explanations. The accuracy is affected by partial occultations of some joints inherent to the motion capture device. In addition, we observed certain inconsistences in the judgment of the therapists, which limit the reliability of the human reference.

Second, a HMM approach is tested to detect variance within movement, caused by errors or compensatory movements that may occur during the completion of the therapeutic exercise. HMMs are trained on these errors and compensatory actions. Although the setting of the experiment was controlled, the classification also included intrapersonal and interpersonal variances, as a model that classified a determined subject was merely trained with the data of the other participants. It suggests that the proposed assessment algorithm has a fair capability of generalization. A high classification accuracy of the movements is obtained by building a general model that can be applied to any subject. A real-time analysis enables us to detect four out of five faulty movements, when these errors briefly occur in the beginning, middle or end of a correct execution of the exercise. The same level of accuracy is maintained whatever the detection rate. These findings demonstrate that the HMM is an appropriate method to provide real-time feedback regarding the correctness of the rehabilitation movement performed by a patient. This approach is successfully applied on a real-time assessment of components of the movement, which are discriminated in several classes that differ on extremely subtle aspects.

Both methods, DTW and HMM, have advantages and disadvantages. It is not necessary to collect lots of data to perform an assessment based on DTW, because just a single reference is required to apply the technique. On the contrary, HMM is a probabilistic approach, in which the accuracy of the classification depends on the quantity of available data. The bigger is the dataset, the higher is the precision. This aspect is particularly relevant if you presume a difficult access to collect enough data to train the model. On the other hand, HMM is more adapted than DTW to perform a real-time evaluation, as it creates a model that can be dynamically generated and adjusted. Another advantage of utilizing HMM is the fact that it is more robust than DTW when the quantity of features to discriminate increases.

Finally, the usability of the platform is positively assessed by end users. The empirical results based on subjective perception and self-reported feedback show that the application is useful, effective, efficient, and easy to use. In addition, the evaluation of the user experience enables us to identify usability aspects that should be implemented, in order to improve the visual interface. The experiment indicates that the error messages should be as detailed as possible. Our results suggest that providing the patients with a systematic and non-ambiguous feedback is a critical aspect to ensure a perfect acceptance of a tele-rehabilitation system.

The main contribution of this manuscript is to provide a holistic description of a solution to implement a tele-rehabilitation platform that presents three advantages rarely available in other similar systems. The first is the implementation of a scalable and modular architecture to facilitate (i) the adaptation to other physical rehabilitation programs, and (ii) the evolution of the system for integrating new software (e.g., game engines) and hardware (e.g., motion capture sensor) technologies.

The second is the integration of an artificial intelligence (AI) module that assesses the quality of the movement through two possible solutions: DTW or HMM. This aspect, which is absent in comparable applications [12,33,34], is however crucial to ensure the efficiency and safety of a remote motor rehabilitation. The third is the gamification of the therapeutic exercises, in order to enhance the motivation of the patients to complete the rehabilitation program at home.

Nevertheless, the current version of the platform presents certain limitations that will be overcome in the future. The vision-based motion capture implies occultation issues that alter the accuracy of the assessment algorithms. A possible solution would be to implement a hybrid system that integrates both Kinect and inertial sensors [35]. In addition, it will be necessary to include additional features to get a more advanced discrimination of the movements assessed by a HMM approach. In particular, these features should stand for kinematic variables related to the upper part of the body, which will improve the identification of compensatory movements. In terms of evaluation of the AI algorithms, the future experimental protocols will simplify the assessment tasks of the therapists, in order to reduce the discrepancies. For instance, this assessment could be based on videos and not performed on the fly, and/or each expert could have to gauge fewer parameters simultaneously. Finally, we are aware that it is required to carry out usability tests on real patients and during the whole completion period of the rehabilitation program, as indicated in [36]. For this purpose, we plan to apply usability questionnaires specifically designed to measure the user experience with e-Health platforms, such as USEQ [36] and TUQ [37].

To conclude, we would like to highlight the fact that the application is built considering both the health professional requirements and the patient limitations. The architecture of the system is modular and flexible enough to be integrated in a global smart home. In addition, the proposed approach intends to deliver a therapeutic program as a service over the Internet. It means that the therapists can implement a personalized rehabilitation program that their patients will be able to execute anywhere through the platform. In that sense, the system promotes a smart medical environment, in which both patients and health professionals can interact remotely from home, for the former, and the medical office, for the latter; transforming the application into a ubiquitous tool to support the patient's recovery.

Author Contributions: Conceptualization, Y.R., J.L.P.M. and D.E.; methodology, Y.R., J.L.P.M. and L.L., software, K.J., L.L., Y.R. and J.L.P.M.; validation, Y.R., L.L. and J.L.P.M.; data curation, L.L., J.L.P.M. and D.E.; data analysis, Y.R., L.L., J.L.P.M. and M.G.; writing and editing, Y.R., J.L.P.M., L.L. and K.J.; project administration, Y.R.; funding acquisition, Y.R.

Funding: This research was funded by REDCEDIA, grant number CEPRA XI-2017-15.

Conflicts of Interest: The authors declare no conflict of interest.

References

1. Rybarczyk, Y.; Kleine Deters, J.; Cointe, C.; Esparza, D. Smart web-based platform to support physical rehabilitation. *Sensors* **2018**, *18*, 1344. [CrossRef] [PubMed]
2. Rybarczyk, Y.; Goncalves, M.J. WebLisling: A web-based therapeutic platform for rehabilitation of aphasic patients. *IEEE Latin Am. Trans.* **2016**, *14*, 3921–3927. [CrossRef]
3. Mani, S.; Sharma, S.; Omar, B.; Paungmali, A.; Joseph, L. Validity and reliability of Internet-based physiotherapy assessment for musculoskeletal disorders: A systematic review. *J. Telemed. Telecare* **2017**, *23*, 379–391. [CrossRef] [PubMed]
4. Rybarczyk, Y.; Kleine Deters, J.; Gonzalvo, A.; Gonzalez, M.; Villarreal, S.; Esparza, D. ePHoRt project: A web-based platform for home motor rehabilitation. In Proceedings of the 5th World Conference on Information Systems and Technologies, Madeira, Portugal, 11–13 April 2017; pp. 609–618. [CrossRef]
5. Kleine Deters, J.; Rybarczyk, Y. Hidden Markov Model approach for the assessment of tele-rehabilitation exercises. *Int. J. Artif. Intell.* **2018**, *16*, 1–19.

6. Rybarczyk, Y.; Kleine Deters, J.; Aladro Gonzalo, A.; Esparza, D.; Gonzalez, M.; Villarreal, S.; Nunes, I.L. Recognition of physiotherapeutic exercises through DTW and low-cost vision-based motion capture. In Proceedings of the 8th International Conference on Applied Human Factors and Ergonomics, Los Angeles, CA, USA, 17–21 July 2017; pp. 348–360. [CrossRef]

7. Fortino, G.; Gravina, R.A. Cloud-assisted wearable system for physical rehabilitation. In *Communications in Computer and Information Science*; Barbosa, S.D.J., Chen, P., Filipe, J., Kotenko, I., Sivalingam, K.M., Washio, T., Yuan, J., Zhou, L., Eds.; Springer: Heidelberg, Germany, 2015; Volume 515, pp. 168–182.

8. Fortino, G.; Parisi, D.; Pirrone, V.; Fatta, G.D. BodyCloud: A SaaS approach for community body sensor networks. *Future Gener. Comput. Syst.* **2014**, *35*, 62–79. [CrossRef]

9. Bonnechère, B.; Jansen, B.; Salvia, P.; Bouzahouene, H.; Omelina, L.; Moiseev, F.; Sholukha, V.; Cornelis, J.; Rooze, M.; Van Sint Jan, S. Validity and reliability of the Kinect within functional assessment activities: Comparison with standard stereophotogrammetry. *Gait Posture* **2014**, *39*, 593–598. [CrossRef] [PubMed]

10. Pedraza-Hueso, M.; Martín-Calzón, S.; Díaz-Pernas, F.J.; Martínez-Zarzuela, M. Rehabilitation using Kinect-based games and virtual reality. *Procedia Comput. Sci.* **2015**, *75*, 161–168. [CrossRef]

11. Morais, W.O.; Wickström, N. A serious computer game to assist Tai Chi training for the elderly. In Proceedings of the 1st IEEE International Conference on Serious Games and Applications for Health, Washington, DC, USA, 16–18 November 2011; pp. 1–8. [CrossRef]

12. Lin, T.Y.; Hsieh, C.H.; Der Lee, J. A kinect-based system for physical rehabilitation: Utilizing Tai Chi exercises to improve movement disorders in patients with balance ability. In Proceedings of the 7th Asia Modelling Symposium, Hong Kong, China, 23–25 July 2013; pp. 149–153. [CrossRef]

13. Hoang, T.C.; Dang, H.T.; Nguyen, V.D. Kinect-based virtual training system for rehabilitation. In Proceedings of the International Conference on System Science and Engineering, Ho Chi Minh City, Vietnam, 21–23 July 2017; pp. 53–56. [CrossRef]

14. Okada, Y.; Ogata, T.; Matsuguma, H. Component-based approach for prototyping of Tai Chi-based physical therapy game and its performance evaluations. *Comput. Entertain.* **2017**, *14*, 1–20. [CrossRef]

15. Da Gama, A.; Chaves, T.; Figueiredo, L.; Teichrieb, V. Guidance and movement correction based on therapeutic movements for motor rehabilitation support systems. In Proceedings of the 14th Symposium on Virtual and Augmented Reality, Rio de Janeiro, Brazil, 28–31 May 2012; pp. 28–31. [CrossRef]

16. Brokaw, E.B.; Lum, P.S.; Cooper, R.A.; Brewer, B.R. Using the Kinect to limit abnormal kinematics and compensation strategies during therapy with end effector robots. In Proceedings of the 2013 IEEE International Conference on Rehabilitation Robotics, Seattle, WA, USA, 24–26 June 2013; pp. 24–26. [CrossRef]

17. Zhao, W.; Reinthal, M.A.; Espy, D.D.; Luo, X. Rule-based human motion tracking for rehabilitation exercises: Realtime assessment, feedback, and guidance. *IEEE Access* **2017**, *5*, 21382–21394. [CrossRef]

18. Antón, D.; Goñi, A.; Illarramendi, A. Exercise recognition for Kinect-based telerehabilitation. *Methods Inf. Med.* **2015**, *54*, 145–155. [CrossRef] [PubMed]

19. Gal, N.; Andrei, D.; Nemes, D.I.; Nadasan, E.; Stoicu-Tivadar, V. A Kinect based intelligent e-rehabilitation system in physical therapy. *Stud. Health Technol. Inf.* **2015**, *210*, 489–493. [CrossRef]

20. López-Jaquero, V.; Rodríguez, A.C.; Teruel, M.A.; Montero, F.; Navarro, E.; Gonzalez, P. A bio-inspired model-based approach for context-aware post-WIMP tele-rehabilitation. *Sensors* **2016**, *16*, 1689. [CrossRef] [PubMed]

21. Rybarczyk, Y.; Vernay, D. Educative therapeutic tool to promote the empowerment of disabled people. *IEEE Lat. Am. Trans.* **2016**, *14*, 3410–3417. [CrossRef]

22. Jaiswal, S.; Kumar, R. *Learning Django Web Development*; O'Reilly: Sebastopol, CA, USA, 2015; ISBN 978-1783984404.

23. Riehle, D. Composite design patterns. In Proceedings of the 12th ACM SIGPLAN ACM Conference on Object-Oriented Programming, Systems, Languages, and Applications, Atlanta, GA, USA, 5–9 October 1997; pp. 218–228. [CrossRef]

24. Hillar, G.C. *Django RESTful Web Services: The Easiest Way to Build Python RESTful APIs and Web Services with Django*; Packt: Birmingham, UK, 2018; ISBN 978-1788833929.

25. Kinectron: A Realtime Peer Server for Kinect 2. Available online: https://kinectron.github.io/docs/server. html (accessed on 5 April 2018).

26. Jakobus, B. *Mastering Bootstrap 4: Master the Latest Version of Bootstrap 4 to Build Highly Customized Responsive Web Apps*; Packt: Birmingham, UK, 2018; ISBN 978-1788834902.

27. Wu, Q.; Xu, G.; Li, M.; Chen, L.; Zhang, X.; Xie, J. Human pose estimation method based on single depth image. *IET Comput. Vis.* **2018**, *12*, 919–924. [CrossRef]
28. Yamato, J.; Ohya, J.; Ishii, K. Recognizing human action in time-sequential images using Hidden Markov Model. In Proceedings of the 1992 IEEE Computer Society Conference on Computer Vision and Pattern Recognition, Champaign, IL, USA, 15–18 June 1992. [CrossRef]
29. Fiosina, J.; Fiosins, M. Resampling based modelling of individual routing preferences in a distributed traffic network. *Int. J. Artif. Intell.* **2014**, *12*, 79–103.
30. Yao, A.; Gall, J.; Fanelli, G.; Van Gool, L. Does human action recognition benefit from pose estimation? In Proceedings of the 22nd British Machine Vision Conference, Dundee, UK, 29 August–2 September 2011. [CrossRef]
31. Smyth, P. Clustering using Monte Carlo cross-validation. In Proceedings of the 2nd International Conference on Knowledge Discovery and Data Mining, Portland, OR, USA, 2–4 August 1996.
32. Lewis, J.R. IBM computer usability satisfaction questionnaires: Psychometric evaluation and instructions for use. *Int. J. Hum. Comput. Interact.* **1995**, *7*, 57–78. [CrossRef]
33. Antón, D.; Berges, I.; Bermúdez, J.; Goñi, A.; Illarramendi, A. A telerehabilitation system for the selection, evaluation and remote management of therapies. *Sensors* **2018**, *18*, 1459. [CrossRef] [PubMed]
34. Antón, D.; Kurillo, G.; Goñi, A.; Illarramendi, A.; Bajcsy, R. Real-time communication for kinect-based telerehabilitation. *Future Gener. Comput. Syst.* **2017**, *75*, 72–81. [CrossRef]
35. Gowing, M.; Ahmadi, A.; Destelle, F.; Monaghan, D.S.; O'Connor, N.E.; Moran, K. Kinect vs. low-cost inertial sensing for gesture recognition. In Proceedings of the 20th International Conference on Multimedia Modeling, Dublin, Ireland, 6–10 January 2014. [CrossRef]
36. Gil-Gómez, J.A.; Manzano-Hernández, P.; Albiol-Pérez, S.; Aula-Valero, C.; Gil-Gómez, H.; Lozano-Quilis, J.A. USEQ: A short questionnaire for satisfaction evaluation of virtual rehabilitation systems. *Sensors* **2017**, *17*, 1589. [CrossRef] [PubMed]
37. Parmanto, B.; Lewis, A.N., Jr.; Graham, K.M.; Bertolet, M.H. Development of the telehealth usability questionnaire (TUQ). *Int. J. Telerehabil.* **2016**, *8*, 3–10. [CrossRef] [PubMed]

Article

Spline Function Simulation Data Generation for Walking Motion Using Foot-Mounted Inertial Sensors

Thanh Tuan Pham and Young Soo Suh *

Electrical Engineering Department, University of Ulsan, Ulsan 44610, Korea; josephpham1194@gmail.com
* Correspondence: yssuh@ulsan.ac.kr; Tel.: +82-52-259-2196

Received: 22 October 2018; Accepted: 20 December 2018; Published: 23 December 2018

Abstract: This paper investigates the generation of simulation data for motion estimation using inertial sensors. The smoothing algorithm with waypoint-based map matching is proposed using foot-mounted inertial sensors to estimate position and attitude. The simulation data are generated using spline functions, where the estimated position and attitude are used as control points. The attitude is represented using B-spline quaternion and the position is represented by eighth-order algebraic splines. The simulation data can be generated using inertial sensors (accelerometer and gyroscope) without using any additional sensors. Through indoor experiments, two scenarios were examined include 2D walking path (rectangular) and 3D walking path (corridor and stairs) for simulation data generation. The proposed simulation data is used to evaluate the estimation performance with different parameters such as different noise levels and sampling periods.

Keywords: motion estimation; inertial sensors; simulation; spline function; Kalman filter

1. Introduction

Motion estimation using inertial sensors is one of the most important research topics that is increasingly applied in many application areas such as medical applications, sports, and entertainment [1]. Inertial measurement unit (IMU) sensors are commonly used to estimate human motion [2–5]. Inertial sensors can be used alone or combined with other sensors such as cameras [6,7] or magnetic sensors [8]. In personal navigation and healthcare applications [9–11], foot-mounted inertial sensors without using any additional sensors is a key enabling technology since it does not require any additional infrastructure. If additional sensors (other than inertial sensors) are also used, sensor fusion algorithms [12,13] can be used to obtain more accurate motion estimation.

To evaluate the accuracy of any motion estimation algorithm, it is necessary to compare the estimated value with the true value. The estimated value is usually verified through experiments with both IMU and optical motion tracker [14,15]. In [2], the Vicon optical motion capture system is used to evaluate the effectiveness of human pose estimation method and its associated sensor calibration procedure. An optical motion tracking is used as a reference to compare with motion estimation using inertial sensors in [15].

Although the experimental validation gives the ultimate proof, it is not only more convenient but also more important to work with simulation data, which is statistically much more relevant for testing and the development of algorithms. For example, the effect of gyroscope bias on the performance of an algorithm cannot be easily identified in experiments. In this case, simulation using synthesized data is more convenient since gyroscope bias can be changed arbitrarily.

In [16–18], IMU simulation data are generated using optical motion capture data for human motion estimation. In [19], IMU simulation data is generated for walking motion by approximating walking trajectory as simple sinusoidal functions. In [20–22], IMU simulation data are also generated for flight motion estimation using an artificially generated trajectory. There are many different methods to represent attitude and position simulation data. Among them, the spline function is the most popular approach [23]. The B-spline quaternion algorithm provides a general curve construction scheme that extends the spline curves [24]. Reference [25] presents an approach for attitude estimation using cumulative B-splines unit quaternion curves. Position can be represented by any spline function [23]. Usually, position data are represented using cubic spline functions. The cubic spline function gives a continuous position, velocity, and acceleration. However, the acceleration is not sufficiently smooth. This is a problem for the inertial sensor simulation data generation since the smooth accelerometer data cannot be generated. Thus, we use the eighth-order spline function for position data since it gives position data with smooth acceleration, whose jerk (third derivative) can be controlled in the optimization problem.

In this paper, we use cumulative B-spline for attitude representation and eighth-order algebraic spline for position representation. The eighth-order algebraic spline is a slightly modified version of the spline function from a previous study [26].

The aim of this paper is to obtain simulation data combining inertial sensors (accelerometer and gyroscope) and waypoint data without using any additional sensors. A computationally efficient waypoint-based map matching smoothing algorithm is proposed for position and attitude estimation from foot-mounted inertial sensors. The simulation data are generated using spline functions, where the estimated position and attitude are used as control points. This paper is an extended version of a work published in the conference paper [27], where a basic algorithm with a simple experimental result is given.

The remainder of the paper is organized as follows. Section 2 describes the smoothing algorithm with waypoint-based map matching to estimate motion for foot-mounted inertial sensors. Section 3 describes the computation of the spline function to generate simulation data. Section 4 provides the experiment results to verify the proposed method. Conclusions are given in Section 5.

2. Smoothing Algorithm with Waypoint-Based Map Matching

In this section, a smoothing algorithm is proposed to estimate the attitude, position, velocity and acceleration, which will be used to generate simulation data in Section 3.

Two coordinate frames are used in this paper: the body coordinate frame and the navigation coordinate frame. The three axes of the body coordinate frame coincide with the three axes of the IMU. The z axis of the navigation coordinate frame coincides with the local gravitational direction. The choice of the x and y axes of the navigation coordinate frame can be arbitrarily chosen. The notation $[p]_n$ ($[p]_b$) is used to denote that a vector p is represented in the navigation (body) coordinate frame.

The position is defined by $[r]_n \in R^3$, which is the origin of the body coordinate frame expressed in the navigation coordinate frame. Similarly, the velocity and the acceleration are denoted by $[v]_n \in R^3$ and $[a]_n \in R^3$, respectively. The attitude is represented using a quaternion $q \in R^4$, which represents the rotation relationship between the navigation coordinate frame and the body coordinate frame. The directional cosine matrix corresponding to quaternion q is denoted by $C(q) \in SO(3)$.

The accelerometer output $y_a \in R^3$ and the gyroscope output $y_g \in R^3$ are given by

$$y_a = C(q)\tilde{g} + a_b + n_a,$$
$$y_g = \omega + n_g,$$

(1)

where $\omega \in R^3$ is the angular velocity, $a_b \in R^3$ is the external acceleration (acceleration related to the movement, excluding the gravitational acceleration) expressed in the body coordinate frame, and $n_a \in R^3$ and $n_g \in R^3$ are sensor noises. The vector $\tilde{g}$ is the local gravitational acceleration vector. It is assumed that $\tilde{g}$ is known, which can be computed using the formula in [28]. The sensor biases are assumed to be estimated separately using calibration algorithms [29,30].

Let T denote the sampling period of a sensor. For a continuous time signal $y(t)$, the discrete value is denoted by $y_k = y(kT)$. The discrete sensor noise $n_{a,k}$ and $n_{g,k}$ are assumed to be white Gaussian sensor noises, whose covariances are given by

$$R_a = E\left\{n_{a,k}n_{a,k}^T\right\} = r_a I_3 \in R^{3\times3},$$
$$R_g = E\left\{n_{g,k}n_{g,k}^T\right\} = r_g I_3 \in R^{3\times3}. \tag{2}$$

where $r_a > 0$ and $r_g > 0$ are scalar constants.

We assume that a walking trajectory consists of straight line paths, where the angle between two adjacent paths can only take one of the following angle $\{90°, -90°, 180°\}$. An example of a walking trajectory is given in Figure 1, where there is $90°$ turn at P_2 and $-90°$ turn at P_3. Waypoints are denoted by $P_m \in R^3$ ($1 \le m \le M$), which include positions with turn events (P_2 and P_3 in Figure 1), the initial position (P_1) and the final position (P_4).

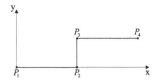

Figure 1. Example of waypoints ($P_1 \sim P_4$).

2.1. Standard Inertial Navigation Using an Indirect Kalman Filter

In this subsection, q, r, and v are estimated using a standard inertial navigation algorithm with an indirect Kalman filter [31].

The basic equations for inertial navigation are given as follows:

$$\dot{q} = \tfrac{1}{2}\Omega(\omega)q,$$
$$\dot{v}_n = a_n = C^T(q)a_b, \tag{3}$$
$$\dot{r}_n = v_n,$$

where symbol Ω is defined by

$$\Omega(\omega) = \begin{bmatrix} 0 & \omega^T \\ \omega & -[\omega\times] \end{bmatrix},$$

and $[\omega\times] \in R^{3\times3}$ denotes the skew symmetric matrix of ω:

$$[\omega\times] = \begin{bmatrix} 0 & -\omega_z & \omega_y \\ \omega_z & 0 & -\omega_x \\ -\omega_y & \omega_x & 0 \end{bmatrix}.$$

Let $\hat{q}_k$, $\hat{r}_k$ and $\hat{v}_k$ be the estimated values of q, r and v using (3), where ω and a_b are replaced by y_g and $y_a - C(\hat{q})\tilde{g}$:

$$\dot{\hat{q}} = \tfrac{1}{2}\Omega(y_g)\hat{q},$$
$$\dot{\hat{v}} = C^T(\hat{q})y_a - \tilde{g}, \tag{4}$$
$$\dot{\hat{r}} = \hat{v}.$$

Coriolis and Earth curvature effects are ignored since we use a consumer grade IMU for limited walking distances where these effects are below the IMU noise level [32].

When the initial attitude ($\hat{q}_0$) is computed, the pitch and roll angles can be computed from $y_{a,0}$. However, the yaw angle is not determined since there is no heading reference sensor such as a magnetic sensor. In the proposed algorithm, the initial yaw angle can be arbitrarily chosen since the yaw angle is automatically adjusted later (see Section 2.3).

$\bar{q}_e$, r_e and v_e denote the estimation errors in $\hat{q}$, $\hat{r}$, and $\hat{v}$, which are defined by

$$
\begin{aligned}
\bar{q}_e &\triangleq q \otimes \hat{q}_k^*, \\
r_e &\triangleq r_n - \hat{r}_k, \\
v_e &\triangleq v_n - \hat{v}_k,
\end{aligned}
\tag{5}
$$

where $\otimes$ is the quaternion multiplication and q^* denotes the quaternion conjugate of a quaternion q. Assuming that $\bar{q}_e$ is small, we can approximate $\bar{q}_e$ as follows:

$$
\bar{q}_e \approx \begin{bmatrix} 1 \\ q_e \end{bmatrix}.
\tag{6}
$$

The state of an indirect Kalman filter is defined by

$$
x \triangleq \begin{bmatrix} q_e \\ r_e \\ v_e \end{bmatrix} \in R^{9 \times 1}.
\tag{7}
$$

The state equation for the Kalman filter is given by [31]:

$$
\dot{x} = \begin{bmatrix} [-y_g \times] & 0 & 0 \\ 0 & 0 & I_3 \\ -2C(\hat{q})^T[y_a \times] & 0 & 0 \end{bmatrix} x + w
\tag{8}
$$

where the covariance of the process noise w is given by

$$
E\{ww^T\} = \begin{bmatrix} 0.25R_g & 0 & 0 \\ 0 & 0 & 0 \\ 0 & 0 & C(\hat{q})^T R_a C(\hat{q}) \end{bmatrix}.
$$

The discretized version of (8) is used in the Kalman filter as in [31].

Two measurement equations are used in the Kalman filter: the zero velocity updating (ZUPT) equation and the map matching equation.

The zero velocity updating uses the fact that there is almost periodic zero velocity intervals (when a foot is on the ground) during walking. If the following conditions are satisfied, the discrete time index k is assumed to belong to zero velocity intervals [31]:

$$
\begin{aligned}
\|y_{g,i}\| &\leq B_g, & k - \tfrac{N_g}{2} \leq i \leq k + \tfrac{N_g}{2} \\
\|y_{a,i} - y_{a,i-1}\| &\leq B_a, & k - \tfrac{N_a}{2} \leq i \leq k + \tfrac{N_a}{2}
\end{aligned}
\tag{9}
$$

where B_g, B_a, N_g and N_a are parameters for zero velocity interval detection. This zero velocity updating algorithm is not valid when a person is on a moving transportation such as an elevator. Thus, the proposed algorithm cannot be used when a person is on a moving transportation.

During the zero velocity intervals, the following measurement equation is used:

$$
0_{3 \times 1} - \hat{v}_k = \begin{bmatrix} 0_{3 \times 3} & 0_{3 \times 3} & I_3 \end{bmatrix} x_k + n_v,
\tag{10}
$$

where n_v is a fictitious measurement noise representing a Gaussian white noise with the noise covariance R_v.

The second measurement equation is from the map matching, which is used during the zero velocity intervals. From the assumption, a straight line path is parallel to either x axis or y axis. If a path is parallel to $x(y)$ axis, $y(x)$ position is constant and this can be used in the measurement equation.

Let $e_i \in R^{3\times1} (1 \le i \le 3)$ be the unit vector whose i-th element is 1 and the remaining elements are 0. Suppose a person is on the path $[P_m, P_{m+1}]$ and

$$e_j^T(P_{m+1} - P_m) = 0, \quad j = 1 \text{ or } 2. \tag{11}$$

For example, (11) is satisfied with $j = 1$ if the path is parallel to the y axis.

When (11) is satisfied with j ($j = 1$ or 2), then the map matching measurement equation is given by

$$e_j^T(P_m - \hat{r}_k) = \begin{bmatrix} 0_{1\times3} & e_j^T & 0_{1\times3} \end{bmatrix} x_k + n_{r,12}, \tag{12}$$

where $n_{r,12}$ is the horizontal position measurement noise whose noise covariance is $R_{r,12}$.

If the path is level (that is, $e_3^T(P_{m+1} - P_m) = 0$), the z axis value of r_k is almost the same in the zero velocity intervals when the foot is on the ground. In this case, the following z axis measurement equation is also used:

$$e_3^T(P_m - \hat{r}_k) = \begin{bmatrix} 0_{1\times3} & e_3^T & 0_{1\times3} \end{bmatrix} x_k + n_{r,3}, \tag{13}$$

where $n_{r,3}$ is the vertical position measurement noise whose noise covariance is $R_{r,3}$.

The proposed filtering algorithm is illustrated in Figure 2. To further reduce the estimation errors of the Kalman filter, the smoothing algorithm in [31] is applied to the Kalman filter estimated values.

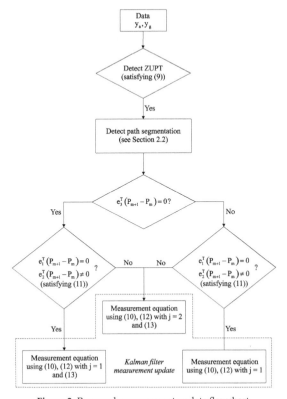

Figure 2. Proposed measurement update flowchart.

2.2. Path Identification

To apply map matching measurement Equation (12), a current path must be identified. Using the zero velocity intervals, each walking step can be easily determined. Let S_l be the discrete time index of the end of l-th zero velocity interval (see Figure 3).

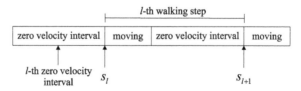

Figure 3. Walking step segmentation.

Let ψ_{S_l} be the yaw angle at the discrete time S_l and $\triangle\psi_l$ be defined by

$$\triangle\psi_l \triangleq \psi_{S_{l+1}} - \psi_{S_l}. \tag{14}$$

Please note that $\triangle\psi_l$ denotes the yaw angle change during l-th walking step.

The turning (that is, the change of a path) is detected using $\triangle\psi_l$. Suppose a current path is $[P_m, P_{m+1}]$. Then the next turning angle is determined by two vectors $P_{m+1} - P_m$ and $P_{m+2} - P_{m+1}$. For example in Figure 1, if a current path is $[P_1, P_2]$, the next turning angle is 90°. Let δ be the next turning angle. Turning is determined to occur at l-th walking step if the following condition is satisfied:

$$\left| \sum_{j=l-M_l}^{l+M_l} \triangle\psi_j - \delta \right| < \psi_{\text{th}}, \tag{15}$$

where ψ_{th} is a threshold parameter and M_l is a positive integer parameter. Equation (15) detects the turning if the summation of the yaw angle changes during $2M_l + 1$ walking steps is similar to the next expected turning angle δ. The use of parameter M_l is due to the fact that turning does not occur during a single step. Once turning is detected in (15), a current path is modified to $[P_{m+1}, P_{m+2}]$ from $[P_m, P_{m+1}]$.

2.3. Initial Yaw Angle Adjustment

The initial yaw angle is arbitrarily chosen and adjusted as follows. Suppose the first N_{first} walking steps belong to the first path $[P_1, P_2]$. Let x_l and y_l ($1 \leq l \leq N_l$) be defined by

$$\begin{bmatrix} x_l \\ y_l \end{bmatrix} = \begin{bmatrix} e_1^T \\ e_2^T \end{bmatrix} \hat{r}_{S_l}, \quad 1 \leq l \leq N_l. \tag{16}$$

The line equation representing (x_l, y_l) is computed using the following least squares optimization:

$$\min_{a,b,c} \sum_{l=1}^{N_l} \|ax_l + by_l + c\|_2^2. \tag{17}$$

The angle between the line (defined by the line equation a, b, c) and $[e_1 \ e_2]^T (P_2 - P_1)$ is computed. Using this angle, the initial yaw angle is adjusted so that the walking direction coincides with the direction dictated by the waypoints.

3. Spline Function Computation

In this section, spline function $\bar{q}(t)$ (quaternion spline) and $\bar{r}(t)$ (position spline) are computed using $\hat{q}_k$, $\hat{r}_k$ and $\hat{v}_k$ as control points.

3.1. Cumulative B-Splines Quaternion Curve

Since the quaternion spline $\bar{q}(t)$ is computed for each interval $[kT, (k+1)T)$, it is convenient to introduce $\bar{q}_k(u)$ notation, which is defined by

$$\bar{q}(t) = \bar{q}_k(u) \triangleq \bar{q}(kT + u), \ t \in [kT, (k+1)T), \ 0 \leq u < T. \tag{18}$$

To define $\bar{q}_k(u)$, $\hat{w}_k$ is defined as follows:

$$\hat{w}_k \triangleq \frac{1}{T} \log(C(\hat{q}_{k+1})C^T(\hat{q}_k)), \tag{19}$$

where the logarithm of an orthogonal matrix is defined in [33]. Please note that $\hat{w}_k$ is a constant angular velocity vector, which transform from $\hat{q}_k$ to $\hat{q}_{k+1}$.

Cumulative B-spline basis function is used to represent the quaternion spline, which is first proposed in [24] and also used in [34].

$$\bar{q}_k(u) = (\prod_{i=1}^{3} S_i(u))\hat{q}_{k-1} \tag{20}$$

where

$$S_i(u) \triangleq \exp(\frac{1}{2}\tilde{B}_i(u)\Omega(\hat{w}_{k-2+i})).$$

The cumulative basis function $\tilde{B}_i(u) \in R^3$ $(1 \leq i \leq 3)$ is defined by

$$\begin{bmatrix} \tilde{B}_1(u) \\ \tilde{B}_2(u) \\ \tilde{B}_3(u) \end{bmatrix} = D \begin{bmatrix} 1 \\ \frac{u}{T} \\ \frac{u^2}{T^2} \\ \frac{u^3}{T^3} \end{bmatrix} \tag{21}$$

where D is computed using the matrix representation of the De Boor–Cox formula [34]:

$$D = \frac{1}{6} \begin{bmatrix} 5 & 3 & -3 & 1 \\ 1 & 3 & 3 & -2 \\ 0 & 0 & 0 & 1 \end{bmatrix}.$$

To generate the gyroscope simulation data, the angular velocity spline $\bar{w}(t)$ is required. From the relationship between $\bar{q}(t)$ and $\bar{w}(t)$ [35], $\bar{w}(t)$ is given by

$$\bar{w}(t) = 2\Xi(\bar{q}(t))\mathring{q}(t) \tag{22}$$

where

$$\Xi(q) \triangleq \begin{bmatrix} -q_1 & -q_2 & -q_3 \\ q_0 & -q_3 & q_2 \\ q_3 & q_0 & -q_1 \\ -q_2 & q_1 & q_0 \end{bmatrix}.$$

The derivative of $\bar{q}(t)$ $(kT \leq t < (k+1)T)$ is given by

$$\mathring{q}(t) = \frac{d\bar{q}_k(u)}{du} = (\dot{S}_3 S_2 S_1 + S_3 \dot{S}_2 S_1 + S_3 S_2 \dot{S}_1)\hat{q}_{k-1} \tag{23}$$

where

$$\dot{S}_i = \frac{dS_i(u)}{du} = \frac{1}{2}\dot{B}_i(u)\Omega(\hat{\omega}_{k-2+i})S_i$$

$$\dot{B}(u) = \begin{bmatrix} \dot{B}_1(u) \\ \dot{B}_2(u) \\ \dot{B}_3(u) \end{bmatrix} = D \begin{bmatrix} 0 \\ \frac{1}{T} \\ \frac{2u}{T^2} \\ \frac{3u^2}{T^3} \end{bmatrix}.$$

3.2. Eighth-Order Algebraic Splines

The position $\bar{r}(t)$ is represented by eighth-order algebraic spline [26], where k-th spline segment is given by

$$\bar{r}(t) = \bar{r}_{k,m}(u) = \sum_{j=0}^{7} p_{kj,m}u^j, \quad t \in [kT, (k+1)T). \tag{24}$$

where $p_{kj,m}$ ($0 \le k \le N, 0 \le j \le 7, 1 \le m \le 3$) are the coefficients of the k-th spline segment of the m-th element of $\bar{r}_k$ (for example, $\bar{r}_{k,1}$ is the x position spline). Continuity constraints up to third derivative of $\bar{r}_{k,m}(u)$ are imposed on the coefficients.

Let $\hat{a}_k$ be the estimated value of the external acceleration in the navigation coordinate frame, which can be computed as follows (see (3))

$$\hat{a}_k = C^T(\hat{q}_k)y_{a,k} - \tilde{g}. \tag{25}$$

The coefficients $p_{kj,m}$ are chosen so that $\bar{r}(kT)$, $\dot{\bar{r}}(kT)$ and $\ddot{\bar{r}}(kT)$ are close to $\hat{r}_k$, $\hat{v}_k$ and $\hat{a}_k$. An additional constraint is also imposed to reduce the jerk term (the third derivative of $\bar{r}(t)$), which makes $\bar{r}(t)$ smooth rather than jerky. Thus, the performance index for m-th element ($1 \le m \le 3$) of $\bar{r}(t)$ is defined as follows:

$$\begin{aligned} J_m = &\alpha_1 \sum_{k=0}^{N} (\bar{r}_{k,m}(T) - \hat{r}_{k,m})^2 + \alpha_2 \sum_{k=0}^{N} (\dot{\bar{r}}_{k,m}(T) - \hat{v}_{k,m})^2 \\ &+ \alpha_3 \sum_{k=0}^{N} (\ddot{\bar{r}}_{k,m}(T) - \hat{a}_{k,m})^2 + \beta \sum_{k=0}^{N} \int_0^T (\dddot{\bar{r}}_{k,m}(t))^2 dt. \end{aligned} \tag{26}$$

This minimization of J_m can be formulated as a quadratic minimization problem of the coefficients $p_{kj,m}$ as follows:

$$\min_X J_m = X^T M_1 X + 2M_2 X + M_3 \tag{27}$$

where $M_1 \in R^{8(N-1) \times 8(N-1)}$, $M_2 \in R^{1 \times 8(N-1)}$ and $M_3 \in R$ can be computed from (26).

Although the matrix size of M_1 could be large, it is a banded matrix with a bandwidth of 7. An efficient Cholesky decomposition algorithm is available for matrices with a small bandwidth [36] and (27) can be solved efficiently.

Let $\bar{p}_{kj,m}$ be the minimization solution of (26). Then $\bar{r}$ can be computed by inserting $\bar{p}_{kj,m}$ into (24) and $\bar{v}$, $\bar{a}$ can be computed by taking the derivatives.

The weighting factors α_i ($1 \le i \le 3$) and β determine the smoothness of $\bar{r}$, $\bar{v}$ and $\bar{a}$. If β is large, we obtain smoother $\bar{r}$, $\bar{v}$ and $\bar{a}$ curves at the sacrifice of nearness to the control points $\hat{r}$, $\hat{v}$ and $\hat{a}$.

Let $\bar{y}_a$ and $\bar{y}_g$ be accelerometer and gyroscope output generated using the spline functions. These values can be generated using (1), where q, a_b, ω are replaced by $\bar{q}$, $C(\bar{q})\bar{a}$, $\bar{\omega}$ with appropriate sensor noises. An overview of the simulation data generation system is shown in Figure 4.

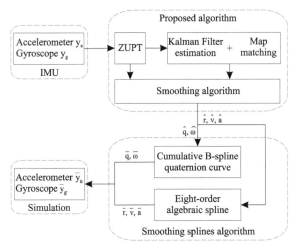

Figure 4. System overview for simulation data generation.

4. Experiment and Results

In this section, the proposed algorithm is implemented through indoor experiments. An inertial measurement unit MTi-1 of XSens was attached on the foot with the sampling frequency of 100 Hz. The parameters used in the proposed algorithm are given in Table 1.

Table 1. Parameters used in the proposed algorithm

Parameters	Values	Related Equations
r_a	0.0015	(2)
r_g	0.00001	
B_g	0.8	
B_a	1.5	(9)
N_g, N_a	30	
n_v	0.01	(10)
$n_{r,12}$	0.0004	(12)
$n_{r,3}$	0.0004	(13)
ψ_{th}	30°	(15)
$\alpha_1, \alpha_2, \alpha_3$	1	(26)
β	0.00001	

Two experiment sets of scenarios are conducted: (1) walking along a rectangular path for 2D walking data generation; and (2) walking on corridors and stairs for 3D walking data generation.

4.1. Walking along a Rectangular Path

In this experimental scenario, the subjects walked five laps at normal speed along a rectangular path with dimensions of 13.05 m by 6.15 m. The total distance for five laps on the path was 192 m.

The standard Kalman filter results without map matching are given in Figure 5. The errors in Figure 5 were primarily driven by the errors in the orientation estimation as well as run bias instability of the inertial sensors leading to the position error of 1 m. As can be seen that the maximum error was almost 2 m at the end of the walking.

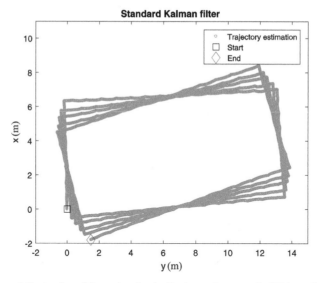

Figure 5. Rectangle walking estimation for five laps using a standard Kalman filter.

The navigation results in Figure 6 were obtained from the proposed smoothing algorithm with map matching. It can be seen that the results are improved due to the map matching.

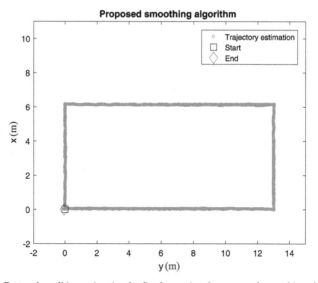

Figure 6. Rectangle walking estimation for five laps using the proposed smoothing algorithm.

The z axis spline data (for the three walking steps out of the rectangle walking steps) is given in Figure 7.

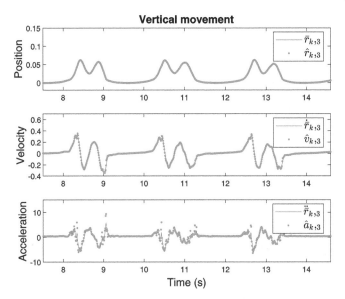

Figure 7. z axis spline functions of the rectangle walking.

4.2. Walking along a 3D Indoor Environment

In the second experimental scenario, a person walked along a 3D indoor environment corridors and stairs.

Figure 8 shows the walking along a 3D trajectory results with a waypoint P_1 is the starting point whose coordinate is $(0, 0, 0)$. The coordinates of waypoints P_1 to P_{14} are known, and the starting waypoint P_1 coincides with the end waypoint P_{14} on the projection plane. The routes are as follow: starting from the third floor waypoint P_1, walking along the floor to collect data with normal speed then turning $180°$ in P_2 and turning on the right in P_3, then going up the stairs through the floor by the same way as the other floors, finally reaching the fifth floor waypoint P_{14}, after that turning $180°$ and walking along the floor to coming back the starting waypoint P_1. The total length of the path line is approximately 562.98 m.

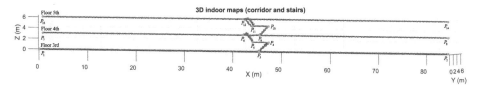

Figure 8. 3D path indoor estimation with the proposed smoothing algorithm.

4.3. Evaluation of Simulation Data Usefulness

The simulation data used to test specific performance of a certain algorithm. In this subsection, the standard Kalman filter without map matching is evaluated using the simulation data generated in Section 4.1. The algorithm is tested 1000 times with different noise values (walking motion data is the same).

Let $\bar{r}_{xy,\text{final},i}$ be the estimation error of the final position value (x and y components) of i-th simulation, where $1 \leq i \leq 1000$. Since the mean value of $\bar{r}_{xy,\text{final},i}$ is not exactly zeros, its mean value is subtracted.

The accuracy of an algorithm can be evaluated from the distribution of $\bar{r}_{xy,\text{final},i}$. Consider an ellipse whose center point is the mean of $\bar{r}_{xy,\text{final},i}$ and which include 50% of $\bar{r}_{xy,\text{final},i}$ (see Figure 9). Let a be the length of the major axis and b be the length of the minor axis. Smaller values of a and b indicate that the error of a certain algorithm is smaller.

4.3.1. Affects of Sampling Rate on the Estimation Performance

The simulation results for the final position estimated errors with different sampling rates are given in Table 2. As an example, Figure 9 shows the estimation error of the final position value with a sampling rate of 100 Hz, where an ellipse represents the boundary of 50% of probability. As can be seen, the final position errors of the different sampling rates are almost the same except for the result with a sampling rate of 50 Hz. This simulation result suggests that the sampling rate is smaller than 100 Hz is not desirable. Also, there is no apparent benefit using the sampling rate higher than 100 Hz.

Table 2. Final position errors with different sampling rates.

Sampling Rate	Mean of $\bar{r}_{xy,\text{final}}$ (m)		Radius (m)	
	$\bar{x}_{\text{final}}$	$\bar{y}_{\text{final}}$	a	b
50 Hz	−1.5217	−0.5428	0.7605	0.0215
100 Hz	0.6639	0.4745	0.0554	0.0034
150 Hz	0.6955	0.4558	0.0594	0.0032
200 Hz	0.7156	0.4520	0.0582	0.0042

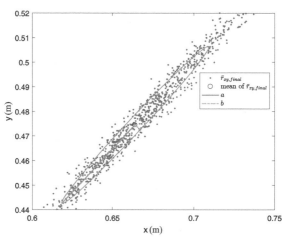

Figure 9. Estimation error of the final position value with a sampling rate 100 Hz [ellipse with 50% of probability radius].

4.3.2. Gyroscope Bias Effect

The simulation results for the final position estimated errors with different gyroscope bias are given in Table 3. As can be seen, the final position errors change significantly when the gyroscope bias becomes to change larger.

Table 3. Final position errors with different gyroscope bias.

r_g	Mean of $\bar{r}_{xy,\text{final}}$ (m)		Radius (m)	
	$\bar{x}_{\text{final}}$	$\bar{y}_{\text{final}}$	a	b
0	0.7023	0.6122	0.133	0.0226
0.00001	0.6568	0.4696	0.0595	0.0035
0.0001	−0.2038	−0.0280	0.5952	0.0309
0.001	−6.3768	0.5568	3.5123	1.0306

5. Conclusions

In this paper, simulation data is generated for walking motion estimation using inertial sensors. The first step to generate simulation data is to perform a specific motion, which you want to estimate. The attitude and position are computed from inertial sensors data using a smoothing algorithm. The spline functions are generated using the smoother estimated values as control points. B-spline function is used for the attitude quaternion, and eighth-order algebraic spline function is used for the position.

The spline simulation data generated from the proposed algorithm can be used to test a new motion estimation algorithm by easily changing the parameters such as noise covariance, sampling rate and bias terms.

The shape of generated spline function depends on the weighting factors, which control the constraint on the jerk term. It is one of future research topic to investigate how to choose the optimal weighting factors, which give the most realistic simulation data.

Author Contributions: T.T.P. and Y.S.S. conceived and designed this study. T.T.P. performed the experiments and wrote the paper. Y.S.S. reviewed and edited the manuscript.

Funding: This work was supported by the 2018 Research Fund of University of Ulsan.

Conflicts of Interest: The authors declare no conflict of interest.

References

1. Zhou, H.; Hu, H. Human motion tracking for rehabilitation—A survey. *Biomed. Signal Process. Control* **2008**, *3*, 1–18.10.1016/j.bspc.2007.09.001. [CrossRef]
2. Tao, Y.; Hu, H.; Zhou, H. Integration of vision and inertial sensors for 3D arm motion tracking in home-based rehabilitation. *Int. J. Robot. Res.* **2007**, *26*, 607–624.10.1177/0278364907079278. [CrossRef]
3. Raiff, B.R.; Karataş, Ç.; McClure, E.A.; Pompili, D.; Walls, T.A. Laboratory validation of inertial body sensors to detect cigarette smoking arm movements. *Electronics* **2014**, *3*, 87–110.10.3390/electronics3010087. [CrossRef] [PubMed]
4. Fang, T.H.; Park, S.H.; Seo, K.; Park, S.G. Attitude determination algorithm using state estimation including lever arms between center of gravity and IMU. *Int. J. Control Autom. Syst.* **2016**, *14*, 1511–1519.10.1007/s12555-015-0251-4. [CrossRef]
5. Ahmed, H.; Tahir, M. Improving the accuracy of human body orientation estimation with wearable IMU sensors. *IEEE Trans. Instrum. Meas.* **2017**, *66*, 535–542.10.1109/TIM.2016.2642658. [CrossRef]
6. Suh, Y.S.; Phuong, N.H.Q.; Kang, H.J. Distance estimation using inertial sensor and vision. *Int. J. Control Autom. Syst.* **2013**, *11*, 211–215.10.1007/s12555-011-9205-7. [CrossRef]
7. Erdem, A.T.; Ercan, A.Ö. Fusing inertial sensor data in an extended Kalman filter for 3D camera tracking. *IEEE Trans. Image Process.* **2015**, *24*, 538–548.10.1109/TIP.2014.2380176. [CrossRef] [PubMed]
8. Zhang, Z.; Meng, X. Use of an inertial/magnetic sensor module for pedestrian tracking during normal walking. *IEEE Trans. Instrum. Meas.* **2015**, *64*, 776–783.10.1109/TIM.2014.2349211. [CrossRef]
9. Ascher, C.; Kessler, C.; Maier, A.; Crocoll, P.; Trommer, G. New pedestrian trajectory simulator to study innovative yaw angle constraints. In Proceedings of the 23rd International Technical Meeting of the Satellite Division of the Institute of Navigation (ION GNSS 2010), Portland, OR, USA, 21–24 September 2010; pp. 504–510.

10. Jiménez, A.R.; Seco, F.; Prieto, J.C.; Guevara, J. Indoor pedestrian navigation using an INS/EKF framework for yaw drift reduction and a foot-mounted IMU. In Proceedings of the 7th Workshop on Positioning, Navigation and Communication, Dresden, Germany, 11–12 March 2010; pp. 135–143.10.1109/WPNC.2010.5649300. [CrossRef]

11. Fourati, H. Heterogeneous data fusion algorithm for pedestrian navigation via foot-mounted inertial measurement unit and complementary filter. *IEEE Trans. Instrum. Meas.* **2015**, *64*, 221–229.10.1109/TIM.2014.2335912. [CrossRef]

12. Rodger, J.A. Toward reducing failure risk in an integrated vehicle health maintenance system: A fuzzy multi-sensor data fusion Kalman filter approach for IVHMS. *Expert Syst. Appl.* **2012**, *39*, 9821–9836. [CrossRef]

13. He, C.; Kazanzides, P.; Sen, H.T.; Kim, S.; Liu, Y. An Inertial and Optical Sensor Fusion Approach for Six Degree-of-Freedom Pose Estimation. *Sensors* **2015**, *15*, 16448–16465.10.3390/s150716448. [CrossRef] [PubMed]

14. Kim, A.; Golnaraghi, M.F. Initial calibration of an inertial measurement unit using an optical position tracking system. In Proceedings of the PLANS 2004. Position Location and Navigation Symposium (IEEE Cat. No.04CH37556), Monterey, CA, USA, 26–29 April 2004; pp. 96–101.10.1109/PLANS.2004.1308980. [CrossRef]

15. Enayati, N.; Momi, E.D.; Ferrigno, G. A quaternion-based unscented Kalman filter for robust optical/inertial motion tracking in computer-assisted surgery. *IEEE Trans. Instrum. Meas.* **2015**, *64*, 2291–2301.10.1109/TIM.2015.2390832. [CrossRef]

16. Karlsson, P.; Lo, B.; Yang, G.Z. Inertial sensing simulations using modified motion capture data. In Proceedings of the 11th International Conference on Wearable and Implantable Body Sensor Networks (BSN 2014), ETH Zurich, Switzerland, 16–19 June 2014.

17. Young, A.D.; Ling, M.J.; Arvind, D.K. IMUSim: A simulation environment for inertial sensing algorithm design and evaluation. In Proceedings of the 10th ACM/IEEE International Conference on Information Processing in Sensor Networks, Chicago, IL, USA, 12–14 April 2011; pp. 199–210.

18. Ligorio, G.; Sabatini, A.M. A simulation environment for benchmarking sensor fusion-based pose estimators. *Sensors* **2015**, *15*, 32031–32044.10.3390/s151229903. [CrossRef] [PubMed]

19. Zampella, F.J.; Jiménez, A.R.; Seco, F.; Prieto, J.C.; Guevara, J.I. Simulation of foot-mounted IMU signals for the evaluation of PDR algorithms. In Proceedings of the 2011 International Conference on Indoor Positioning and Indoor Navigation, Guimaraes, Portugal, 21–23 September 2011; pp. 1–7.10.1109/IPIN.2011.6071930. [CrossRef]

20. Parés, M.; Rosales, J.; Colomina, I. *Yet Another IMU Simulator: Validation and Applications*; EuroCow: Castelldefels, Spain, 2008; Volume 30.

21. Zhang, W.; Ghogho, M.; Yuan, B. Mathematical model and matlab simulation of strapdown inertial navigation system. *Model. Simul. Eng.* **2012**, *2012*, 264537.10.1155/2012/264537. [CrossRef]

22. Parés, M.E.; Navarro, J.A.; Colomina, I. On the generation of realistic simulated inertial measurements. In Proceedings of the 2015 DGON Inertial Sensors and Systems Symposium (ISS), Karlsruhe, Germany, 22–23 September 2015; pp. 1–15.10.1109/InertialSensors.2015.7314268. [CrossRef]

23. Schumaker, L. *Spline Functions: Basic Theory*, 3 ed.; Cambridge Mathematical Library, Cambridge University Press: Cambridge, UK , 2007; doi:10.1017/CBO9780511618994.

24. Kim, M.J.; Kim, M.S.; Shin, S.Y. A general construction scheme for unit quaternion curves with simple high order derivatives. In Proceedings of the 22nd Annual Conference on Computer Graphics and Interactive Techniques, Los Angeles, CA, USA, 6–11 August 1995; ACM: New York, NY, USA, 1995; pp. 369–376.10.1145/218380.218486. [CrossRef]

25. Sommer, H.; Forbes, J.R.; Siegwart, R.; Furgale, P. Continuous-time estimation of attitude using B-Splines on Lie groups. *J. Guid. Control Dyn.* **2016**, *39*, 242–261.10.2514/1.G001149. [CrossRef]

26. Simon, D. Data smoothing and interpolation using eighth-order algebraic splines. *IEEE Trans. Signal Process.* **2004**, *52*, 1136–1144.10.1109/TSP.2004.823489. [CrossRef]

27. Pham, T.T.; Suh, Y.S. Spline function simulation data generation for inertial sensor-based motion estimation. In Proceedings of the 2018 57th Annual Conference of the Society of Instrument and Control Engineers of Japan (SICE), Nara, Japan, 11–14 September 2018; pp. 1231–1234.

28. Pavlis, N.K.; Holmes, S.A.; Kenyon, S.C.; Factor, J.K. The development and evaluation of the Earth Gravitational Model 2008 (EGM2008). *J. Geophys. Res. Solid Earth* **2012**, *117*. [CrossRef]

29. Metni, N.; Pflimlin, J.M.; Hamel, T.; Souères, P. Attitude and gyro bias estimation for a VTOL UAV. *Control Eng. Pract.* **2006**, *14*, 1511–1520.10.1016/j.conengprac.2006.02.015. [CrossRef]

30. Hwangbo, M.; Kanade, T. Factorization-based calibration method for MEMS inertial measurement unit. In Proceedings of the 2008 IEEE International Conference on Robotics and Automation, Pasadena, CA, USA, 19–23 May 2008; pp. 1306–1311.10.1109/ROBOT.2008.4543384. [CrossRef]

31. Suh, Y.S. Inertial sensor-based smoother for gait analysis. *Sensors* **2014**, *14*, 24338–24357.10.3390/s141224338. [CrossRef]

32. Placer, M.; Kovačič, S. Enhancing indoor inertial pedestrian navigation using a shoe-worn marker. *Sensors* **2013**, *13*, 9836–9859. [CrossRef]

33. Gallier, J.; Xu, D. Computing exponential of skew-symmetric matrices and logarithms of orthogonal matrices. *Int. J. Robot. Autom.* **2002**, *17*, 1–11.

34. Patron-Perez, A.; Lovegrove, S.; Sibley, G. A spline-based trajectory representation for sensor fusion and rolling shutter cameras. *Int. J. Comput. Vis.* **2015**, *113*, 208–219. [CrossRef]

35. Markley, F.L.; Crassidis, J.L. *Fundamentals of Spacecraft Attitude Determination and Control*; Springer: New York, NY, USA, 2014.

36. Golub, G.H.; Van Loan, C.F. *Matrix Computations*; Johns Hopkins University Press: Baltimore, MD, USA, 1983.

Article

Data-Adaptive Coherent Demodulator for High Dynamics Pulse-Wave Ultrasound Applications

Stefano Ricci * and Valentino Meacci

Information Engineering Department (DINFO), University of Florence, Florence 50139, Italy;
valentino.meacci@unifi.it
* Correspondence: stefano.ricci@unifi.it

Received: 29 October 2018; Accepted: 13 December 2018; Published: 14 December 2018

Abstract: Pulse-Wave Doppler (PWD) ultrasound has been applied to the detection of blood flow for a long time; recently the same method was also proven effective in the monitoring of industrial fluids and suspensions flowing in pipes. In a PWD investigation, bursts of ultrasounds at 0.5–10 MHz are periodically transmitted in the medium under test. The received signal is amplified, sampled at tens of MHz, and digitally processed in a Field Programmable Gate Array (FPGA). First processing step is a coherent demodulation. Unfortunately, the weak echoes reflected from the fluid particles are received together with the echoes from the high-reflective pipe walls, whose amplitude can be 30–40 dB higher. This represents a challenge for the input dynamics of the system and the demodulator, which should clearly detect the weak fluid signal while not saturating at the pipe wall components. In this paper, a numerical demodulator architecture is presented capable of auto-tuning its internal dynamics to adapt to the feature of the actual input signal. The proposed demodulator is integrated into a system for the detection of the velocity profile of fluids flowing in pipes. Simulations and experiments with the system connected to a flow-rig show that the data-adaptive demodulator produces a noise reduction of at least of 20 dB with respect to different approaches, and recovers a correct velocity profile even when the input data are sampled at 8 bits only instead of the typical 12–16 bits.

Keywords: Cascaded-Integrator-Comb (CIC) filter; FPGA; fixed point math; data adaptive demodulator

1. Introduction

The velocity of blood flowing in an artery can be investigated by detecting the Doppler frequency shift that the moving particles produce on the energy pulses of 0.5–10 MHz periodically transmitted in the medium. This is a technique normally exploited by biomedical echographs for echo-Doppler exams [1]. Modern Pulse-Wave Doppler (PWD) electronics systems (including most of the clinical echographs) are nowadays based on the numerical approach for data processing. In these systems, the signal is converted to the digital domain as near as possible to the signal source, i.e., directly at the receiver front-end [2–5], while the analog conditioning is maintained at a minimum. This trend is common to most modern electronics [6,7]. The availability of relatively economic high-speed Analog-to-Digital (AD) converters working at several hundreds of MHz, and digital devices like Field Programmable Gate Arrays (FPGAs) [8] capable of in-line processing the high amount of data produced by the AD converters, foster the full-digital approach. In a PWD system, after the AD conversion, the signal is processed through coherent demodulation [9]. In the digital approach, a perfect match of the in-phase (I) and quadrature (Q) channels is easily achieved, with no need for compensation [10]. After demodulation, the signal is further processed through spectral analysis to detect the Doppler shift and, finally, the fluid velocity [1].

Fostered by the successful application in clinical echographs, the Doppler velocimetry [11] has been applied in detecting the velocity profile of industrial fluids flowing in pipes. The final application ranges from the accurate volume flow monitoring to the in-line rheological characterization of the fluids [12,13]. In industrial applications, the weak echoes produced by the fluid are acquired together with the strong reflections generated by the interface between the pipe wall and the fluid. This problem is similar to that present in a biomedical application with respect to blood and the vessel wall [14]. The pipe echoes are typically 30–40 dB stronger than the fluids', and this ratio can be even higher for special ultrasound transducers that investigate the fluid through the steel pipe surface [15,16]. This technique, which avoids cutting the pipe steel for creating an access "window", is employed in the food or pharmaceutical industries [17] where windows are not usable due to hygienic constraints.

The simultaneous presence of the high echo from the wall and the weak signal from flow imposes severe constraints to the dynamics of the processing chain in the PWD system. Moreover, the correct detection of both signals is necessary for assessing the Wall Shear Rate. Wall Shear Rate represents the velocity gradient in the radial direction evaluated at the wall position. It is a parameter widely used in rheology and in biomedical application [18].

Further challenges are imposed by the industrial environment: The PWD system is supposed to operate autonomously or with minimum intervention of operators. The system should be as robust as possible at the different conditions that can arise, for example, from the use of fluids with different ultrasound attenuation. In summary, the demodulator should not saturate at the high amplitude signal from the pipe, it should feature high dynamics, and should work in different conditions. The architecture of the demodulator should be carefully designed to accommodate these constraints.

In this paper, we present a coherent demodulator designed for high dynamics and suitable to be efficiently integrated into FPGA [19]. It is based on a modified Cascaded-Integrator-Comb (CIC) filter architecture [20]. The CIC, employing no multipliers but adders only, is attractive for FPGA implementation [21]. The proposed architecture includes barrel-shifters in the strategic positions where the dynamics of data bus-widths must be reduced. The barrel-shifters scale-down the bus-width by translating the most suitable section of the original bus, so that the resulting signal is maintained below but near the saturation. The barrel-shifter settings are automatically selected by a simple and quick procedure that occurs immediately before the PWD measurement. This procedure is based on the analysis of the actual data stream, therefore the demodulator is "data-adaptive" since its internal dynamics settings depend on the data to be processed [22].

The proposed data-adaptive demodulator was implemented in a PWD ultrasound system designed for the detection of the velocity profile of fluids moving in industrial pipes [23], whose final aim is the rheological characterization of industrial fluids [24]. The performance of the proposed demodulator was compared to the performance attainable by non-data adaptive approaches in simulation and experiments on flow-rig. Results show that the data-adaptive approach outperforms the other methods in the presence of high pipe wall echoes and for signals with reduced input dynamics.

This paper is organized as follows: Section 2 clarifies the processing chain of the PWD Doppler signal and presents the basics of the CIC filter architecture; Section 3 describes the proposed method, details the filter architecture, reports the procedure for the management of the dynamics in the filter stages; in Section 4 the error produced by the fixed-point numerical representation is evaluated and it is shown how the error affects the detection of the velocity profiles in fluids; Section 5 discusses and concludes the work.

2. Background and Motivation

2.1. Pulse Wave Signals in Industrial Echo-Doppler Applications and Their Processing

In PWD measurements a burst of ultrasounds with a central frequency F_T is transmitted in the medium to be investigated every Pulse Repetition Interval (PRI) through a suitable transducer [1]. The ultrasonic burst travels in the medium at velocity c, and when it encounters a scatter, part of its energy is reflected towards the transducer. If the scatter moves at velocity v, the echoes from subsequent transmissions are returned from slightly different positions. Thus, they are affected by a phase-shift. The echo signal sampled at the same distance from the transducer and from subsequent pulses presents a phase variation that corresponds to the frequency f_d described by the Doppler equation [1]:

$$f_d = 2\frac{v}{c} \cdot F_T \cdot cos(\theta) \tag{1}$$

where θ is the angle between the directions of the ultrasound wave and the scatter velocity, and the factor 2 in front of the formula accounts for the forth-back path the sound travels between the transducer and the target. Figure 1a reports an example of the signal acquired at 100 Ms/s, 16 bits resolution, from a fluid moving in an 8 mm diameter pipe and investigated with 5-cycle, 6 MHz ultrasound bursts. The 2 strong echoes located at 5 μs and 16 μs are the reflections of the static pipe walls, while the weak signal in-between, barely discernible from noise, is the echo of the moving fluid. In this example, the fluid signal is 27 dB below the pipe echoes. As the pipe is relatively still with respect to the transducer, the pipe echoes are stationary or quasi-stationary in the PRI sequence, at least for a temporal interval of several minutes. This is an important feature that will be exploited later to optimize the data-adaptive strategy (See Section 3.2).

The received signal feeds a coherent demodulator that removes the carrier frequency F_T. For example, Figure 1b reports in blue and red the I/Q components produced after coherent demodulation of the signal shown in Figure 1a.

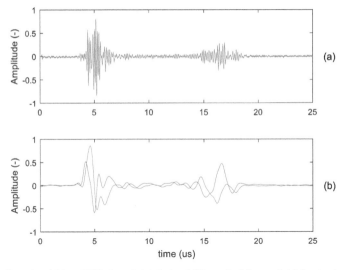

Figure 1. Raw signal (**a**) and I/Q demodulated signal (**b**) acquired from a fluid flowing in an 8 mm diameter pipe investigated with 6 MHz bursts. The strong echoes visible at 5 μs and 16 us are the reflections of the pipe walls; the useful signal of the moving fluid is barely visible in-between the pipe echoes.

As stated before, the acquisition system, and in particular the analog front-end, the AD converter, and the first step of the numerical data processing chain should accommodate the high signal from the wall and, simultaneously, the low echoes from the fluid. If the dynamics management of the demodulator is not appropriate, the low useful signal fades below the mathematical noise generated by the internal data truncations. This makes the demodulator a critical element in this application.

After demodulation, the I/Q components are processed through spectral estimation to detect f_d. The spectral analysis is performed through the efficient Fast Fourier Transform (FFT) [25–27] or more sophisticated adaptive estimators [28–30]. The demodulated ultrasound echoes are typically organized in the memory of the processing system along the columns of a matrix. The spectral analysis correlates the signal sampled at the same depth, i.e., proceeding along the rows of such a matrix and producing the power spectra matrix. The latter, color-coded, represents an intuitive picture of the flow profile in the pipe. Its rows report the Doppler shifts, which are proportional to the flow velocity through Equation (1); the columns report the depths inside the pipe. Some examples of spectral matrices are reported later in the experimental section of this paper.

2.2. Coherent Demodulator and CIC Filter Basics

The coherent demodulation [9] is typically obtained by multiplying the input signal $s_i(t)$ with two sinusoids of frequency F_T, affected by a 90° phase difference. In PWD applications the frequency F_T typically matches the transmission carrier. Each multiplier is followed by a low-pass filter that eliminates the spectral replica generated by the multiplication. The filtered signals, $I(t)$ and $Q(t)$, represent the phase and quadrature components of the complex output.

The two low-pass filters, implemented in FPGA, process the input signal at the AD converter rate, which can be up to 100 Ms/s. In this condition, the CIC architecture [20] has clear implementation advantages with respect to the standard Finite Impulse Response (FIR) filter [9]. With reference to the Z-domain [9], the basic CIC filter unit is a single integrator-comb (IC) cell, that can be realized as depicted in the graph reported in Figure 2a, where Z^{-i} represents an i-position delay. Basically, the integrator accumulates all of the input samples, while the comb removes from the accumulation the sample delayed of K-positions. The result is the summation of the latest K-samples. The IC cell is described with the following time-discrete equation, corresponding to the Z-domain transfer function $H(Z)$:

$$y(n) = y(n-1) + x(n) - x(n-K) \Leftrightarrow H(Z) = \frac{Y(Z)}{X(Z)} = \frac{1 - Z^{-K}}{1 - Z^{-1}} \qquad (2)$$

From Equation (2) it is apparent that the filter cell features a low-pass behavior with transmission zeroes in $1 - Z^{-K} = 0$, i.e., where the normalized frequency f_N is i/K, with I = 1,2,3, etc. The side lobes have an amplitude of -13 dB. An example of the cell filter mask is reported in Figure 3b for a cut-off normalized frequency of $F_L = 0.04$, obtained with K = 15.

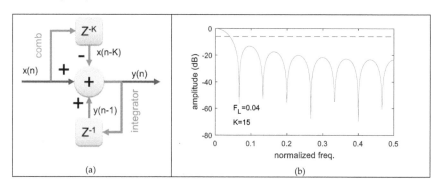

(a)   (b)

Figure 2. (a) Integrated-comb (IC) cell of cascaded-IC (CIC) filter and (b) an example of frequency mask obtained for K = 15, which corresponds to normalized cut-off frequency $F_L = 0.04$. Horizontal dashed line represents the -6 dB level.

In order to overcome the limited performance attainable by a single cell, the decimator CIC filter is normally based on several cells. It is typically realized by separating the integrator and the comb of the single IC cell and rearranging the sequence by cascading several integrators/combs separated by a decimator. The graph of the filter is reported in Figure 3a.

An example of the frequency mask referred to the normalized input frequency, i.e., before applying the spectrum folding due to the decimation, is shown in Figure 3b. For a better comparison, the cut-off frequency is the same as the previous example, i.e., $F_L = 0.04$, now obtained with $D \cdot K = 8$. The transfer function is:

$$H(Z) = \frac{(1 - Z^{-DK})^N}{(1 - Z^{-1})^N} \qquad (3)$$

As demonstrated in reference [20], the filter mathematics should allow a word-growth that corresponds to the gain of the filter, i.e., $(D \cdot K)^N$. In other words, if n is the number of bits used in input to the filter, all of the filter calculations and delay registers should work with a number of bits of:

$$m = n + \text{ceil}[N \cdot \log_2(D \cdot K)] \qquad (4)$$

where ceil(x) is the nearest integer higher than x. For example, the resources for a 4-section complex CIC with $K = 64$, $D = 16$ and input data at $n = 28$ bits include 8 adders at 54 bits and $64 \cdot 4 \cdot 54 = 13824$ bits of memory employed by the delay registers. Although this architecture can be realized in modern FPGA, it is onerous. In fact, the adders of the integrator sections work at the front-end clock frequency that can reach hundreds of MHz. Hogenauer in reference [20] describes how the number of bits can be safely reduced by truncating the least-significant part of the word. However, the method depends on the specific filter parameters (like K, D, F_L, etc.) and is not suitable for a programmable CIC whose FPGA architecture should work with different parameter sets.

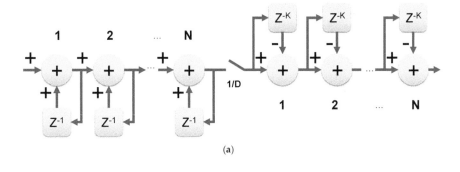

(a)

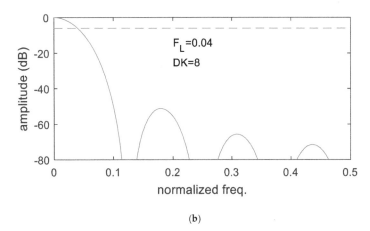

(b)

Figure 3. (a) 4-cell CIC filter and (b) an example of filter masks with DK = 8 for cut-off frequency $F_L = 0.04$. Horizontal dashed line represents the −6 dB level.

2.3. Demodulator Desired Features

The target for the numerical demodulator is the detection of the velocity profiles of fluids flowing in industrial pipes. In general, the demodulator includes the multiplication section and the following filter. However, in practice, the multiplication section is almost ideal and not critical, and all of the complexity resides in the filter. The filter should feature:

- Cut-off frequency programmable in a wide range of frequencies;
- Input dynamic range sufficient for accommodating both the strong pipe echoes and weak fluid signal;
- Low mathematical noise;
- Reasonable FPGA resource utilization;
- Up to 100 MHz working frequency.

3. Methods

3.1. Modified-CIC Filter Aarchitecture

In order to face the aforementioned challenges, in this work, we implemented a slightly different CIC filter architecture, as reported in Figure 4. The filter employs 4 single IC cells numbered C_1–C_4, which include both the integrator and the comb, alternated to 4 decimators. At the output of each cell, a barrel shifter is added. The "Settings Manager" block sets the $K_{0\text{-}3}$ and $D_{1\text{-}4}$ values which establish the mask filter shape; while the "Dynamics Manager" block monitors the data amplitude at every cell output and sets the barrel-shifter according to a control strategy that is detailed in the next section. The transfer function of the modified filter, referred to the input frequency, is:

$$H(z) = \frac{1 - z^{-K_0}}{1 - z^{-1}} \cdot \frac{1 - z^{-K_1 D_1}}{1 - z^{-D_1}} \cdot \frac{1 - z^{-K_2 D_1 D_2}}{1 - z^{-D_1 D_2}} \cdot \frac{1 - z^{-K_3 D_1 D_2 D_3}}{1 - z^{-D_1 D_2 D_3}} \tag{5}$$

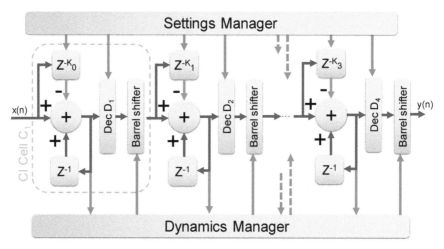

Figure 4. Modified CIC architecture based on Combo-Integrator sections interconnected by a barrel-shifter and a decimator. A dynamics manager monitors the dynamics in output of every section and operates the barrel-shifters.

An example of a filter mask is reported in Figure 5. It is obtained with $K_0 = 9$, $K_1 = 5$, $K_2 = 10$, $K_3 = 3$, $D_1 = 1$, $D_2 = 1$, $D_3 = 2$, $D_4 = 1$. The normalized cut-off frequency is $F_L = 0.04$ and it can be compared with the corresponding filter mask shown in Figure 3b produced by the standard CIC with 4 cells and B·K = 8. Both filters achieve an attenuation higher than 50 dB outside the main lobes.

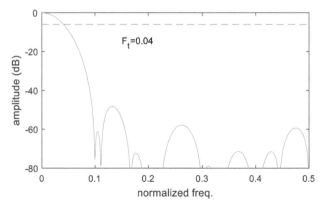

Figure 5. Filter mask obtained by the CIC architecture of Figure 6 with $K_0 = 9$, $K_1 = 5$, $K_2 = 10$, $K_3 = 3$, $D_1 = 1$, $D_2 = 1$, $D_3 = 2$, $D_4 = 1$. The cut-off normalized frequency is $F_L = 0.04$. Horizontal dashed line represents the –6 dB level.

3.2. Dynamics Management

The dynamics of the filter is one of the key-points for this application. The dynamics management is performed by setting the positions of the barrel-shifters inserted after each IC cell. The goal is to optimize the signal dynamics before the reduction of the bus-width operated on the output of each IC cell. This optimization is in charge of the "Dynamics Manager" block, which can operate according to the 3 different strategies described below. Although the data-adaptive is clearly the approach that grants the best result, coefficient-adaptive and non-adaptive approaches are described as well because they are typically employed in standard CIC and are used in this work for comparison. The strategies are:

(a) Non-adaptive

The most significant bits of the accumulator are selected in output. This is the simplest strategy, and the barrel shifters can be totally removed to save resources in the FPGA. However, bad performance is expected.

(b) Coefficient-adaptive

The barrel shifter position is selected according to the number of accumulations K programmed in the IC cell, i.e., the DC gain of the cell. The maximum word-growth for each cell in bit is ceil(log2(K)). The barrel-shifter is set to accommodate this growth regardless of the dynamics of the actual input data.

(c) Data-adaptive

The barrel-shifters are positioned to accommodate the effective dynamics of the data that are processed. However, the barrel-shifter positions must not change during the PWD measurement session in order to avoid gain steps. Fortunately, the dynamics of the input signal can be considered constant (see Section 2.1) during the duration of a measurement session (typically up to a few minutes). A quick training session was added before the measurement session. First of all the "Settings Manager" block sets the filter parameters (K_i and D_i) to establish the filter mask, gain, etc. Then the training session starts. During the first 10 PRIs, the "Dynamics manager" block monitors the data amplitude at the output of the first IC cell, i.e., C_1, and saves the maximum value. The "Dynamics manager" block uses the read value to tune the first barrel-shifter at the output of C_1. Then, the next 10 PRIs are acquired, and now the "Dynamics manager" block observes the data out of C_2, saves the maximum amplitude, and sets the second barrel-shifter. The procedure is repeated in sequence for C_3 and C_4 and, after 40 PRIs all the barrel-shifters are set for optimal performance. These first PRIs, corrupted by gain steps, are not suitable for Doppler analysis and thus are discarded, but the following are acquired and processed without even stopping the PRIs sequence between the training and acquisition sessions. In a typical set-up, a single PRI lasts about 100–1000 µs, while a complete Doppler measurement involves the acquisition and processing of several thousands of PRIs. Thus, the training session takes no more than 0.1 s of the several hundreds of second that take the whole measurement. The delay due to the filter training is negligible and not perceivable by the final user.

For reader convenience the training procedure is summarized below:

1)   "Setting Manager" block program K_0, K_1, K_2, K_3, and D_1, D_2, D_3, D_4
2)   Repeat for IC_i cells I = 1 to 4:

    a.   Detect the maximum data amplitude on 10 PRIs, M=max(abs(Data))
    b.   Calculate the bits necessary to represent data: J=ceil(log2(M))+1
    c.   Set the shifter so that J is the most significant bit
    d.   Discard the PRIs used for training

3)   Start normal data acquisition and processing

3.3. FPGA Implementation

The demodulator with the modified-CIC architecture was implemented in an FPGA of the Cyclone V family (Intel/Altera, San Jose, CA). The architecture of the single IC cell is detailed in Figure 6. The IC cell is designed to accommodate the worst case of K_i = 64, although the cell can be set for a lower K_i value. The input data bus of width BI_i bits feeds a First Input First Output (FIFO) memory and an adder that constitutes the accumulator together with the following register. The delay of K-sample is obtained by generating with the suitable clock-delay the "write" and "read" commands of the FIFO memory that holds the data stream. The adder sums up the input data to the accumulator register value and subtracts the delayed samples coming from the FIFO.

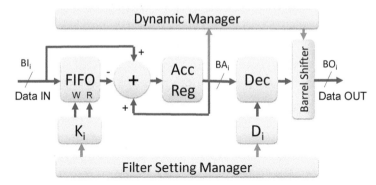

Figure 6. Details of the IC cell as implemented in the field programmable gate array (FPGA).

The FIFO is sized for holding, in the worst case, $64 \cdot BI_i$ bits of input data. An integration factor of K corresponds to a maximum gain of the same value K. The maximum data word-growth is 6 bits. Thus, the adder and the accumulation register work with a bit-width of:

$$BA_i = BI_i + 6 \tag{6}$$

The output of the accumulator is decimated by a programmable factor D_i.

In each stage of the filter the IC_i cell is designed to reduce the input-to-output bus width of 3 bits, i.e.,:

$$BO_i = BI_i - 3 \tag{7}$$

where BO_i is the bus-width in output. The combination of Equations (6) and (7) produces:

$$BO_i = BA_i - 9 \tag{8}$$

Thus, a barrel-shifter with 10 positions covers all of the possible shifts between the accumulator and the output bus. For reader convenience, Figure 7 summarizes the relation among the accumulator, the output bus, and the possible barrel-shifter positions for the three dynamics management strategies reported in Section 3.2.

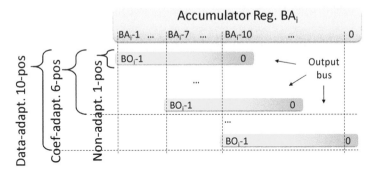

Figure 7. Barrel-shifter positions for the three different dynamics management strategies. The accumulator of the cell C_i features BA_i bits numbered from $BA_i -1$ to 0. The output bus features BO_i bits numbered from $BO_i -1$ to 0. The shifter has 1, 6, 10 positions for non-, coeff-, data- adaptive strategies, respectively.

The IC cell is integrated into the demodulator with the bus-widths reported in Figure 8. The data stream $s_i(t)$ sampled up to 100 Ms/s at 16-bit enters the demodulator. The coherent sin/cos sources are represented at 13-bit. The 2 multipliers produce an output at $16 + 13 - 1 = 28$ bits that feed the 2 identical filters composed by 4 sections for the phase and quadrature channels. The filters take in input the 2 buses at 28 bits, and, since each IC stage decreases the bus width of 3 bits, the I/Q signals are outputted at 16 bits. The number of words in FIFO (Mw), the total memory bits in FIFO (Mb), the adder, and accumulator width (BA), and the barrel-shifter positions for data-adaptive strategy (BS) are reported in Figure 8 inside the graphical blocks of each specific IC cell in the filter chain.

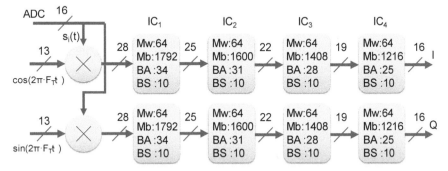

Figure 8. Architecture of the data-adaptive demodulator. IC cells report the memory words (Mw), the memory bits (Mb), the accumulator width (BA), and the barrel-shifter (BS) positions. The bus-widths in input and output of each IC cell are reported as well.

4. Experiments and Results

4.1. Resources Utilization

The first experiment aimed at evaluating the resource utilization of the proposed solutions. The demodulator of Figure 8 was implemented in an FPGA of the Cyclone V family (Altera/Intel,

San Jose, CA, USA) in all of the three configurations for dynamics management described in Section 3.2. The design was targeted for a clock up to 100 MHz, a goal easily reached for all of the implementations. The results are listed in Table 1, distinguished for Adaptive Logic Modules (ALM), Adaptive Look-up-Tables (ALUT), Registers (REG), Memory bits, and Digital Signal Processors (DSP) blocks. In all of the implementations two DSP blocks are employed for the two multipliers of the demodulator (see, e.g., Figure 8). The memory bits (17,700 for the proposed architecture) are more than the sum of the memory bits listed in Figure 8. This is due to the internal organization of FPGA memory. The data-adaptive and coeff-adaptive approaches have a similar resource utilization, while the non-adaptive approach employs fewer resources since the barrel-shifters are removed.

Table 1. Demodulator resources utilization in FPGA implementation.

Device	Cyclone V				
	ALM	**ALUT**	**Reg**	**Memory Bits**	**DSP**
data-adaptive demodulator	831	1271	871	17700	2
coeff-adaptive demodulator	818	1056	869	17700	2
non-adaptive demodulator	523	758	803	17700	2

4.2. Demodulator Noise Performance

This experiment aimed to evaluate the noise produced by the finite number representation in the mathematical calculations of the filter. The system for rheological fluid characterization described in reference [23] was connected to a flow-rig. A fluid composed by demineralized water with added specific ultrasonic scatters flowed in an 8 mm diameter pipe moved by a gear pump. The pipe was immersed in a water tank where a cylindrical ultrasound transducer was directed towards the pipe at an angle of 60° with respect to the pipe axis. The transducer was excited by the system with bursts composed by 5 cycles at 6 MHz, repeated with a PRIs of 200 μs. The received echoes were sampled at 16 bits 100 Ms/s. The analog gain of the front-end of the system was accurately tuned with a manual try-and-check procedure to exploit the full 16 bits dynamic range of the AD converter. An example of the signal acquired in a PRI is shown in Figure 1a.

The acquired signal was used to generate three different test signals. The first, hereafter named 'S_{16}' was the original signal itself, the second and the third signals, named 'S_{12}' and 'S_{08}' were obtained by reducing the dynamics of the original signal to 12 and 8 bits, respectively. This was obtained by dividing the data to 2^4 and 2^8 but maintaining the 16 bits word representation. These last two signals mimic a non-optimal tuning of the analog input gain of the front-end of the system.

The demodulators were coded in VHDL language and implemented in Modelsim® (Mentor Graphics Corp. Wilsonville 97070 OR). The filter parameters were set to obtain $F_L = 0.01$, that, for a 100 MHz sampling frequency, corresponds to a 1 MHz bandwidth. The employed parameters are detailed in Table 2.

Table 2. Filter parameter employed in experiments.

Parameters K_i	Parameters D_i	Cut-off Frequency (Normalized)	Cut-off Frequency
$K_0 = 32, K_1 = 17, K_2 = 9, K_3 = 14$	$D_1 = 1, D_2 = 3, D_3 = 1, D_4 = 1$	$F_L = 0.01$	1 MHz

The 3 test signals were processed according to all of the 3 strategies for dynamics management. The corresponding demodulated outputs were named SDxx, where xx is 16, 12, and 08 and indicate the corresponding input signal. The demodulator was implemented in Matlab® (The Mathworks, Natick, MA, USA) as well, and used to process the test signals in double precision. These results were considered as reference and named SDRxx. The signals were compared in Matlab® by computing the Signal-to-Noise ratio with the following metric:

$$\text{SNR} = 10 \cdot \log_{10}\left[\frac{\sum_i SDxx^2(i)}{\sum_i (SDxx(i) - SDRxx(i))^2}\right] \qquad (9)$$

Please note that the reference output signals SDRxx were generated by the ideal Matlab® demodulator with the Sxx signals quantized at 16, 12, 08 bits. Thus, the quantization input noise is not included in the SNR evaluated by (9). SNR calculated by Equation (9) accounts for the mathematical noise of the demodulator and the final 16-bit quantization noise. The results, expressed in dB, are listed in Table 3. In addition, the maximum SNR achievable for the signals present in this application was further calculated in Matlab®. The output of the ideal demodulator SDRxx with in input the S_{16} signal was normalized at full dynamics and quantized at 16 bits. The SNR due to this quantization was calculated and reported in the last column of Table 3 (Reference). Note that the typical formula $6.02 \cdot N + 1.76$ (where N is the number of bits) [9] results in SNR = 98.1 dB instead of 85.0 dB for N = 16 bits. In fact, the aforementioned formula is valid for a full-dynamics sinusoidal signal, while the actual signal used here exploits the full dynamics only for a small part of the acquired period (see Figure 1a).

Table 3. Signal-to-noise ratio (SNR) Performance of the demodulator–input quantization excluded.

SNR (dB)	Non-Adaptive	Coeff-Adaptive	Data-Adaptive	Reference
S_{16}	24.7	60.2	83.4	85.0
S_{12}	5.7	36.3	83.4	85.0
S_{08}	0.0	14.2	83.4	85.0

The performance in non-adaptive approach (see Table 3) is particularly bad, being the maximum SNR = 25 dB only. Since that the ratio between pipe and fluid echoes is up to 30–40 dB, the non-adaptive approach is not suitable for the application. The coef-adaptive strategy grants much better performance and reaches SNR = 60 dB in the best condition. However, the SNR degrades quickly when the input data scales-down. The coef-adaptive strategy is sensitive to input data dynamics and thus it is not so robust for industrial applications. The data-adaptive approach produces the best performance achieving an SNR = 84 dB. Most importantly, the performance does not depend on the input dynamics even at 8 bits of input data. Moreover, the predominant noise is generated by the 16 bits quantization in output, and not from the finite numerical representation of the filter mathematics. This confirms that data-adaptive performance is quite close to the reference (see Table 3).

The noise performance of the demodulators is further confirmed by positions of the barrel shifter present during the experiment and listed in Table 4. Each BS_i column reports the position of the barrel-shifter at the end of the cell IC_i. A value of m in the table means that the shifter scales the signal by 2^{-m}.

Table 4. Scaling positions of the barrel shifters.

	Non-Adaptive				Coeff-Adaptive				Data-Adaptive			
	BS_1	BS_2	BS_3	BS_4	BS_1	BS_2	BS_3	BS_4	BS_1	BS_2	BS_3	BS_4
S_{16}	9	9	9	9	8	8	7	7	7	7	6	6
S_{12}	9	9	9	9	8	8	7	7	3	7	6	6
S_{08}	9	9	9	9	8	8	7	7	0	6	6	6

In non-adaptive strategy, the scaling is fixed to 2^{-9}, i.e., the 6 positions related to the maximum filter gain (K_i up to 64) plus 3 for the bus-width reduction (7). In the coeff-adaptive approach, the positions correspond to the actual filter settings, plus the 3 positions for bus-width reduction. For example, since $K_0 = 32$ (see Table 2), $BS_1 = \text{ceil}(\log2(32)) + 3 = 8$. However, the settings are the same regardless of the input signal Sxx. In a data-adaptive approach the filter positions change for different rows of Table 4, i.e., they depend on the signal dynamics. BS_1 scales 7 positions for the strong signal S_{16}, but 0 positions for S_{08}, thus recovering 7 bits of dynamics. BS_2 scales 6 positions for S_{08} and 7 for the other signals. BS_3 and BS_4 have the same behavior for all the signals. This means that the dynamics of S_{08} is recovered mostly by BS_1 and BS_2. Then BS_3 and BS_4 scale 6 positions like for the other signals. This explains how the demodulator achieves the best performance of 83.4 dB when processing S_{08} (see Table 3).

4.3. Flow Simulation

The performance of the demodulator was tested in a flow simulation. The simulation was carried out in Matlab® through the Field II ultrasound simulator [31,32], freely available at https://field-ii.dk. Field II, given the position of a set of scattering particles, the transducer characteristics, and the TX pulse, simulates the echo data acquired in each PRI. In this test, a piston transducer transmitted bursts of 5 cycles at 6 MHz in a 45 mm diameter pipe. The positions of the scattering particles were updated every PRI to mimic the typical parabolic profile of a Newtonian fluid flowing in a straight pipe [33]. The peak velocity was set to 1 m/s. A 16-bit AD converter was simulated by scaling the amplitude of the data generated by Field II and by applying the 16 bits fixed point representation. Two data sets were generated: The first was composed by the echoes from the particles in the flow only, while the other included the echoes from the static pipe wall as well. The power ratio between echoes from pipe wall and from flow particles was 35 dB.

The two data sets were processed by both the non-adaptive and by the data-adaptive demodulators. The demodulators were programmed with the same integration and decimation parameters used in the previous experiment. Four power spectral matrices were obtained and reported in Figure 9 in color code. The vertical axes show the depth along the pipe diameter, while the horizontal axes report the velocity obtained by converting the Doppler shift through (1).

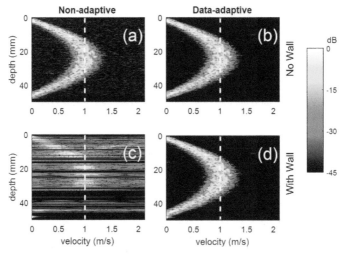

Figure 9. Power spectral matrices obtained for a simulated parabolic flow with 1 m/s peak velocity in a 45 mm diameter pipe. In (**c,d**) the signal from a static pipe-wall is added with a power 35 dB higher than the flow signal; in (**a,b**) the only flow signal is present. (**a,c**) are obtained with non-adaptive demodulator; (**b,d**) with data-adaptive demodulator. Horizontal axes report the Doppler shift converted to velocity. Vertical dashed lines correspond to the simulated peak velocity.

The simulated signal without the pipe wall echoes produces spectral matrices where the parabolic profile can be clearly detected (Figure 9a,b). When the pipe wall signal is added, the data-adaptive demodulator produces a spectral matrix (Figure 9d) that is identical to the case without the wall signal (Figure 9b). On the other hand, the non-adaptive demodulator does not produce a detectable profile when the pipe wall is added (Figure 9c). Background noise is quite high and several regions (black horizontal bands) are below the filter sensitivity. Moreover, whenever the velocity profile is detected (Figure 9a,b,d) the velocity that corresponds to the parabola peak is located with an accuracy of ±2.2%. For comparison, the reference velocity of 1 m/s is reported by the vertical dashed lines.

4.4. Example of Application

The proposed demodulator was included in the processing chain of the system for the detection of the velocity profile of fluids flowing in pipes described in reference [34]. The system was connected to the flow-rig as described in Section 4.2. The demodulator was programmed with the same integration and decimation parameters used in the previous experiment. The analog gain of the front-end was tuned to reproduce the 16, 12, 08 bits input signal dynamics, and the filter was set for non-, coeff-, data-adaptive approaches. Frames of power spectral matrices elaborated in real-time by the system were captured and reported in Figure 10.

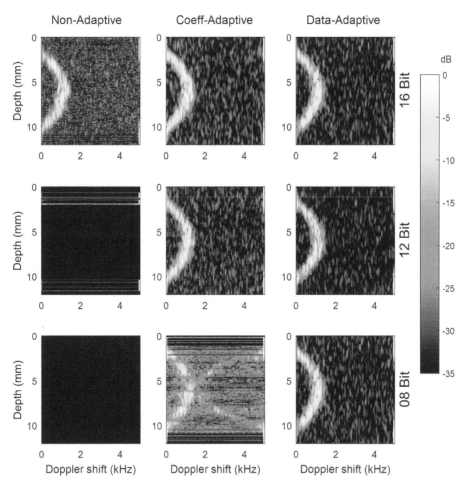

Figure 10. Power spectral matrices calculated by the system, including the proposed demodulator. Horizontal and vertical axes report Doppler shift and depth, respectively. Matrices processed with non-, coeff-, data- adaptive strategies are reported in columns; input signal equivalent to 16, 12, 08 bits are reported in rows.

The spectral matrices show the typical parabolic profile of a Newtonian fluid. When the input gain is tuned for exploiting the full dynamics of the AD converter (16 bits, first row in Figure 10), the parabolic profile is clearly detected regardless of the dynamic's management employed in the filter. The non-adaptive configuration features a higher noise level, the other two cases are similar. When the input signal covers 12 bits of the AD dynamics, coef- and data- adaptive approaches do not show appreciable deterioration, while a non-adaptive approach shows no usable signal. With input dynamics at 8 bits, coeff-adaptive approach features a very high noise level, while data-adaptive showed no visible difference with respect to previous analysis. In other words, non-adaptive demodulator produces a good signal only when the full input dynamics is exploited; data-adaptive demodulators produce the same high-quality signal even if the input dynamics is reduced to only 8 bits. The coeff-adaptive approach produces intermediate results.

5. Discussion and Conclusion

In this work, a data-adaptive demodulator for PWD applications is presented. A "training phase" is used to read the dynamics of the actual signal and tune accordingly the internal barrel-shifters. It is followed by the "running phase" where the signal is effectively processed with the gain parameters set in the training phase. The training phase is very quick and precedes the normal acquisition phase without impact to the final application.

The superior performance of the proposed method is evident in presence of strong pipe-wall echoes, as shown in the simulation of Section 4.3. The simulation highlights that the non-adaptive demodulator fails while the data-adaptive detects the correct velocity profile. In fact, in the presence of a strong pipe wall echo, the dynamics of the useful flow signal is reduced proportionally to the amplitude of the disturbing echo. If the dynamics are reduced beyond the SNR limits reported in Table 3, the profile detection is prevented because the signal is concealed in the noise. The high SNR performance of the data-adaptive approach is confirmed also in the experiment on a real pipe flow, whose results are shown in Figure 10. The data-adaptive approach allows us to recover the optimal signal at the demodulator output even when the signal at the AD converter input uses only 8 bits. In this condition, nor the coeff-adaptive, neither the non-adaptive approaches, can produce any usable signal. This is a very important feature in industrial applications, where the PWD system is expected to work with minimal tuning and to be robust to a wide range of conditions.

The data-adaptive approach can also be implemented with a single barrel-shifter at the end of a standard 4-stage CIC architecture, however, this approach would require more FPGA resources. Floating point mathematical calculations [35–37] would grant even better performance. However, although recent high-end FPGAs integrates floating-point hard-processors, the resources needed are by far higher than those employed in the proposed solution. Thus, floating point approach is, at present, not cost-effective.

The presented demodulator fulfils the requirements reported in Section 2.3. It includes a filter with a programmable mask, it can be easily implemented in low-cost FPGA, and it features a data throughput up to 100 Ms/s. Most importantly, the data-adaptive approach is not affected by the strong pipe echoes and is capable of auto-tuning for the widest range of input conditions, reducing the intervention of specialized workers. The proposed demodulator can represent a valuable processing block for industrial applications where high dynamics is an essential precondition.

Author Contributions: Conceptualization, methodology, writing paper, funding acquisition: S.R.; software, investigation, data curation: V.M.

Funding: This work is funded by the Ministero dell'Istruzione, dell'Università e della Ricerca (MIUR) of Italy Government.

Acknowledgments: Authors thank Johan Wiklund for his advice about fluid rheology.

References

1. Evans, D.H.; McDicken, W.N. *Doppler Ultrasound Physics, Instrumentation and Signal Processing*; Wiley: Chichester, UK, 2000; ISBN 978-0471970019.
2. Vogt, M. Direct sampling and baseband conversion in Doppler systems for high-frequency ultrasound blood flow measurements. *Electron. Lett.* **2005**, *41*, 189–790. [CrossRef]
3. Weibao, Q.; Zongying, Y.; Yanyan, Y.; Yan, C.; Liyang, C.; Peitian, M.; Guofeng, L.; Congzhi, W.; Yang, X.; Jiyan, D.; et al. A Digital Multigate Doppler Method for High Frequency Ultrasound. *Sensors* **2014**, *14*, 13348–13360. [CrossRef]
4. Boni, E.; Bassi, L.; Dallai, A.; Meacci, V.; Ramalli, A.; Scaringella, M.; Guidi, F.; Ricci, S.; Tortoli, P. Architecture of an Ultrasound System for Continuous Real-Time High Frame Rate Imaging. *IEEE Trans. Ultrason. Ferroelectr. Freq. Control* **2017**, *64*, 1276–1284. [CrossRef] [PubMed]
5. Jensen, J.A.; Nikolov, S.I.; Yu, A.C.H.; Garcia, D. Ultrasound Vector Flow Imaging-Part II: Parallel Systems. *IEEE Trans. Ultrason. Ferroelectr. Freq. Control* **2016**, *63*, 722–1732. [CrossRef] [PubMed]
6. Hervás, M.; Alsina-Pagès, R.M.; Salvador, M. An FPGA Scalable Software Defined Radio Platform Design for Educational and Research Purposes. *Electronics* **2016**, *5*, 27. [CrossRef]
7. Koulamas, C.; Lazarescu, M.T. Real-Time Embedded Systems: Present and Future. *Electronics* **2018**, *7*, 205. [CrossRef]
8. Rodriguez-Andina, J.J.; Moure, M.J.; Valdes, M.D. Features, design tools, and application domains of FPGAs. *IEEE Trans. Ind. Electron.* **2007**, *54*, 1810–1823. [CrossRef]
9. Richard, L. *Understanding Digital Signal Processing*, 2nd ed.; Prentice Hall: Upper Saddle River, NJ, USA, 2004; ISBN 978-0-13-702741-5.
10. Mohsin, A.; Fadhel, M.G.; Mohamed, H. Blind Compensation of I/Q Impairments in Wireless Transceivers. *Sensors* **2017**, *17*, 2948. [CrossRef]
11. Ricci, S.; Matera, R.; Tortoli, P. An improved Doppler model for obtaining accurate maximum blood velocities. *Ultrasonics* **2014**, *7*, 2006–2014. [CrossRef]
12. Wiklund, J.; Stading, M. Application of in-line ultrasound Doppler-based UVP–PD rheometry method to concentrated model and industrial suspensions. *Flow Meas. Instrum.* **2008**, *19*, 171–179. [CrossRef]
13. Birkhofer, B.; Debacker, A.; Russo, S.; Ricci, S.; Lootens, D. In-line rheometry based on ultrasonic velocity profiles: Comparison of data processing methods. *Appl. Rheol.* **2012**, *22*, 44701. [CrossRef]
14. Morganti, T.; Ricci, S.; Vittone, F.; Palombo, C.; Tortoli, P. Clinical validation of common carotid artery wall distension assessment based on multigate Doppler processing. *Ultras. Med. Biol.* **2005**, *31*, 937–945. [CrossRef] [PubMed]
15. Shamu, T.J.; Kotzé, R.; Wiklund, J. Characterization of acoustic beam propagation through high-grade stainless steel pipes for improved pulsed ultrasound velocimetry measurements in complex industrial fluids. *IEEE Sens. J.* **2016**, *16*, 5636–5647. [CrossRef]
16. Kotzé, R.; Ricci, S.; Birkhofer, B.; Wiklund, J. Performance tests of a new non-invasive sensor unit and ultrasound electronics. *Flow Meas. Instrum.* **2016**, *48*, 104–111. [CrossRef]
17. Qwist, P.K.; Sander, C.; Okkels, F.; Jessen, V.; Baldursdottir, S.; Rantanen, J. On-line rheological characterization of semi-solid formulations. *Eur. J. Pharm. Sci.* **2019**, *128*, 36–42. [CrossRef] [PubMed]
18. Ricci, S.; Swillens, A.; Ramalli, A.; Segers, P.; Tortoli, P. Wall Shear Rate Measurement: Validation of a new Method through Multi-physics Simulations. *IEEE Trans. Ultrason. Ferroelectr. Freq. Control* **2017**, *64*, 66–77. [CrossRef] [PubMed]
19. Meacci, V.; Matera, R.; Ricci, S. High dynamics adaptive demodulator for ultrasound applications: FPGA implementation. In Proceedings of the 1st New Generation of CAS, NGCAS, Genoa, Italy, 6–8 September 2017.
20. Hogenauer, E. An economical class of digital filters for decimation and interpolation. *IEEE Trans. Acoust. Speech Signal Process.* **1981**, *29*, 155–162. [CrossRef]
21. Peilu, L.; Xinghua, L.; Haopeng, L.; Zhikun, S.; Hongxu, Z. Implementation of High Time Delay Accuracy of Ultrasonic Phased Array Based on Interpolation CIC Filter. *Sensors* **2017**, *17*, 2322. [CrossRef]
22. Pilato, L.; Fanucci, L.; Saponara, S. Real-Time and High-Accuracy Arctangent Computation Using CORDIC and Fast Magnitude Estimation. *Electronics* **2017**, *6*, 22. [CrossRef]

23. Ricci, S.; Meacci, V.; Birkhofer, B.; Wiklund, J. FPGA-based System for In-Line Measurement of Velocity Profiles of Fluids in Industrial Pipe Flow. *IEEE Trans. Ind. Electron.* **2017**, *64*, 3997–4005. [CrossRef]

24. Ricci, S.; Liard, M.; Birkhofer, B.; Lootens, D.; Brühwiler, A.; Tortoli, P. Embedded Doppler System for Industrial in-Line Rheometry. *IEEE Trans. Ultrason. Ferroelectr. Freq. Control* **2012**, *59*, 1395–1401. [CrossRef]

25. Cooley, J.W.; Tukey, J.W. An algorithm for the machine calculation of complex Fourier series. *Math. Comput.* **1965**, *19*, 297–301. [CrossRef]

26. Minotta, F.; Jimenez, M.; Rodriguez, D. Automated Scalable Address Generation Patterns for 2-Dimensional Folding Schemes in Radix-2 FFT Implementations. *Electronics* **2018**, *7*, 33. [CrossRef]

27. Nguyen, H.N.; Khan, S.A.; Kim, C.H.; Kim, J.M. A Pipelined FFT Processor Using an Optimal Hybrid Rotation Scheme for Complex Multiplication: Design, FPGA Implementation and Analysis. *Electronics* **2018**, *7*, 137. [CrossRef]

28. Ricci, S. Adaptive Spectral Estimators for Fast Flow Profile Detection. *IEEE Trans. Ultrason. Ferroelectr. Freq. Control* **2013**, *60*, 421–427. [CrossRef] [PubMed]

29. Elif, D.Ü.; Hakan, I.; İnan, G. Application of FFT and Arma Spectral Analysis to Arterial Doppler Signals. *Math. Comput. Appl.* **2003**, *8*, 311–318. [CrossRef]

30. Larsson, E.; Stoica, P. Fast implementation of two-dimensional APES and Capon spectral estimators. *Multidimens. Syst. Signal Process.* **2002**, *13*, 35–54. [CrossRef]

31. Jensen, J.A.; Svendsen, N.B. Calculation of pressure fields from arbitrarily shaped, apodized, and excited ultrasound transducers. *IEEE Trans. Ultrason. Ferroelect. Freq. Control* **1992**, *39*, 262–267. [CrossRef] [PubMed]

32. Jensen, J.A. Field: A Program for Simulating Ultrasound Systems. *Med. Biol. Eng. Comp.* **1996**, *34*, 351–353.

33. Granger, R.A. *Fluid Mechanics*; Dover: Mineola, NY, USA, 1995; ISBN 978-0486683560.

34. Meacci, V.; Ricci, S.; Wiklund, J.; Birkhofer, B.; Kotze, R. Flow-Viz—An integrated digital in-line fluid characterization system for industrial applications. In Proceedings of the 11th IEEE Sensors Applications Symposium (SAS), Catania, Italy, 13–15 April 2016; pp. 128–133.

35. 754-2008—IEEE Standard for Floating-Point Arithmetic. 2008. Available online: https://doi.org/10.1109/IEEESTD.2008.4610935 (accessed on 12 December 2018).

36. Al Kadi, M.; Janssen, B.; Huebner, M. Floating-Point Arithmetic Using GPGPU on FPGAs. In Proceedings of the IEEE Computer Society Annual Symposium on VLSI, ISVLSI, Bochum, Germany, 3–5 July 2017; pp. 134–139.

37. Sanchez, A.; Todorovich, E.; De Castro, A. Exploring the Limits of Floating-Point Resolution for Hardware-In-the-Loop Implemented with FPGAs. *Electronics* **2018**, *7*, 219. [CrossRef]

Article

Parallel K-Means Clustering for Brain Cancer Detection Using Hyperspectral Images

Emanuele Torti [1,*], Giordana Florimbi [1], Francesca Castelli [1], Samuel Ortega [2], Himar Fabelo [2], Gustavo Marrero Callicó [2], Margarita Marrero-Martin [2] and Francesco Leporati [1]

[1] Department of Electrical, Computer and Biomedical Engineering, University of Pavia, I-27100 Pavia, Italy; giordana.florimbi01@ateneopv.it (G.F.); francesca.castelli02@ateneopv.it (F.C.); francesco.leporati@unipv.it (F.L.)

[2] Institute for Applied Microelectronics (IUMA), University of Las Palmas de Gran Canaria (ULPGC), 35017 Las Palmas de Gran Canaria, Spain; sortega@iuma.ulpgc.es (S.O.); hfabelo@iuma.ulpgc.es (H.F.); gustavo@iuma.ulpgc.es (G.M.C.); margarita@iuma.ulpgc.es (M.M.-M.)

* Correspondence: emanuele.torti@unipv.it; Tel.: +39-0382-985678

Received: 9 October 2018; Accepted: 26 October 2018; Published: 30 October 2018

Abstract: The precise delineation of brain cancer is a crucial task during surgery. There are several techniques employed during surgical procedures to guide neurosurgeons in the tumor resection. However, hyperspectral imaging (HSI) is a promising non-invasive and non-ionizing imaging technique that could improve and complement the currently used methods. The HypErspectraL Imaging Cancer Detection (HELICoiD) European project has addressed the development of a methodology for tumor tissue detection and delineation exploiting HSI techniques. In this approach, the K-means algorithm emerged in the delimitation of tumor borders, which is of crucial importance. The main drawback is the computational complexity of this algorithm. This paper describes the development of the K-means clustering algorithm on different parallel architectures, in order to provide real-time processing during surgical procedures. This algorithm will generate an unsupervised segmentation map that, combined with a supervised classification map, will offer guidance to the neurosurgeon during the tumor resection task. We present parallel K-means clustering based on OpenMP, CUDA and OpenCL paradigms. These algorithms have been validated through an in-vivo hyperspectral human brain image database. Experimental results show that the CUDA version can achieve a speed-up of ~150× with respect to a sequential processing. The remarkable result obtained in this paper makes possible the development of a real-time classification system.

Keywords: Graphics Processing Units (GPUs); CUDA; OpenMP; OpenCL; K-means; brain cancer detection; hyperspectral imaging; unsupervised clustering

---

1. Introduction

One of the most diffused types of cancer is the brain tumor, which has an estimated incidence of 3.4 per 100,000 subjects [1]. There are different types of brain tumors; the most common one concerns the *glial* cells of the brain and is called *glioma*. It accounts from the 30% to the 50% of the cases. In particular, in the 85% of these cases, it is a malignant tumor called *glioblastoma*. Moreover, these kind of *gliomas* are characterized by fast-growing invasiveness, which is locally very aggressive, in most cases unicentric and rarely metastasizing [2].

Typically, the first diagnosis is performed through the Magnetic Resonance Imaging (MRI) and the Computed Tomography (CT). Those techniques are capable to highlight possible lesions. However, it is not always possible to use them, since they can, for example, make interference with pacemakers or other implantable devices. Moreover, the certainty of the diagnosis only comes from the histological and pathological analyses, which require samples of the tissue. In order to obtain this tissue, an *excisional biopsy* is necessary, which consists in the removal of tissue from the living body through surgical cutting. It is important to notice that all those approaches have some disadvantages; in particular they are not capable of providing a real-time response and, most important, they are invasive and/or ionizing.

The clinical practice for brain cancers is the tumor resection, which can cure the lowest grade tumors and prolongs the life of the patient in the most aggressive cases. The main issue about this approach is the inaccuracy of the human eye in distinguishing between healthy tissue and cancer. This is because the cancer often infiltrates and diffuses into the surrounding healthy tissue and this is particularly critical for brain cancers. As a consequence, the surgeon can unintentionally leave behind tumor tissue during a surgery routine potentially causing tumor recurrence. On the other hand, if the surgeon removes too much healthy tissue, a permanent disability to the patient can be provoked [3].

The HELICoiD European project aims at providing to the surgeon a system which can accurately discriminate between tumor and healthy tissue in real-time during surgery routines [4,5]. Traditional imaging techniques feature a low grade of sensitivity and often cannot clearly determine the tumor region and its boundaries. Therefore, the HELICoiD project exploits Hyperspectral Imaging (HSI) techniques in order to solve this critical issue. Hyperspectral images (HS) can be acquired over a wide range of the electromagnetic spectrum, from visible to near-infrared frequencies and beyond. Hyperspectral sensors acquire the so-called *HS cube* where the spatial information is in the *x*-axis and in the *y*-axis, while the spectral information is in the *z*-axis. Thus, a single hyperspectral pixel can be seen as a mono-dimensional vector, which contains the spectral response across the different wavelengths. Moreover, it is important to notice that the spectral information is strictly correlated with the chemical composition of the specific material. It is possible to say that each hyperspectral pixel contains the so-called *spectral signature* of a certain substance. Thus, different substances can be distinguished by properly analyzing those images [6].

A previous study [4,7] proposed a processing chain for hyperspectral image analysis acquired during brain surgery. The framework developed in this work is depicted in Figure 1.

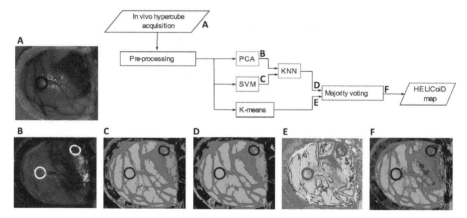

Figure 1. Hyperspectral brain cancer detection algorithm proposed in [7]. After acquiring (**A**) and pre-processing the image, the system performs a supervised classification through Principal Component Analysis (PCA) (**B**), Support Vector Machine (SVM) (**C**) and K-Nearest Neighbor (KNN) (**D**). Moreover, it generates a segmentation map through the K-means (**E**). The (**D,E**) maps are merged using the majority voting (**F**).

First, the acquired HS cube (Figure 1A) is pre-processed in order to perform a radiometric calibration, reduce the noise and the dimensionality of the HS image and normalize it. After this preparatory step, the image is analyzed using the supervised and unsupervised classification. The former is performed exploiting the Principal Component Analysis (PCA), the Support Vector

Machine (SVM) and the K-Nearest Neighbor (KNN). The KNN filters the spatial information given by the PCA (Figure 1B) and the classification map generated by the SVM (Figure 1C). Its output (Figure 1D) is a map where tissues are displayed with different colors representing the associated classes. The unsupervised classification is based on the K-means algorithm. Despite the supervised classification output, the unsupervised result is a segmentation map (Figure 1E), whose clusters are semantically meaningless. However, the K-means provides a good delimitation of the different areas present in the scene. Since the goal of the system is to accurately delineate the tumor borders, the K-means plays a crucial role for its ability to clearly separate different areas. For these reasons, it is important to merge the two outputs in order to exploit the benefits of the two approaches. The majority voting provides the final output combining the supervised and unsupervised classifications (Figure 1F).

While the PCA, the SVM and the KNN filter are executed through a fixed number of steps, the K-means algorithm iterates until a certain condition is satisfied. In order to provide the real-time classification during surgery, parallel computing is required, since the computational load of the algorithms is extremely high. The other algorithms of this framework have been already developed in parallel, in particular the SVM [8] and the KNN filtering [9] have been recently proposed in the literature. Those works target Graphics Processing Units (GPUs) technology since the considered algorithms have an intrinsically parallel structure. Previously, other parallel technologies have been evaluated in order to provide faster implementations of the PCA [10], SVM [11] and KNN [12] compared to the serial ones. Despite this, in our work we choose to exploit GPUs since they assure higher performance. Moreover, GPUs are going to be increasingly used for real-time image processing [13–15], together with other scientific applications related to simulation and modeling or machine learning in biomedical applications [16,17].

In this paper, we present the parallelization of the K-means algorithm on different parallel architectures in order to evaluate which one is more suitable for real-time processing. In particular, we consider multi-core CPUs through the OpenMP API and the GPU technology using NVIDIA CUDA framework. We also propose OpenCL-based implementations in order to address code portability.

In other words, the work performed allows identifying the best suitable parallel approach between one that could be more appealing since it requires low programming effort and another one more efficient but also more demanding in terms of optimization and tuning. A tool that allows intra-architectures portability (OpenCL) was also considered but due to its lower performance it is not competitive with the other two approaches.

The paper is organized as follows: Section 2 describes the K-means algorithm for hyperspectral images, while Section 3 details the different parallel versions. Section 4 contains the experimental results and their discussion, making comparisons between the different approaches described in this paper. Section 5 concludes the papers and addresses some possible future research lines.

2. K-Means Algorithm for Hyperspectral Images

As already said, the K-means algorithm, unlike the other ones of the hyperspectral brain cancer detection algorithm, is not performed through a fixed number of steps. It performs an unsupervised learning since no previous knowledge of the data is needed. The algorithm separates the input data into K different clusters with a K value fixed a priori. Data are grouped together on the basis of feature similarity. The first step of the algorithm is the definition of K *centroids*, one for each cluster. Using those centroids, a first grouping is performed on the basis of the distance of each point to the centroids. A point is associate to the cluster represented by the nearest centroid. At this moment, each k *centroid* is updated as the baricenter of the group it represents. This process iterates until the difference between the centroids of two consecutive iterations are smaller than a fixed threshold or if the maximum number of iterations is reached.

The pseudo-code of the K-means algorithm is shown in Algorithm 1, where Y indicates a hyperspectral image made up of N pixels and L bands. Therefore, the hyperspectral image can be seen as an $N \times L$ matrix. The number of clusters to produce is determined by K, the threshold error by min_error and the maximum number of iterations by max_iter. The K-means algorithm produces as a result a $K \times L$ array containing the centroids, which will be referred as cluster_centroids in Algorithm 1 and an N-dimensional array containing the label of the cluster assigned to each pixel. This array is denoted by assigned_cluster.

Algorithm 1 K-means

Input: Y, K, min_error, max_iter

1: Pseudo-random initialization of cluster_centroids
2: Initialize previous_centroids at 0   ▷ previous_centroids is an $K \times L$ array
3: n_iter ← 0   ▷ initialize the iteration counter to 0
4: Initialize actual_error with a huge value
5: **while** actual_error > min_error and n_iter < max_iter **do**
6:     **for** i:=1 to N **do**
7:         Initialize centroid_distances to 0   ▷ centroid_distances is a K-dimensional array
8:         **for** j:=1 to K **do**
9:             centroid_distance$_j$ ← distance between the j-th centroid and the i-th pixel
10:         **end for**
11:         assigend_cluster$_i$ ← index of min centroid_distance
12:     **end for**
13:     previous_centroids ← cluster_centroids
14:     update cluster_centroids
15:     actual_error ← $\frac{\sum_{i=1}^{K} \sum_{j=1}^{L} |\text{previous\_centroids}_{i,j} - \text{cluster\_centroids}_{i,j}|}{K \cdot L}$
16:     n_iter ← n_iter + 1
17: **end while**

Output: assigned_cluster, cluster_centroids

In Algorithm 1, lines 1 and 2 contain the initialization of the variables. In particular, cluster_centroids is initialized with K different hyperspectral pixels pseudo-randomly chosen from the input image Y. The variable actual_error is initialized with a huge value in order to ensure that the main loop of the algorithm (from line 5 to 17) is performed at least one time. Inside this main loop there are two *for* loops that iterate over the number of pixels N and the number of clusters K (lines from 6 to 12). For each pixel, a temporary array centroid_distances is set to 0, used for storing the distances between the considered hyperspectral pixel and the centroids. The distance metric used for hyperspectral pixels is usually the *Spectral Angle* (SA) which is defined as:

$$SA = \theta(x,y) = \cos^{-1}\left(\frac{\sum_{h=1}^{L} x_h y_h}{\left(\sum_{h=1}^{L} x_h^2\right)^{1/2} \left(\sum_{h=1}^{L} y_h^2\right)^{1/2}}\right) \qquad (1)$$

where x and y are the spectral vectors and x_h and y_h represent the response of the h-th band of x and y respectively, being L the number of bands.

The label assigned to the i-th pixel corresponds to the group represented by the centroid with the minimum SA value, as shown in line 11. This phase is repeated for each pixel.

After these steps, the centroids used for the SAs computation are stored in the previous_centroids array. Successively, the centroids are updated by computing the barycenter of each group that is computing the mean value, for each band, of the pixels belonging to the group. Using the updated centroids and the previous ones, it is possible to evaluate the variation from the previous iteration. It represents how much the centroids have changed and it can be used as a stopping criterion when these variations become small (line 15). The last step of the *while* loop is the increment of the n_iter variable, used for controlling the maximum number of iterations performed by the algorithm.

The next section describes the serial and the parallel versions of this algorithm that we developed using different parallel approaches, together with a code profiling carried out in order to identify the heaviest code parts from the computational point of view.

3. Parallel K-Means Implementations

First, we developed a serial version of the K-mean algorithm written in C code. It serves both as reference for validating the results of the parallel implementations and for performing a careful code profiling needed to identify the most complex code parts. The numerical representation used is the IEEE-754 floating-point single precision.

3.1. Serial Code Profiling

The code profiling was performed using a dataset formed by real HS images and assuming $K = 24$, min_error $= 10^{-3}$ and max_iter $= 50$. This K value was stablished during the development of the HS brain cancer algorithm presented in [7]. Using this configuration, the execution of the algorithm never reached the maximum number of iterations. The characteristics of the dataset are shown in Table 1, while Figure 2 shows the RGB representation of the images.

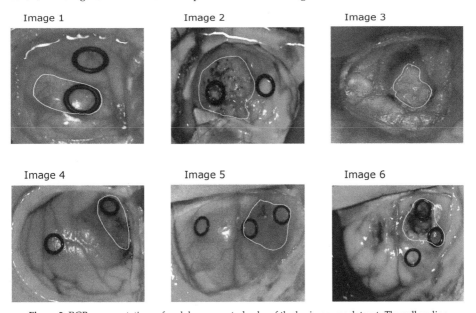

Figure 2. RGB representations of each hyperspectral cube of the brain cancer dataset. The yellow line represents the tumor location identified by the neurosurgeon.

Table 1. Dataset characteristics.

Image ID	# of Rows	# of Columns	Total # of Pixels	# of Bands	Size (MB)
Image 1	329	379	124,691	128	60.88
Image 2	493	376	185,368	128	90.51
Image 3	402	472	189,744	128	92.65
Image 4	496	442	219,232	128	107.05
Image 5	548	459	251,532	128	122.82
Image 6	552	479	264,408	128	129.11

The profiling highlighted that the heaviest code parts are the computation of distances, which are evaluated between each hyperspectral pixel and each centroid. In the considered cases, the *for* loops of lines 6–12 (Algorithm 1) take from 94 to 98% of the time for the smallest and the biggest image, respectively. Notice that these computations can be performed in parallel, since there is no dependency between the evaluations needed by a single pixel and the others.

3.2. OpenMP Algorithms

OpenMP (https://www.openmp.org/) is a parallel programming framework capable of exploiting multi-core architectures. It is based on a set of simple *#pragma* statements used for code annotations that indicates to the compiler which parts should be parallelized. An example is the *#pragma omp parallel for* statement, which generates a set of parallel threads and assigns to each one a group of iterations. It is also possible to indicate to the compiler which variables should be shared among the threads and which ones are private through the *shared* and *private* clauses, respectively. Finally, it is possible to choose the scheduling algorithm to use through the *schedule* option. The supported scheduling algorithms are *static*, *dynamic* and *guided*. In the first case, the number of iterations are equally or as equal as possible subdivided among the threads. Thus, each thread performs the same number of iterations. The *dynamic* scheduling uses the internal work queue to give a chunk-sized block of loop iterations to each thread. When a thread finishes, it retrieves the next block of loop iterations from the top of the work queue. The default value of the chunk size is 1, but it is possible to change it by a proper command. Finally, the *guided* scheduling is similar to the *dynamic* one, but the chunk size starts from a big value and then decreases in order to manage load imbalance between different iterations.

We developed two different OpenMP versions of the K-means algorithm. The first one parallelizes the *for* loop which iterates over the hyperspectral pixels (line 6, Algorithm 1). In this way, at each iteration of the main *while* loop, a set of parallel threads are generated and each one computes the SA between a certain group of pixels and the centroids. All the other operations are performed in a serial way. The shared arrays are the cluster_centroids and the input image Y, while all the other variables are private. In this version, the parallel region is created and destroyed at each iteration of the main *while* loop.

Concerning the second implementation, the majority of the operations are performed in parallel. The operations that continue to be performed sequentially are the actual_error computation and the increment of n_iter, at lines 15 and 16 of Algorithm 1, respectively. A barrier must be placed after the actual_error computation, in order to prevent the other threads to evaluate the *while* condition with an inconsistent old value. In this case, also the centroid_distance is declared as shared. Notice that, in this version, the parallel region is created and destroyed only once, at the beginning and at the end of the main *while* loop. However, in this case, it is necessary to introduce a barrier in order to ensure the correct execution of the program.

3.3. CUDA Algorithms

CUDA (https://developer.nvidia.com/cuda-zone) is a parallel programming framework developed by NVIDIA to exploit GPU computing power. In this framework, the GPU, also called *device*, is seen as a parallel co-processor, with separated address space with respect to the CPU, also called *host*. The execution of a CUDA program always begins from the host, using a serial thread. When it is necessary to perform a parallel operation, the host allocates memory on the GPU and transfers the data to that memory. Those two operations are performed through the *cudaFree* and *cudaMemcpy* routines. At this point, the GPU generates thousands of parallel threads, which cooperate in order to perform the desired computation. The function performed by the GPU is called *kernel*. When the kernel execution ends, the CPU retrieves the results from the GPU memory through memory transfer (*cudaMemcpy* routine). The GPU memory is then deallocated by the *cudaFree* routine. The execution proceeds then in a serial way.

The threads generated by the GPU are grouped into *blocks*, which form the *grid*. The blocks can be mono-dimensional, bi-dimensional, or three-dimensional and the number of threads within a block can be chosen by the programmer.

The typical bottleneck of GPU applications is represented by memory transfers. Therefore, it is necessary to properly manage them in order to achieve the best performance.

In this work, we present three different parallel versions of the K-means algorithm. The first one is based on the parallelization of the distance computation. In this case, the thread performs the computation of the distance between the assigned pixel and the K centroids. This kernel takes as inputs the hyperspectral image Y and the K centroids stored in the cluster_centroids variable. It produces as output a $N \times K$ array which contains the distances between each pixel and each centroid. In particular, the i-th row and the j-th column of this array store the distance between the i-th pixel and the j-th centroid. Therefore, it is necessary to add a supplementary temporary array ($N \times K$) with respect to the serial implementation. The schematization of this implementation is shown in Figure 3.

The hyperspectral image Y is copied to the GPU memory only once, before the beginning of the main *while* loop. This has been done since the image is not modified by the algorithm. At every iteration, the only data transferred to the GPU is the matrix containing the centroids, that is used, together with the image, to compute the distances, stored in a temporary matrix (distances_array in Figure 3). Data are sent back to the host, which computes the minimum distance for each pixel (i.e., each row of this matrix) and then updates the centroids and computes the error in order to evaluate convergence.

The second CUDA version has been developed in order to avoid the limit of the amount of data transferred during each iteration of the main *while* loop. Therefore, the minimum distance computations, the centroids update, and the error evaluation have been performed on the GPU side. Since the distances are stored in an $N \times K$ array, the kernel used to find the index of the minimum distance is executed by N threads. The i-th thread performs a *for* loop in order to evaluate the minimum distance of the i-th centroid. In other words, this task has been parallelized by assigning to each thread the computation of the minimum distance for one pixel. The index of the minimum distance is stored in the *assigned_cluster* array, which contains the classification obtained at the current iteration of the main loop. The update of the centroids has been performed by a simple kernel where the i-th thread computes the update of the i-th centroid. Concerning the error evaluation, it is possible to use the highly optimized routines offered by the CUBLAS library. In particular, it is possible to use the *cublasSasum* routine, which calculates the sum of the absolute values stored in the input array. Before activating this kernel the element-wise difference between the values stored in the *actual_centroids* and *previous_centroids* arrays must be computed. This is done by a kernel in which a single thread computes the difference between two elements. The sum computed by the *cublasSasum* routine is returned to the host, which performs the final division needed for error evaluation and increments the number of iterations. The schematization of this CUDA version is shown in Figure 4.

It is important to notice that, in this version, only a single precision floating-point value is transferred at each iteration of the main loop. However, an additional data transfer at the end of the main loop must be performed, since it is necessary to retrieve the *assigned_cluster* that contains the hyperspectral pixel classification.

The last CUDA version developed in this work exploits the *dynamic parallelism* introduced by CUDA 6.0. This allows to use a thread inside a kernel in order to generate a grid which executes another kernel. In the proposed case, it is possible to take advantage of dynamic parallelism by moving the main *while* loop inside the kernel. In other words, this version is made up of a single kernel executed on the GPU by a single thread, which manages the activation of the kernels already described for the second CUDA version. In this case, the only memory transfers are performed before (the hyperspectral image *Y*) and after the main loop (the classified pixels *assigned_cluster*). However, it is worth noting that the activation of a kernel from another kernel requires a launching overhead, which will be discussed in Section 4.

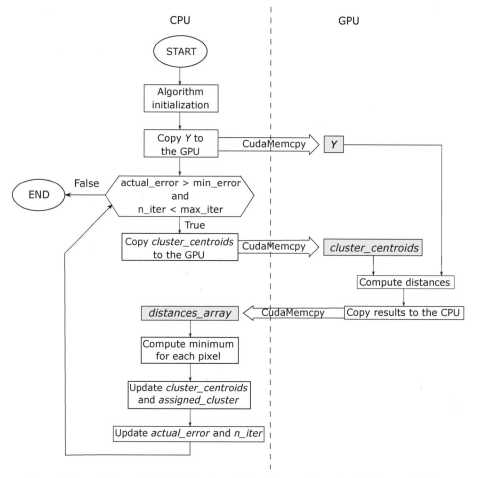

Figure 3. Schematization of the first GPU implementation. The operations are in white boxes, while data are in yellow boxes.

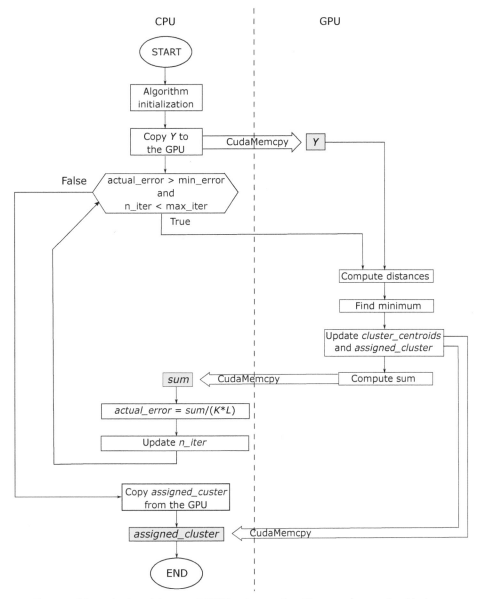

Figure 4. Schematization of the second GPU implementation. The operations are in white boxes, while data are in yellow boxes.

3.4. OpenCL Algorithms

OpenCL (https://www.khronos.org/opencl/) is a parallel programming framework maintained by the Khronos Group which addresses the issue of portability between devices from different vendors. It assumes a model similar to CUDA, with the difference that the blocks are called *working groups* and the threads are called *working items*. The computing platforms that can be programmed using OpenCL range from multi-core CPUs to manycore GPU and finally to Field Programmable Gate Arrays (FPGAs). Similarly to CUDA, this paradigm assumes that the computing platform is made up of a serial processor, called *host*, and one or more parallel *devices*. At the beginning of an OpenCL application, it is important to correctly initialize the execution context. This has the effect of pointing out to the OpenCL environment which devices will be used in the case that there are more than one OpenCL compatible boards installed on the same machine. Data that must be processed by the devices are stored into *buffers*, which can be of different types, depending on the targeting devices of the implementation. In particular, considering a generic GPU as a device, a buffer is a portion of the device memory where data are copied from the host memory. On the other hand, if we consider as a device a multi-core CPU or an integrated GPU which shared the RAM memory with the host, the buffer is only a reference to the RAM portion where data are stored. Notice that, in this last case, there will be no data transfers between host and device since the RAM address space is shared. An important difference when compared with CUDA is the absence of dynamic parallelism, thus, it is not possible to activate a kernel from another one. Therefore, we only developed two versions based on OpenCL. The first one performs the parallel computation of the distances on the device while the other operations are performed on the host. The second version performs all the operations inside the main *while* loop on the device, as we implemented in the second CUDA version already described. However, it is not possible to exploit the CUBLAS library, since it is strictly correlated with the adoption of NVIDIA devices. Therefore, we exploit the *clBLAS* library which is very similar to CUBLAS. In particular, we use the *clblasSasum* routine which performs the summation of all the elements stored in a given array. All the other operations have been performed as described for the second CUDA version.

4. Experimental Results and Discussion

All the parallel implementations have been tested with the hyperspectral dataset already used for serial code profiling and shown in Table 1. The images have been employed both to evaluate the processing times of the different versions and to validate the results. All the parallel versions have obtained the same results than the serial one when removing the random initialization. In other words, if the serial and the parallel versions have the same initialization, they perform the same number of iterations and produce the same outputs.

To graphically analyze the classification results, Figure 5A–F shows the RGB images where the tumor is highlighted. Moreover, Figure 5G–L depicts the supervised classification maps where the tumor is indicated with the red color, the healthy tissue in green, the hypervascularized in blue and the background in black. Images in Figure 5M–R are the segmentation maps produced by the K-means algorithm. As can be seen from the images, this algorithm is capable of distinguishing blood vessels, different tissue regions and the ring markers (used by neurosurgeons to label the image for the supervised classification). As said before, the algorithm defines with high accuracy the boundaries of each area, but the clusters do not correspond to specific classes. Moreover, colors are randomly assigned to each cluster. For this reason, it is crucial to combine this segmentation map with the supervised classification result in obtain the final output, shown in Figure 5S–X.

4.1. OpenMP Performance Evaluation

First, for each OpenMP implementation, several tests have been conducted in order to establish the optimal number of threads to be generated, using the biggest image (Image 6). These tests have been performed on an Intel i7 6700 processor working at 3.40 GHz equipped with 32 GB of RAM. The codes have been compiled with the *vc140* compiler, using compilation options to indicate the target architecture (i.e., x64 processor) and to maximize the processing speed. The processing times have been measured through the *omp_get_wtime* routine. The obtained results are shown in Figure 6.

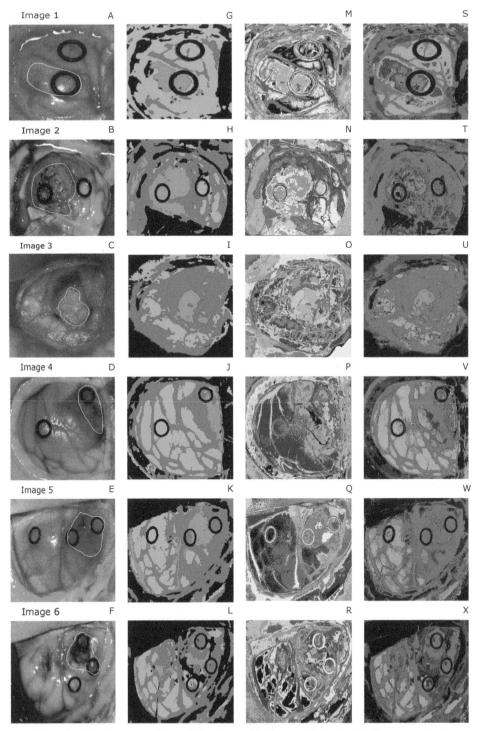

Figure 5. RGB representations of the dataset (**A–F**), supervised classification maps (**G–L**), segmentation maps (**M–R**), final output (**S–X**).

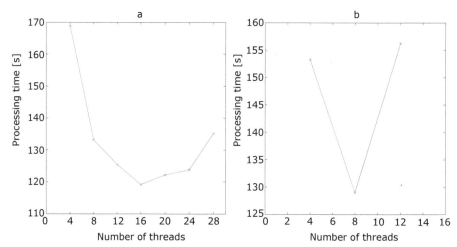

Figure 6. Processing time for Image 6 with respect to the number of threads for the first (**a**) and for the second (**b**) OpenMP version.

It is important to highlight that the experiments have been conducted with the same initialization, and they provide the same number of iterations and the same classification results. For the first OpenMP implementation, we measured the processing time from 4 to 28 threads. We did not test the application with more threads since the processing time begins to significantly grow after 28 threads. By analyzing Figure 6a, it is possible to see that the optimal number of threads for the first OpenMP version is 16. These measures have also been performed for the second OpenMP version, but in this case the maximum number of threads tested was 12 since the processing times begins to grow. In this case, as highlighted by Figure 6b, the optimal number of threads is 8.

After establishing the optimal number of threads, we tested the two OpenMP versions on the entire dataset presented in Table 1. In order to allow a direct comparison between the serial and the parallel versions, we initialized the algorithm with the same values for a given image. The obtained results, together with the speed-up values, are reported in Table 2, where OpenMPv1 indicates the first version (the parallelization of the distance metric computation), while OpenMPv2 indicates the second one (the whole main loop parallelized). Those results, together with the others obtained by the CUDA and OpenCL versions, will be discussed in Section 4.4.

Table 2. Comparison between the serial and the OpenMP versions of the algorithm. The speed-up is reported between brackets.

Image ID	# of Iterations	Serial [s]	OpenMPv1 [s]	OpenMPv2 [s]
Image 1	32	272.20	73.18 (3.72×)	75.88 (3.59×)
Image 2	13	162.37	44.42 (3.65×)	45.80 (3.55×)
Image 3	23	289.64	77.81 (3.72×)	81.35 (3.56×)
Image 4	10	151.50	40.98 (3.70×)	43.42 (3.49×)
Image 5	13	214.52	59.00 (3.64×)	63.09 (3.40×)
Image 6	25	465.51	118.31 (3.93×)	136.99 (3.40×)

4.2. CUDA Performance Evaluation

The three CUDA versions have been compiled using the NVIDIA *nvcc* compiler, which is part of the CUDA 9.0 environment. Compilation options have been chosen in order to maximize the execution speed. The tests have been conducted using two different GPUs. The first one is a NVIDIA Tesla K40 GPU equipped with 2880 CUDA cores working at 750 MHz and with 12 GB of DDR5 RAM.

It is based on the Kepler architecture that does not have a graphical output port since it is optimized for scientific computations. The second GPU is a NVIDIA GTX 1060 equipped with 1152 CUDA cores working at 1.75 GHz and with 3 GB of DDR5 RAM. This GPU is more recent than the first one and it is based on the Pascal architecture, having a graphical output port. In order to take full advantage of the specific architecture of each GPU, we indicate to the compiler which is the target micro-architecture. Specifically, we used the options *sm_35* and *compute_35* for the Tesla K40 GPU and the options *sm_60* and *compute_60* for the GTX 1060, where the values 35 and 60 represent the Kepler and the Pascal architecture, respectively. The results obtained using the Tesla K40 GPU are reported in Table 3, while the results obtained by the GTX 1060 GPU are reported in Table 4.

Table 3. Comparison between the serial and the CUDA versions of the algorithm on a Tesla K40 GPU. The speed-up is reported between brackets.

Image ID	# of Iterations	Serial [s]	CUDAv1 [s]	CUDAv2 [s]	CUDAv3 [s]
Image 1	32	272.20	87.48 (3.11×)	4.52 (60.22×)	4.87 (55.89×)
Image 2	13	162.37	54.51 (2.98×)	2.97 (54.67×)	3.34 (48.61×)
Image 3	23	289.64	100.67 (2.88×)	4.99 (58.04×)	5.12 (56.57×)
Image 4	10	151.50	56.41 (2.69×)	2.96 (51.18×)	3.47 (43.66×)
Image 5	13	214.52	79.74 (2.69×)	3.99 (53.76×)	4.14 (51.82×)
Image 6	25	465.51	159.77 (2.91×)	7.45 (62.48×)	7.83 (59.45×)

Table 4. Comparison between the serial and the CUDA versions of the algorithm on a GTX 1060 GPU. The speed-up is reported between brackets.

Image ID	# of Iterations	Serial [s]	CUDAv1 [s]	CUDAv2 [s]	CUDAv3 [s]
Image 1	32	272.20	80.84 (3.37×)	2.37 (114.85×)	4.21 (64.66×)
Image 2	13	162.37	44.54 (3.65×)	1.94 (83.70×)	2.93 (55.42×)
Image 3	23	289.64	98.61 (2.94×)	2.66 (108.89×)	2.96 (97.85×)
Image 4	10	151.50	52.47 (2.89×)	2.02 (75.00×)	3.25 (46.62×)
Image 5	13	214.52	75.00 (2.86×)	2.41 (89.01×)	3.48 (61.64×)
Image 6	25	465.61	147.50 (3.16×)	3.16 (147.34×)	3.69 (126.18×)

In both tables, CUDAv1 indicates the version where only the distance computation is computed on the GPU, CUDAv2 indicates the version where all the operations are performed in parallel and, finally, CUDAv3 indicates the version exploiting dynamic parallelism.

Concerning the GPU implementation, we also conducted a profiling using the NVIDIA Visual Profiler. This tool allows to profile the code execution on GPU together with memory transfers, in order to evaluate the efficiency of the implementation. Figure 7 shows the results obtained by profiling the Image 1 (the most demanding one) processing on the GTX 1060 with the CUDAv1 (a) and CUDAv2 (b) codes. Concerning the CUDAv2, in Figure 7b the different kernels executions percentage on the GPU are detailed. Profiling of CUDAv3 is not shown since it is very similar to CUDAv2 as well as the code profiling on the NVIDIA Tesla K40 GPU.

4.3. OpenCL Performance Evaluation

OpenCL codes have been compiled using vendor-specific compilers. In particular, the OpenCL version without memory transfers have been tested on an Intel i7 6700 processor working at 3.40 GHz, equipped with 32 GB of RAM and on an Intel HD Graphics 530 integrated GPU with 16 cores working at 350 MHz. The integrated board shares the RAM with the CPU. Concerning the OpenCL version which performs memory transfers, it has been tested on the NVIDIA GTX 1060 GPU. Results obtained by the OpenCL versions are reported in Table 5.

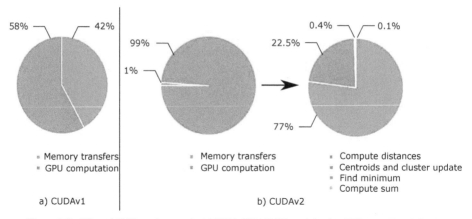

Figure 7. Profiling of GPU versions on the NVIDIA GTX 1060 board for the CUDA v1 (**a**) and CUDA v2 (**b**) versions.

Table 5. Comparison between the serial and the OpenCL versions of the algorithm. The speed-up is reported between brackets.

Image ID	# of Iterations	Serial [s]	Intel i7 [s]	Intel HD 530 [s]	GTX 1060 [s]
Image 1	32	272.20	74.13 (3.67×)	183.96 (1.48×)	57.61 (4.72×)
Image 2	13	162.37	44.32 (3.66×)	114.24 (1.42×)	35.61 (4.56×)
Image 3	23	289.64	79.52 (3.64×)	203.62 (1.42×)	63.75 (4.54×)
Image 4	10	151.50	40.52 (3.74×)	113.82 (1.33×)	35.36 (4.28×)
Image 5	13	214.52	59.92 (3.58×)	156.56 (1.37×)	47.03 (4.56×)
Image 6	25	465.51	121.59 (3.83×)	312.68 (1.49×)	93.65 (4.97×)

4.4. Comparisons and Discussion

The OpenMP version that offers the better results is the one where only the distance evaluations are processed in parallel. In this version, a parallel region is created and then destroyed at every iteration of the main loop, while in the second version the parallel region is created only once before the beginning of the main loop and is destroyed after the end of the main loop. However, the second version requires synchronization barriers between the threads, since there are operations that should be performed sequentially to obtain correct results. As an example, the increment of the number of iterations and the check of the conditions for repeating or not the main loop should be performed by a single thread. This is a critical issue since the advantage of creating and destroying the parallel region only once is thwarted by the synchronization bottleneck. The result analysis shows that the processing times are very similar, but the processor manages better the first version (OpenMPv1). Moreover, the speed-up values of the two versions are similar. Finally, it is important to highlight that the considered processor is equipped with 4 physical cores and the obtained speed-up is always greater than 3.5×. This means that the parallelization efficiency is close to the theoretical value.

Concerning the CUDA versions, by analyzing Tables 3 and 4, it is possible to observe that, for both GPU boards, the first CUDA version (CUDAv1) performs worse than the OpenMP ones. The reason is highlighted in Figure 7a, where the profiling results show that the memory transfers take about 42% of the time and only the remaining 58% is used for the computation. This is the typical bottleneck of GPU computing since the memory transfers are performed by the PCI-express external bus. The second CUDA version (CUDAv2) is not affected by this issue since the amount of data transferred at each main iteration is significantly lower than in the previous case. It is possible to parameterize the amount of transferred data at each iteration for these two versions. In the first case (CUDAv1), the data transferred is the distance_array matrix, which is made up of $N \times K$ elements represented in single precision floating-point arithmetic, while in the second case (CUDAv2) only one single precision floating-point value is copied back to the host. In the third case (CUDAv3), when dynamic parallelism is used, there are no data transfers inside the main loop. Therefore the third CUDA version is the one which transfers the minimum possible amount of data, but it does not perform better than the second version. This is because the dynamic parallelism produces an overhead due to the GPU switch between the main kernel and the subroutine kernel. This overhead affects every sub-kernel activation. In this specific case, four different sub-kernels are activated at every iteration. This overhead is not negligible and, as it can be seen form the results of Tables 3 and 4, it takes longer than the copy of a single float value from device to host. In other words, the time needed by the GPU to manage the generation of four sub-kernels (CUDAv3) is comparable with the time taken by a single value copy from the host to the device memory (CUDAv2). Finally, for all the CUDA versions, the GTX 1060 board performs better than the Tesla K40, even if the last board is optimized for scientific computations. This is because the first board is equipped with a more recent architecture which has better CUDA cores working at a higher frequency than the Tesla GPU.

The analysis of the OpenCL versions highlight that, considering the Intel i7, the processing times are close to the OpenMP ones. For what concerns the Intel HD 530 integrated GPU, the performance is very poor, and the speed-ups are negligible. This is probably due to the low-end integrated GPU with a working frequency of 350 MHz and only 16 parallel processing elements. Therefore, it is not possible to obtain a significant speed-up compared to the serial version. Comparing the OpenCL version and the CUDA versions running on the GTX 1060 GPU, it is possible to notice that the OpenCL version performs better than the CUDAv1, but is significantly slower than the other two CUDA versions. These CUDA versions (CUDAv2 and CUDAv3) employ highly optimized routines, which exploits all the hardware features of a GPU. Moreover, the CUDA versions have been compiled using compilation options in order to produce an executable code which fully exploits the specific target architecture. This is not possible in OpenCL since it targets portability between different devices as main feature.

We also performed a comparative study between the three best performing versions of the three considered technologies in order to characterize how the speed-up varies with respect to the number of clusters. In particular, we performed experiments using Image 6 and K values varying from 2 to 50. The speed-ups of the OpenMP, CUDA and OpenCL best versions with respect to the serial implementation are shown in Figure 8 using a semi-logarithmic scale. It is possible to see that the CUDA version has a speed-up that ranges from $10\times$ to $\sim150\times$ and from 12 clusters on it becomes nearly constant. On the other hand, the solutions based on a multi-core processor have speed-ups that are close to $4\times$.

In the literature, there are different works about parallel K-means.

Baramkar et al. [18] performed a review of different parallel GPU-based K-means, but the considered works where focused only on general classification, without considering high data dimensionality, which is the case explored in our work. Therefore it is hard to perform direct comparisons with these works, which achieve very different speed-ups ranging from $11\times$ to $220\times$.

Zechner et al. [19] proposed a parallel implementation of this algorithm using both CPU and GPU. In particular, the GPU was only employed for distance computation, while centroids update was left to the CPU. They classified an artificial dataset with two-dimensional elements ranging from 500 to 500, 000. The maximum speed-up achieved was $14\times$, lower than the one obtained in our work. This is because the optimization proposed in [19] is only valid for low-dimensional data and cannot be employed for classifying high-dimensional data such as hyperspectral images.

A similar approach is shown in [20,21], with the difference that also the clusters update has been performed on the GPU. However, between the distance computation and centroids update they performed host computation for updating each pixel label. This choice leads to a maximum speed-up of 60 in both works, lower than our one, since we moved all the computation on the device side.

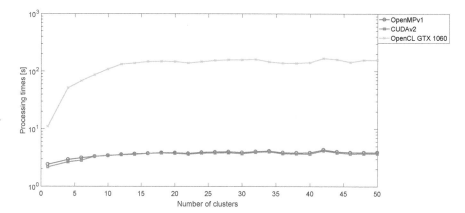

Figure 8. Speed-ups achieved by the three best parallel implementations (one for each evaluated parallel technology) with respect to the number of clusters.

In [22], a GPU-based K-means algorithm is proposed, with a distance computation that is evaluated through a simple Cartesian distance. Under this assumption, they classify 1,000,000 pixels with 32 features in 1.15 s. In our case, the bigger image has 264,408 pixels, the features (i.e., the bands) are 128 and it is processed in ~3.56 s. Moreover, the distance metric that we adopt (the spectral angle) is more complex than the one proposed in [22].

Baydoun et al. [23] developed a parallel K-means for RGB images classification. They adopted as metric a simple Cartesian distance and they parallelize only this computation, achieving a maximum speed-up of ~25×. In this case, the metric and the data dimensionality are very different compared to this work.

In [24], the K-means algorithm was modified to further reduce the distance computation. The speed-up varies from 4× to 386×, but also, in this case, it is not possible to perform a direct comparison since there are not enough details about the dataset composition. Finally, in [25], the K-means algorithm was developed on GPU with the Cartesian distance. They adopt a modern GPU with 1536 CUDA cores obtaining a maximum speed-up of 88×, which is very similar to our results.

Lutz et al. [26] proposed a parallel K-means implementation using an NVIDIA GTX 1080 GPU. They perfomed only experiments producing four groups and no further details are given in the paper about the dataset. They achieved a maximum speed-up of 18.5× which is nearly an order of magnitude smaller than one of our implementations.

A comparative analysis similar to the one we conducted is reported in [27]. Authors exploited GPUs, OpenMP, Message Passing Interface (MPI) and FPGAs. However, also in this case, they considered only a dataset made up of 10-dimensional points, therefore the computational complexity of the distance computation is lower than our one. On the other hand, the results were not as good as our ones, since the maximum GPU speed-up achieved is ~60×. They also demonstrated that the speed-up could reach a value up to 200× if the number of clusters to produce was significantly increased (i.e., more than 2000 clusters), but a study of how this speed-up varied also with respect to the data dimensionality were not carried out. Concerning OpenMP, the classification of 20,000 10-dimensionality points took ~3 s. Our smallest image is 6 times bigger than this one and with a dimensionality 18 times greater than the one considered. Keeping this in mind, the performance of our best OpenMP version is quite similar to this one. Finally, concerning the FPGA implementation, experiments were reported only with a 17,692 9-dimensionality dataset. Classification time is ~100 ms, but, as stated in [27], the FPGA resources, especially memory banks, were not enough to process bigger datasets. The authors of this work do not use external DDR memory, therefore the FPGA performance is limited due to this design choice.

The comparison between our work and the literature is summarized in Table 6.

Table 6. Comparison between the proposed work and the literature.

Paper	Maximum Image Size	Data Dimensionality	Technology	Speed-Up
[18]	2,000,000	8	GPU NVIDIA GTX 280	220
[19]	500,000	2	GPU NVIDIA 9600 GT	14
[20]	1,000,000	2	GPU NVIDIA 8800 GTX	60
[21]	15,052,800	3	4 × GPU NVIDIA GTX 750Ti	60
[22]	1,000,000	32	GPU NVIDIA GTX 280	N. A.
[23]	16,777,216	3	GPU NVIDIA Tesla C2050	25
[24]	245,057	4	GPU NVIDIA GeForce 210	386
[25]	500,000	16	GPU NVIDIA Quadro K5000	88
[26]	N. A.	N. A.	GPU NVIDIA GTX 1080	18.5
[27]	20,000	10	2 × AMD Opteron quad-core	8
[27]	65,536	10	GPU NVIDIA Tesla 2050	60
[27]	17,692	9	Mitrion MVP FPGA Simulator	N. A.
Our work	264,408	128	GPU NVIDIA GTX 1060	126

5. Conclusions

In this paper, we presented different parallel implementations of the K-means algorithm for hyperspectral medical image clustering. In particular, we evaluated multi-core CPUs and manycore GPUs through the OpenMP and CUDA frameworks, respectively. Moreover, we also addressed the problem of code portability by developing OpenCL-based versions. We performed experiments with a dataset made up of *in-vivo* hyperspectral human brain images. Those experiments validated the results of all the proposed parallel implementations. Among them, CUDA achieved the better performance, outperforming OpenMP implementations. The cost of the better performance is the parallelization effort, which is significantly greater when working with CUDA. In fact, the development of the CUDA versions required the development of custom kernels and ad-hoc memory transfer management, while OpenMP only required code annotations with suitable pragmas. Code portability has also been addressed with OpenCL. However, this technology is not yet competitive with OpenMP or CUDA, achieving the worst results among the developed parallel applications. Moreover, OpenCL guarantees portability among different devices, but, for obtaining the best performance from a given device, it is necessary to tune the code with respect to specific hardware features. The comparison of the proposed implementations shows that the best one is based on CUDA and executed on the GTX 1060 board, achieving a maximum speed-up of ~125×. In particular, the best CUDA version performs all the computations on the GPU without exploiting dynamic parallelism.

We also made comparisons with other recent works in the literature, that only in one case achieved results comparable but not better than ours, except for the FPGA solution proposed in [27]. However, FPGA memory constraint does not allow to process images with more than 17, 692 pixels. This limits the use of this technology and, in particular, it makes FPGAs not suitable for our target application.

Summarizing, the proposed work confirms that the GPU technology is the best solution for these class of problems, even when considering a data dimensionality bigger than the ones considered before. It also highlights that the GPU algorithm has a good scalability with respect to the number of clusters (*K*). Moreover, when considering high data dimensionality, the parallelization of the distance computation is not enough, since also the centroids update, and the error computation can be parallelized. This ensures a supplementary speed-up. Finally, the technological evolution of GPUs offers increasing computing power at relatively low cost. In our case, a consumer GPU sold at about \$200 outperforms a more expensive Tesla K40 GPU (~\$5000) of a previous generation, but optimized for scientific computations.

In conclusion, this work provides an efficient GPU implementation of the K-means algorithm, that will be included in the parallel version of the complete system already shown in Figure 1. Since the K-means is one of the most computational demanding algorithms in the system, this remarkable result is essential to satisfy the real-time constraint.

Future research will be focused on integrating this parallel algorithm in more complicated classification frameworks, such as the one proposed in [5,7].

Author Contributions: E.T. performed the GPU implementations, the algorithms optimizations, designed and performed experiments and wrote the manuscript. G.F. designed experiments and edited the manuscript. F.C. performed the GPU implementations and experiments. S.O., H.F. performed the serial algorithm implementation and edited the manuscript. G.M.C., M.M.-M., F.L. supervised the project and edited the manuscript.

Funding: This work has been supported in part by the Canary Islands Government through the ACIISI (Canarian Agency for Research, Innovation and the Information Society), ITHACA project "Hyperspectral Identification of Brain Tumors" under Grant Agreement ProID2017010164 and it has been partially supported also by the Spanish Government and European Union (FEDER funds) as part of support program in the context of Distributed HW/SW Platform for Intelligent Processing of Heterogeneous Sensor Data in Large Open Areas Surveillance Applications (PLATINO) project, under contract TEC2017-86722-C4-1-R. Additionally, this work was completed while Samuel Ortega was beneficiary of a pre-doctoral grant given by the "Agencia Canaria de Investigacion, Innovacion y Sociedad de la Información (ACIISI)" of the "Conserjería de Economía, Industria, Comercio y Conocimiento" of the "Gobierno de Canarias", which is part-financed by the European Social Fund (FSE) (POC 2014–2020, Eje 3 Tema Prioritario 74(85%)). Finally, this work has been also supported in part by the 2016 PhD Training Program for Research Staff of the University of Las Palmas de Gran Canaria.

Acknowledgments: The authors would like to thank NVIDIA Corporation for the donation of the NVIDIA Tesla K40 GPU used for this research.

Conflicts of Interest: The authors declare no conflict of interest.

References

1. Ferlay, J.; Soerjomataram, I.; Ervik, M.; Dikshit, R.; Eser, S.; Mathers, C.; Rebelo, M.; Parkin, D.M.; Forman, D.; Bray, F. *Cancer Incidence and Mortality Worldwide: IARC CancerBase No. 11*; International Agency for Research on Cancer: Lyon, France, 2013.
2. Louis, D.N.; Perry, A.; Reifenberger, G.; von Deimling, A.; Figarella-Branger, D.C.; Webster, K.; Ohgaki, H.; Wiestler, O.D.; Kleihues, P.; Ellison, D.W. The 2016 World Health Organization Classification of Tumors of the Central Nervous System: A summary. *Acta Neuropathol.* **2016**, *131*, 803–820. [CrossRef] [PubMed]
3. Sanai, M.; Berger, M.S. Operative techniques for gliomas and the value of extent of resection. *Neurotherapeutics* **2009**, *6*, 478–486. [CrossRef] [PubMed]
4. Fabelo, H.; Ortega, S.; Kabwama, S.; Callicó, G.M.; Bulters, D.; Szolna, A.; Pineiro, J.F.; Sarmiento, R. HELICoiD project: A new use of hyperspectral imaging for brain cancer detection in real-time during neurosurgical operations. *Proc. SPIE Int. Soc. Opt. Eng.* **2016**, *12*, 9860. [CrossRef]
5. Fabelo, H.; Ortega, S.; Lazcano, R.; Madronal, D.; Callicó, G.M.; Juárez, E.; Salvador, R.; Bulters, D.; Bulstrode, H.; Szolna, A.; et al. An intraoperative visualization system using hyperspectral imaging to aid in brain tumor delineation. *Sensors* **2018**, *18*, 430. [CrossRef] [PubMed]
6. Chang, C.-I. *Hyperspectral Data Processing: Algorithm Design and Analysis*; John Wiley & Sons: Hoboken, NJ, USA, 2013; ISBN 978-0-471-69056-6.
7. Fabelo, H.; Ortega, S.; Ravi, D.; Kiran, B.R.; Sosa, C.; Bulters, D.; Callicó, G.M.; Bulstrode, H.; Szolna, A.; Pineiro, J.F.; Kabwama, S.; et al. Spatio-spectral classification of hyperspectral images for brain cancer detection during surgical operations. *PLoS ONE* **2018**, *13*, e0193721. [CrossRef] [PubMed]
8. Torti, E.; Fontanella, A.; Florimbi, G.; Leporati, F.; Fabelo, H.; Ortega, S.; Callicó, G.M. Acceleration of brain cancer detection algorithms during surgery procedures using GPUs. *Microprocess. Microsyst.* **2018**, *61*, 171–178. [CrossRef]
9. Florimbi, G.; Fabelo, H.; Torti, E.; Lazcano, R.; Madronal, D.; Ortega, S.; Salvador, R.; Leporati, F.; Danese, G.; Báez-Quevedo, A.; et al. Accelerating the K-Nearest Neighbors Filtering Algorithm to Optimize the Real-Time Classification of Human Brain Tumor in Hyperspectral Images. *Sensors* **2018**, *18*, 2314. [CrossRef] [PubMed]
10. Lazcano, R.; Madronal, D.; Salvador, R.; Desnos, K.; Pelcat, M.; Guerra, R.; Fabelo, H.; Ortega, S.; Lopez, S.; Callico, G.M.; et al. Porting a PCA-based hyperspectral image dimensionality reduction algorithm for brain cancer detection on a manycore architecture. *J. Syst. Archit.* **2017**, *77*, 101–111. [CrossRef]
11. Madronal, D.; Lazcano, R.; Salvador, R.; Fabelo, H.; Ortega, S.; Callico, G.M.; Juarez, E.; Sanz, C. SVM-based real-time hyperspectral image classifier on a manycore architecture. *J. Syst. Archit.* **2017**, *80*, 30–40. [CrossRef]

12. Domingo, R.; Salvador, R.; Fabelo, H.; Madronal, D.; Ortega, S.; Lazcano, R.; Juarez, E.; Callico, G.M.; Sanz, C. High-level design using Intel FPGA OpenCL: A hyperspectral imaging spatial-spectral classifier. In Proceedings of the 2017 12th International Symposium on Reconfigurable Communication-centric Systems-on-Chip (ReCoSoC), Madrid, Spain, 12–14 July 2017; pp. 1–8. [CrossRef]

13. Fontanella, A.; Marenzi, E.; Torti, E.; Danese, G.; Plaza, A.; Leporati, F. A suite of parallel algorithms for efficient band selection from hyperspectral images. *J. Real-Time Image Process.* **2018**, 1–17. [CrossRef]

14. Marenzi, E.; Carrus, A.; Danese, G.; Leporati, F.; Callicó, G.M. Efficient Parallelization of Motion Estimation for Super-Resolution. In Proceedings of the 2017 25th Euromicro International Conference on Parallel, Distributed and Network-based Processing (PDP), St. Petersburg, Russia, 6–8 March 2017; pp. 274–277. [CrossRef]

15. Lopez-Fandino, J.; Heras, D.B.; Arguello, F.; Dalla Mura, M. GPU Framework for Change Detection in Multitemporal Hyperspectral Images. *Int. J. Parallel Program.* **2017**, 1–21. [CrossRef]

16. Florimbi, G.; Torti, E.; Danese, G.; Leporati, F. High Performant Simulations of Cerebellar Golgi Cells Activity. In Proceedings of the 2017 25th Euromicro International Conference on Parallel, Distributed and Network-based Processing (PDP), St. Petersburg, Russia, 6–8 March 2017; pp. 527–534. [CrossRef]

17. Feng, X.; Jin, H.; Zheng, R.; Zhu, L.; Dai, W. Accelerating Smith-Waterman Alignment of Species-Based Protein Sequences on GPU. *Int. J. Parallel Program.* **2015**, *43*, 359–380. [CrossRef]

18. Baramkar, P.P.; Kulkarni, D.B. Review for K-Means On Graphics Processing Units (GPU). *Int. J. Eng. Res. Technol.* **2014**, *3*, 1911–1914.

19. Zechner, M.; Granitzer, M. K-Means on the Graphics Processor: Design and Experimental Analysis. *Int. J. Adv. Syst. Meas.* **2009**, *2*, 224–235. [CrossRef]

20. Hong-tao, B.; Li-li, H.; Dan-tong, O.; Zhan-shan, L.; He, L. K-Means on Commodity GPUs with CUDA. In Proceedings of the WRI World Congress on Computer Science and Information Engineering, Los Angeles, CA, USA, 31 March–2 April 2009; pp. 651–655. [CrossRef]

21. Fakhi, H.; Bouattane, O.; Youssfi, M.; Hassan, O. New optimized GPU version of the k-means algorithm for large-sized image segmentation. In Proceedings of the Intelligent Systems and Computer Vision, Fez, Morocco, 17–19 April 2017; pp. 1–6. [CrossRef]

22. Li, Y.; Zhao, K.; Chu, X.; Liu, J. Speeding up k-Means algorithm by GPUs. *J. Comput. Syst. Sci.* **2013**, *79*, 216–229. [CrossRef]

23. Baydoun, M.; Dawi, M.; Ghaziri, H. Enhanced parallel implementation of the K-Means clustering algorithm. In Proceedings of the 3rd International Conference on Advances in Computational Tools for Engineering Applications (ACTEA), Beirut, Lebanon, 13–15 July 2016; pp. 7–11. [CrossRef]

24. Saveetha, V.; Sophia, S. Optimal Tabu K-Means Clustering Using Massively Parallel Architecture. *J. Circuits Syst. Comput.* **2018**, In press. [CrossRef]

25. Cuomo, S.; De Angelis, V.; Farina, G.; Marcellino, L.; Toraldo, G. A GPU-accelerated parallel K-means algorithm. *Comput. Electr. Eng.* **2017**, 1–13. [CrossRef]

26. Lutz, C.; Bress, S.; Rabl, T.; Zeuch, S.; Markl, V. Efficient k-means on GPUs. In Proceedings of the 14th International Workshop on Data Management on New Hardware, Huston, ID, USA, 11 June 2018. [CrossRef]

27. Yang, L.; Chiu, S.C.; Liao, W.K.; Thomas, M.A. High Performance Data Clustering: A Comparative Analysis of Performance for GPU, RASC, MPI, and OpenMP Implementations. *J. Supercomput.* **2014**, *70*, 284–300. [CrossRef] [PubMed]

Article

i-Light—Intelligent Luminaire Based Platform for Home Monitoring and Assisted Living

Iuliana Marin [1], Andrei Vasilateanu [1,*], Arthur-Jozsef Molnar [2], Maria Iuliana Bocicor [2,*], David Cuesta-Frau [3,4], Antonio Molina-Picó [3] and Nicolae Goga [1,5,*]

[1] Faculty of Engineering in Foreign Languages, University Politehnica of Bucharest, 060042 Bucharest, Romania; iuliana.marin@upb.ro

[2] S.C. Info World S.R.L., 023828 Bucharest, Romania; arthur.molnar@infoworld.ro

[3] Innovatec Sensing & Communication S.L., 03801 Alcoi, Spain; dcuestaf@innovatecsc.com (D.C.-F.); amolina@innovatecsc.com (A.M.-P.)

[4] Technological Institute of Informatics, Polytechnic University of Valencia, Alcoi Campus, Plaza Ferrandizy Carbonell 2, 03801 Alcoi, Spain

[5] Molecular Dynamics Group, University of Groningen, Nijneborgh 7, 9747 AG Groningen, The Netherlands

[*] Correspondence: andrei.vasilateanu@upb.ro (A.V.); iuliana.bocicor@infoworld.ro (M.I.B.); nicolae.goga@upb.ro (N.G.)

Received: 9 September 2018; Accepted: 25 September 2018; Published: 28 September 2018

Abstract: We present i-Light, a cyber-physical platform that aims to help older adults to live safely within their own homes. The system is the result of an international research project funded by the European Union and is comprised of a custom developed wireless sensor network together with software services that provide continuous monitoring, reporting and real-time alerting capabilities. The principal innovation proposed within the project regards implementation of the hardware components in the form of intelligent luminaires with inbuilt sensing and communication capabilities. Custom luminaires provide indoor localisation and environment sensing, are cost-effective and are designed to replace the lighting infrastructure of the deployment location without prior mapping or fingerprinting. We evaluate the system within a home and show that it achieves localisation accuracy sufficient for room-level detection. We present the communication infrastructure, and detail how the software services can be configured and used for visualisation, reporting and real-time alerting.

Keywords: ambient assisted living; intelligent luminaires; wireless sensor network; indoor localisation; indoor monitoring

---

1. Introduction

Ambient Assisted Living (AAL) systems are designed to offer support for people with various diseases or disabilities, or older adults, thus enabling them to live as independently as possible in their own homes. Such systems create intelligent environments in people's personal residences and are able to monitor the indoor ambient, people's activities, behaviour and even health status. They were conceived to adapt independently to the needs of their users and to offer timely assistance in case of emergency or problematic situations, thus improving the quality of life [1].

AAL systems appeared in recent years, in the current context of profound demographic transformations. As shown by the 2012 European Commission report on ageing [2], the ratio between the inactive population aged 65 to active persons (aged 15–64) will "rise significantly from around 39% in 2010 to 71% in 2060" [2]. Similar transformations are expected to take place in the rest of the world: in wide areas of Asia and North America, more than 30% of the population will be 60 or older by 2050 [3]. While members of the geriatric population can opt to live at home or in nursing homes, the favoured choice for most of them is to continue living autonomously in their own homes and communities, with support from family, friends and caregivers.

Depending on their functionality and design, AAL systems can be used for various purposes: monitoring at home, intervention in case of emergency, or telehealth services. They all have the same goal of allowing older adults to maintain an autonomous lifestyle in safety and with optimised costs by discarding the need for constant caregiver supervision. To provide the required features, the majority of systems comprise wireless sensor networks, medical devices and software applications for monitoring and reporting. However, in many cases, these systems are cumbersome to deploy and maintain, leave an unwanted visual footprint in the monitored person's home and can be a source of frustration or stress through the visible indicators of the person being constantly monitored.

This paper describes the first prototype of i-Light, a pervasive cyber-physical system targeted toward older adult supervision and home monitoring [4,5]. The system is being developed under the umbrella of European Union research funding. One of its innovative aspects, as described in the present paper, is that all system components are embedded in unobtrusive luminaires, providing the following capabilities:

- Continuous supervision of the monitored person's indoor whereabouts and activities through localisation.
- Constant monitoring of indoor ambient conditions in order to ensure the safety of monitored persons.
- Real-time alerts and notifications provided to the monitored person and selected caregivers in case of emergency situations.
- Interoperability with third-party medical devices for telehealth purposes.

To achieve all these, the system is composed of a wireless network of sensors and a suite of multi-platform software applications for indoor localisation, ambient data monitoring and analysis, reporting and real-time alerting. In addition, an important innovation brought by i-Light is that the nodes of the wireless network are custom developed energy-efficient luminaire devices embedded with sensing, localisation and communication capabilities. As such, system deployment is simple and inexpensive, requiring only the replacement of existing electrical illumination devices in the household with the intelligent luminaires. This creates a pervasive and complete home monitoring scheme, while removing current adoption barriers related to deployment complexity and associated costs. Nevertheless, the system's main advantage remains that it ensures timely assistance from family members, friends and caregivers in case of emergency.

The present work details the intelligent luminaires embedded with lighting and sensor modules, the system's software components, its communication capabilities and hardware-software integration. Luminaires can be either smart or dummy, depending on their purpose. Both types are described within the present paper. Software applications were conceived for indoor localisation, sensor data collection, aggregation and analysis, as well as creation and visualisation of reports. Furthermore, the system can create and send real-time alerts to monitored persons and designated caregivers in case of emergency or undesired ambient conditions.

2. State of the Art

Research required for the presented system spans several topics including ambient assisted living, interior localisation and intelligent luminaires. We provide a concise account of the current state of the art related to all three research directions, with particular emphasis on state of the art AAL systems.

2.1. Ambient Assisted Living

Current technological solutions are targeted towards monitoring and offering support for several vulnerable categories including people in nursing homes, people suffering from disease or disability, or older adults living in their own homes.

Of these systems, we find the most relevant to be those designed for residential homes. The electronic Medication Administration Record system (eMAR), a product of Extended Care Pro company [6], provides alerts and reminders for taking prescribed medication, signalling medication errors or missed follow-ups, performs various analyses and synchronises medication changes with an associated pharmacy. Carevium Assisted Living Software [7] provides features for medication administration, activity tracking, alerts and progress notes, appointments, physician communications, pharmacy interactions and others. Yardi offers a senior living suite of solutions, among which the Yardi EHR [8] and the Yardi eMAR [9] are of interest. The first one, an electronic health record system enables senior living providers to enhance operations and care, to manage medication and streamline caregivers' tasks, while the second one helps improving resident care by ensuring safe medication intake, enabling connections with pharmacies and consolidating medication management.

Further, we focus on systems that target users living in their personal homes and who need supervision due to specific conditions such as disease, disability or old age. The Necessity intelligent system [10] includes an adaptive mechanism that considers the monitored person's routines and detects abnormal situations. Lynx [11] uses a wireless network of heterogeneous sensors to collect data about the monitored person's environment and daily activities. The data are used to infer activities and identify behaviour patterns, which are subsequently employed by an expert knowledge system to detect dangerous situations and send real-time alerts to caregivers. Considering these solutions, Lynx is similar to the system we are proposing in regards to the provided features. However, its deployment necessitates the installation of a multitude of heterogeneous sensors, while our system's deployment is easy, as existing light bulbs must only be replaced by the system's intelligent luminaires. This also reduces the supervised person's mental discomfort, given that they will not feel constantly observed. Another advantage of i-Light is given by its location detection algorithms that run uninterruptedly, while in Lynx indoor positioning is achieved using presence sensors and sensors detecting door opening. Finally, from a medical point of view, the two systems are quite different: while Lynx extracts information from medical records to find correlations between the patient's diagnosis, disease and treatment, i-Light provides communication with third-party medical devices for monitoring the person's health status.

Other systems which aim to determine a person's activities for behavioural pattern identification are described in [12–14]. These use either acoustic wireless sensor networks, comprised of audio and ultrasound receivers, or video data. Acoustic features extracted from data allow the identification of the monitored person's current activity with a high degree of accuracy [12], automatic assessment of the risk of falling (a serious threat to older adults' well-being) [13] and the detection of gait related parameters [14], which can be employed to determine user activity. From the point of view of the final goal (person supervision and risk reduction), these systems are similar to the one we are proposing. However, they achieve it by inferring current activities from several parameters measured via acoustic or video devices, which should be installed within the residence, while our system uses the embedded intelligent luminaires, which replace the existing light bulbs. Furthermore, i-Light is more complex, as it monitors the environment for an increased level of safety and it communicates with standards-compliant third-party medical devices to transmit data to a server, where it can be accessed by caregivers and health professionals.

In the area of home monitoring of neurological patients suffering from conditions such as epilepsy, Parkinson's and Alzheimer's, the literature provides examples of solutions comprising sensors and decision support systems for assisting both patients and doctors. Accelerometers attached to the supervised person's extremities and an unsupervised learning method contribute to seizure detection in epileptic children [15,16]. Behavioural patterns of Alzheimer's patients are identified via a probabilistic approach [17], while hardware devices with pressure sensors and accelerometers that measure tremor and a screening system including data analysis using feature selection and artificial neural networks classification are used to provide decision support in case of Parkinson's patients [18]. A proof of concept for a digital assistant which provides clinical support to patients and facilitates medical and caregiver intervention via smart voice recognition is presented in [19]. Considering patient self-assessment provided using voice, the system provides feedback in the form of advice or warnings and can trigger interventions in case of risk detection.

There are also a few commercially available solutions. Healthsense [20] offers a service for monitoring senior persons' behaviour and activities via sensor networks and remotely alerts caregivers about changes in routine, which could mean potentially dangerous situations. Although not present in the current version, our system will also include an intelligent component, for which we have already started research [21], to analyse activity patterns and to detect any deviations from them. Additionally, the advantage of i-Light compared to Healthsense is represented by the intelligent luminaires, which involve reduced deployment costs and by the supplementary feature of ambient monitoring. Philips' in-home monitoring devices [22] allow patients to take and transmit their own vital signs and measurements to a server. Medtronic CareLink Network [23] uses specific devices such as the Medtronic CareLink Home Monitor to allow sending data over a standard phone line or the Internet to the clinic, connecting cardiac device patients with their clinician. The aforementioned devices are focused on health monitoring, which is also one of i-Light features. This will be achieved within the system via communication between the intelligent luminaires and medical standards compliant devices that send data to the bulbs, which further forward them to the platform's server.

2.2. Indoor Positioning

The standard positioning service used for outdoor localisation is the well known Global Positioning System (GPS), developed within the United States, and available globally. Competing systems are the Russian GLONASS and the European Union developed Galileo system, expected to become fully functional in 2019. A common limitation of these systems is that none work reliably when indoors, due to interference caused by buildings and surrounding objects. While indoor positioning systems have been developed, none of them are regarded as standard.

The i-Light system uses well established wireless technologies to enable indoor localisation, and therefore our focus in this section falls on similar efforts. However, we briskly mention other types of indoor localisation techniques that have been proposed. One alternative to using wireless technology is visible light communication using LED or OLED-based lighting [24], employed in systems such as those offered by GE Lighting [25] or Acuity Brands [26]. In [27], the positions of laser points shot by an unmanned aerial vehicle, in an indoor environment, are used to compute the vehicle's location. Acoustic background fingerprinting [28] or user movement [29] are other techniques proposed for indoor positioning.

The main difference between these systems and ours remains that wireless signal, unlike light, is in most implementations omni-directional and it passes through walls and other obstacles. There are two techniques exploited for this type of localisation: *triangulation*, i.e. angle calculation between node and anchor points; and *trilateration*, i.e. distance measurement. Trilateration is usually preferred, as it is less complex and less expensive. Most systems employ trilateration via the received strength signal index (RSSI) [30], time of arrival (ToA) [31] or time difference of arrival, which can achieve precision of up to a few centimetres [32]. Our choice for indoor localisation is trilateration, considering its benefits mentioned above. Compared to the work in [32], our positioning algorithms obtain a higher error (Section 6), but the aforementioned paper uses mobile nodes embedded in the person's clothes. As opposed to this method, our approach is less interfering, as the monitored persons do not need to wear "smart" clothes and will not feel constantly observed given that our nodes are embedded within the light bulbs. Therefore, we consider this error—guinea pig effect trade-off—advantageous for our system. "Fingerprinting" is an approach that can be used with both Wi-Fi and Bluetooth technology and which involves recording the RSSI in multiple locations within the indoor environment and later the user's location is computed using a prerecorded map [33]. The effectiveness of the newer Bluetooth Low Energy (BLE) standard for indoor positioning has also been studied [34]. By exploring a variety of algorithms and approaches, Dahlgren [34] concluded that BLE is suitable for indoor localisation, offering reasonable accuracy and inexpensive deployment. Wi-Fi based fingerprinting and trilateration have been experimented with for indoor localisation in [35]. Other methods based on trilateration, using both Wi-Fi and BLE technologies with RSSI measurements are presented in [36–38], together with means for noise and bias elimination, as well as for obtaining a good trade-off between accuracy, deployment cost and effort.

Finally, we also mention a few commercially available solutions. Zonith's real time location system [39] is capable of locating persons, as long as they always wear a discoverable Bluetooth device. Similar systems, based on Bluetooth or Wi-Fi beacons, or even ultra-wideband technology [40] are provided by many companies, such as BlooLoc [41], Senion [42], Estimote [43], Pozyx [40] or Infsoft [44].

2.3. Intelligent Luminaires

Light emitting diodes (LEDs) have revolutionised illumination technology, becoming the most suitable candidates for new, intelligent illumination devices. Intelligent luminaires are relatively new products and so far research and development have mostly been oriented towards somewhat basic tasks, such as controlling light intensity. There are several bulbs on the market that allow remote control of light intensity and colour. Using Wi-Fi technology, the Lifx bulb [45] can be controlled using a smart phone, can change its colors and allows creating lighting schedules. The Lumen Smart Bulb [46] is energy efficient, can create light in a spectrum of 16 million colours and can be controlled from a mobile application using Bluetooth. Philips [47] and Elgato [48] offer similar products: as opposed to other smart lights, Elgato Avea can also be controlled by Apple Watch via Bluetooth, while Philips Hue provides lighting for security and the possibility of setting up timers and geofences. Additional sensing is integrated in the iLumi smart bulb [49], which can detect presence and automatically light users' path inside their homes.

Luminaires presented in [50] address the next level of complexity. Using incorporated photosensors, they respond to daylight changes in the indoor environment, by dimming or increasing light levels. Furthermore, these devices also have built-in occupancy sensors which allow them to determine when a person is in the room and fade or switch off whenever necessary, leading to significant energy savings.

The group of applications presented above is characterised by lighting control with smartphones for security or energy-saving purposes, but not more. Our solution has a clear, innovative advantage over the aforementioned existing solutions by: harnessing the current electrical and lighting infrastructure to decrease the cost of the product and deployment; pervasive individual monitoring to provide timely assistance to family members, friends, and informal and formal carers; and interoperability with third-party devices. The intelligent luminaires composing the hardware element of our platform include three main parts: an illumination module, a sensing module and a processing unit (for more details, we refer the reader to Section 4). These components, together with the software system of the i-Light platform, collaborate to achieve its final purpose: home monitoring, assisted living and ensuring the safety of the monitored older adults.

3. Platform Overview

The high-level architecture of the cyber-physical system is illustrated in Figure 1. This section presents the general overview of the platform, while details about its hardware and software components are provided in Sections 4 and 5. The i-Light system [5] has two main components:

- *Ambient tracking network*: Sensors and hardware devices that perform ambient monitoring and interior localisation of supervised persons.
- *Multiplatform software applications*: A software suite that includes Android and web applications for ambient data monitoring, indoor localisation, analysis, reporting and real time alerting.

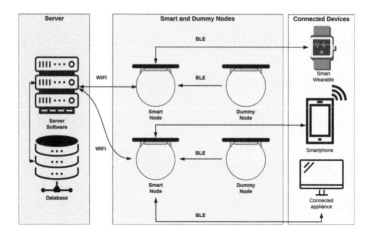

Figure 1. High-level architecture of the system.

The system employs two types of luminaires dubbed *dummy* and *smart*. Together, they create an area-wide coverage in which the signal strength from BLE emitting devices such as smartphones, smart bracelets or Bluetooth beacons are recorded and used for positioning. As opposed to dummy bulbs, which are simply used for light dimming and, indirectly, for indoor localisation purposes, smart luminaires are also capable of environment sensing through an incorporated module, as well as receiving data from medical devices. The luminaires are described in more detail in Section 4.

The system also includes all the required software components to leverage the available hardware. The server web application is responsible for securely storing user profile data including the deployment location's layout, user preferences, notification settings and designated caregiver permissions. The server also houses the data store, as well as data acquisition and client facing subsystems which expose a web interface for customising preferences and managing smart bulbs. Other substantial capabilities worth mentioning are the visualisation and reporting functionalities available over the same web interface. Notifications and real time alerts can be received via short message service or a smartphone application.

Our method of choice for indoor localisation is trilateration [36–38]. Our system uses at least three nodes with known positions and the user's coordinates are trilaterated using the received signal strength indices. With regard to the technology employed, our experiments have shown that Bluetooth appears more accurate for short distances, while Wi-Fi signal is better suited once the distance is increased or when obstacles are added [37].

Smart nodes contain a sensor module, which includes sensors for monitoring various conditions. For complex measurements, several physical measurements are aggregated. Abnormal values are first validated with data acquired from the closest smart nodes, to rule out the possibility of errors. There are three types of sensors in the module: environmental, presence and location. All readings are sent to the server which stores them for creating alerts or for further analyses.

An essential component of the system is the real time alerting module. It continuously verifies data received from sensors and checks them against a number of predefined system rules, as well as user defined rules. In case readings are outside the permitted range, an additional reading is taken to rule out the possibility of errors. If the reading is confirmed, an alert is generated by the system, and transmitted according to preferences recorded within the system.

4. Wireless Network of Intelligent Luminaires

This section details the most significant hardware components of the i-Light system. To ensure the system is cost-effective, it consists of two kinds of luminaires: *dummy bulbs* and *smart bulbs*. Both device types share the capability of dimming the LEDs, but they differ with regard to CPU power, available communication interfaces and installed sensor array.

4.1. Dummy Bulbs

Dummy bulbs are built around a Bluegiga BLE112 Bluetooth Low Energy module [51] which is used to establish connection with smart bulbs and accept commands from them. Dummy bulbs have the capability of managing the intensity of their LEDs according to a value provided by the smart bulb they are connected to. In addition, dummy bulbs perform Bluetooth scans in order to detect other nearby devices and report their physical addresses and signal strength. Thus, these types of luminaires are employed for indoor localisation, but only indirectly, by collecting RSSI values and sending them to a smart bulb over Bluetooth.

4.2. Smart Bulbs

Smart bulbs are built around a single Raspberry Pi 3 board [52]. They share the capabilities for LED intensity management with the dummy bulbs, as well as the capability of performing BLE scans for detecting signal strength. In addition, they incorporate several sensing stages to sense temperature, humidity, CO_2, dust and volatile organic compound (VOC) gases, as well as ambient light intensity. Furthermore, smart bulbs incorporate a passive infrared sensor for detecting movement. Smart bulbs can establish communication with the software server using both Wi-Fi and Ethernet connection. Signal strength recorded by several bulbs is forwarded using a smart bulb to the software server, which runs the localisation algorithm. Finally, an important functionality of smart bulbs is that, when connected over BLE with a medical device implementing Bluetooth medical protocols or ISO/IEEE 11073 [53], measured data are captured, aggregated and forwarded to the designated software endpoint over a secure connection.

4.3. Lighting Module

Both smart and dummy bulbs contain an LED-based lighting module. LEDs were chosen due to their efficacy, low energy consumption, reduction of electronic waste and suitability for being controlled via software. Our project aims to advance the state of the art by augmenting these bulbs with computing and communication resources to make them more useful, without significant additional expense. To achieve this, the considered LED will employ a constant current driver that provides longer operating life and less wasted heat than an alternative constant voltage driver.

The LED management stage is built around the Zetex ZXLD1366 [54] integrated circuit. It is designed for driving single or multiple series connected LEDs with great efficiency from a voltage source higher than the LED voltage. The device operates using an input between 6 V and 60 V. This voltage range allows for the creation of several kinds of luminaires, in different sizes and number of LEDs. Figure 2 shows the schematic of this LED dimming stage. The different elements of the circuit are:

- **P8** is a screw connection used to connect the LED set.
- **VDD_IN** is the power signal provided by the LED driver. The LED driver output can be up to 60 V and it is obtained from the mains. This signal is introduced to the PCB board using a screw connection.
- **R8** is a resistor that sets the nominal current provided to the LEDs.
- **PWM** is the signal provided by the BLE module that sets the desired dimming applied to the LED set.
- **C19**, **L3** and **D1** are electronic components required for proper operation of the ZXLD1366 circuit.

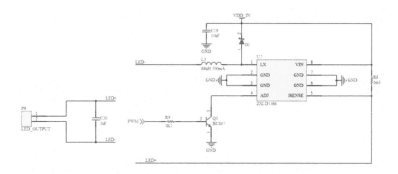

Figure 2. Schematic of the LED dimming stage.

To achieve the LED dimming stage in both dummy and smart bulbs, the components are placed both at the top and at the bottom of the printed circuit board to meet placement constraints required for the proper operation of the ZXLD1366 and to reduce the board size, thus facilitating the printed circuit board's integration into different luminaire designs.

4.4. Sensor Module

Smart nodes are endowed with a sensor module containing sensors that can be classified in three main categories: environmental, presence and location. The module senses ambient light, temperature, humidity, dust, volatile organic compounds and carbon dioxide gas. Furthermore, it also senses the presence of people as well as nearby BLE devices. Sensor data formats and interfaces are different. There are sensors that offer an analog output that must be digitally converted, while others allow connection and internal register readings using serial communication protocols. In terms of power supply, most sensors accept a specific range of voltages, so two power supply levels are required: 3.3 V and 5 V. Table 1 illustrates all implemented sensor types together with their characteristics.

Table 1. Sensors and their characteristics.

Sensor	Magnitude	Output Type	Required Power Supply (V)	Applied Power Supply (V)
SHT21 [55]	Humidity and temperature	Digital I2C	2.1 to 3.6	3.3
AMS302 [56]	Ambient light	Analog	3.3	3.3
Winsen WSP2110 [57]	Air quality	Analog	5	5
Winsen MG812 [58]	CO_2	Analog	5	5
GP2Y1010AU0F [59]	Smoke/Dust	Analog	4.5 to 5	5
EKMC1601111 [60]	Presence	Digital GPIO	3.3	3.3
GridEye [61]	Presence and location	Digital I2C	3.3 or 5, depending on the mounted version	Both correct

4.5. Communication Interface

As illustrated in Figure 1, data flow in the direction of smart nodes, and from smart nodes to the software server. Inter-node communication is achieved via Bluetooth, while smart node to server communication is achieved using Wi-Fi or Ethernet, depending on deployment location.

4.5.1. Communication between Smart and Dummy Luminaires

Bluetooth Low Energy (BLE) is the chosen technology for inter-bulb communication. Its suitability is proven by its reduced power and cost requirements, as well as proper range and transmission speed. The dependable range for BLE is up to 50 m line of sight, but this requires increased transmission power and affects battery life. An effective range for BLE that provides good balance with battery life is between 2 and 5 m. This also depends on device and antenna design, as well as the presence of obstacles between and around communicating devices [62].

To establish a BLE connection, one device must act as a master and the other device as a slave. Typically, the dummy bulb advertises itself and the smart bulb performs a scan to detect dummy bulbs nearby. Once detected, the pairing process occurs and the connection is established, so the smart bulb acts as master and the dummy bulb as slave. The master device cannot emit advertising packets as it has no sense in this role. This limitation is a problem as one of the dummy bulb's tasks is to scan the environment and maintain information regarding other nearby devices. To achieve this, dummy bulbs need to act as master but, in parallel, they need to accept connections from smart bulbs. The adopted solution has been to change the dummy bulb role in time, defining a period to act as master and a period to act as slave. During its master period it scans the environment searching for nearby devices, after which it advertises itself in order to establish a connection with a smart bulb and act as data producer. This mechanism adds complexity to the dummy bulb firmware as there is a software timer and a counter that controls when the scans take place, when they are stopped, and when device role must change. Moreover, when changing device role, several actions must be performed to make the gathered information available.

The Bluetooth SIG defines the Attributes Protocol [63] for BLE devices, a client/server protocol where attributes are configured and grouped into services using the Generic Attribute Profile (GATT) [63]. The profile describes a use case, roles and general behaviours based on the GATT functionality. Services are collections of characteristics and relationships to other services that encapsulate the behaviour of part of a device. Profiles and services that describe node capabilities are developed and customised as part of the project to enable power-efficient data transfer. The GATT database is defined using an XML file. The GATT structure implements one or more profiles, each profile consists of one or more services and each service has of one or more characteristics. Some examples of services that have been defined are: the LED dimming control, which has only one characteristic that corresponds to the PWM value; the BLE devices detected nearby (see Figure 3)—this service has ten characteristics, one for each device in the list, all characteristics are readable and each one occupies 6 bytes; the RSSI level of the BLE devices, which has ten characteristics, one for each device in the list; and a service that offers a counter for each detected BLE device in the list.

```
<!-- DETECTED DEVICES MAC -->
<service uuid="db6222ab-eeea-4779-b2fc-bc326e8e290d" advertise="true">
    <description>Devices mac</description>
    <characteristic uuid="de22d3f0-703d-4894-9b3a-7362a899691d" id="gatt_mac01">
        <description>mac 01</description>
        <properties read="true"/>
        <value length="6"/>
    </characteristic>
    <characteristic uuid="e9378c8c-5b2c-48fd-a293-561c75844ca2" id="gatt_mac02">
        <description>mac 02</description>
        <properties read="true"/>
        <value length="6"/>
    </characteristic>
    [ ... ]
    <characteristic uuid="0fa9e6b9-bcc2-4274-9480-5263217cbba2" id="gatt_mac10")
        <description>mac 10</description>
        <properties read="true"/>
        <value length="6"/>
    </characteristic>
</service>
```

Figure 3. Sample from ten position service list storing detected BLE devices.

Dummy nodes will be installed within range of a smart node to ensure accurate tracking as well as suitable battery life. Additional consideration will be given to trilateration to ensure that the signal coverage is adequate for obtaining the desired precision. This is facilitated by the fact that dummy nodes are powered using long-life batteries, which allows their deployment to be less constrained by location.

4.5.2. Communication between Smart Bulbs and the Server

The sensor network communicates with the software server over Wi-Fi. In opposition to BLE, Wi-Fi is long-range and has much higher data rate. Conversely, it also presents high power consumption [64,65]. Wi-Fi equipped smart luminaires are socketed and replace the lighting system within the deployment location. Considering its relatively high transmission power, and operation in the 2.4 Ghz band, Wi-Fi networks can cause interference with other wireless technologies, including BLE. Our project addresses this issue by ensuring that enough physical separation exists between nodes, while on-site testing the deployment. Most luminaires are ceiling-mounted, therefore we expect low interference for smart node Wi-Fi. In addition, given that smart nodes are also BLE enabled, interferences within a node are addressed using software. As dummy nodes are small size and battery operated, they can be located out of the Wi-Fi interference range.

Communication between smart nodes and the software server is neither bandwidth nor power limited, thus data are transferred using the JavaScript Object Notation (JSON) format [66]. Each message includes the sender's unique identifier, timestamp, the reading value and unit of measurement. An example JSON for temperature reading is shown in Figure 4. Similar messages are used for humidity, smoke, dust, air quality, CO_2 level, ambient light and presence.

```
{ "mac":"1D:35:62:25:17:81",
  "timestamp":"2018-06-28T09:12:28.000+0000",
  "sensor":"1",
  "value":"25.4",
  "units":"ºC" }
```

Figure 4. Smart bulb reading in JSON format

Given the sensitive nature of transmitted data, security and privacy are paramount. This is especially important in light of the EU-level adoption of the General Data Protection Regulation [67], which represents a large reformation with regard to data protection and which aims to address privacy issues in the digital domain. While Wi-Fi provides data encryption, existing research demonstrates its insufficiency [68]. Our system addresses this by including an additional layer of application-level encryption over all transmitted data. Data sent between dummy and smart bulbs, as well as from the smart bulbs to the server, are encrypted using the Advanced Encryption Standard (AES) [69]. This prevents access of outside actors to transmitted data, and also prevents man-in-the-middle attacks. Furthermore, application level encryption provides greater flexibility for system deployment, as data remain safe even when transmitted over unencrypted networks.

4.6. Processing Unit

The processing unit within the smart bulbs was designed considering the following factors:

- Easy integration into an LED-based luminaire.
- Correct positioning of the sensor module in order to avoid interference generated by other luminaires, as well as to provide accurate readings.
- Metallic components of the luminaire must not provide interference with the processing unit's wireless communication chip.

The processing unit's current prototype is built around a Raspberry Pi 3 Model B [52] main board. Compared to other board types, the Raspberry Pi proved to be more powerful, complex, reliable and suitable to our requirements. Furthermore, it includes communication interfaces for Wi-Fi and Bluetooth.

Taking into account previously mentioned factors, the processing unit uses a modular design and consists of two main components. It incorporates three boards that can be connected using board to board connectors or just wires so that they can be adapted to almost any LED luminaire design. The first component is the Raspberry Pi board and the power management stage; the second integrates two printed circuit boards that comprise all available sensor types. Ensuring proper communication between smart and dummy bulbs, as well as between bulbs and other devices was one of the major reasons that drove us towards a two-component design. As such, the Raspberry Pi and antenna, which must be free of metallic parts that could cause signal shielding effects, are mounted upside down. This is done given that most luminaires are affixed to the ceiling and that devices they communicate with are located physically underneath them.

This modular approach provides the required flexibility for placing composing elements within the luminary design. In the case of a round luminaire, for instance, the sensor module could be placed in the centre and the main board at the periphery. Moreover, the modular design avoids situations in which the heat emitted by the Raspberry Pi unit would cause the temperature and humidity sensors to read distorted values.

The final prototype, illustrated in Figure 5 incorporates the required stage to get the appropriate power supply from the mains, as well as an AC/DC transformer that provides 5 V DC output. In this board, the Raspberry Pi is mounted upside down to facilitate the assembly process and to put the antenna upside down for maximum signal strength. The sensor module is comprised of two boards, one of which is mounted vertically and the other horizontally. The components of the device are connected to the Raspberry Pi using its expansion header. The pins in this connector can be grouped as follows:

- **Power and earth pins:** The Raspberry Pi board outputs two different voltage levels: 3.3 V and 5 V. The first one is generated by an internal step-down regulator from the original 5 V level. Normally, the board is fed connecting an external power supply to the micro USB connector. However, this is not a suitable option in our case. Thus, we provide an external 5 V voltage level using this connector. Unfortunately, if done in this way, a protection stage is bypassed. Thus, this protection stage has been replicated and placed in the main board. Finally, there are several ground connections, all of them are routed to the main board earth.
- **General purpose digital inputs and outputs:** These can be used as common digital inputs or outputs or as a method to enable or disable certain stages.

- **Universal Asynchronous Receiver/Transmitter:** There are two pins dedicated to this. By default, this interface is used to provide a Unix shell. In this case, this feature is disabled and we use this interface to gather debugging data.
- **I2C PORT:** This port is used to communicate with the humidity, temperature and GridEye sensors.
- **SPI PORT:** The port is used to communicate with the analog to digital converter (for the sensor module).

Figure 6 shows how the different components of the design are connected. All components are connected to the Raspberry Pi using its expansion header. The processing unit executes a software application which currently provides the following features, with existing possibility for further extension:

- Sensor module management. Each sensor has its own software library and the information must be accessed in different ways, using either digital interfaces or analog outputs.
- Dummy bulb management, and reception of the devices detected by the bulb.
- Room illumination management, according to the user's configuration, for the bulb itself together with all connected dummy bulbs.
- Management of communication with devices following the IEEE 11073 standard.

Figure 5. Printed circuit board and processing unit.

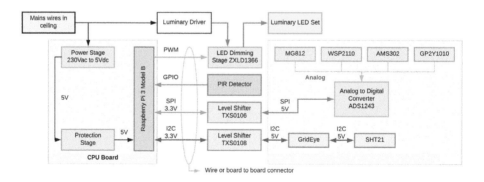

Figure 6. Connections between the different components of the design.

5. Software Architecture

The general architecture of the system is shown in Figure 7. The system has a distributed architecture, with information gathered and processed across different system levels and components.

The components are deployed on different devices: smart and dummy luminaires, the software server and client devices such as smartphones or other wearables. In the present section, we detail each component.

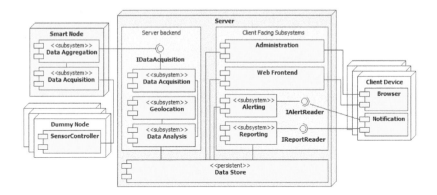

Figure 7. Software architecture of the system [5] (IEEE 978-1-5386-3368-7/17/$31.00 © 2017).

5.1. Administration

The administration component is essential for all other elements of the software system, which are described subsequently in this section. Management of system users and their residences, as well as managing and configuring the intelligent luminaires are all centrally handled by this component. Entering a new residence involves entering user data and building a two-dimensional representation of their home. The system provides functionality for drawing walls, adding furniture, labeling rooms and generating a three-dimensional plan of the dwelling. A particular step in the process is adding the smart and dummy bulbs to the location plan. Luminaires can be placed and configured directly from within the application; both bulb types require providing a MAC address, and for smart bulbs available sensors must be selected from a list. Smart bulbs must also be configured in order to enable connecting them to the user's home wireless network.

5.2. Geolocation

The Geolocation Component is responsible for indoor localisation of tracked persons or objects that have a Bluetooth emitter attached. A series of experiments have been performed to identify the best solution for indoor localisation [4,36,37,70,71]. Each of the luminaires captures Bluetooth signal strength from emitting devices together with their MAC address and timestamp. Dummy luminaires forward these data to the smart ones which aggregate signal strength readings and forward the information to the software server. The software server aggregates received data with the location layout and performs the trilateration to obtain the current position of the target, which is persisted in the system's data store. For the trilateration algorithm, we have used a non-linear least squares optimisation, the Levenberg–Marquardt Optimiser, which finds a local minimum by interpolating between the Gauss–Newton algorithm and the method of gradient descent [72]. Running trilateration on the server-side allows fine-tuning the algorithm by setting individual correction constants per location in order to improve its accuracy.

5.3. Reporting

The Reporting subsystem is responsible with creating relevant and customisable reports based on administrative, sensor and alert data. The reports can be textual or visual, conveying optimal visualisation for better insight. Various filters can be applied to aggregate corresponding data for queries such as start and end dates, indoor location or ambient condition type. The system currently provides the following report types:

- *User report.* It includes administrative data such as user name, email, telephone number, age, and deployed device identifiers; this report can only be requested by the system administrator.
- *Interior localisation report.* The report displays indoor localisation information relevant for caregivers. It includes location, start and end times and total period spent in each particular location. This is available for caregivers and administrators.
- *Environmental data report.* It can be requested by all user types and shows data regarding ambient conditions such as temperature, humidity, smoke and gases.
- *Alerts report.* This report is available to administrators and caregivers and presents a summary about generated alerts and notifications, including alert type, source, destinations and alert time.

The reporting component is deployed on the software server and can be accessed by the client device application. Accessing the reports requires authentication and authorisation according to preset permissions.

5.4. Data Analysis

The data analysis component is responsible for collecting, processing, aggregating and analysing received sensor readings to generate alerts, notifications or infer behaviours. Any abnormal readings are first validated with data from other close-by smart nodes to check for sensor malfunction before issuing a real time alert. For example, in the case of an abnormal high temperature, an increased temperature should also be read from close-by sensors. Currently, the hardware provides the following data for analysis [5]:

1. Environmental measurements:

    - Temperature, measured in degrees Celsius.
    - Relative humidity, measured as a percentage.
    - Ambient light, measured as a percentage.
    - Smoke presence, measured as a boolean value.
    - Air quality, measured in parts per million by volume; this includes the concentration of carbon dioxide and volatile organic compounds.

2. Presence is detected using the GridEye sensor, which produces a matrix of values. The raw sensor data must be processed to detect human presence based on the difference in detected infrared signature.
3. Location is computed starting from RSSI combined with device MAC addresses.

Abnormal readings are identified using a predefined set of default rules, available for each measurement. System users can redefine these rules, or provide additional ones to customise the system. When data analysis reveals that sensor readings do not comply with at least one of the defined rules, an action is taken in real time. This can either be passive, i.e. setting a software flag that will be seen by the system administrator or a designated caregiver in the application, or active, in which case a real-time alert is generated and forwarded to the monitored person and their caregivers. While the default set of rules covers typical values for a residential building, additional rules can be created for each deployment location.

5.5. Real-Time Alerts

This component is responsible for sending real-time alerts to monitored persons as well as their registered caregivers. In the current implementation, alerts are created when sensor readings are outside the permitted range for at least one of the defined rules. Each alert is stored on the server as a record containing the device responsible for the reading, the measurement type and value, its severity and the timestamp of the reading.

To send alerts, a database listener is triggered every time an alert is stored. As mentioned in the previous section, the actions taken for an alert are specified within the rule(s) that were used to generate it. Alerts can either result in a software notification that can be consulted through the application's web interface, or they are sent in the form of a text message to the monitored person as well as their designated caregivers. In addition, as part of the project, a prototype smartphone application that employs push notifications to receive alerts was implemented and is expected to be available in an upcoming system version.

6. System Validation

The current implementation of the cyber-physical system was deployed to a real environment. Intelligent luminaires were placed for evaluation in three rooms: one bedroom, a study room and a hallway.

The main objective of the deployment was to evaluate whether the most significant technical challenges were fully addressed within the technical work. These included ensuring that intelligent luminaire design and assembly does not interfere with data readings, that sensor readings are consistent and correct, interior localisation is accurate and that the hardware-software connection is reliable. This was achieved using a combination of real-life and simulated data transmitted over the Wi-Fi network.

6.1. System Integration

The experimental evaluation was undertaken within three rooms of a dwelling, namely a 2.50 m × 3.30 m bedroom, a 2.50 m × 1 m study room and a 2.40 m × 2.22 m hallway. The dwelling also includes a kitchen and bathroom, but these have not been considered in our evaluation. Both indoor and outdoor walls are brick and reinforced concrete. This is particularly significant for the positioning algorithm, as these materials strongly influence RSSI values.

The first step in installing the system is to set up a smart bulb to which dummy bulbs are associated. When first deployed, the smart bulb creates a wireless network through which the system exposes a web application where the user can set up the location and house plan. The location of all deployed bulbs must be entered for accurate indoor localisation, as illustrated in Figure 8. In addition, the web application allows providing the capabilities of smart and dummy bulbs as well as registering the monitored person and their designated caregivers. The final step is to configure the Wi-Fi network through which the system will connect to the cloud-based software server.

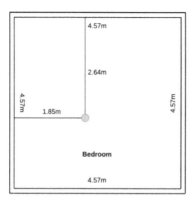

Figure 8. Bulb placement.

After initial configuration the user can customise the system, ask for reports or obtain real-time status for the monitored buildings they have access rights to. Figure 9 illustrates the monitoring dashboard that provides information about current ambient conditions and past values.

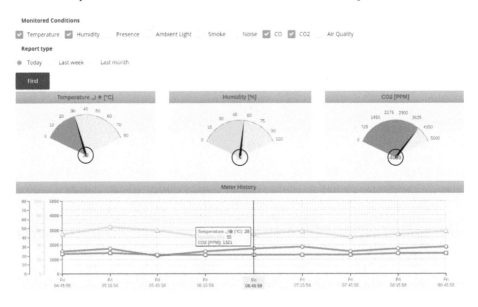

Figure 9. Example of daily ambient report for temperature, humidity and carbon dioxide.

The system also provides an option to show the evolution of ambient conditions over past weeks or months, as shown in Figure 10, using charts and tables. Reports are also available for existent users, person location and activities, as well as alerts.

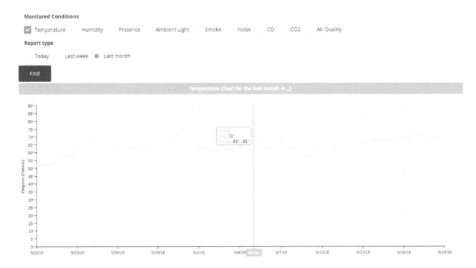

Figure 10. Monthly ambient report—temperature.

6.2. Positioning

Achieving accurate indoor positioning represents one of the most innovative parts of the system, with significant associated technical risk. As such, to reach a suitable implementation, experimentation with positioning algorithms and methods was performed using dedicated prototypes and testing scenarios from the first phases of the project. Experimentation results are detailed in [36–38]. The experiments used various settings, covering many real-world scenarios, including setting anchor points on different floors or in the corner of the rooms [37], performing the tests in locations with heavy wireless interferences [36] or choosing an asymmetric placement of anchor points [38]. These experiments used rudimentary versions of the system's nodes, as they were targeted particularly towards indoor localisation, given that the goal was to improve the positioning algorithms to be used in the system prototype. Results showed that detection with room-level accuracy can be achieved using either Bluetooth or Wi-Fi, without prior location fingerprinting. In addition, we observed that the presence, configuration and materials walls are built from have a larger effect on localisation results than that of enclosure size. Therefore, we undertook our evaluation in a smaller physical location, but one having reinforced concrete and brick walls. Basic trilateration with one bulb per room was considered suitable for the project's requirements. Improved accuracy is possible using a more refined algorithm that employs corrections, as presented in [38].

This article describes indoor localisation testing as a subsystem of the i-Light system, having tested the localisation independently as mentioned in the previous paragraph . We employed a complete workflow that includes installation, room and bulb setup, positioning feedback and reporting. A smart luminaire was set-up in each room and different positioning scenarios were tested. In the first three scenarios, the tracked person is in the middle of each room, close to the respective luminaire. In the fourth and fifth scenarios, the tracked person is in equal range of the three luminaires; in the fourth, the doors are opened, while, in the fifth, the doors are closed. The application's real time output is illustrated in Figures 11 and 12. For this test, we used direct trilateration. To obtain the distance from the strength of the signal, we used the RSSI lognormal model described in [73], in which the distance can be inferred as:

$$d = 10^{(A-RSSI)} / (10 * n) \tag{1}$$

where n represents the path-loss exponent and ranges between 2 to 6 for indoor environments. We used $n = 2$ for our experiments. A is the received signal strength expressed in dBm measured at one meter, and is known for each luminaire. Signal strength was recorded every 6 s over a 5 min interval, during three different intervals of time and then averaged. Outliers were discarded. The figures show luminaire placement, as well as both the correct and inferred positions of the monitored person.

Scenario 1 is illustrated in Figure 11 (left). The monitored person is sitting on the bed, and is detected with an average error of 64 cm.

In Scenario 2, illustrated using Figure 11 (middle), the average localisation error is of 85 cm, and provides correct room-level detection. Scenario 3 is illustrated in Figure 11 (right), with the person standing in the hallway, localised with an average error of 131 cm.

Scenarios 4 and 5 are shown in Figure 12. The person is at equal distance from all luminaires. In Scenario 4 (Figure 12, left), interior doors are open and the person is localised with an average error of 66 cm. Scenario 5 repeats Scenario 4, but with closed doors. Accuracy slightly decreases and the person is localised with an average error of 84 cm.

Table 2 summarises the obtained experimental results. As the results have shown, achieved positioning is correct for room-level localisation in most probable settings, without any a priori set up or signal fingerprinting.

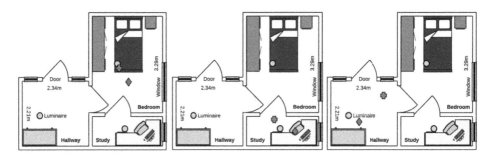

Figure 11. Localisation tests. Luminaires are represented using yellow circles with black border, the person's real position is represented using the green cross shape and the detected position is shown using the red diamond.

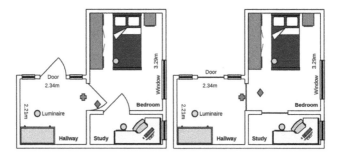

Figure 12. Open and closed-door localisation tests. Person at equal distance from all luminaires. Luminaires are represented using yellow circles with black border, the person's real position is represented using the green cross shape and the detected position is shown using the red diamond.

Table 2. Positioning details, for all analysed scenarios.

	Real Location	Computed Location	Error
Scenario 1	(547, 44)	(506, −6)	64 cm
Scenario 2	(583, 208)	(506, 171)	85 cm
Scenario 3	(314, 182)	(410, 96)	131 cm
Scenario 4	(523, 125)	(457, 124)	66 cm
Scenario 5	(523, 125)	(440, 138)	84 cm

6.3. Alerting

Ambient condition information is periodically sampled by the smart bulbs and transmitted to the software server. At a predefined time interval (currently 15 s), all recorded values, for all types of environment conditions, are analysed and compared against the correct values defined by the default or custom business rules. Should any inadequacy be identified, an alert is immediately created and stored in the database. Each such alert contains information about: the timestamp when it was generated, the type, value and unit of measurement for the involved ambient condition, the MAC address of the smart node that recorded the abnormal value, and the room where this node is located. In addition to anomalous environment conditions, person presence in certain locations and for certain periods of time may also indicate a risky situation. For instance, if the monitored person spends more hours in the bathroom or in the bedroom, but not on the bed or on a chair, he/she might be in need of help. Such situations are also regulated by the system and new custom rules can be added to handle them. Person location is computed by the system in real time and, furthermore, verification is made at a predefined time interval (currently 15 s) to detect whether the position has unchanged. Alerts are then generated according to the rules and the modification in person position, in a similar manner to the environment conditions.

Alerts generated by the corresponding component are sent using short text message service by integrating a K4505 GSM broadband modem and the Gammu SMS Daemon [74] with the application server. Figure 13 illustrates two examples of alerts sent by the system. The first involves the temperature parameter, which exceeded the maximum allowed value. This was generated using simulated data, as during system testing there were no interior environment anomalies. The second alert involves the monitored person's prolonged presence in the bathroom. This was generated as a consequence of an existing business rule which states that presence within such a room should not be longer than one hour.

Along with sending the alerts via SMS, the system also shows these notifications within the application's web interface, where they can be consulted at will. However, sending a real-time message to the user's and the caregiver's telephones is not only more effective, but even indispensable in the case of dangerous scenarios. In addition to these two types of communication, a prototype smartphone application to receive alerts is also being developed.

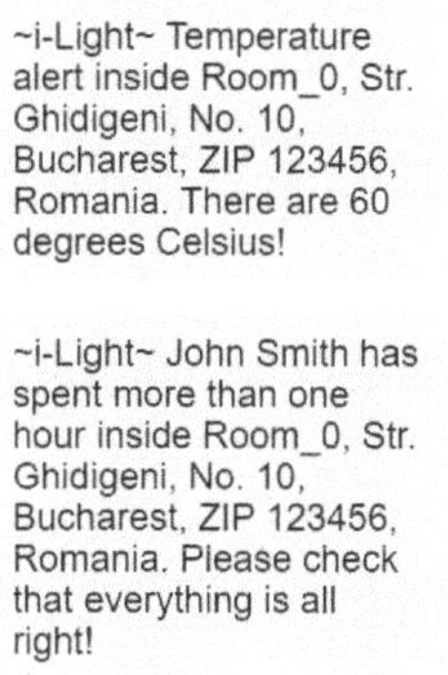

~i-Light~ Temperature
alert inside Room_0, Str.
Ghidigeni, No. 10,
Bucharest, ZIP 123456,
Romania. There are 60
degrees Celsius!

~i-Light~ John Smith has
spent more than one
hour inside Room_0, Str.
Ghidigeni, No. 10,
Bucharest, ZIP 123456,
Romania. Please check
that everything is all
right!

Figure 13. Received SMS alerts regarding the temperature parameter and prolonged presence in a room where presence time should be shorter (bathroom).

7. Conclusions

The current trend in population ageing, as well as increasing costs of geriatric healthcare require adaptive, intelligent, innovative technology to lessen the burden on both seniors and their primary caregivers. This paper presents the design and implementation of the i-Light system for ambient condition and indoor monitoring of older adults in their own residences. The system incorporates a wireless network of custom developed intelligent luminaires, a software server and a suite of mutiplatform software applications and its proper functioning relies on an impeccable cooperation between all these components.

i-Light is the product of collaboration between industry and academia under the framework of the Eureka Eurostars research funding program. The current system implementation provides ambient condition monitoring, room-accurate indoor localisation, configuration capabilities for alert generation and severity using customisable business rules together with generation and transmission of real-time alerts.

Compared to other ambient assisted living systems, i-Light's innovation includes the design and implementation of novel, energy efficient luminaires, with embedded sensing, indoor localisation and communications electronic system that enable a pervasive, seamless, and inexpensive home monitoring scheme. Using these intelligent luminaires as network nodes allows harnessing the electrical infrastructure and decreases deployment costs. Furthermore, given that the network's nodes replace existing light bulbs and are not mounted as separate devices, monitored persons will not feel constantly observed, reducing the level of mental discomfort. Another compelling advantage of i-Light is the real-time alerting feature: the system generates and sends alerts to caregivers for any detected potentially dangerous situations, whether this involves the indoor environment or the monitored person. Thus, it ensures timely assistance in case of emergency.

The system prototype has been deployed to a real environment, consisting in three rooms within an apartment. All the system's features have been evaluated: configuration, indoor positioning, reporting and real-time alerts generation and transmission. This paper illustrates all obtained results in terms of person localisation and environment monitoring. Real-time alerting, a critical aspect of the platform, is also described and exemplified using simulated data that creates dangerous conditions.

Future work on the system will focus on developing an intelligent component for analysing human activity patterns to detect the onset and evolution of chronic diseases or conditions such as frailty. This component might use sensor collected location data to identify behavioural patterns and, more importantly, atypical activities of the monitored older adults, which might indicate early signs of disease.

Author Contributions: All authors contributed equally to this work. "Conceptualization, A.V., A.-J.M., D.C.-F., M.I.B., N.G; Methodology, A.V., D.C.-F, N.G.; Software, A.V., A.M.-P., I.M.; Validation, A.-J.M., D.C.-F., M.I.B., I.M., N.G.; Formal Analysis, A.V., A.M.-P., I.M.; Investigation, A.V., A.M-P., A.-J.M., M.I.B., I.M.; Resources, A.M.-P., I.M.; Data Curation, A.M.-P., I.M.; Writing—Original Draft Preparation, A.V., A.M.-P., A.-J.M., M.I.B.; Writing—Review & Editing, A.V., A.M.-P., A.-J.M., D.C.-F., M.I.B., I.M., N.G.; Visualization, A.-J.M., M.I.B.; Supervision, D.C.-F., N.G.; Project Administration, D.C.-F., N.G.; Funding acquisition, D.C.-F., N.G."

Funding: This work was funded by a grant of the Romanian National Authority for Scientific Research and Innovation, CCCDI- UEFISCDI, project number 46E/2015, *i-Light—A pervasive home monitoring system based on intelligent luminaires.*

Conflicts of Interest: The authors declare no conflict of interest.

References

1. Darwish, M.; Senn, E.; Lohr, C.; Kermarrec, Y. A comparison between ambient assisted living systems. In *Smart Homes and Health Telematics*; Bodine, C., Helal, S., Gu, T., Mokhtari, M., Eds.; Lecture Notes in Computer Science; Springer: New York, NY, USA, 2015; Volume 8456, pp. 231–237.

2. European Commission; Economic Policy Committee. *The 2012 Ageing Report. Economic and Budgetary Projections for the 27 EU Member States (2010–2060)*; European Economy: Brussels, Belgium, 2012.

3. World Health Organization. World Report on Ageing and Health. 2015. Available online: http://apps.who.int/iris/bitstream/10665/186463/1/9789240694811_eng.pdf?ua=1 (accessed on 28 August 2018).

4. Draghici, I.C.; Mihailescu, M.N.; Guta, L.I.; Vasilateanu, A.; Pavaloiu, B.; Bocicor, I.; Molnar, A.; Goga, N. A quantitative research to decide the user requirements for the i-Light System. In Proceedings of the 21st International Conference on Control Systems and Computer Science (CSCS21), Bucharest, Romania, 29–31 May 2017.

5. Bocicor, M.I.; Cuesta Frau, D.; Draghici, I.C.; Goga, N.; Molnar, A.J.; Valor Perez, R.; Vasilateanu, A. Cyber-Physical System for Assisted Living and Home Monitoring. In Proceedings of the IEEE International Conference on Intelligent Computer Communication and Processing (ICCP2017), Cluj-Napoca, Romania, 7–9 September 2017.

6. ECP. ECP Makes Switching to eMAR Easy. 2017. Available online: http://extendedcarepro.com/products/ (accessed on 28 August 2018).

7. Carevium. Carevium Assisted Living Software. 2017. Available online: http://www.carevium.com/carevium-assisted-living-software/ (accessed on 28 August 2018).

8. Yardi. Yardi EHR. 2017. Available online: http://www.yardi.com/products/ehr-senior-care/ (accessed on 28 August 2018).

9. Yardi. Yardi eMAR. 2015. Available online: http://www.yardi.com/products/emar/ (accessed on 28 August 2018).

10. Botia, J.A.; Villa, A.; Palma, J. Ambient Assisted Living system for in-home monitoring of healthy independent elders. *Expert Syst. Appl.* **2102**, *39*, 8136–8148. [CrossRef]

11. Lopez-Guede, J.M.; Moreno-Fernandez-de Leceta, A.; Martinez-Garcia, A.; Grana, M. Lynx: Automatic Elderly Behavior Prediction in Home Telecare. *BioMed Res. Int.* **2015**, *2015*, 201939. [CrossRef] [PubMed]

12. Vuegen, L.; Van Den Broeck, B.; Karsmakers, P.; hamme, V.; Hugo Vanrumste, B. Automatic monitoring of activities of daily living based on real-life acoustic sensor data: A preliminary study. In Proceedings of the Workshop on Speech and Language Processing for Assistive Technologies (SLPAT-2013), Grenoble, France, 21–22 August 2013; pp. 113–118.

13. Baldewijns, G.; Debard, G.; Mertens, M.; Devriendt, E.; Milisen, K.; Tournoy, J.; Croonenborghs, T.; Vanrumste, B. Semi-automated Video-based In-home Fall Risk Assessment. In *Assistive Technology: From Research to Practice*; Encarnação, P., Azevedo, L., Gelderblom, G., Newell, A., Mathiassen, N., Eds.; IOS Press: Amsterdam, The Netherlands, 2013; pp. 59–64.

14. Van Den Broeck, B.; Vuegen, L.; Van hamme, H.; Moonen, M.; Karsmakers, P.; Vanrumste, B. Footstep Localization based on In-home Microphone-array Signals. In *Assistive Technology: From Research to Practice*; Encarnação, P., Azevedo, L., Gelderblom, G., Newell, A., Mathiassen, N., Eds.; IOS Press: Amsterdam, The Netherlands, 2013; pp. 90–94.

15. Luca, S.; Karsmakers, P.; Cuppens, K.; Croonenborghs, T.; de Vel, A.V.; Ceulemans, B.; Lagae, L.; Huffel, S.V.; Vanrumste, B. Detecting rare events using extreme value statistics applied to epileptic convulsions in children. *Artif. Intell. Med.* **2014**, *60*, 89–96. [CrossRef] [PubMed]

16. Cuppens, K. Detection of Epileptic Seizures based on Video and Accelerometer Recordings. Ph.D. Thesis, University of Leuven, Leuven, Belgium, 2012.

17. Zhang, S.; McClean, S.; Scotney, B.; Hong, X.; Nugent, C.; Mulvenna, M. Decision Support for Alzheimer's Patients in Smart Homes. In Proceedings of the 21st IEEE International Symposium on Computer-Based Medical Systems (CBMS '08), Jyvaskyla, Finland, 17–19 June 2008.

18. Chiuchisan, I.; Geman, O. An Approach of a Decision Support and Home Monitoring System for Patients with Neurological Disorders using Internet of Things Concepts. *WSEAS Trans. Syst.* **2014**, *13*, 460–469.

19. Bafhtiar, G.; Bodinier, V.; Despotou, G.; Elliott, M.T.; Bryant, N.; Arvanitis, T.N. Providing Patient Home Clinical Decision Support using Off-the-shelf Cloud-based Smart Voice Recognition. In Proceedings of the WIN 2017 Conference CDS Stream, Coventry, UK, 24 January 2017.

20. Healthsense. Better Health Assessments Every Day, for Better Everyday Living. 2017. Available online: http://healthsense.com/ (accessed on 18 June 2016).

21. Bocicor, M.I.; Molnar, A.J.; Marin, I.; Goga, N.; Valor Perez, R.; Cuesta Frau, D. Intelligent Decision Support for Pervasive Home Monitoring and Assisted Living. In Proceedings of the IEEE International Conference on Intelligent Computer Communication and Processing (ICCP2018), Cluj-Napoca, Romania, 6–8 September 2018.

22. Philips. Home Telehealth. 2017. Available online: https://www.usa.philips.com/healthcare/solutions/enterprise-telehealth/home-telehealth (accessed on 28 August 2018).

23. Medtronik. The Carelink Network. 2017. Available online: http://www.medtronic.com/us-en/healthcare-professionals/products/cardiac-rhythm/managing-patients/information-systems/carelink-network.html (accessed on 28 August 2018).

24. Haigh, P.A.; Bausi, F.; Ghassemlooy, Z.; Papakonstantinou, I.; Le Minh, H.; Flechon, C.; Cacialli, F. Visible light communications: real time 10 Mb/s link with a low bandwidth polymer light-emitting diode. *Opt. Express* **2014**, *22*, 2830–2838. [CrossRef] [PubMed]

25. GE Lighting. Indoor Positioning System. 2017. Available online: http://www.gelighting.com/LightingWeb/na/solutions/control-systems/indoor-positioning-system.jsp (accessed on 28 August 2018).

26. AcuityBrands. Indoor and Outdoor Lighting Solutions. 2017. Available online: http://www.acuitybrands.com/solutions/featured-spaces (accessed on 28 August 2018).

27. Mohamed, M.K.; Patra, S.; Lanzon, A. Designing simple indoor navigation system for UAVs. In Proceedings of the 19th Mediterranean Conference on Control and Automation, Corfu, Greece, 20–23 June 2011; pp. 1223–1228.

28. Tarzia, S.P.; Dinda, P.A.; Dick, R.P.; Memik, G. Indoor localization without infrastructure using the acoustic background spectrum. In Proceedings of the 9th International Conference on Mobile Systems, Applications, and Services, Bethesda, MD, USA, 28 June–1 July 2011; p. 155.

29. Tarrio, P.; Cesana, M.; Tagliasacchi, M.; Redondi, A.; Borsani, L.; Casar, J.R. An energy-efficient strategy for combined RSS-PDR indoor localization. In Proceedings of the IEEE International Conference on Pervasive Computing and Communications Workshops (PERCOM Workshops), Seattle, WA, USA, 21–25 March 2011; pp. 619–624.

30. Huang, C.N.; Chan, C.T. ZigBee-based indoor location system by k-nearest neighbor algorithm with weighted RSSI. *Procedia Comput. Sci.* **2011**, *5*, 58–65. [CrossRef]

31. Ciurana, M.; Cugno, S.; Barcel-Arroyo, F. WLAN Indoor Positioning Based on TOA with Two Reference Points. In Proceedings of the 4th Workshop on Positioning, Hannover, Germany, 22–22 March 2007; pp. 23–28.

32. Charlon, Y.; Fourty, N.; Campo, E. A telemetry system embedded in clothes for indoor localization and elderly health monitoring. *Sensors* **2013**, *13*, 11728–11749. [CrossRef] [PubMed]

33. Chandrasekharapuram, R.H.; Gupta, S. Patient/Elderly Activity Monitoring Using WiFi-Based Indoor Localization. 2010. Available online: https://wiki.cc.gatech.edu/designcomp/images/3/3d/HHH_Report.pdf (accessed on 20 February 2016).

34. Dahlgren, E. Evaluation of Indoor Positioning Based on Bluetooth Smart Technology. Master's Thesis, Chalmers University of Technology, Göteborg, Sweden, 2014.

35. Chan, S.; Sohn, G. Indoor Localization using Wi-Fi based Fingerprinting and Trilateration Techniques for LBS Applications. In Proceedings of the 7th International Conference on 3D Geoinformation, Quebec, QC, Canada, 16–17 May 2012.

36. Goga, N.; Vasilateanu, A.; Mihailescu, M.N.; Guta, L.; Molnar, A.; Bocicor, I.; Bolea, L.; Stoica, D. Evaluating indoor localization using WiFi for patient tracking. In Proceedings of the International Symposium on Fundamentals of Electrical Engineering, Bucharest, Romania, 30 June–2 July 2016.

37. Vasilateanu, A.; Goga, N.; Guta, L.; Mihailescu, M.N.; Pavaloiu, B. Testing Wi-Fi and Bluetooth Low Energy technologies for a hybrid indoor positioning system. In Proceedings of the IEEE International Symposium on Fundamentals of Electrical Engineering, Edinburgh, UK, 3–5 October 2016.

38. Draghici, I.C.; Vasilateanu, A.; Goga, N.; Pavaloiu, B.; Guta, L.; Mihailescu, M.N.; Boiangiu, C.A. Indoor positioning system for location based healthcare using trilateration with corrections. In Proceedings of the International Conference on Engineering, Technology and Innovation (ICE), Funchal, Portugal, 27–29 June 2107.

39. Zonith. Real Time Location System. 2017. Available online: http://zonith.com/products/rtls/ (accessed on 28 August 2018).

40. Pozyx. Accurate Positioning. 2017. Available online: https://www.pozyx.io/ (accessed on 28 August 2018).

41. Blooloc. yooBee System Overview. 2017. Available online: https://www.blooloc.com/over-yoobee (accessed on 28 August 2018).

42. Senion. The Top Indoor Location Engine for Smart Apps. 2017. Available online: https://senion.com/ (accessed on 28 August 2018).

43. Estimote. Locating People, Way-Finding, and Attendance Tracking. 2017. Available online: https://estimote.com/products/ (accessed on 28 August 2018).

44. Infsoft. Indoor Navigation, Indoor Positioning, Indoor Analytics and Indoor Tracking. 2017. Available online: https://www.infsoft.com/ (accessed on 28 August 2018).

45. Lifx. Lighting Reimagined. 2017. Available online: https://www.lifx.com/ (accessed on 28 August 2018).

46. Tabu. Lumen. Simply Brighter. 2012. Available online: http://www.lumenbulb.net/ (accessed on 28 August 2018).

47. Plilips. Philips Hue. 2017. Available online: http://www2.meethue.com/en-us (accessed on 28 August 2018).

48. Elgato. Elgato Avea. 2017. Available online: https://www.elgato.com/en/avea (accessed on 28 August 2018).

49. Indiegogo. iLumi—The World's Most Intelligent Light Bulbs. 2017. Available online: https://www.indiegogo.com/projects/ilumi-the-world-s-most-intelligent-light-bulbs--5#/ (accessed on 28 August 2018).

50. Radetsky, L.C. *Easily Commissioned Lighting Controls. A Report of BPA Energy Efficiency's Emerging Technologies Initiative*; Rensselaer Polytechnic Institute: Troy, NY, USA, 2015.

51. Labs, S. Bluegiga BLE112 Bluetooth® Smart Module. 2017. Available online: http://www.silabs.com/products/wireless/bluetooth/bluetooth-low-energy-modules/ble112-bluetooth-smart-module (accessed on 28 August 2018).

52. Halfacree, G.; Upton, E. *Raspberry Pi User Guide*; Wiley: Chichester, UK, 2012; ISBN 978-1118464465.

53. International Organization for Standardization. ISO/IEEE 11073. 2016. Available online: https://www.iso.org/standard/67821.html (accessed on 28 August 2018).

54. Diodes Incorporated. Description. 2016. Available online: https://www.diodes.com/assets/Datasheets/ZXLD1366.pdf (accessed on 28 August 2018).

55. Sensirion—The Sensor Company. Digital Humidity Sensor SHT2x. 2017. Available online: https://www.sensirion.com/en/environmental-sensors/humidity-sensors/humidity-temperature-sensor-sht2x-digital-i2c-accurate/ (accessed on 28 August 2018).

56. Panasonic. Photo IC Type High Sensitive Light Sensor. 2015. Available online: https://industrial.panasonic.com/cdbs/www-data/pdf/ADD8000/ADD8000CE2.pdf (accessed on 20 June 2017).

57. Winsen. WSP2110 VOC Gas Sensor. 2017. Available online: http://www.winsen-sensor.com/products/flat-surfaced-gas-sensor/wsp2110.html (accessed on 28 August 2018).

58. Winsen. Low Power-Consumption CO_2 Sensor. 2016. Available online: http://www.winsen-sensor.com/d/files/PDF/Solid%20Electrolyte%20CO2%20Sensor/MG812%20CO2%20Manual%20V1.1.pdf (accessed on 28 August 2018).

59. Sharp. GP2Y1010AU0F Compact Optical Dust Sensor. 2006. Available online: http://www.sharp-world.com/products/device/lineup/data/pdf/datasheet/gp2y1010au_e.pdf (accessed on 28 August 2018).

60. Panasonic. EKMC (VZ) Series. 2017. Available online: http://www3.panasonic.biz/ac/e/control/sensor/human/vz/index.jsp (accessed on 28 August 2018).

61. Panasonic. Sensors for Automotive & Industrial Applications: Grid-EYE Infrared Array Sensor. 2017. Available online: https://na.industrial.panasonic.com/products/sensors/sensors-automotive-industrial-applications/grid-eye-infrared-array-sensor (accessed on 28 August 2018).

62. Shhedi, Z.A.; Moldoveanu, A.; Moldoveanu, F.; Taslitchi, C. Real-time hand hygiene monitoring system for HAI prevention. In Proceedings of the 2015 E-Health and Bioengineering Conference (EHB), Iasi, Romania, 19–21 November 2015; pp. 1–4. doi:10.1109/EHB.2015.7391474. [CrossRef]

63. Bluetooth. Generic Attributes. 2017. Available online: https://www.bluetooth.com/specifications/gatt (accessed on 28 August 2018).

64. Coskun, V.; Ok, K.; Ozdenizci, B. *Near Field Communication: From Theory to Practice*; Wiley: Berlin/Heidelberg, Germany, 2012. [CrossRef]

65. Matsuoka, H.; Wang, J.; Jing, L.; Zhou, Y.; Wu, Y.; Cheng, Z. Development of a control system for home appliances based on BLE technique. In Proceedings of the 2014 IEEE International Symposium on Independent Computing (ISIC), Orlando, FL, USA, 9–12 December 2014; pp. 1–5. [CrossRef]

66. Ecma Intenational. Standard ECMA-404. The JSON Data Interchange Format. 2013. Available online: http://www.ecma-international.org/publications/files/ECMA-ST/ECMA-404.pdf (accessed on 28 August 2018).

67. EU GDPR. The EU General Data Protection Regulation. 2017. Available online: http://www.eugdpr.org/ (accessed on 28 August 2018).

68. Tews, E.; Beck, M. Practical Attacks against WEP and WPA. In Proceedings of the Second ACM Conference on Wireless Network Security (WiSec '09), Zurich, Switzerland, 16–19 March 2009; ACM: New York, NY, USA, 2009; pp. 79–86. [CrossRef]

69. Farooq, U.; Aslam, M. Comparative analysis of different AES implementation techniques for efficient resource usage and better performance of an FPGA. *J. King Saud Univ.* **2017**, *29*, 295–302. [CrossRef]

70. Marin, I.; Goga, N.; Vasilateanu, A. A Novel Indoor Positioning using Smart Luminaires. In Proceedings of the 9th International Conference on Information, Intelligence, Systems and Applications, Zakynthos, Greece, 23–25 July 2018.

71. Marin, I.; Goga, N.; Draghici, I.; Pavaloiu, I.; Nitu, M. Ambient Assisted Control using Smart Luminaires. In Proceedings of the Zooming Innovation in Consumer Electronics International Conference, Novi Sad, Serbia, 30–31 May 2018.

72. Luo, X.L.; Liao, L.Z.; Tam, H.W. Convergence Analysis of the Levenberg-Marquardt Method. *Optim. Methods Softw.* **2007**, *22*, 659–678. [CrossRef]

73. Dong, Q.; Dargie, W. Evaluation of the reliability of RSSI for indoor localization. In Proceedings of the IEEE International Conference on Wireless Communications in Unusual and Confined Areas (ICWCUCA), Clermont Ferrand, France, 28–30 August 2012; pp. 1–6.

74. Gammu. Wammu. 2018. Available online: https://wammu.eu/gammu/ (accessed on 28 August 2018).

Article

A Plug and Play IoT Wi-Fi Smart Home System for Human Monitoring

Marco Bassoli, Valentina Bianchi * and Ilaria De Munari

Department of Engineering and Architecture, University of Parma, Parco Area delle Scienze, 181/A, 43124 Parma, Italy; marco.bassoli@studenti.unipr.it (M.B.); ilaria.demunari@unipr.it (I.D.M.)
* Correspondence: valentina.bianchi@unipr.it; Tel.: +39-0521-906284

Received: 27 August 2018; Accepted: 14 September 2018; Published: 16 September 2018

Abstract: The trend toward technology ubiquity in human life is constantly increasing and the same tendency is clear in all technologies aimed at human monitoring. In this framework, several smart home system architectures have been presented in literature, realized by combining sensors, home servers, and online platforms. In this paper, a new system architecture suitable for human monitoring based on Wi-Fi connectivity is introduced. The proposed solution lowers costs and implementation burden by using the Internet connection that leans on standard home modem-routers, already present normally in the homes, and reducing the need for range extenders thanks to the long range of the Wi-Fi signal. Since the main drawback of the Wi-Fi implementation is the high energy drain, low power design strategies have been considered to provide each battery-powered sensor with a lifetime suitable for a consumer application. Moreover, in order to consider the higher consumption arising in the case of the Wi-Fi/Internet connectivity loss, dedicated operating cycles have been introduced obtaining an energy savings of up to 91%. Performance was evaluated: in order to validate the use of the system as a hardware platform for behavioral services, an activity profile of a user for two months in a real context has been extracted.

Keywords: smart homes; Internet of Things (IoT); Wi-Fi; human monitoring; behavioral analysis

1. Introduction

The concept of a Smart Home has evolved remarkably over the past few decades. Initially, the Smart Home coincided with Home Automation intended as technological solutions applied to the home environment to automatically manage some situations (e.g., open doors/curtains, control thermostat) and detect dangerous events (e.g., fire, flood), freeing the user from manual control [1]. Now, the evolution of ICT (Information and Communication Technologies) has allowed for the addition of many advanced features to smart homes over time, extending the possible applications. Among the advancements, the monitoring of human activity in the home environment has particular importance. Modern systems exploit human monitoring mainly to improve the energy management of the building [2–7]. However, data related to the users and how they live in their own home environment can find straightforward applications in health management, allowing for early detection of behavioral trends and anomalies possibly relevant to one's wellbeing [8–14].

To accomplish this task, some new devices have to be developed [15] aimed at considering the interaction of the user with the home environment (e.g., armchair sensors to monitor inactivity periods, toilet sensors, etc.). These devices must be able to send data over the Internet so that, once processed, they can be accessed by the various professionals involved, for example, medical doctors, caregivers, relatives, and the users themselves.

Applications based on such a system have been presented in past works. For example, an infrastructure based on a Passive InfraRed (PIR), bed and temperature sensors was reported in [16]. In this case, data transmission was based on the X10 wireless protocol, and a home server was exploited to process data and to send analyses and alerts to a third person (i.e., the clinician) through emails. Another monitoring system based on temperature, pressure, PIR sensors, and actuators was described in [17]. Sensors communicated with a local computer by means of a wireless ZigBee protocol. Data were processed to monitor the activities of elders, and the results determined which actions were taken. The system proposed in [18] leans on a mix of ZigBee and Power Line Communication (PLC) transmission protocols. The architecture was conceived with distinct ZigBee Wireless Sensor Networks (WSNs) in each room, which communicate with a central management station through a PLC. An infrastructure exploiting a custom wireless protocol, the so called Wellness protocol, was presented in [19]. The implementation was based on temperature, pressure sensors, PIR sensors, a manual alert button, and actuators. Another example of such a system was CARDEA (Computer-Aided, Rule-based Domestic Environment Assistant), developed at the University of Parma and specifically aimed at behavioral analysis. Originally based on the Ethernet protocol [20,21], the system's strength is flexibility. It is conceived to integrate different kinds of sensors and to support smart interfaces [22,23], in order to tailor the system's functions to the specific users' needs. By supporting a wireless protocol (i.e., IEEE 802.15.4/ZigBee) as well, further kinds of devices were introduced; the most remarkable is the wearable sensor MuSA (MUltiSensor Assistant) [24–27], designed for user motion analysis (e.g., fall monitoring) and for localization and identification purposes [28,29].

Most of the systems presented in the literature based their connectivity on wireless protocols, typically ZigBee [30–32], due to the low cost and power consumption. Coupling the low power required by a ZigBee transmission with recent developments in the field of energy harvesting, it is now possible to develop battery-less Internet of Things (IoT) nodes [33,34]. However, powering the ZigBee protocol tasks for prolonged periods of time (i.e., >10 s) with energy harvesters is not recommended [35]. Some advanced functions (e.g., localization or identification [36]), useful in smart home systems conceived for the continuous monitoring of the individual and for behavioral analysis, can be prevented. Moreover, the disadvantage of the ZigBee approach is mainly the necessity of a completely new and dedicated infrastructure in each home in which the system is going to be deployed, since, typically, a network compliant with these standards is not already present. Furthermore, a gateway device has to be considered as an interface between the home protocol and the Ethernet, in addition to a number of range extenders due to the low range featured by ZigBee [37].

In this paper, we present a new home monitoring system entirely based on Wi-Fi connectivity, in a fashion strictly compliant with the Internet of Thing (IoT) paradigm. Sensors connect to the Internet through a standard Wi-Fi home router, which is quite often already present in the homes. Some manufacturers are already producing chips for routers which are able to support Wi-Fi, Bluetooth, and ZigBee protocols in parallel (e.g., Qualcomm QCA4020 and QCA4024 [38]). These solutions could simplify the adoption of multiple protocols in the near future, but do not eliminate the need for building a complete infrastructure for the ZigBee sensors and in particular for deploying range extenders in the environment. On the contrary, Wi-Fi features a much wider range than ZigBee, so that no (or fewer) network extenders are needed, simplifying the overall approach, lowering the costs, and making the whole system more scalable. These characteristics open the market to the system making it particularly attractive to consumers. This, of course, comes at the expense of increasing power consumption, which may harm battery lifetime. Therefore, we carefully designed sensor platforms for low-power operation. An extensive account for the exploited design methodologies is given in [39], where it is shown that the obtained battery lifetimes are suitable for practical exploitation.

Based on such preliminary studies, we developed a complete set of specific sensor prototypes, providing expressive information relevant to behavioral inference. In [16,40–42] some examples on how the sensor data can be processed and elaborated to extract patterns in the behaviors of home occupants are given. The present work is an extension of a published conference paper [43] where a brief description of the sensors is given. Here, more details about the developed hardware are given, and the proposed system hardware infrastructure is validated. The sensors have been tested both in a laboratory and in a real home environment. Some measurements about the power consumption are presented.

Moreover, during the tests, the sensors' data were logged to carry out a possible activity profile of the users in order to test the system performance. It is worth stressing that the aim of this work is not to develop and demonstrate a new behavioral analysis method, but to present a new hardware architecture conceived to collect data usable by behavioral analysis models developed elsewhere [16,40–42]. These tests show the usability and convenience of data collected and demonstrate that it is possible to take advantage of the flexibility of the Wi-Fi platform while eliminating costs given by the need of additional hardware (i.e., home servers and routers, adopted in [13–16]).

The paper is organized in four sections. After an introduction, a detailed description of the Wi-Fi architecture is presented in Section 2. In Section 3, experimental results are discussed, then in Section 4, conclusions are drawn.

2. Materials and Methods: The Wi-Fi System

2.1. System Architecture

The general system architecture is sketched in Figure 1. It includes a set of sensing devices, a Wi-Fi router, and services installed on a cloud environment. We currently exploit the IBM Bluemix Watson IoT platform (IBM, Armonk, NY, USA). The system is open to third-party and new device addition. We plan to integrate both custom-designed and commercial Wi-Fi devices in a seamless fashion.

Figure 1. CARDEA (Computer-Aided, Rule-based Domestic Environment Assistant) Wi-Fi system architecture. IoT = Internet of Things.

Here, we discuss the custom design of a subset of sensors specifically aimed at behavioral analysis. Based on outcomes of previous European projects in which the ZigBee version was exploited [44], we defined the following device list:

- Armchair (or Bed) occupancy sensor, to monitor inactivity periods or sleep disorders;
- Passive InfraRed (PIR), to monitor the movements inside the house;
- Toilet sensor, to monitor the toilet accesses;
- Magnetic contact, to detect door and windows opening/closing. The same device can be used to monitor interaction with other meaningful objects (e.g., a cupboard door, to monitor feeding habits, or the medicine cabinet, for monitoring compliance with therapy prescriptions).

All sensors are directly and individually connected to the Internet through the Wi-Fi home router. The commissioning procedure is very simple and relies on the Wi-Fi Protected Setup (WPS) standard. No technical skill is required, so that consumers themselves could manage the installation procedure. Data are sent to the Watson IoT platform, inside the IBM Bluemix cloud services, via MQTT (Message Queue Telemetry Transport) protocol with a Quality of Service (QoS) equal to 2. This ensures the necessary reliability of the transmission process, since the protocol itself ensures that the message is received by the broker once and once only. The payload of the message is a string in a JSON (JavaScript Object Notation) format, reporting the sensor status. The device firmware, nevertheless, is suitable for connecting to other platforms as well (e.g., Amazon AWS (Amazon Web Services) (Amazon, Seattle, WA, USA), Microsoft Azure (Microsoft, Redmond, WA, USA), Thingspeak (MathWorks, Natick, MA, USA), etc.).

2.2. Sensors Prototypes

A Wi-Fi certified system-on-chip (SoC) (CC3200, Texas Instruments, Dallas, TX, USA [45]) was chosen as the core of all sensors. It integrates an 80 MHz clock MCU (MicroController Unit) with a 32-bit architecture and a network processor (compliant with the IEEE 802.11b/g/n network radio protocol).

For prototyping purposes, commercial development boards were exploited as the motherboard for all the devices. By connecting the same motherboard to different sensing devices, different sensors were built, sharing the architecture, thus reducing development costs. The sensors are shown in Figure 2.

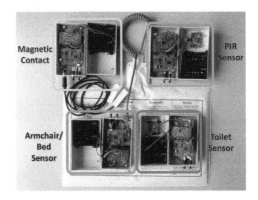

Figure 2. The sensors prototypes. PIR = Passive InfraRed.

All the devices can be powered from an AC (Alternating Current) outlet (through a standard USB port). This possibility eliminates the need to control and replace the batteries. However, the sensors' position is very important to efficiently monitor the users' activities. This position has to be independent of where the outlets have been set up in the house, but, at the same time, it is necessary to avoid wires in the room or to modify the existing home electrical system. For this reason, the devices are also conceived for battery-powered operation. In order to preserve battery lifetime, careful management of the energy budget was implemented. In particular, simple sensors do not need to fully exploit the Wi-Fi data transmission rate, since a limited quantity of data have to be exchanged over time. So, taking advantage of such an overabundant data rate, sleep phases are introduced in the operating cycle. The devices alternate active (data processing and transmission) and sleep intervals. Among available low power modes of the MCU, the Low-Power Deep Sleep (LPDS) and the HIBERNATE modes were exploited. In LPDS mode, the MCU stops its main clock while the radio module is active and maintains the connection with the network. The device is more reactive to external interrupts and features low wake up times. In HIBERNATE mode, the radio section is also turned off. Hence, HIBERNATE is the most effective in power saving, but, when awakening from hibernation, the device needs to re-connect to the network. Wake up times are in the order of tens of seconds, so hibernation is convenient when the sleep time is long enough. In our previous study [39], it was shown that the overall power performance of LPDS mode is better than HIBERNATE whenever a large enough frequency of messages (higher than 150 message/day) is to be managed. Considering the fact that all the sensors need to send a keep-alive message (every 15 minutes, in the application at hand), hibernation turns out to be practical whenever only a few tens of actual "events" per day are expected to occur. Among the sensors presented in this first implementation of the Wi-Fi system, this characteristic may fit with Armchair/Bed sensors, Toilet sensors and the several uses of the Magnetic contact. On the other hand, LPDS mode may be a better fit for higher frequency events, as happens for the PIR sensor. Based on such general assumptions, in the following specific implementation, details are given for each device.

- Armchair/Bed sensor: In [46], a characterization of three different chair sensor elements is presented: a strain gauge, a mechanical switch, and a vibration sensor. Highest detection accuracy is reported for the mechanical switch, but this kind of sensor is more difficult to integrate in an ordinary home chair/bed since it is not straightforward to cover the whole sitting area. For our application, the strain gauge seems the most indicated choice. Indeed, resistive pressure pads are being commercialized which can be placed under the bed mattress or over the chair seat. These pads have been selected as sensing elements. Resistance change is assessed through a simple voltage divider, which drives a binary threshold comparator. This, in turn, generates an interrupt to wake up the MCU. As mentioned, given the relatively low expected number of events, the HIBERNATE sleep mode is exploited during idle phases.
- Magnetic Contact: The sensing element is a reed switch, coupled to a magnet. When the two components are close to each other, the switch opens. This configuration is particularly convenient when drawers/doors are supposed to stay closed most of the time. Since the reed switch is open when they are closed, the sensor drains no current while in this state. Interrupts are generated to signal both transitions (close to open, open to close). In this case, selection of sleep mode depends on the actual device function. If, for instance, applied to the home main door, the HIBERNATE mode seems to be more effective again.
- Toilet sensor: The sensing element is a distance/proximity sensor. The sensor purpose is to allow for counting toilet visits (which may be relevant to many medical conditions), distinguishing them from generic bathroom presence (due to washing, for instance), which could be assessed though a PIR sensor. A short-enough, personalized reading range is therefore needed to cope with the actual placement of the sensor itself. The device has a reading range from 10 cm to 150 cm. The analog reading is fed to a comparator, which generates an interrupt signal to the system core. In our experiments, we found that calibrating the sensor threshold at 65 cm distance was effective in discriminating toilet actual usage from generic bathroom presence. The nature of this sensor should make it suitable to exploit the benefits of the HIBERNATE mode. However, due to the high current consumption of the sensing element during its on state, the system core needs to power it on only when a distance reading is needed, keeping it in the off state otherwise. In our tests, we found that a period of 3 seconds for power off followed by 0.5 s of power on gives the optimal system reactivity. Since the sensing element duty cycle is driven by the MCU, LPDS mode had to be adopted.
- PIR sensor: the sensing device is a standard passive-infrared motion sensor. It requires a supply voltage in the range of 3.3–5 V. In order to allow the system to be powered by AA batteries (as a common feature of all devices), a boost DC-DC regulator (direct current to direct current power converter that steps up voltage) has been added. The device already has embedded converters and provides a digital output signal, which is used to wake up the system core whenever a movement is detected. To avoid communication overload, PIR data are filtered on board; only status changes are transmitted, besides keep-alive messages. In the envisaged scenario, however, this results in a number of daily messages exceeding the above-mentioned threshold, which makes the adoption of hibernation not suitable and makes the adoption of LPDS mode preferable.

3. Results and Discussion

To evaluate the system, field tests were performed for two months.

For standby battery-lifetime evaluation, a full set of sensors was installed in a laboratory environment. The power consumption depended on the frequency of the occurring interactions with the sensor events. To determine a figure that allows for the comparison between sensors, only power consumption caused by the keep-alive events sent every 15 minutes were considered.

In order to estimate the battery lifetime in a working condition similar to the real one, another full set of sensors was installed in a real home environment inhabited by a family.

The sensors were deployed accordingly to their purpose:

- Armchair sensor: Sensor pad placed on a lunchroom chair.
- Magnetic contact: On the bedroom door.
- Toilet sensor: Inside the bathroom to sense toilet interactions.
- PIR sensor: Inside the bedroom.

The performance of the whole system was investigated, manually registering the user-sensor interactions and comparing them with the events reported by the sensors themselves.

Test details and results are given in the following subsections.

3.1. Power Consumption Analysis

In a previous work [39], preliminary laboratory tests about the sensors' power consumption were carried out. In this paper, we report an actual characterization of the system.

In the tests shown in [39], we assumed that the connection to the Wi-Fi network and to the Internet were reasonably stable. In real operation, this is not always true, and in order to consider possible disruptions that a consumer may experience, two main issues were evaluated:

- Sensor unable to connect to the Wi-Fi network: The system, after power on, is configured to search for the previously known network (through the WPS procedure) until connection succeeds; if the network connection is broken (e.g., because of a blackout), the device performs a reboot. The system always experiences an energy-expensive boot-loop until the network is restored;
- Sensor connected to the Wi-Fi network but without an active Internet access (e.g., because of Internet provider issues): This situation arises only after the previous condition is met. After power on, the device searches and connects to the known network; it tries to establish a connection with the online cloud. If the procedure fails (e.g., because the Internet connection is lost), a reboot is performed. The result is the same, with the system always in an energy-expensive boot-loop until the internet connection is restored.

To better understand the consequences of this behavior on the actual current consumption, each scenario was reproduced and current measurements were carried out using a digital oscilloscope with a bandwidth of 350 MHz, an ADC (Analog to Digital Converter) resolution of 12 bit, and a maximum sample rate of 1.25 GS/s. To measure the sensors current, a probe with a bandwidth of 50 MHz and a minimum sensitivity of 10 mA/div was exploited.

Results are shown in Figure 3. In Figure 3a, the device settles at an almost constant current absorption of 14.2 mA while waiting for the network connection, with an averaged 71.4 mA current while searching for a Wi-Fi connection. In Figure 3b, phases in which the system is not using the radio module (during reboot) with a 101 mA peak current absorption can be identified, as well as a 74.3 mA peak current when the Wi-Fi connection succeeded and tried to establish connection to the cloud.

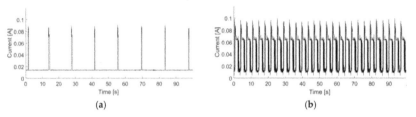

(a)　　　　　　　　　　　(b)

Figure 3. Current absorption measurements: (**a**) scenario with missing Wi-Fi network connection; (**b**) scenario with sensor connected to Wi-Fi but without internet access.

By the analysis of those data, a total mean current of 17.3 mA can be extracted for the first scenario, and a total mean current of 34.5 mA for the second one. This behavior can significantly degrade sensors' energy performance. To overcome this problem, and hence to extend battery lifetime, the device is forced to follow a duty-cycled sequence of searching and sleeping phases, as shown in Figure 4.

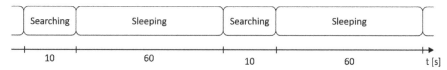

Figure 4. Working phases for both Wi-Fi and Internet absence scenarios.

The device is allowed to check for the presence of the Wi-Fi network or the Internet connectivity for a maximum period of 10 s. After this time, if the task fails, the system enters in a HIBERNATE sleep mode for 60 s to save energy and preserve battery charge. After the sleeping phase, a new search phase begins. This behavior has been tested and compared with the standard one for the same scenarios. The new current measurements are shown in Figure 5.

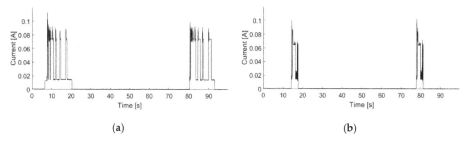

Figure 5. Current absorption measurements of sensors running with the introduced sleep periods: (a) scenario with missing Wi-Fi network connection; (b) scenario with sensor connected to Wi-Fi but without internet access.

After a larger initial current peak needed by the device to boot up, some current peaks are experienced during the Wi-Fi/Internet check phase and they reach the minimum in the sleep phase. In this case, the total mean currents over the period are 7.3 mA in the first scenario and 3.1 mA in the second one. Due to the unpredictability of these situations, the advantage in terms of battery lifetime is not quantifiable; however, with this method, the system is able to reduce the energy consumption by 42% in the case of Wi-Fi network absence and by 91% in the case of Internet connectivity absence. Hence, this behavior has been adopted for all sensors, and the actual battery lifetime during real operation has been evaluated.

As stated before, the sensors' energy performance was evaluated in both laboratory and home environments. All sensors were powered with parallel-series of four AA LR6 alkaline batteries. In the laboratory test, due to the different activity profile expected in a public environment, we tested only the stand-by power consumption. The only signals sent were periodic (15 min) keep-alive messages. In the real home environment, instead, the sensors were stressed during the day by three different members of a family.

After two months of testing, only the toilet sensor ran out of battery: For the other sensors, the laboratory set shows a residual charge of about 46%, while in the home environment this value is lower at 34%. It is worth considering that the battery lifetime in a real home environment strongly depends on the actual interaction with the sensors (e.g., the Magnetic contact can be stressed by more than one user, affecting the expected daily events and the sensor energetic performance). Moreover, as expected, the toilet sensor has a higher energy consumption because of the usage of LPDS mode and due to the higher power consumption of the sensible element. For this reason, the toilet battery lifetime was 30 days.

3.2. Behavioral Tests and Results

To evaluate the system accuracy, sensitivity, and specificity, one user manually took note of his interactions with the sensors for two months. These data were compared with the events generated by the sensors and automatically collected into the cloud platform. This analysis could effectively be done, in our scenario, only with the chair sensor, in fact, data for the Magnetic contact, Toilet and PIR sensors cannot be univocally assigned to a specific person, in an environment populated by more than one end-user. To resolve this situation a user identification mechanism should be considered [36,47].

In the case of the chair sensor, a total of 218 events were detected as follows: 99 True Positives (TP), 109 True Negatives (TN), 0 False Positives (FP), and 10 False Negatives (FN). Then, the accuracy, sensitivity, and specificity were carried out [48]:

$$Accuracy = \frac{TP + TN}{TP + TN + FP + FN} = 95\% \tag{1}$$

$$Sensitivity = \frac{TP}{TP + FN} = 91\% \tag{2}$$

$$Specificity = \frac{TN}{TN + FP} = 100\% \tag{3}$$

where TP, TN, FP, and FN are defined as reported in Table 1.

Table 1. Definition of True Positives (TP), True Negatives (TN), False Positives (FP), and False Negatives (FN).

Symbol	Position of the User	Where the User is Identified
TP	user seated on the chair	user detected as seated on the chair
TN	user not seated on the chair	user not detected as seated on the chair
FP	user not seated on the chair	user detected as seated on the chair
FN	user seated on the chair	user not detected as seated on the chair

The results presented show that our sensor is definitely capable of providing occupancy information in a real context. In [46], the reported averaged accuracy for a resistive strain gauge was 94%. This value is compatible with our results. We can conclude that the performance of our sensors are attributable to the resistive pressure pad. Nowadays, the pressure pad is the best choice due to its commercial availability and because it does not require specialized installation. Better performance could be obtained by replacing the sensing element, without affecting the system architecture.

Some elaborations on the data acquired from all the sensors has been performed to demonstrate the possibility of identifying patterns in the user's activity. For each sensor, two different cases have been considered:

- Daily activity: the distribution of the user-sensor interactions during a 24 h period was analyzed. In Figures 6a, 7a, 8a and 9a the probability of an event in a certain hour of the day is plotted. Values were obtained through the analysis of the activity per hour of every test day. The relative probability v_i was calculated with the equation

$$v_i = \frac{c_i}{N} \tag{4}$$

where c_i is the number of events that occurred in the hour, \ and N is the total number of events observed during the test.

- Weekly activity: the interaction was assessed during a week, counting the events registered in different three-hour intervals in the same day of the week (Figures 6b–9b).

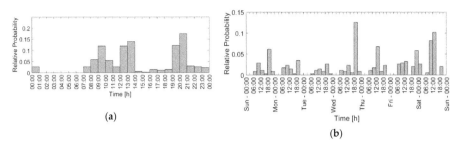

Figure 6. Armchair sensor activity during the day (**a**) and during the week (**b**).

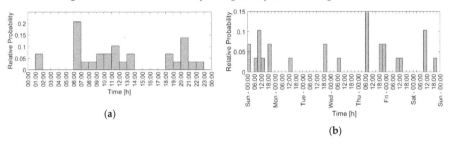

Figure 7. Magnetic contact (door sensor) activity during the day (**a**) and during the week (**b**).

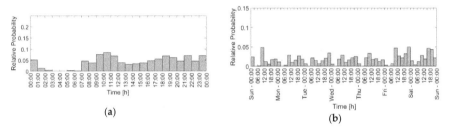

Figure 8. PIR sensor activity during the day (**a**) and during the week (**b**).

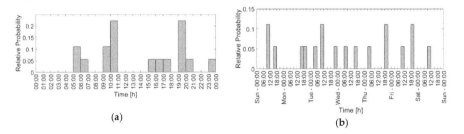

Figure 9. Toilet sensor activity during the day (**a**) and during the week (**b**).

Although the aim of this paper was not to present a complete behavioral analysis module, simple trend information might be extracted from the results, demonstrating data convenience. For instance, a high lunchroom chair interaction can be seen during meals; the door openings are concentrated during the weekend, when the user is usually not at work. This fact can be confirmed by the PIR weekly graphs, in which the activity distribution shows a higher presence starting from Friday. Looking at the Toilet sensor activity, a periodic usage can be seen around meal times and in the early morning after waking up. Moreover, as expected, no sensors recorded activities during nighttime, when the user is supposed to be sleep.

4. Conclusions

In this paper, a new Smart Home system architecture conceived for behavioral analysis and based on Wi-Fi connectivity has been presented. The aim is to present an alternative architecture compared to the more traditional ones based on protocols such as ZigBee. The ZigBee solutions are not typically already present in the home environment, and this causes some problems in the practical deployment, mainly due to the necessity of the set-up fo a new and complete network infrastructure for every system installation.

In the proposed architecture, the sensors are connected to the Internet through a standard Wi-Fi router, in an IoT compliant fashion, without the need to add a dedicated home gateway to ensure connectivity or the range extenders often needed when using other standard protocols. A complete set of new devices conceived to acquire data related to users' behaviors has been designed and developed.

Since the principal drawback of the Wi-Fi connectivity is the higher power consumption, low power design strategies have been considered and applied to demonstrate the possibility of using this architecture in the context of smart homes for behavioral monitoring. The whole system has been tested in a real environment to evaluate the feasibility of adopting it in a real situation.

For this study, two sets of sensors. composed of an Armchair sensor, a Magnetic contact, a Toilet sensor, and a PIR sensor, were run for two months. The first set was used to evaluate stand-by battery lifetime while the second one was placed in a real home environment, inhabited by a family, to evaluate real battery lifetime. After the two months of testing, only the Toilet sensor ran out of battery. For the other sensors, the laboratory set shows a residual charge of about 46%, while in the home environment this value was 34%. Furthermore, in some cases, the network could undergo connectivity issues; in these situations, dedicated operating cycles were introduced, instead of the standard ones, to reduce the impact on the battery lifetime. This lead to a reduction in the current absorption of 42% in the case of Wi-Fi network absence and of 91% in the case of a lack of Internet connectivity.

Moreover, in order to validate the possibility of using this system as a hardware platform for behavioral services, we have extracted, from the set of sensors installed in the home environment, a possible activity profile of an occupant. A user was assigned to take note of each interaction with the sensors for two months to test the system performance. The accuracy, sensitivity, and specificity were evaluated for the chair sensor (whose interaction, in our environment, can definitely be attributable to a single person) resulting in 95%, 91%, and 100%, respectively. These results show that our sensor is definitely capable of providing occupancy information in a real context.

In conclusion, exploiting Wi-Fi as an infrastructure for smart home systems conceived for human monitoring is a possible alternative to other systems based on protocols such as ZigBee, due to the low cost and ease of installation and use. The power consumption does not affect the usability, and the performance is not influenced by the system architecture.

Author Contributions: Conceptualization, V.B., I.D.M.; Methodology, V.B., I.D.M; Software, M.B.; Validation, V.B.; Formal Analysis, V.B., M.B.; Investigation, V.B., M.B.; Data Curation, V.B., M.B.; Writing-Original Draft Preparation, V.B., M.B.; Writing-Review and Editing, V.B., M.B., I.D.M.; Visualization, V.B., M.B, I.D.M.; Supervision, I.D.M; Project Administration, I.D.M.; Funding Acquisition, I.D.M.

Funding: This research received no external funding.

Acknowledgments: The authors would like to acknowledge Federico Mendogni for the help with the experiments and prof. Paolo Ciampolini for his scientific guidance and advice.

Conflicts of Interest: The authors declare no conflict of interest.

References

1. Yerrapragada, C.; Fisher, P.S. Voice controlled smart house. In Proceedings of the IEEE 1993 International Conference on Consumer Electronics Digest of Technical, Rosemont, IL, USA, 8–10 June 1993. [CrossRef]
2. Shih, H.C. Automatic building monitoring and commissioning via human behavior recognition. In Proceedings of the 2016 IEEE 5th Global Conference on Consumer Electronics, Kyoto, Japan, 11–14 October 2016.

3. Hwang, I.K.; Lee, D.S.; Baek, J.W. Home network configuring scheme for all electric appliances using ZigBee-based integrated remote controller. *IEEE Trans. Consum. Electron.* **2009**, *55*, 1300–1307. [CrossRef]

4. Chen, C.-Y.; Liu, C.-Y.; Kuo, C.-C.; Yang, C.-F.; Chen, C.-Y.; Liu, C.-Y.; Kuo, C.-C.; Yang, C.-F. Web-Based Remote Control of a Building's Electrical Power, Green Power Generation and Environmental System Using a Distributive Microcontroller. *Micromachines* **2017**, *8*, 241. [CrossRef]

5. Lobaccaro, G.; Carlucci, S.; Löfström, E. A review of systems and technologies for smart homes and smart grids. *Energies* **2016**, *9*. [CrossRef]

6. Brusco, G.; Burgio, A.; Menniti, D.; Pinnarelli, A.; Sorrentino, N.; Scarcello, L.; Brusco, G.; Burgio, A.; Menniti, D.; Pinnarelli, A.; et al. An Energy Box in a Cloud-Based Architecture for Autonomous Demand Response of Prosumers and Prosumages. *Electronics* **2017**, *6*, 98. [CrossRef]

7. Froiz-Míguez, I.; Fernández-Caramés, T.; Fraga-Lamas, P.; Castedo, L.; Froiz-Míguez, I.; Fernández-Caramés, T.M.; Fraga-Lamas, P.; Castedo, L. Design, Implementation and Practical Evaluation of an IoT Home Automation System for Fog Computing Applications Based on MQTT and ZigBee-WiFi Sensor Nodes. *Sensors* **2018**, *18*, 2660. [CrossRef] [PubMed]

8. Ceccacci, S.; Generosi, A.; Giraldi, L.; Mengoni, M. An user-centered approach to design smart systems for people with dementia. In Proceedings of the 2017 IEEE 7th International Conference on Consumer Electronics-Berlin (ICCE-Berlin), Berlin, Germany, 3–6 September 2017.

9. Pal, D.; Funilkul, S.; Charoenkitkarn, N.; Kanthamanon, P. Internet-of-Things and Smart Homes for Elderly Healthcare: An End User Perspective. *IEEE Access* **2018**, *6*, 10483–10496. [CrossRef]

10. Vechet, S.; Hrbacek, J.; Krejsa, J. Environmental data analysis for learning behavioral patterns in smart homes. In Proceedings of the 2016 17th International Conference on Mechatronics-Mechatronika (ME), Prague, Czech Republic, 7–9 December 2016.

11. Thapliyal, H.; Nath, R.K.; Mohanty, S.P. Smart Home Environment for Mild Cognitive Impairment Population: Solutions to Improve Care and Quality of Life. *IEEE Consum. Electron. Mag.* **2018**, *7*, 68–76. [CrossRef]

12. Grossi, F.; Matrella, G.; De Munari, I.; Ciampolini, P. A flexible home automation system applied to elderly care. In Proceedings of the 2007 Digest of Technical Papers IEEE International Conference on Consumer Electronics, Las Vegas, NV, USA, 10–14 January 2007.

13. Saponara, S.; Donati, M.; Fanucci, L.; Celli, A.; Saponara, S.; Donati, M.; Fanucci, L.; Celli, A. An Embedded Sensing and Communication Platform, and a Healthcare Model for Remote Monitoring of Chronic Diseases. *Electronics* **2016**, *5*, 47. [CrossRef]

14. Sasakawa, D.; Honma, N.; Nakayama, T.; Iizuka, S.; Sasakawa, D.; Honma, N.; Nakayama, T.; Iizuka, S. Human Posture Identification Using a MIMO Array. *Electronics* **2018**, *7*, 37. [CrossRef]

15. Losardo, A.; Grossi, F.; Matrella, G.; De Munari, I.; Ciampolini, P. Exploiting AAL environment for behavioral analysis. *Assist. Technol. Res. Ser.* **2013**, *33*, 1121–1125. [CrossRef]

16. Skubic, M.; Guevara, R.D.; Rantz, M. Automated health alerts using in-home sensor data for embedded health assessment. *IEEE J. Transl. Eng. Heal. Med.* **2015**, *3*. [CrossRef] [PubMed]

17. Nag, A.; Mukhopadhyay, S.C. Occupancy Detection at Smart Home Using Real-Time Dynamic Thresholding of Flexiforce Sensor. *IEEE Sens. J.* **2015**, *15*, 4457–4463. [CrossRef]

18. Li, M.; Lin, H.-J. Design and Implementation of Smart Home Control Systems Based on Wireless Sensor Networks and Power Line Communications. *IEEE Trans. Ind. Electron.* **2015**, *62*, 4430–4442. [CrossRef]

19. Ghayvat, H.; Liu, J.; Mukhopadhyay, S.C.; Gui, X. Wellness Sensor Networks: A Proposal and Implementation for Smart Home for Assisted Living. *IEEE Sens. J.* **2015**, *15*, 7341–7348. [CrossRef]

20. Grossi, F.; Bianchi, V.; Matrella, G.; De Munari, I.; Ciampolini, P. Internet-Based Home Monitoring and Control. In *Assisted Technology: From Adapted Equipment to Inclusive Environment*; Assistive Technology Research Series; IOS Press: Amsterdam, The Netherlands, 2009; ISBN 9781607500421.

21. Losardo, A.; Bianchi, V.; Grossi, F.; Matrella, G.; De Munari, I.; Ciampolini, P. Web-Enabled Home Assistive Tools. In *Everyday Technology for Independence and Care*; Assistive Technology Research Series; IOS Press: Amsterdam, The Netherlands, 2011; Volume 29, pp. 448–455. [CrossRef]

22. Bianchi, V.; Grossi, F.; De Munari, I.; Ciampolini, P. *Multi-Modal Interaction in AAL Systems*; Assistive Technology Research Series; IOS Press: Amsterdam, The Netherlands, 2011; ISBN 9781607508137.

23. Mora, N.; Bianchi, V.; De Munari, I.; Ciampolini, P. Simple and efficient methods for steady state visual evoked potential detection in BCI embedded system. In Proceedings of the 2014 IEEE International Conference on Acoustics, Speech and Signal Processing (ICASSP), Florence, Italy, 4–9 May 2014.

24. Bianchi, V.; Grossi, F.; Matrella, G.; De Munari, I.; Ciampolini, P. A wireless sensor platform for assistive technology applications. In Proceedings of the 11th EUROMICRO Conference on Digital System Design Architectures, Methods and Tools, Parma, Italy, 3–5 September 2008.

25. Bianchi, V.; Guerra, C.; De Munari, I.; Ciampolini, P. A wearable sensor for AAL-based continuous monitoring. In *International Conference on Smart Homes and Health Telematics*; Springer: Cham, Switzerland, 2016; Volume 9677, pp. 383–394. [CrossRef]

26. Bianchi, V.; Grossi, F.; De Munari, I.; Ciampolini, P. MuSA: A multisensor wearable device for AAL. In Proceedings of the 2011 Federated Conference on Computer Science and Information Systems (FedCSIS), Szczecin, Poland, 18–21 September 2011; pp. 375–380.

27. Bianchi, V.; Grossi, F.; De Munari, I.; Ciampolini, P. Multi sensor assistant: A multisensor wearable device for ambient assisted living. *J. Med. Imaging Heal. Inform.* **2012**, *2*, 70–75. [CrossRef]

28. Montalto, F.; Guerra, C.; Bianchi, V.; De Munari, I.; Ciampolini, P. MuSA: Wearable multi sensor assistant for human activity recognition and indoor localization. *Biosyst. Biorobotics* **2015**, *11*, 81–92. [CrossRef]

29. Guerra, C.; Bianchi, V.; De Munari, I.; Ciampolini, P. CARDEAGate: Low-cost, ZigBee-based localization and identification for AAL purposes. In Proceedings of the 2015 IEEE International Instrumentation and Measurement Technology Conference (I2MTC) Proceedings, Pisa, Italy, 11–14 May 2015.

30. Gill, K.; Yang, S.H.; Yao, F.; Lu, X. A ZigBee-based home automation system. *IEEE Trans. Consum. Electron.* **2009**, *55*, 422–430. [CrossRef]

31. Hwang, K.; Choi, B.J.; Kang, S.H. Enhanced self-configuration scheme for a robust zigbee-based home automation. *IEEE Trans. Consum. Electron.* **2010**, *56*, 583–590. [CrossRef]

32. Zualkernan, I.A.; Al-Ali, A.R.; Jabbar, M.A.; Zabalawi, I.; Wasfy, A. InfoPods: Zigbee-based remote information monitoring devices for smart-homes. *IEEE Trans. Consum. Electron.* **2009**, *55*, 1221–1226. [CrossRef]

33. Cho, J.Y.; Kim, K.-B.; Jabbar, H.; Sin Woo, J.; Ahn, J.H.; Hwang, W.S.; Jeong, S.Y.; Cheong, H.; Yoo, H.H.; Sung, T.H. Design of optimized cantilever form of a piezoelectric energy harvesting system for a wireless remote switch. *Sens. Actuators A* **2018**, *280*, 340–349. [CrossRef]

34. Mallick, S.; Bin Habib, A.-Z.S.; Ahmed, A.S.; Alam, S.S. Performance appraisal of Wireless Energy Harvesting in IoT. In Proceedings of the 2017 3rd International Conference on Electrical Information and Communication Technology (EICT), Khulna, Bangladesh, 7–9 December 2017.

35. Amaro, J.P.; Cortesão, R.; Ferreira, F.J.T.E.; Landeck, J. Device and operation mechanism for non-beacon IEEE802.15.4/Zigbee nodes running on harvested energy. *Ad Hoc Networks* **2015**, *26*, 50–68. [CrossRef]

36. Bianchi, V.; Ciampolini, P.; De Munari, I. RSSI-Based Indoor Localization and Identification for ZigBee Wireless Sensor Networks in Smart Homes. *IEEE Trans. Instrum. Meas.* **2018**, 1–10. [CrossRef]

37. Al-Sarawi, S.; Anbar, M.; Alieyan, K.; Alzubaidi, M. Internet of Things (IoT) communication protocols: Review. In Proceedings of the 2017 8th International Conference on Information Technology (ICIT), Amman, Jordan, 17–18 May 2017.

38. QCA4020 | Qualcomm. Available online: https://www.qualcomm.com/products/qca4020 (accessed on 12 September 2018).

39. Bassoli, M.; Bianchi, V.; De Munari, I.; Ciampolini, P. An IoT approach for an AAL Wi-Fi-based monitoring system. *IEEE Trans. Instrum. Meas.* **2017**, *66*, 3200–3209. [CrossRef]

40. Moraru, S.; Perniu, L.; Kristaly, D.M.; Ungureanu, D.A.; Sandu, F.; Mo, A.A. Proceedings of the 2017 25th Mediterranean Conference on Control and Automation (MED), Valletta, Malta, 3–6 July 2017.

41. Kristaly, D.M.; Moraru, S.-A.; Stefan Petre, V.; Parvan, C.A.; Ungureanu, D.E.; Mosoi, A.A. A Solution for Mobile Computing in a Cloud Environment for Ambient Assisted Living. In Proceedings of the 2018 26th Mediterranean Conference on Control and Automation (MED), Zadar, Croatia, 19–22 June 2018.

42. Lago, P.; Roncancio, C.; Jiménez-Guarín, C. Learning and managing context enriched behavior patterns in smart homes. *Futur. Gener. Comput. Syst.* **2019**, *91*, 191–205. [CrossRef]

43. Bassoli, M.; Bianchi, V.; De Munari, I.; Ciampolini, P. An unobtrusive Wi-Fi system for human monitoring. In Proceedings of the IEEE International Conference on Consumer Electronics, Berlin, Germany, 3–6 September 2017.

44. Grossi, F.; Bianchi, V.; Matrella, G.; De Munari, I.; Ciampolini, P. Senior-friendly kitchen activity: The FOOD Project. *Gerontechnology* **2014**, *13*, 200. [CrossRef]

45. CC3200 SimpleLink Wi-Fi® and Internet-of-Things solution, a Single-Chip Wireless MCU | TI.com. Available online: http://www.ti.com/product/CC3200# (accessed on 12 September 2018).

46. Labeodan, T.; Aduda, K.; Zeiler, W.; Hoving, F. Experimental evaluation of the performance of chair sensors in an office space for occupancy detection and occupancy-driven control. *Energy Build.* **2016**, *111*, 195–206. [CrossRef]

47. Bianchi, V.; Guerra, C.; Bassoli, M.; De Munari, I.; Ciampolini, P. The HELICOPTER project: Wireless sensor network for multi-user behavioral monitoring. In Proceedings of the 2017 International Conference on Engineering, Technology and Innovation: Engineering, Technology and Innovation Management Beyond 2020: New Challenges, New Approaches, Funchal, Portugal, 27–29 June 2017.

48. Fawcett, T. An introduction to ROC analysis. *Pattern Recognit. Lett.* **2006**, *27*, 861–874. [CrossRef]

MDPI

St. Alban-Anlage 66

4052 Basel

Switzerland

Tel. +41 61 683 77 34

Fax +41 61 302 89 18

www.mdpi.com

Electronics Editorial Office

E-mail: electronics@mdpi.com

www.mdpi.com/journal/electronics